OATHS AND OUTFITS

OATHS AND OUTFITS

MAGICAL GIRL UNDERGRAD – BOOK 2

Aest Belequa

Podium

This is a work of fiction. Names, characters, places, and incidents are either products of the author's imagination or used fictitiously. Any resemblance to actual events, locales, or persons, living, dead, or undead, is entirely coincidental.

Cover design by Kittra McBriar

ISBN: 978-1-0394-7036-1

Published in 2024 by Podium Publishing
www.podiumentertainment.com

OATHS AND OUTFITS

PART ONE

1

Green Christmas

Even superheroes have to work holidays sometimes.

I dashed through Tottergarten's halls, The Cloud bobbing behind me like a Christmas-themed balloon on his leash. "Hurry, Understuffy! The Present Pilferer is getting away!"

The Present Pilferer was fast, but I was faster. Hopefully. "I'm running as fast as I can!" I shouted back. The chrome camera drone followed us around a corner, filming everything for the studio.

I also wore holiday finery, though I wasn't Understudy right now. The Cloud loved my Rainy Day costume, and he threw a fit every time I tried to transform, so I'd given up trying to switch out of my sixth-grade form. It was easier to give the pint-sized superhero what he wanted. I did have an ugly sweater over the top, though.

The Narrator wouldn't give us the full stories of why The Cloud and Kaiju Kid were here on Christmas Day. Supposedly, their parents had to work, same as me, and The Narrator was more than happy to hang on to them for the morning. She *had* briefed us both on Kaiju Kid's power, though. Fursona had to stop her from eating refined sugar by any means necessary. Otherwise? Two-hundred-foot plasma-breathing lizard. Someday, she'd learn to control it and catapult to the major leagues, but not today.

"The Grinch's Christmas" had been a standard Tottergarten G-rated Episode, as The Narrator had made clear from the start. Fanfic was . . . The Narrator's clone? Evil twin? Alter ego? No one had been specific, but part of her studio's price for unleashing the villain was our service today. So here Fursona, my sidekick and girlfriend, and I were working on Christmas.

We'd caught Teacher's Pet and Pranky Jones trying to get the doors open for the Anti-Naptime League's getaway car, busted them, and heard about a brand-new villain: The Present Pilferer. Then, instead of immediately hunting him down, 'Mrs. N' taught a lesson on sharing but also respecting others' belongings. Now, we

were finally in hot pursuit of The Present Pilferer and his lieutenant, who I was 95%
sure was Jungle Jim in a yeti suit.

God, Rated-G Episodes were ridiculous.

Wham!

I ran face-first into a gigantic wall of fur. The hulking figure turned a moment
later and roared an icy roar at me. "RAUGH! Who dares challenge The Abomina-
Bill Snowman?"

It could *only* be Jungle Jim in that suit. It was massive, easily seven feet tall, and
so wide its arms rubbed the hall's walls. Jim's costume sported vicious-looking claws
that, if I had to guess, were rubber. The teeth probably were, too, especially since
Jim's face glared between them. Still, The Abomina-Bill Snowman's costume would
probably make my kangaroo-themed sidekick jealous. I had to beat him before Fursona
showed up, or she'd probably want *this* for Christmas. And I hadn't gotten her *this*.

"Magic Girl Understuffy's gonna take you down!" The Cloud shouted.

I facepalmed. Then I ducked away as the wall of white fur surged toward us.
"[**Stellar Ray**]!" I shouted, waving my blue and gold-white wand at The Abomina-
Bill Snowman. The bubble ray—a Rainy Day special—shot out, popping against the
yeti's fur. Each explosion shoved him back just a tiny bit. It hit as hard as a boxer's
punch, but Jungle Jim had been Brick House before he retired. I couldn't *actually*
hurt him.

[You Hurt Someone! +1 Sad Point]

G-rated Episodes overrode the Style System and made it all little-kiddy, but that
was a Drama point. I'd been earning points all Episode on my way to the fifty I'd
need to roll for another skill. The skills flowed a lot faster in Tokyexico, but I had a
long way to go.

The gigantic yeti juggernauted toward me, filling the hall. The further it ran,
though, the more a headwind pushed it back. I looked up. The Cloud was . . .
blowing? Yep, he was blowing as hard as he could. His face went red as more air
than should be possible rushed from his lungs, tossing The Abomina-Bill Snowman
back.

As the yeti somersaulted through the hall, I saw an odd look on Jungle Jim's
face—pride.

"Cool! I'm a windstorm!" The Cloud panted.

The Abomina-Bill Snowman crashed through the double doors and tumbled into
the playroom. He picked himself up with a theatrical groan, standing next to a green-
furred monster. Though similar to the yeti, this one was thin and smirking. The
smirk faded as someone slammed through a different door—a toddler in a dinosaur
suit. Fursona followed the little girl through, trying desperately to take something
from her.

Something shiny. With a straw.

"Oh **[Beep!]**," The Abomina-Bill Snowman muttered. Then he started shouting. "Narrator! *Narrator!*"

I had just enough time to wonder what his censorship penalty would be. Then, the little girl started to *change*. Spines grew from her back, the suit's teeth sharpened, and she began to grow. The childish roars turned guttural and feral, and she stomped a foot. The building shook. Her head reached the ceiling, pushing ceiling tiles away.

"And then everyone calmed down," The Narrator's voice echoed from a loudspeaker, "and Kaiju Kid took a nap instead of drinking the juice box."

Someone slammed through a different door—a toddler in a dinosaur suit. She yawned and curled up on the playroom's rubber mat, an unopened Capri Sun in her hand. Fursona burst through a moment later. She paused, then gingerly pulled the juice box away from the kid. Everyone sighed in relief.

Crisis averted.

"Forget this," the green-furred villain said. She fled toward the door Kaiju Kid had just come from, with The Abomina-Bill Snowman following closely behind. The bag full of presents they'd been stealing sat on the playroom floor, abandoned.

"Yay! We stopped them from ruining Christmas!" The Cloud shouted, waking up Kaiju Kid, who started looking for her juice box. Fursona hid it in her pouch, whistling fake-innocently.

I cleared my throat as the camera drone hovered in front of me, waiting for my prepackaged line. "No, Cloud—"

"The Cloud!"

". . . The Cloud. The spirit of Christmas is giving and togetherness. As long as we have each other, our friends and family, and those we care about, The Present Pilferer and The Abomina-Bill Snowman can't ever ruin the holidays."

God, I hated G-rated Episodes so much.

[Episode Finished!]
[Episode: Short: The Grinch's Christmas! - G]
[Penalties: N/A]
[Short Finished! +3 of each Style Point]
[Winner Winner! +2 of each Style Point]
[Role Focus: Sad + Strong - Goal Unmet!]
[Alias - Understudy] [Archetype - Magical Girl] [Community Rank - 348/523]
[HP 5/7]
[Styles and Skills]
▶Archetype Skill - Transformation Sequence
▶Badass (46)
▶Cunning (48)
▶Drama (51) (Skill Roll Available)

▶Hometown Heroine 1
▶Bit-Part Barrage 1
▶Flamboyance (14)
▶Signature Skill - Adaptive Armoire
▶Stored Costumes: (Rainy Day, Lab Assistant Panic)
▶Spotlight Strike 1
▶Starwave Sail 1
▶Flickerform 1
▶Grit (16)
[Drama Credit Used. Rolling Skill!]
[Rank-Up! Thunderhead 1Corre: The storm rolls in more quickly, reducing time to power up the next attack]

Bianca pulled the Capri Sun out of her pouch and took off her fursuit while I untransformed. She grabbed her backpack and slipped through the maintenance door before I could stop her, heading for the bedroom. She had shorts and a T-shirt on; it was hot in the suit. I wore a blue wool dress and leggings—not holiday-themed, but wintery enough. I hadn't taken my skill roll; I had a lot on my mind today, and I'd do it later.

I was pretty sure we had Walnut Tower's whole thirteenth floor to ourselves. Most people headed home for the holidays; Man vs. Nature Five had screwed that up for anyone *not* from Tokyexico City, but most people had friends to spend Christmas with. Bee and I had plans with our friend Su-Bin's family, but that wasn't for a few hours.

I'd learned something new about Bianca over winter break: She was a present-hunter. A dirty, filthy present-hunter.

I'd first caught her just after our Superpower Ethics final. She'd slipped out of bed, waking me up, and raided my closet, looking for . . . something. There wasn't anything to find yet, though. I'd blown it off as a one-off. It was not. For the next almost three weeks, I'd been in a battle of minds with my girlfriend. I'd put off my purchase as long as I could. Then, I'd hidden it in different spots—usually ones I knew she'd already looked in. When that stopped working, I built a special hanger, and the already wrapped gift now hung inside my skull T-shirt in my closet.

She hadn't found it yet, and I'd asked her to stop looking after I hid it there, so she probably didn't know what it was. I fished the tiny box out with one hand, hiding it behind my back, and sat on the couch.

Bee stepped out of the bathroom a few minutes later, combing her curly black hair furiously and narrowing her brilliant blue eyes at my hidden hand She ducked down, hurried back to my secret base, and returned a moment later. Unlike me, she now wore a suitably Christmasy outfit: a green ugly sweater with a reindeer that looked more like a moose, jeans, and heavy-duty wool socks. As always, she smelled like green apples, and she had a gift of her own in one hand. She sat beside me, put her free hand around my waist, and started feeling around.

"Hey now, don't get grabby," I complained a moment before her hand clamped down on the present. I grappled with her, hand behind my back, trying to keep it away from her, but eventually, she outmaneuvered me and hurried off to the couch's far side. I grimaced dramatically and stood up. "At least wait a minute, okay? I need to make some hot chocolate."

"Awwwww, fine. Make some for me."

I could hear her shaking the damn box as I slowly walked into the kitchen and read the hot chocolate instructions out loud. "Hurry up, dammit," she complained.

I measured out *just* the right amount of water for each mug, double-checked the chocolate powder scoop to ensure it was *perfect*, and then thought of an even more evil idea. I sat on the counter and hummed "White Christmas" the whole time the microwave ran. It dinged. I grabbed the mugs and started walking back.

I'd almost reached the couch when I paused, looking thoughtful. "The marshmallows! I forgot the marshmallows!"

Bianca grabbed her mug before I could turn around. She glared daggers of pure hate at me, and I grinned sheepishly. "I guess I could skip the marshmallows for now?"

"Damn right you could," she said. She ripped into the wrapping paper, which flew everywhere. My gift was unwrapped almost before I could blink. She clipped it around her neck, and just as I'd suspected, the shiny silver necklace hung low enough that the kangaroo wouldn't be visible.

"You can loop it twice, too, if you want it to be a choker," I said.

"No thanks. It'd be harder to keep my secret identity. *Some* heroes actually care about that." She stuck her tongue out at me.

"Look, I thought I was doing a good job!"

"Yeah, you sure fooled everyone." Bianca laughed. She had a nice laugh, and she'd gotten over the awkwardness again after revealing her identity—and that my attempts to keep a secret had fooled no one.

"Teach me your ways, oh full-body-covering fursuit girl," I teased back. She wasn't wrong. I hadn't worried too much about my secret identity back home; Peter and Collidus had both known, and it'd been easy to . . . not hang out with too many people. Here, it was different, and I'd need to be careful.

She handed me my present, which I set on my lap.

I tore the wrapping paper off Bianca's box, which was much wider than mine, though similar in height. Then I popped the white cardboard open, expecting a similar necklace to the one I'd given her. Instead, I saw a tarot deck and a cat's collar. The same collar Pataki had included on her improved Fursona fursuit.

We needed to see Rocko. Now.

She'd given me a piece of her costume.

2

A Piece of Her Costume

I didn't pay much attention to Rocko as the four-armed, otter-furred alien movie executive rocketed up from his desk and knucklewalked toward me. I was far too busy basking in the gift's glow.

Sure, it was a cat collar, which made me anxious. I wasn't ready to be a furry, even as a Costume. Honestly, I had no idea how Bianca dealt with her gimmick. I guess if no one knew who you were, it'd be fine. But I'd be transforming on-screen. If I got a catgirl costume, no one would ever be able to take Understudy seriously. And it'd probably still look like a Magical Girl; I'd be Magical Girl Here Kitty Kitty or something.

God, that'd be the worst.

Most of my brain was still fuzzing up, though. I thought back to when Peter finally gave me his goggles, and how nice it was to wear something of his. This felt just as nice. Maybe even nicer because I *could* wear a cat collar with certain outfits. I'd just be another eccentric theater girl on campus. There were dozens of us—dozens!—and our numbers grew daily. Gifts had always been a weakness for me; unlike *some* people, I wasn't a present-poacher, but I *loved* getting little trinkets and doodads, especially if they meant something.

"DuPont, you're daydreaming," Rocko snapped.

I sucked in a breath, blinking. My hand gripped the collar, squeezing it like a stress ball. The Ilneat handed me a water bottle; I set the collar in my lap so I could take a sip.

"Now that you're with us, I have an even better Christmas present than Marino here does," Rocko said. "But first, results."

They hopped back onto their chair and pressed a remote. The screen showed the big finish to my Series Finale—specifically, the part where I dive-bombed Professor Panic's TERROR Mech and used [**Bit-Part Barrage**] to break into the cockpit, then landed on the professor and punched him in the face. They paused it. "Top ratings in the little league for the first two weeks, third now. Not bad at all, DuPont, Marino. Not. At. All. We're starting to recover from all the losses I took *getting* that Episode running in the first place."

"What, exactly, did you have to do?" I asked.

"I sold the rights to the *Small-Town Super* spin-off with Collidus, arranged a new contract for him and Professor Panic, and I owe . . . let's see . . . two more favors to major-league studios. Plus, I emptied Rocko Studios's coffers. I've got two super contracts unfilled and no budget for 'em, but that doesn't matter. Know why?"

"No, why?" Bianca asked. She winked at me. I grinned back, but I was processing. He'd gotten Professor Panic a new contract. We wouldn't fight again. Not unless one of us guest-starred on the other's show. Relief washed over me.

"Har har. Because I've got you two." They fiddled with their computer, and the screen changed. The network's schedule appeared. They'd shown me this before, but this time, they typed again, eliminating 95% of the shows. The remaining ones included *Heroics 101*, *Infinity Stellar Saga Redux*, *Sugar and Chili Powder*, *Crimson Crescent*, and a few others. All were Magical Girl–led shows.

Infinity Stellar Saga Redux was highlighted in red.

"Is that . . . ?"

"Yep." The Ilneat grinned predatorily. "One of the minor-league Magical Girls is set to drop leagues—super's choice, not the studio's. She's not hacking it in the minors and wants back on their old show. That leaves an opening. So, Merry Christmas. I told you I'd get you a shot at the minors by next season. Here it is."

"This is . . . This is great!" I stood up and gave Rocko a big, sweaty hug. "Thanks!"

"Hold on, DuPont," they said. "This is just a shot. *You've* gotta do the work side of it. See, there's one *teeny tiny* problem."

They messed with the screen again. "You two kick back for a bit, eh? Just enjoy the show, like your Superpower Ethics class, but a little different."

I stared at the screen. The Broadway Mall, where I'd patrolled with Tele-Portal, was in chaos. Shattered glass covered the ground, and a villainess laughed maniacally as she piled clothes into a henchman's arms. "The Shoppe-Lifter strikes again!" she yelled.

I facepalmed. This *had* to be a little-league villain. She was probably a bruiser, judging by her bulging biceps and by the deep red, sleeveless costume designed to showcase them. She was ripped; if she had that kind of strength and was robbing shopping malls, she wasn't a minor leaguer.

The scene switched as a figure jumped from one rooftop to another, closing in on Mid-Town. Every time he jumped, a dozen shining crystals bobbed up and down around him, bathing his white outfit and the plaid scarf around his neck in a multicolored light. The boy—he wasn't a college student, no way—pulled a jet-black wand from his pocket as he ran. He stopped on an overlooking rooftop, watching the madness unfold below.

I recognized him from somewhere. I *knew* it. I just couldn't place where.

A title popped across the screen. *Vowsworn*: Season Two, Episode One: "Broadway Blitz." This was an actual, publicly aired Episode, not one of the unpublished cuts from Superpower Ethics or a half-edited Rocko project. I hadn't heard about *Vowsworn* before. Back home, I'd been focused on *my* show or the minors and majors I wanted to be like, not on other little leaguers. And since I got here, I'd been playing catch-up or watching those same major leaguers with Bee, not keeping up on other little-league heroes.

"Who's he?" Bianca asked Rocko.

The Ilneat paused the screen. "Your competition. His Alias is Magical Boy Vigilant Vow. He's an up-and-comer with a **[Signature Skill]** that's almost as unique as Understudy's and a lot more powerful up front. He's only been on the little-league circuit for two years, but he's on his way up. That's the issue. Vigilant Vow's forty points ahead on the community rank board, and that board is *the* number three decider in offering minor-league spots, just behind archetype and marketability. It's not enough to be a camera magnet with your skills, or sell lots of toys, which you both do. You've gotta *win*. This kid's got all three. Watch what he does."

They pressed play, and the action started. I sighed. I'd been about to explain that we *had* been winning.

Vigilant Vow touched an opalescent crystal with the onyx wand and rattled off an oath. "I swear to defend Tokyexico in starlight and under new moon. To stand against evil and corruption. And, above all, to remain true to what's right and just. So witness star, so witness moon."

I blinked. Bianca gasped. That was Magical Girl Stella-Lunar's oath—everyone knew that. I leaned forward, eager to see what happened next.

The crystal broke. Light pooled and swirled below it. Something formed from the light, becoming increasingly solid by the second until Stella-Lunar's familiar, Iyago, suddenly stood there. The two-headed albino owl opened his two beaks and hooted once, then flew up to sit on Vigilant Vow's shoulder.

He cracked four more crystals, ending up with two cats, a weasel, and a fish that swam through the air around Iyago. Then he dropped to the ground, letting the owl slow his descent.

"Look, we could watch the whole Episode, but no one's got time for that. You've got a dinner, and I've got investors to schmooze. Let me sum it up from here. Vigilant Vow punches a few mooks. The army of damn familiars he's contracted with uses their original girls' powers to flatten The Shoppe-Lifter—not sure how that works, exactly, but holy shit do I wish I'd signed VV instead of Collidus when I had the chance. You two would already be minor leaguers with his familiar army and you as his sidekick."

Rocko tapped the pause button, leaving Vigilant Vow frozen mid-charge. I took a moment to compose myself. "How does his power work? It has something to do with the oaths, right?"

"Right. But we ain't focused on Vigilant Vow right now. We're focused on Understudy. Specifically, rebranding."

"Rebranding? Like, a new oath and costume?" I grinned. This Christmas kept getting better and better; it almost made it worth not being home.

"On the platform, feet on the *X*'s," Pataki drawled at me. Bee sat nearby, watching as I stepped into the scanner. I held my hands out, waited for the tickling sensation, and held still while the machine built a hard-light mannequin of me. It took way too long, but the model eventually finished, and Pataki waved me off. "Step out of the scanner, DuPont. We don't need yours, Marino. The suit's dimensions stay the same."

"Alright, alright, toss her normal costume up there," Rocko ordered. My pastel pink-and-blue dress covered the electronic mannequin, white tights and gloves on its limbs, and bows in its "hair."

"What's first?" I asked. I had some ideas, but I wanted to see what Rocko came up with.

Surprisingly, though, they pointed at Pataki. "Ideas. Go."

The costume designer took a long drag from their ever-present cigarette and spoke into their translator. "First off, ditch the little-league look. It's been great for you, but you're moving up, and your costume should reflect that. Let's pull up Stella-Lunar's Star Form outfit as a baseline."

Stella-Lunar's Star Form costume appeared on another mannequin. Pataki waved several hands at my outfit. "Get rid of that. Duplicate Star Form, resized for DuPont," Rocko said. They seemed more intense than usual, staring at it. I wasn't great at reading Ilneats' body language, but I thought I could hear the cash register sounds in their head.

"Done." Before I could protest, Pataki pulled the outfit off my hard-light copy, then quickly covered it with Stella-Lunar's dress. It looked nothing like my frilly, bow-festooned outfit. Instead, my model was encased in overlapping, semirigid plates, each covered in silk. The skirt only reached my upper thighs, and boots met it at the hemline instead of tights. It looked dangerous. Powerful. And—I blushed a bit at the thought—sexy.

It also featured a tiara instead of bows, which I approved of.

"You're still running the Magical Girl Understudy moniker, right?" Pataki asked.

"Yes," I said.

"No," Rocko interrupted at the same time. "How about Magical Girl Spotlight Star? More adult, more confident, kinda evokes Golden Goose and her powerset. Could be good."

"No," Bianca said quickly. I glanced at her questioningly. "You don't want that kind of reputation."

"Why not? She makes millions for her studio, and she's amazing at stopping supervillains," Rocko said.

As they argued about Golden Goose's relative merits, I pondered. Golden Goose *did* win her fights, and Rocko said we needed wins. Lots of wins. If I built a reputation as the little league's Golden Goose, I could win Episodes before they even started. That'd be powerful. But . . . that wasn't me, and even though it was still theater-themed, Spotlight Star didn't fit what my power *did*. I wasn't a star. Not a spotlight-hogging one. [**Adaptive Armoire**] let me fill any role easily, but I wasn't an expert bot-builder, a powerful elementalist, or great at anything else. I was the backup actor—able to do it all.

"I'm sticking with Understudy," I said, interrupting their argument. "It fits my [**Signature Skill**], and you said it'd be what got me to the majors, right?"

Rocko sighed. "Fine. Fine. You wanna stick with a little-league name, be my guest. It's only our shot at the minors on the line. Now, let's talk oaths and outfits. That's what *really* needs to change. Gimme your oath."

"'I swear on my family, who I love very much, that I'll stand up against Professor Panther, his minions, and evil all over Riverside! I'll fight for justice, peace, and hope! And I'll never stop 'til evil does first,'" I recited. "Then I go through the sequence. Can we fix the sequence, too?"

"Maybe. I've got appointments."

"Got it. Then, after the sequence, it's 'Don't fear! Magical Girl Understudy is here! I swear to defend the weak against evil and uphold truth and love!'"

"Wow." Bianca laughed. "I've never paid attention to exactly what you say. Yeah, that's gotta change."

3

That's Gotta Change

Bianca looked happy, but Rocko was *pissed*.

Somehow, my new outfit had even *more* frills on the skirts than the previous one. The blue had almost disappeared, replaced by a pastel purple, and in contrast to Magical Girl Stella-Lunar's Star Form battle dress, it seemed even less armored than my old outfit. Not that armor mattered; I had superhero damage to mitigate injuries.

The two big changes, however, were the tiara and the golden filigree. The first sat just below the hard-light dummy's hairline, pushing it up and out of its face. It featured a tall crest in the center, prominently displaying the comedy and tragedy masks and a row of stars descending on each side. I wasn't sure why Magical Girls all needed stars on everything, but I wasn't complaining. The dress's bodice was off-white now, with golden patterning around my chest and down the tights. I'd chosen to replace the thigh-highs with proper hose, and apparently, that came with gold. So did the domino mask.

I'd made a few other minor changes to the dress. The poofy shoulders *had* to go. Rocko had replaced them with scarlet off-the-shoulder mini-sleeves, which, shockingly, looked terrific. And I'd replaced the sapphire and bow with a purple amethyst, which sat in the gold filigree's center.

"Dammit, DuPont. I said like Stella-Lunar, not . . . whatever this is," Rocko complained.

"Actually, this is based on late-little-league Stella's outfit, with a touch of Scarlet Star's for spice," Pataki corrected. "The ballerina-esque skirts give it some class and a lot of leg, which looks older, and the gold—and your red—offer some maturity as well. It's still a little-league Magical Girl outfit, but it's modeled on what successful would-be-minor-league girls have worn in the past. And it doesn't have a cape. I approve."

Well, if it was good enough for Pataki, it was good enough for me. I nodded. "How quickly can you have this in the System?"

"An hour or two. You won't be able to transform at all while I work. And give me that collar. I've got an idea," Pataki rasped.

I handed the collar over, and Pataki started fiddling on their keyboard. Then they glared at Rocko. "Get out. I don't want an audience for this one."

"Fine. But Pataki, the ratings better be through the roof, or it'll be outta your paycheck!" Rocko stood up. "DuPont, Marino, waiting room. We'll work through the oath."

I followed. I knew something Rocko either hadn't caught on to or, for once, was too tactful to mention. The new dress showed some actual cleavage above the new amethyst gemstone. Not much; in fact, it was downright modest compared to half my college outfits. But against the old dress, and in the role of heroine, it felt almost scandalous. I'd made sure to add it, which was one reason Bianca was probably thrilled.

Ratings were going up.

Rocko drummed their fingers against a chair. "Oath. That oath ain't gonna cut it. It's been good for *Small Town Super* and early *Heroics 101* pilots, but we're launching a proper Season One now. Ditch the family, ditch some of the love, ditch the named villain—you don't have a rival anymore—and please, please, don't say 'Don't fear! Magical Girl Understudy is here!'"

Bianca snorted. I whirled in my plastic seat. "Oh please. You call yourself the Marsupial of Justice."

"That's clicking with older audiences better than your oath," Rocko said.

"Shit." I took a deep breath. "How about 'The spotlight shines on darkness and villainy'? That feels more in line with what my powers do now, and it's more—"

"It's better than 'love' and 'truth' and 'peace,' but we can do better." Rocko pulled a paper and started scribbling. "Okay, you gotta hit three ideals. You gotta have a catchphrase. You gotta name the community you're part of, but we'll let it flex this time. And then you need the post-sequence stinger."

"'I swear to upstage villains and put justice in the spotlight across Tokyexico'? That's better, right?"

"That's too short," Bianca said. "This shit's your big spotlight moment, no pun intended. You've gotta go big. How about 'I swear to upstage villains and put justice in the limelight, from opening night to curtain call. To stand against evil, greed, and villainy. And to stay true to love and hope?'"

"That'll work. We can refine it after Season One, but it's functional. And the postsequence vow? That can be more of a catchphrase. Yeah, a catchphrase would be best."

"'I'll always be your star, Tokyexico!'"

Rocko put their face in three hands, holding their cigar carefully away so they didn't knock it to the ground. "Seriously? I give you creative freedom, and *that's* the line you come up with? It's not on-theme, it's not clever, and it's not minor-league. Back to the drawing board."

Then they got an evil-looking grin. "Even better. Marino! What's your catchphrase?"

"Have no fear, Justice-Roo is here."

Rocko shook their head. "That's stupid, but it's better than 'I'll always be your star.' It's on-brand for you, and it evokes pre–Launch Day superheroes. You want that catchphrase to be snappy. Something people will remember. Justice-Roo is memorable. Goofy and little league as all get out, but memorable. Try again."

"'Villains, exit stage left'? 'The curtains close on evil'? 'Shining a light on crime'?" I had no idea what to do.

But, shockingly, Rocko nodded. "The first one's not bad. You might even earn a Badass point or two if you say it right. So, run me through the whole thing from the top. Action!"

"I swear to upstage the villains and put justice in the limelight from opening night until curtain call. To stand against evil, greed, and cruelty. And to stay true to love and hope." I did a little spin and jazz-hands; Backstage, the System was off, and Pataki'd said I couldn't transform even if I wanted to. "Villains, time to exit stage left!"

"That works," Rocko said. They puffed a cloud of clove-scented smoke. "Time to work on yours, Marino!"

A couple hours later, Bee and I slipped through the Backstage door and into my green room. "Show me, show me, show me," she said, bouncing up and down excitedly.

I held the collar in my hand. "Fine, but get out, just in case the sequence is incredibly embarrassing."

"What, worse than Squirt's?"

"Shut up!" I held the maintenance door to my apartment open and stared until she walked out. Then I stared at the collar in my hand for a full minute. Pataki had said it was a surprise, and the Ilneat costume designer refused to elaborate, which meant the new Costume was either incredibly dumb or ridiculously cool. I ran through my new oath, the same old transformation to Understudy, and my new catchphrase. Then I fastened the collar around my neck and held Tails high.

"Transform meow!"

<Transform meow!>

The plushie cat hovered in front of me. She lifted a paw at the same time I raised my hand. I spun and so did she, mirroring my movements. Then, as I bowed at her, she leaped out of the air and onto my head. I flinched from the sudden pounce and reached up to steady her. But I couldn't feel her.

I *could* feel two ears, though.

And two tails.

"Oh my god!" I screamed, locking the maintenance door.

"It's been fifteen minutes, Annie! I know you're done changing!" Bianca knocked on the door, thumping on it over and over.

A small part of me noted how mundane that sentence sounded out of context. A normal relationship was probably full of moments like that; one partner hogging the bathroom while the other banged desperately on the door, or a locked bedroom door keeping someone from their nap.

Most normal relationships weren't powered, though. And of the ones that were, one partner usually didn't turn into a catgirl.

Which was precisely what Pataki's costume design had done to me.

I had two cat ears, white plushie fur across my face, and whiskers. The dress, similar in design to my old Understudy outfit, pressed even more plush down. And, worst of all, were the tails—two of them, just like my familiar. I'd taken one look and screamed again. Thank god, the door was locked. I'd never hear the end of this as it was, but at least I had time to think about how I'd explain this to Bee.

<Okay,> I thought. Or maybe Tails thought. I wasn't sure where she ended and I began anymore. *<Let's take a nap for a bit and think this through. The Ilneat who built this had a wonderful idea, and nya-ow we're one person. Do you feel like fish? I feel like fish.>*

"Stop talking about food, Tails. I'm going to be sick."

The domino mask formed a black pattern around my eyes. I couldn't see why. No one was *ever* going to recognize me like this.

<You should look at your new powers meow!>

"Come on, I wanna see!" Bianca said from behind the door. She sounded frustrated, but I couldn't explain this. No. Way.

"J-just a minute!" I shouted. I pulled up the catgirl Costume's powers. Then I groaned. "Bianca, I'm going to kill you! These power names are so stupid!"

"I know, right? Open the door and let me see!"

"Gimme a minute!"

"You've had like twenty!"

[**Leaping Leopards**] was a gap-closer. It was a pounce. A full-on pounce. It had a cooldown, but no restriction on the uses per act. I could use it to leap to prey—er, villains—from far away. Simple, practical, and, frankly, kind of uninteresting. But it was a functional Badass power, and since Fursona was Badass/Grit, I needed to try it out. Her version must've been whatever she'd used to hop onto the van during "You're Super-Suited for This Job" during the job fair.

[**Cat-Scratch Fever**] seemed much more interesting. A combination of damage over time and a double-vision debuff, I could only use it once per Act. It paired well with [**Leaping Leopards**], though. *Really* well. Against a more powerful villain like Theseus, I could use [**Hometown Heroine**], leap into melee with [**Leaping Leopards**], and [**Cat-Scratch Fever**] before running away. I wasn't sure which of Fursona's powers this copied. I looked at my paws and extended the half-inch claws.

Yeah. I had paws, too.

The last power was the reason I told Bianca the power names were stupid. [**Fursonal Furcefield**] gave me a 20% chance to ignore damage as long as I wore my fursuit. There was just one problem.

"Tails, I don't *have* a fursuit."

"Oh my god you got that power this is amazing!" Bianca said from the door. I was glad we had the thirteenth floor to ourselves since her voice echoed around my apartment. She'd have blown at least one of our covers otherwise.

<I'm your fursuit meow!> Tails said in my mind. I paused. I had no idea how that'd work with this power, and that meant it was the most important one to test. If it *did* work, would Tails take damage? I'd had Pataki make sure she was fine after the Series Finale, but I didn't want to get her hurt.

All told, my new Costume looked pretty solid mechanically—but also totally embarrassing visually.

[Costume - Copy Cat]
[HP 7/7]
[Styles and Skills]
▶Archetype Skill - Transformation Sequence
▶Badass
▶Leaping Leopards 0
▶Cunning
▶Drama
▶Cat-Scratch Fever 0
▶Hometown Heroine 1
▶Flamboyance
▶Signature Skill - Adaptive Armoire 1
▶Stored Costumes: (Understudy)
▶Spotlight Strike 1
▶Grit
▶Fursonal Furcefield 0

Bianca banged on the door. I gulped, walked over, put my hand on the door, and hesitated. "Don't laugh when you see it, okay?"

"I wear a fursuit for my powers. I'm not gonna laugh."

"Okay. I'm holding you to that." I cracked open the door.

Bianca smiled, but to her credit, she didn't laugh. I explained the powers I'd gotten and the body-merge with Tails as best I could, which was hard when Tails couldn't explain it either. It took a few minutes on the couch to finish the explanation.

When it was over, Bianca leaned in for a quick kiss, but she pulled back with a grossed-out expression. "Eugh! Whisker!"

"Sorry, but that's kinda your fault." I flopped onto the couch, and she ran her hand through my plushie fur. It felt good. Really good.

Then she stopped. "Annie, you're purring. That's really weird. And . . . kinda fun?"

<She can do that anytime!>

I stood up, blushing. "We'll explore this newfound interest of yours later. I'm changing back and getting ready for Christmas Dinner."

4

Christmas Dinner

Su-Bin's parents were from Seoul, an old city from before Launch Day. They'd gotten dumped here in Tokyexico when the Ilneats returned everyone to Earth, but Christmas had been one of their traditions before they'd left. It just hadn't been quite so . . . commercialized.

Mr. Pak laughed over the remains of his ham. "We switched to North American Christmas after we came here. Or, more accurately, Su-Bin smuggled it in."

I looked over my shoulder theatrically and nodded. "She sure did." The apartment's living room was *covered* in wrapping paper, and the tree sat half-tilted from their cat's efforts. They'd cooked all day, and—being completely honest and without any guilt at all—I admitted their Christmas dinner was the best tasting I'd ever had. Mom and Dad couldn't compete; the double-wide trailer's oven wasn't big enough, and Mom wasn't this good of a cook. The whole apartment smelled like honey, cinnamon, and fresh bread.

I leaned back, stuffed. Bianca excused herself and hurried to the bathroom. A moment later, she burped, sounding like a cross between a frog and a cow. Su-Bin and I both laughed while Mr. Pak smiled. The Paks were the kind of people who didn't have first names until you got to know them. He turned to me.

"We've asked Su-Bin, but we're curious. With supervillains on campus and in school-sponsored clubs, do you feel safe on campus?"

"Yes?" Where'd that question come from? I glanced at Su-Bin, who looked apologetic.

I *knew* Su-Bin couldn't possibly know my secret identity; I wasn't that close to her, and Bianca had seen both the superhero and the student. But she *did* know I liked supers a lot. We'd discussed it before, even though she wasn't into them.

"Well, we're not sure Su-Bin is. She's taking Engineering 103 next semester."

"Oh, because of *that* fight. The building was empty, and only part of it collapsed." I realized I was too flippant as soon as I said it, but it was too late. I'd already put my foot in my mouth.

"Anika, right?" Mrs. Pak asked. Her eyes narrowed.

I nodded.

"I don't trust heroes," she said bluntly. "They're in on it with the villains, and it's all a game. The Pherris Report did the digging, and according to them, crime is up 26% from three years ago. There are too many heroes and villains looking to make it big, and none of them care about us. We're just Extras, and—"

"Mom. It's Christmas." Su-Bin looked mortified that the conversation was going this way. "Can we not do this tonight?"

"No, she's right," Mr. Pak said. "I'm just *shocked* that the university didn't do more to keep people safe. There's only so much we can put up with, and things aren't getting better out there. Right, Anika?"

I shot Bianca a look. She'd done a *ton* of research when she got her powers. She nodded just slightly and cleared her throat. "Actually, the streets are statistically safer than they were pre–Launch Day. Things get bad just before Power Wars, but that's only because all the supers look at their competition and start pushing harder."

"That's not true," Mrs. Pak interrupted.

"It's really not. The Pherris Report says it's as bad as it's ever been right now. Should we even allow Power Wars?" Mr. Pak asked. The question sounded like it came from someone else and like he was repeating what he'd heard. "Are superheroes *really* heroes? How can you tell which is which?"

My mouth was open, but Su-Bin cleared her throat before I could say anything. "I'm not sure I feel safe at school either, Dad, but it's Christmas. Please?"

Mrs. Pak looked ready to keep going, but Mr. Pak put his hand on hers. "Sure. We want you to be safe, though, and it's a bigger, scarier world than when we were young."

It didn't seem bigger or scarier to me. Didn't everyone used to live under the threat of nuclear war? We'd watched a whole Episode about nukes last semester, and how dangerous they were. But I let the subject change. "What classes do you have next semester, Su-Bin?"

Su-Bin pounced on the opportunity. "Engineering, Calculus, Child Psychology, Creative Writing, and Post–Launch Day North American History. I'm excited about Calculus and Engineering, but the others sound boring."

"We might share some classes. What time is Child Psychology?"

"Ten o'clock Tuesdays and Thursdays."

"Twinsies!" I held out my hand for a high five. I did *not* tell her about Creative Writing since that was my "cover" class for Combat Style. We probably didn't share that class, but I'd rather have time to find an excuse if we did.

The three of us chatted for a while about our classes. I had Prop Design and Manufacture, Ilneat Politics, Combat Style, Child Psych, and Ilnean 1: Intro to Ilnean Language. Bianca wasn't in any of my regular ones this semester, which kind of sucked. I'd hoped she wanted to stick with the theater theme, but her biology career path locked in a lot of her choices. And, much to my annoyance, she actually seemed interested in it as a career.

"Well, I think that's a great choice," Mr. Pak said approvingly. "And what about you, Anika?"

"I'm thinking either theater or law."

I did *not* mention it was superpower law, but I doubted he'd have been happy if I had.

I rode the elevator—the real one, not my secret one to the green room—up to my apartment. Su-Bin's parents had been nice at first, but it bothered me a ton that they disliked supers so much. They hadn't seemed upset, either. No one had ever wronged them specifically, or if someone had, they hadn't said anything. But they did have real concerns.

The Tokyexico University Student Superhero Association and the Student Supervillain Society routinely put students at risk, often for downright crazy purposes. Not every villain created high-risk Episodes, of course, and most student supers had Codes of Ethics thanks to the Superpower Ethics class. But that didn't mean what the villains were doing was *legal*. And it definitely didn't mean it was *safe*.

Professor Panic and all the other villains without codes were a different story. He didn't have a code. He'd leveled a building on campus and probably made Su-Bin's parents more worried than they'd already been.

I'd talk to Su-Bin sometime and see what she thought.

My computer sat on the coffee table, with a pair of presents next to it. The red one said *Mom*, and the green one said *Dad*. Neither was wrapped *well*; lumps bulged out of the blob-shaped presents, both of which had far too much tape.

I opened up the laptop and found my video chat option. I pressed Call, and then waited while the digital ringing filled the room.

"Merry Christmas, Annie!" Mom and Dad both shouted. Mom held a glass of orange juice, but judging by her rosy cheeks, she'd spiked it with something. For once, she didn't have a cigarette. Dad's drink was nowhere to be seen. He waved into the screen.

"Hi, Mom! Hi, Dad! I missed you a ton at dinner." I rubbed an eye, which had started stinging.

"Us too, Anika," Mom said. "Did you have a good time with your friend?"

"Yeah, kind of." I explained everything as best I could, trying not to sound too confused. I didn't feel like I'd done a good job when I finished.

Mom nodded, though. "There were some people like that in Riverside. Antisuper folks. Before you got powers, I was one of them."

I didn't say anything for a moment. "You were antisuperhero?"

"No. Not antisuperhero. Antisuper. There's a big difference. Superheroes aren't a problem for most people, even the antisupers. It's the villains. Crime *does* spike all the time, but in Riverside, it wasn't as noticeable. The only villain was a little leaguer with an army of robots. There wasn't a Power War going, either." Mom sighed, looking away from the screen. "Look, the fact is that most antisuper people have completely fair concerns. And in an ideal world, I'd rather not have powered people running around. I'd rather not be an Extra."

"But that's not what we have," Dad said. He hurried to fill the conversation before Mom could keep talking. "We've got dangerous villains like that gas guy who attacked us on move-in day—"

"Haze-Matt."

"—Yeah, Haze-Matt. Thanks, Dot. Villains like that need to be stopped, and when they get that powerful, the police aren't enough anymore."

"But you were antisuper?" I asked Mom.

"Yes. I *was* antisuper. I've come around, at least a little bit. We're not getting rid of villains, so getting rid of heroes makes no sense."

"We are *not* ruining this virtual holiday with pro versus antisuper talk," Dad said decisively. He pointed at a pile of wrapped gifts, then attempted to ruin the virtual holiday a different way. "Have your grades come in yet?"

"No." I stiffened. I hadn't put enough effort into my classes, and I was worried about what that report card would say. But that was a problem for tomorrow Anika, not today Anika. "I'll let you know when they do. Let's get to the gift exchange."

"Alright, Dot. Which present do you want us to unwrap first?" Dad asked.

"The one on top." I watched as Mom and Dad slowly unwrapped it, peeking inside and pretending to be excited about what they'd gotten me. We'd been playing this game all month with Advent Calendars, so it wasn't new or anything, and it definitely wasn't as good as being home.

If the option to go to Bianca's house had been on the table, I'd probably have taken it. But not being able to be home—not having Dad's cookies, decorating, or even the stupid drive around Riverside to see the lights? Missing all that was hard, and it'd all just hit me. I was a sniffly mess by the time they'd finished unwrapping the new backpack, which was a pink faux-leather and would probably look fantastic with my new costume.

I grinned through the tears while I unwrapped their gifts. Dad got a model airplane made of wood that he'd have to put together, and Mom got a fabulous multicolored blouse I'd found at Broadway Mall. "I'll . . . hide them in the closet until I can come home," I sniffed.

Being stuck away from home for the holidays sucked.

<Hey Annie. Can we chat for a bit? - Bianca 9:45>
<Yeah. I could use the distraction. Coming over? - Annie 9:46>
<Nope. Too cold out, and I'm tired. Just text - Bianca 9:46>

I wasn't in any condition to have her over right now, but I also wanted to talk. I lay on my bed, halfway under the covers, eating Christmas chocolate. The wrappers sat on the floor and on my blanket while a little-league Episode played. It was Vigilant Vow. I was trying to get a jump on the competition, but my attention kept drifting.

<What's up? - Annie 9:47>
<I miss home - Bianca 9:48>
<Me too - Annie 9:48>
<My mom makes precooked ham every year. It's usually dry - Annie 9:48>
<I'd rather have her ham than Mrs. Paks - Annie 9:49>

My eyes got watery, and I blinked the tears away. On the screen, VV summoned his familiar squad—five again—and ducked into the shadows as the fantastical animals swarmed toward a building where some villain had taken hostages.

<I'm hurting a lot, annie. It's like when I came out here - Bianca 9:50>

I shut the Episode off and squeezed my eyes shut. Figuring out how Vigilant Vow's power worked was important, but I needed to focus on Bee. And on me. The job could wait.

<Tell me about it - Annie 9:51>
<I flew. I had one carry-on and two checked bags. That's it - Bianca 9:52>
<Mom and Dad didn't come with. Busy with working - Bianca 9:52>
<So I had a tough Saturday and Sunday night - Bianca 9:53>
<<3 - Annie 9:53>
<Thanks - Bianca 9:54>
<So I really needed a friend on Monday - Bianca 9:55>
<Thanks again for that btw - Bianca 9:55>

We chatted for another hour, jumping back to talk about her flight, then way ahead to her coming out to me, then back to our first Episode against Jumper and S. By the time Bianca felt tired, I knew more about her than I had about Peter in our first year together, all in text messages. Eventually, though, she texted me one last time.

<Goodnight. Tomorrow we'll do some research - Bianca 11:58>

I didn't fall asleep, unfortunately. I was too worried. I wasn't sure if it was the race for the minor-league role, homesickness, or my impending report card.

5

Report Card

MONDAY, DECEMBER 29

Fall Semester, Freshman Year

Math: Algebra - C-, 1.7

History: Post–Launch Day North American History - C, 2.0

Performing Arts: Intro to Drama - A, 4.0

Political Science: Ilneat Relations - B, 3.0

Ethics: Ethics - Pass, 3.0

Cumulative GPA: 2.74

I hadn't *failed* Algebra, but I wasn't looking forward to telling my parents about my grades. Cs get degrees, but in high school, they'd also gotten my parents mad at me.

I curled up on the couch and tried to think up a way to spin this. Math was expected. And, to be honest, I'd ditched too much of Post–Launch Day North American History to have a shot at an A there. The other two were fine, and Ethics . . . was what it was. I could call the bottom three a victory. History hurt, but I could recover from that, and none of my career options needed any more math. I was fine. I just had to convince my parents.

Easier said than done.

I scrolled to the next email.

Subject: Academic Performance Meeting Request
Magical Girl Understudy,

As your advisor, I'm requesting a meeting to discuss your academic performance this past fall semester. You are not currently in danger of academic probation. However, reports from some of your instructors are troubling, and I would like to head off any future issues.

Are you available for a meeting today at 12:15? I will provide lunch. You don't need to bring anything.

Dr. Mindstorm

Associate Professor of Superpower Studies

"Well, shit," I muttered. "On my break, huh?"

<*It seems so. I'd say nya. You're busy, and school's not in session,*> Tails said, voice echoing in my head. The plushie cat lay unmoving on my bed in the other room, but since our first session as Copy Cat, she'd been much easier to talk to. All. The. Time.

"Yeah. That's what I want to do, but she'll corner me sometime during the first week back if I don't," I answered. "I'll just get it over with."

Subject: RE: Academic Performance Meeting Request

Dr. Mindstorm,

I'm available today at 12:15. I'll see you then.

Magical Girl Understudy

Dr. Mindstorm's office hadn't changed over break, but she wasn't dressed for teaching, supervillainy, *or* lounging on the couch. The retired supervillain wore a sweatshirt with "Friends of Tokyexico Public Library" on the front and a pair of jeans. Two cardboard take-out boxes sat on her desk.

"Sit and . . . enjoy the food," Mindstorm said in her bored, slippery-sounding voice. She slid a box my way: Lo mein and vegetables. I sniffed it as she kept talking. "I'm a vegetarian and was unsure what your . . . eating habits were."

The salty smell of soy filled the tiny room quickly as we ate. Mindstorm took three bites, then stared at me until I paused. "What's this meeting about?" I asked.

"Your academic future at Tokyexico University. I am having a . . . similar meeting with all my mentees. However, your case is my most pressing. Your plans post-school revolve around superhero work . . . correct?"

I nodded and slurped a noodle. "Yeah. I'm taking some theater classes, and Mom wants me in superpower law, but I'm going to be a hero."

"I thought that was the case. Are you familiar with the 'Freshman Fifteen'?"

"Yeah, of course." The Freshman Fifteen was the mythical idea that college students, exposed to tons of free food, inevitably gained weight. It didn't always happen, and I was crossing my fingers—and eating plenty of burritos even though it made it more likely. "What's that got to do with academics?"

"You're also familiar with New Power Boldness Syndrome?"

I nodded. Fursona had mentioned it during our discussion about The Agent and responsibility last semester.

"There's another common issue with superpowered students—actually, most supers, but it's almost . . . universal in students. Superpower Slacking. It's the idea that the rest of a super's life isn't important compared to the mask, cape, or cowl. It happens . . . frequently . . . on campus. The job becomes all-consuming, and super students stop attending classes they really should be at."

I winced. She was talking about me ditching history.

"I'm not talking about your history attendance, though that *is* a warning sign." Mindstorm sighed. "You missed it consistently, according to Teaching Assistant Smith, but Rocko Studios claims you didn't make a single Episode during your truancy. Superpower Slacking is more consistent across all classes, and also . . . impacts your social life."

"If I'm not doing it, why are we talking about it?" I asked. Honestly, this all felt pretty accusatory, and I didn't like that—not from a former supervillain.

"You're currently at high risk for Superpower Slacking in the upcoming semester. Your record of truancy and your . . . flouting of the rules during finals week are both major warning signs. So is your lack of . . . direction relative to your peers. Many super students have majors picked out, or at least directions they're pursuing as covers. Alone, your lack of direction is not a problem. Taken with the other . . . warning signs . . . I have concerns. I also have . . . recommendations."

"Like what?" I narrowed my eyes. "I'm not on academic probation. I did well enough not to be in trouble, so I'm not sure why I'm in trouble anyway."

"You aren't in trouble." Dr. Mindstorm sighed and stared at the ceiling. "Why are the 'good guys' always so hardheaded? This would be easier if I just . . . snipped the slacking out."

I stiffened. "What?"

"Nothing. I recommend an every-other-week check-in to see how classes are going."

"No. I'm fine."

"Magical Girl Understudy, I am not trying to make you miserable. I am trying to help you be successful at Tokyexico University, get your minor in Superpower Studies, and use the skills we teach to springboard your postschool career. You're signed up for Combat Style with Professor Tennyson and me. There are more classes like that, all designed to make you a better super postcollege. But the administration watches supers carefully, and you're on their naughty list after . . . destroying the Engineering and Applied Sciences building and Mister Felsic statue. I helped you and Rocko. I stuck my neck out for you. You need to . . . take advantage of my generosity."

"Ah." I had no interest in meeting with Dr. Mindstorm seven or eight times next semester. But I didn't see a way around it other than just saying no. "Can we make the meeting times between my classes and keep my evenings and weekends free?"

"Yes."

"Then . . . fine." I crossed my arms, feeling like Rainy Day with how stupidly petulant I probably looked.

"Wonderful."

We finished our lo mein in an awkward silence.

My pastel-pink green room smelled like hot chocolate and cinnamon.

And green apples.

"Okay, you're ranked three hundred forty-eighth in Tokyexico. Our friend Magical Boy Vigilant Vow is two hundred ninety-ninth—he moved up again. So, let's make a plan to change that." Bianca had a whiteboard on wheels, probably from a classroom on campus. She wrote 'Rank-Up Plan' in the middle of the board, then drew a big circle around it.

"We need Episodes. Lots of Episodes," I said.

Bianca wrote 'Episodes' and circled it, then linked it to the middle circle. "Yeah. Who do we know? Any likely wins, or anyone that'd be impactful?"

"Easy fights? Honeycomb and Jumper. Tottergarten. Flare and The Crumb. But none of them are . . . good. Maybe we can talk to Gourmet and get her to show up *without* Theseus this time. We could probably beat her now two versus one."

The dry-erase marker flew across the whiteboard; the first three ideas went into a circle labeled 'Filler Episodes,' while Gourmet went into one called 'Headliners.' Both of those connected to the 'Episodes' circle.

"Add 'The SSS' to 'Headliners.' They're big-shot Episodes, even if we join as side-kicks. And I also have patrols with Tele-Portal."

"Yeah, if she doesn't decide to get rid of you after the Season Finale shenani-gans. We'll add to 'Headliners' as we find them, but let's not add to the 'Filler Episodes' unless we have to." Bee nodded thoughtfully. "Any other ideas? No? Then let's move on."

She drew another circle. I groaned. "Training doesn't move the community rank."

Bianca glared at me. "I had six soccer practices for every game in high school. That's how we got to the third playoff round my senior year. Training doesn't move your rank, but it *does* help us fight better together. What are our options there?"

"Tottergarten again." If it worked—kind of—for Honeycomb, it'd work for us. Plus, we wouldn't be relying solely on fighting the Anti-Nap League to get better, and if we talked to The Narrator, she might be willing to accommodate us and set us up with some more challenging fights.

Bianca nodded. She wrote 'Tottergarten' under 'Training.' Then she added 'The Triad.'

"Yeah! They had the training arena. Maybe Tele-Portal will let us run an old Episode or two."

"Maybe. We also have the Combat Style class. There might be something there for fighting with a partner." 'Combat Style' went on the board.

I stood up and started pacing. "So, we have 'Episodes' and 'Training.' How else do we move up the ranks?"

"*We* don't need to move," Bianca said. She shrugged. "I'm currently in the four hundreds. The low four hundreds, but I won't catch up. We need *you* to move, and I have an idea to make that happen in a high-risk, high-reward way."

My danger sense—my nonexistent danger sense, which never worked when I tried something dumb—went off like a fire alarm as she wrote 'Public Relations' on the whiteboard. She circled it. "I'm thinking three fronts. First, PSAs."

"I've done PSAs before." I'd done a couple for the high school "news" channel back home. They barely counted, but it was an option if getting recognized was my goal. "I don't think it's the best option, though."

"Neither do I. That's why I have three options." Bianca wrote 'PSAs.' Then she wrote another option. "KRTU. It's the campus radio station. The three p.m. Tuesday and Thursday DJ runs an Ask Me Anything and Interview segment after his playlist. So far, he's interviewed some heroes and villains, the campus vice president in charge of student affairs, the TU women's soccer coach, and a Tokyexico Council of Heroes representative. That last one was interesting—it was a no-holds-barred discussion about Man vs. Nature and safety issues on campus and across the city."

"Who's the host?"

"No idea. Goes by DJ Smooth—I know it's dumb, but there it is. He's a freshman, and sometimes he arranges roundtables and panel discussions, too. He's shockingly professional for a freshman."

"Okay. I'm in. What's the last one?"

"Television talk shows."

"Nope. That's too much." I sat back down and went for my phone. "I can do radio on campus, but live TV is too much. I'm good at putting my foot in my mouth."

"Ooookay, setting that one in the 'Strong Maybe' pile, then," Bianca said. She wrote 'Strong Maybe' on the board and scribbled 'Talk Shows' underneath it. Then she flopped down, not in her regular chaise lounge, but beside me. I wiggled so my head rested on her leg, and she played with my hair. She'd been doing that a *lot* since I got the Copy Cat Costume.

I knew she wanted me to transform, but I didn't want to. Not right now. I needed my Bee time, not my Bee *and* Tails time. So, instead, I pulled out my phone and started doomscrolling on Followbook. Every time I found a funny video, I made Bee watch it. We bounced other ideas for The Plan off each other, but nothing sounded promising enough to add to the board. And she played with my hair the whole time— almost thirty minutes.

My phone buzzed. So did Bee's, but she blew it off. I read the email and passed the phone to her. "Sound fun?"

She read the email and passed it back. "Yeah, that sounds fun."

Subject: TUSSA New Year's "Rager"
Greetings, Magical Girl Understudy,
According to Hephaestus, it is time for a "rager."
When: December 31, 11:00 p.m.
Where: TUSSA Cave
What: New Year's Party. Tap beer provided. Pizza provided. Music Provided. Show up in costume, but be ready to be accessorized. Keep your New Year's Day open to recover.
Party Hardy, Superheroes,
Ikenga
President, TUSSA

6

Party Hardy, Superheroes

Fursona and I walked furtively through the tunnels, on the lookout for any SSS members. A few of them were back on campus, and if they found out the whole student superhero population was at a party, they might try something.

And it really would be the *whole* population. Vigilantes too. Someone had invited them. I wasn't sure how I felt about that, but I'd spend the time with Springlock and Milo. And Fursona, of course. I enjoyed their company.

"You're such a hottie in the new costume," Fursona said through her voice modulator. "I'm really excited for tonight."

"Me too." I *felt* like a hottie. An added, unforeseen benefit to the Understudy costume was the ballerina-like skirt. Pataki had included a cool function in it, though. The stiffness snapped off with a few moves, leaving me with a passable cocktail-dress-style outfit that swished around mid-thigh. "Sorry that you're not gonna be able to drink or anything."

"Oh, don't worry. Pataki took care of that problem."

We arrived at the door to the TUSSA Cave. Hephaestus stood just outside, next to a table of goofy accessories; New Year's glasses, pointed hats, noisemakers and kazoos, and a pair of glittery spheres with "Take at Your Own Risk" written on the tablecloth beside them. "Don't take those," the Genius said. "If you do, and you use them in there, that's on you. I don't know why Ikenga told me to bring them."

"What do they do?" Fursona asked.

Hephaestus snorted. "What do you think they do? They're glitter bombs. Choose something, come on in, and have fun. The bar opens in eight minutes and thirty-four seconds. Swing by for a free drink."

"Sure. Thanks." I picked a hat with a cartoon baby on it and a noisemaker—the kind you blew to whack your neighbor with the unfurling paper bit. Fursona picked the kazoo and, against *everyone's* better judgment, a glitter bomb.

"Come on in. No powers. Everyone's drinking, so it's better if you don't use anything. We don't want a repeat of what happened last year." Hephaestus shuddered dramatically.

"What happened last year?" Fursona asked as I opened the door. The frenetic pulse of drum-and-bass music roared out toward us, along with shouted conversation. My whole body shook.

"You don't want to know!" Hephaestus shouted back.

The door shut behind us. Fursona wrapped her paw around mine and dragged me toward the dance floor, where two familiar, green-and-purple-suited superheroes bounced up and down with a bunch of people I'd seen at the job fair. I slapped the goofy, cone-shaped party hat on my head and followed her.

Punch caught sight of me before we even started dancing. He turned, uh . . . punched . . . his brother in the shoulder, and pointed right at me. Shit.

The last time I'd seen Punch outside of a class was right here, in the TUSSA Cave. We'd just won the lair-assault Episode in a come-from-behind finish, but he'd been upset at me for . . . I wasn't sure, to be honest. For using my power? Sure, I'd turned into a villain, lost control at the last possible moment, and maybe hit his brother a few times.

No big deal, right?

Wrong.

Punch stormed over, fists balled. The Bruiser superhero also wore a pointy party hat. He said something, but I couldn't hear him. When I cupped my hand over my ear, he started shouting. I couldn't tell if it was angry shouting or just loud shouting. "Underoos, you figured out your villain problem yet?"

"I don't know. It seemed pretty good in my finale, didn't it?" I shouted back.

"You don't have to do this," Fursona said. I only half-heard her, and when she grabbed my hand to pull me to the bar, I didn't move. I did have to do this, not to win, but because Punch wouldn't stop until he got to say his piece.

A pair of vigilante heroes gave us side-eyes. One pointed at the bar, where Hephaestus pushed the table of party props into place. I didn't blame them; I had no intention of fighting another hero, but they didn't know that.

"You may be Ikenga's golden girl for giving Monologue a rough time, but not everyone loves your bullshit, Underoos. You're just another gimmicky Magical Girl, but without that costume-changing trick, what do you have?"

"**[Stellar Ray]**, a cool sailboard, a guided punch, a speed boost, and a massive ranged damage power. How about you?"

"Work. Hard, hard work. Grapple and I train every day to be stronger and faster than the villains we fight, and it's paying off. We don't see you at the gym."

"What time do you go?"

"Five thirty in the morning and six at night, just before dinner. TUSSA has a gym room, so we can work out like supers. Gotta work up an appetite!" He held up a hand for a high five. Grapple gave it to him, but the other twin didn't seem very enthusiastic about it. Punch barely noticed. "Meet us there any day if you want to see how real heroes work. Unless you're too much of a wimpy, noodle-armed Magical Girl."

The joke was on Punch. I'd been working out since October, originally at Fursona's insistence. More recently, though, I'd been doing it for myself. I didn't always love it, but it helped focus me for the day. "I hit up the Roth Arena gym. I didn't know TUSSA had a weight room. That sounds way better."

Fursona shook her head, facepalming dramatically, but I ignored her. "See you there, Punchy," I said loudly.

I didn't have a better conversation ender than that, so I turned and headed for the bar. Before I took three steps, though, a hand clamped down on my shoulder. An insistent hand. One with far more grip than ordinary people had. I stopped—not that I could have pulled away if I wanted to—and turned back to the twins.

Or, more accurately, to Grapple. Punch stomped across the dance floor toward a pair of drinks with plastic covers, but the other twin had stuck around. "Sorry about him!" he shouted in my face.

"He's kind of pissy!" I shouted back. "What's his problem?"

"We're D-rate superheroes, that's what. Punch was so excited to get powers, but there's nothing special about him, and he hates it. Milo's a better wrestler than me, and Iron Fist hits harder than him. I'm okay with being a high little-league or low minor-league hero, but he's got dreams and goals. And you didn't just save the day during the TUEAS dogpile. You had to go and run a finale right after it. Eyes were on you for a month. Not him. Not Springlock—who's damn hot and deserves all the eyes. But you."

"Oh. Yeah, I can see why he's still angry!" He had ambitions, and his circumstances kept holding him back. I got that; I'd been in a little-league show for almost six years. Not moving up wasn't easy, especially when you wanted it so badly.

Still, I couldn't let a challenge go unanswered. Not one like Punch's gym barb. "So, six p.m.? Here at the TUSSA Cave? I'll be there."

"Great. It'll be good for Punch to put you in your place," Grapple said. He winked and left to sit with his brother.

I joined Fursona at the bar. She'd opened up a flap in her costume, revealing an empty tank with a hose leading from it, and she was shouting at Hephaestus. "Just put the damn beer in the bladder, dude! Skip the cup. I'm just gonna dump it in there."

"Nope." Hephaestus pointed up at the sign. "Serving in a nonbar container is against the rules."

I looked up. Sure enough, Rule 4 said, "Beverages may only be served in approved containers." "He's got you there, Fursona. I'll take one too."

Hephaestus poured the drinks while Fursona grumbled. "We're underage too. Isn't *that* against the rules?"

"No."

We sat at the bar, nursing our drinks. At least, I nursed my drink. I heard Fursona's furious sucking through the modulator; she'd filled the bladder up, and now she was working on emptying it. "Why are you picking a fight with Punch?" she asked me.

"I didn't try to pick a fight with him. He did that on his own. But I won't back down just because he's upset. It doesn't help."

"I know it doesn't help, but now's not the time, babe," Fursona said. "Let's enjoy the party instead of posturing, okay?"

I reached out and put an arm around her; my other one held my drink. "Sure, little miss marsupial."

I'd started my third beer, and I felt all three, by the time Ikenga arrived at the New Year's party. The music faded to a low hum.

Milo and Springlock flanked the club president at the door; she sat near the bar as he started talking. She'd opted for those glasses with the year on them and the other glitter bomb. Her Greek wrestler boyfriend interpreted Ikenga's words, fingers flying.

"In just a few minutes, my fellow TUSSA members and vigilante guests, we'll begin another year of superhero work on Tokyexico University's campus. I've been looking forward, and I see a tumultuous year ahead. We face many threats, and not only from our . . . colleagues in the Student Supervillain Society. The Man vs. Nature threat is receding, but a Power War may be on the horizon. When that happens, the burden will fall on us heroes—yes, the powerful major leaguers and our professors, but to us in the minor and little leagues, to help."

I finished my drink. Somehow, another one appeared in front of me. This one was different, though. This one was double-sized. Hephaestus stared right at me, pity in his eyes. "Sorry, Understudy. You'll want this. It's your turn."

"My turn?"

Before the Genius behind the bar could respond, Ikenga kept talking. "Yes, the next year will be filled with challenges, but tonight, we're celebrating old victories and accomplishments. The 'You're Super-Suited for This Job' career fair paired twenty-three intern sidekicks with high-minor or major-league heroes and only created eighty-seven henchmen for the SSS—an acceptable trade. Then we beat them in the TUEAS dogpile Episode. And last spring semester, we won most of our TUSSA versus SSS fights."

He took a deep breath and stared right at me. "We also had new members accomplish big things."

"Shit," I whispered. The double-sized beer sat in front of me. I took a big pull and nodded gratefully to Hephaestus. "Thanks."

"Magical Girl Understudy, in her first semester, finished a Series Finale against her former nemesis, Professor Panic. He'd come here from the small town they're from to seek revenge for something he should *never* have sought revenge for."

"I'm gonna need another." I drank again.

Hephaestus looked me in the eye, then shook his head. "I'm cutting you off."

"Please?"

"Nope."

Ikenga *kept* talking. "Using her power cleverly and staying in her villain form just long enough, Magical Girl Understudy managed to defeat the villainous Genius—and not only that! She conducted the first arrest leading to imprisonment on TU soil in over five years. For that, Magical Girl Understudy is our guest of honor at tonight's New Year's rager!"

Fuck. Shit. I tried to smile happily as the heroes—most of them—clapped politely. The double-sized beer was three-quarters empty.

"Oh, it's happening!" someone shouted, interrupting Ikenga's speech. Sure enough, on the big-screen TV in the corner, the gigantic ball in Confluence Park started dropping.

10, 9, 8

Milo grabbed Springlock's hand and pulled her up from her seat. I stared for a moment, then figured it out. It was the ball drop. That, traditionally, meant kissing your partner on zero.

7, 6, 5

But Fursona had her damn fursuit head on, and even if I wasn't drunk, it took more than five seconds to take it off.

4, 3, 2, 1

I gave her a gigantic hug through the plush. She probably didn't even feel it, but it was the thought that counted, right?

Bang!

"Fuck!" A glitter volcano erupted from Fursona's pocket, coating me with the stuff and launching more into the air. The party also erupted into angry shouts as superheroes fled from the growing glitter storm.

"I guess the party's over," Fursona said. I nodded, grabbed her paw, and headed for the door.

PART TWO

7

Power Weaving

MONDAY, JANUARY 5

Subject: Conditions of Future Enrollment

To Anika DuPont, aka Magical Girl Understudy

Due to your actions in the last month of the fall semester, the Tokyexico University Campus Administration has placed you under a behavioral hold. The destruction levels from the two Episodes you were involved in, "Grant Building Dogpile" and "Absent-Hearted Professor Parts One and Two," represent a significant financial hardship for the university. Further, they put student safety at unacceptable risk.

Tokyexico University takes its students' safety very seriously, as you know. In order to remain enrolled, you must abide by the following rules.

1. You may not commit further acts of violence or aggression on Tokyexico University grounds. You may defend yourself if attacked, but must attempt to either leave campus or find professorial help. Any Episodes started by you will be considered aggression.

2. You must report any superheroic involvement on Tokyexico University grounds within twelve hours, including Episode name, locations, and known participants. Failure to do so will be considered subverting Rule One. This does not include meeting with heroes on your team, TUSSA meetings, or Superpower Studies classes.

3. You must confirm receipt of this email and your intention to follow Rules One and Two.

Note that the Campus Administration's protocols for such destruction typically follow a zero-tolerance policy. The Department of Superpower Studies faculty and your Studio advocated for your continued attendance at Tokyexico University. However, violating these terms will result in your immediate expulsion, as will not responding by Friday, January 9.

We look forward to having you on campus,

Helen Barber

Vice President of Student Services

Tokyexico University

I didn't have much choice in how to respond. Getting kicked out of TU wasn't an option; I needed on-campus resources to boost me to the minor league. But at the same time, losing out on all the on-campus Episodes? That sucked. That sucked a lot. Hopefully, radio shows and PSAs didn't count as Episodes, and I could still work out with Punch and Grapple.

Ilneat Politics was a bust; Dr. Doug Quailman continued to be completely uninspiring, monotoning on and on about the syllabus. However, unlike Ilneat Relations, guest lectures dotted the schedule, including three actual Ilneats. I circled those dates in red pen, even though one was on a weekend after Spring Break. *Those* would be worth something.

Dr. Quailman stopped talking about the syllabus about ten minutes before class ended. "Now, to understand modern Ilneat politics, we must first understand Earth's role in its hierarchy. My research on the Ilneat Empire's political structure shows that it's closest not to a modern monarchy or republic, but to an early feudal European kingdom. To make this analogy work, consider those Ilneats on Earth to be lords or knights of varying ranks."

I raised my hand. The poorly named professor droned on for another few sentences. "Yes, miss . . . DeWalt?"

"No, DuPont. How does that work with the stated role of Earth within the Ilneat Empire? Aren't we a studio world?"

"Yes, but that doesn't change the empire's political structure as I describe it. Now, within this feudal structure are two major factions and dozens or hundreds of smaller ones. The two that matter are the traditionalist Atonement faction and the reformist Collective."

He'd just dismissed my question. Plus, I knew a little about Ilneat politics from Rocko and Pataki; neither had ever mentioned that they were any kind of lord or knight. Hell, Rocko made it sound like they couldn't even afford to pay their mortgage half the time. None of this made any sense to me. I made a note to ask Rocko for a political overview of Ilneat space later, then settled in for the last few minutes of Ilneat Politics. I tuned out Dr. Quailman's voice and focused on the textbook, only to discover he'd also written it.

By the time Ilneat Politics ended, I regretted signing up for it.

<Hey. Got classes between now and this afternoon? - Annie 10:52>
<Nope. Don't hate me though - Bianca 10:53>
<I could never hate you - Annie 10:53>
<What did you do? - Annie 10:53>

Bianca didn't respond. What had she done? We'd *just* cleaned what I *hoped* was the last of the glitter out of my green room. If she was in my apartment making another mess, I'd—

Actually . . . what *would* I do if she trashed my apartment? Probably nothing. But it'd be a bummer.

<You're not making a mess, are you? - Annie 10:56>
<Only of your late January schedule. Sorry - Bianca 10:56>
<What did you DO? - Annie 10:57>
<Green room in 10? - Bianca 10:58>
<Fine - Annie 10:58>

I arrived at my apartment five minutes later. Bianca was already there, helping herself to some coffee. I gave her a quick hug. "*Seriously*, though, what did you do?"

"Remember how I was talking about that radio program on campus? The host turned out to be pretty excited about having you on. He said he'd get a roundtable discussion scheduled for January 22 in the afternoon. Three o'clock, I think. So we have that public relations campaign going."

"Shit." I'd hoped Bee would forget about that. "Any idea who else is invited?"

"No. I just called him an hour ago, and he said he'd need to make some phone calls to see if he could get emails for someone from the SSS and from APPEAL to join in."

I searched APPEAL on my phone. Then, when that *obviously* didn't find anything, I searched "APPEAL TU." *That* got a hit. "The Anti-Power Protestors' and Extras' Advancement League is one of several pro-Extra organizations on campus. We—they—strive to create a world where people are safe from those more powerful than them, starting with Tokyexico University and spanning the globe."

"So they're an antipower organization? That'll be a fun roundtable. Can you imagine you, Monologue, and some know-nothing antipowers person?"

I nodded, feigning enthusiasm. "This isn't until the twenty-second, you said?"

"That's right. So there's plenty of time to prepare."

"Good. Now, I have bad news." I told her all about my email from Helen Barber.

Surprisingly, she nodded. "I got one, too, but mine was just a warning. I'm not on a behavioral hold, and I can still do Episodes freely. They must've decided it was *your* fault. We'll have to figure out how to leverage that."

"Or how to get my ban lifted," I agreed.

"Welcome to Combat Style," the silver-clad superhero said. He couldn't have been more than thirty, and his blonde goatee was immaculate. "I'm Dr. Warp Tennyson, and I coteach this class with Dr. Mindstorm and a rotating guest lecturer. This semester, it's The Underdelver. After our introduction, we'll split into three teams, each with a professor, based on the three major Combat Style groups."

Dr. Mindstorm nodded curtly from her seat behind Warp Tennyson, while The Underdelver's massive mech sat in the corner of the basement classroom. The Underdelver himself grinned and waved.

"This first lesson will be about just what, exactly, Combat Style is," Tennyson continued. "As is tradition in *most* Superpower Studies classes, this is pass/fail, though Mindstorm *insists* on keeping a gradebook. Passing is determined by your mastery of the skills we teach. Now, what's the difference between a minor-league hero and a little leaguer?"

I thought for a moment while The Crumb raised his hand. "Your power?"

"Potential," Punch said, glaring.

"Not quite, but good guesses." Tennyson clapped his hands. "Without a team, my power would only be minor-league-worthy. It's not as versatile as Tele-Portal's, and it's gimmicky. But it has high potential when I'm combined with teammates. With Drs. Mays and Jackson, my power becomes Episode-stopping. I can drop them into a fight, Mays can stop the fighting, and Jackson is unaffected by Mays's power. It's incredibly high potential. But neither of those defines minor-league heroes."

"This class will be about learning how to be a minor-league hero. By the end, you'll have a leg up on other former little leaguers who have to learn these skills independently. But it alone won't mean you're a minor leaguer." He clapped his hands again. "Now, we'll divide up by Combat Style. Geniuses, you'll be learning how to use **[Systematic Chaos]** from The Underdelver. You're in the room to our left. Bruisers, Tanks, Speedsters, and Mindbenders, you'll be with Dr. Mindstorm. Your focus is on **[Power-Chaining]** in the room to our right. And Magical Girls and Elementalists, you're with me. We're learning **[Power-Weaving]**."

"See you later, Fursona," I said.

"Byeeee." Fursona gave me an air high five and left, following Dr. Mindstorm. As the supervillain professor left the room, I couldn't help but feel a little relieved, though that stopped when I looked around.

Besides me and Dr. Tennyson, only three super students remained. A girl in a dark blue dress glowered at me from the corner. In the middle of the room, another blue-clad figure with skin that seemed to ebb and flow like a river stood with his arms crossed over his vest.

And, standing uncertainly by the door, stood Flare. "I'm a hybrid Speedster/Elementalist. I've been mostly focused on the elemental side, though."

"Well, you can choose between Chaining and Weaving." Tennyson strolled over to Flare and put a hand on his shoulder. They talked for a while, and Flare returned to his seat.

"Wonderful. Five is about how many we usually have in the **[Power-Weaving]** team, but four will do." He clapped his hands yet again. "Right. Let's get started. When a super hits the minor leagues, the Style System opens up three new power slots. The first one is free, the second is always **[Combo-Breaker]**, and the last is either **[Systematic Chaos]**, **[Power-Chaining]**, or my favorite, **[Power-Weaving]**. We're unlocking **[Power-Weaving]** for you early so you can practice with it. I need a power type. Any will do."

"Drama!"

"Cunning."

"Grit."

"Flamboyance it is. Excellent choice, class. So, if I start with a Flamboyance power as a little-league super, then I use a Badass power, and both deal one point of damage, how much have I dealt?"

"Uh, two points," the water-skinned guy said.

"Correct! But as a minor-league hero with **[Power-Weaving]**, if I use a Flamboyance power, then a Badass power, I've dealt?"

"Four?" I asked.

"No. Trick question. Still two. But I earn one Flamboyance point for the first power, one Badass point for the second, and one Flamboyance point floats. If I then use a Drama power, I earn a Drama point, and another Flamboyance and Badass point are floating. Then, I can cap the combo with another Flamboyance power. How many points do I get?"

Flare rolled his eyes. "Four Flamboyance, two Badass, and one Drama. It's a lot more points, but how does that help with fighting?"

Dr. Tennyson laughed. "The last ability that closes out a combo hits much harder. The minor league gets much more dangerous when you combine that with **[Environmental Combos]**, known weaknesses, and harder-hitting powers. So, for the next ten minutes, think about your power set and what your most effective combo is, taking into account cooldowns, how you're built, and your finisher's extra two points of superhero damage. No **[Environmental Combos]** unless you can create them yourself."

The watery superhero raised his hand. "Can you run through the process one more time?"

"Sure," Tennyson said. "**[Power-Weaving]** is the most complex combo to maintain. By starting with a power from one Style, then using a second Style, followed by a third, then the original Style, you can gain a lot of Style Points quickly, and get a chunk of bonus damage on your finishing power."

The other students started thinking, but I raised my hand. "Can I have a paper and pen?"

"Why?"

"I have fifteen different powers equipped, and I won't be able to stay organized without it."

"One of those weird Magical Girl signatures, huh? Sure. Go for it. Nine minutes!"

1. Stellar Ray > Quick-Time Change > Speed-Hacker > Bit-Part Barrage

That wasn't bad, but I felt like I'd left a lot on the table. The middle felt weak with a double-utility power streak.

2. Spotlight Strike > Quick-Time Change > Ride the Lightning > NOPE

3. Ride the Lightning > Quick-Time Change > Check the Script > Bit-Part Barrage

That was probably my strongest until I shuffled some powers around. This would take some real work. A thought hit me; what if I ran that combo backward?

4. BPB > CTS > QTC > RTL

Assuming only one hit, that was stronger, but I'd have to aim pretty badly to miss a full [**Bit-Part Barrage**]. It'd probably win out in an [**Environmental Combos**] zone set up for lightning. I was still wasting parts of the combo with utilities, though.

I'd come up with three more by the time Dr. Tennyson stopped us. "Now, we'll introduce ourselves by hero name, the Style we're combo-ing off, and how much potential damage we do."

The other Magical Girl was Candi Crush. I didn't see it; she didn't seem all that strong. There was no way she was really a Badass-based Magical Girl either, but she claimed she could get a respectable seven points out of her combo spread across all four moves.

I had her beat at eight or so, though it was 100% carried by [**Bit-Part Barrage**], so accuracy could hurt.

Flare shocked me at first with a Grit-based combo that somehow did twelve points of damage. When I called bullshit, he grinned. "I've been playing with combos for years. This stuff is new, but with my [**Burn Baby Burn**] power, I can reduce one power's damage to double a different one. You just only let me combo off once when we fought before."

Waterspout, the other Elementalist in the group, could only get five points of damage. He shrugged. "I fight more like a Tank, but I'm technically an Elementalist."

"We've got an arrangement with the System to unlock this power early, so be ready for it."

The other super-students trickled back into the room, and Fursona hopped over to me. "Chaining is so easy. I just use powers from the same style over and over."

I groaned. "Of course yours is super easy. Weaving is all up-front work and then executing it in a fight. I'll need to rebuild all my builds."

8

All My Builds

<Hey Tele-Portal, Fursona and I want to use your training room - Understudy 3:15>

I stared at the phone, one arm around Bee's waist, as we sat on the green room couch. It'd been an hour since my text, and while the snuggling *was* nice, I wanted that phone call. I reached for the phone, and Bianca laughed and grabbed my hand. "She's probably fighting a gigantic buffalo or something. Come on. Let's go *do* something."

"Like what? It's freezing outside."

As Bianca pulled me to my feet, the phone buzzed.

<Elevator - Tele-Portal 4:21>

"Shit. She's here," I said. Bianca sprinted for the bathroom to change into her fursuit, and I started a transformation sequence. It took far too long, but eventually, I finished. I tapped the button to let Tele-Portal onto the elevator, cleared a spot on the chaise lounge—then thought better of it and found an armchair instead—and waited.

We didn't need to wait long. The elevator dinged, and Tele-Portal stepped out. She wasn't alone, but I barely noticed her lawyer. The superheroine looked terrible. One arm was torn off her super-suit, her portal cannon had black burn marks on part of it, and her hair was a mess under her speedskater's helmet. But her eyes caught my . . . eyes . . . right away. Her glare told me she was pissed, sure, but the bags under her eyes scared me more than that. I pointed at the armchair, then at the lounge. "Your choice."

"Thanks." The major leaguer took off her stilts, set the portal cannon down, and dropped onto the chaise lounge. She cleared her throat. "What the hell, Understudy?"

"I'm sorry, but what?" I asked.

"I think you know. Your bullshit with your nemesis drags The Triad onto your campus, then the *second* we turn around to deal with Fanfic, you're out there wrecking stuff again! Then, the second you beat him, you run off to your next class. Okay.

Fine. That one's fair, but fuck! The least you could do is text to schedule another patrol. I've been busy, but holy shit, Understudy."

Mr. Braningham, the lawyer, cleared his throat before she could keep going. "Tele-Portal, please allow me to explain."

"Sure, Edgar, go for it. You're better at this than me."

"What my client is trying to say is that, while she's been busy, the expectation was that you'd patrol once a month with her. Now, I believe it's reasonable to have missed November. Tele-Portal couldn't have patrolled then if she'd wanted to. However, you missed December. As far as my client is concerned, until you make that up, she has no interest in helping you train."

"Damn right," Tele-Portal said from the chaise lounge. She yawned.

Fursona walked through the door, and Tele-Portal jumped to her feet, blinking and reaching for the cannon. "Easy, easy, just the Marsupial of Justice," Fursona said, holding up her paws.

Tele-Portal relaxed. Then she yawned again, and before I could get another word in, she'd fallen asleep on the chaise lounge. I laughed. "Sorry, Fursona. She's got your favorite spot."

"That's fine. I'll stand." Fursona pointed at Tele-Portal. "She's working herself ragged, huh?"

"Yes, quite so." Mr. Braningham frowned. "Unfortunately, some smaller-time villains have decided that a Man vs. Nature is the perfect time to push their luck, and the city's heroes have been working overtime for weeks. Your message reached her during an ambush. A few minor leaguers set a trap for The Triad. They took over the gate and pinned them between the turbo-buffalo herd and the wall. It got ugly, but luckily, she's Tele-Portal. The Triad left, Golden Goose was contacted, and the minor-league villains are . . . dealt with."

I gulped. *Dealt with* meant a totally different thing when it came to Golden Goose. Plus, my internship was almost certainly sunk. I'd just had so much going on, and it'd fallen through the cracks. "She didn't have to come here. She could have just texted and said the internship was off."

"It's not off." Mr. Braningham opened his briefcase. "However, when she contacted me immediately after escaping, I took the liberty of putting together a contract. We were woefully lacking one before, and I blame myself for that."

He pulled out a stack of papers. "This document states that you'll make up the December patrol by the end of January, as well as that you'll participate in monthly patrols. In exchange, your internship will continue, and you'll gain access to The Triad's training room at Tele-Portal's discretion. Right now, that means February."

I looked over the contract as Fursona stared over my shoulder. She nodded, and I reached for a pen. "I wish we had Jennifer and Robert right about now."

"Yeah."

But we didn't have the prelaw Extras. I clicked the pen and signed my name in all the necessary spots.

"Wonderful. Now, your first patrol is this Saturday, from nine to two. It's long, but crucially, Tele-Portal will have had an entire day off to recover. That's important, as this time, you're looking for an ongoing Episode, not just 'schmoozing,' as Tele-Portal might say. Now, as much as my client needs her sleep, she needs to get back to The Triad's base more, and I need to get home."

The moment the elevator door closed, Fursona squealed. "This is so exciting!"

I stared at her. "Calm down. It's not a win. We're not getting into that training room for at least a month—and it could be a lot longer."

"It is *absolutely* a win. We're not in a rush to get training. We both have classes, and you have a public relations campaign to win. Plus, we can hunt villains off campus on the weekends. In some ways, your ban's a blessing, not a curse."

"How so?" It didn't feel like a blessing to me. Not. At. All.

"Well, as long as you're on campus, you can focus on school, and when you're being a superhero, you'll be off campus. My dad's always going on about a healthy work/life balance, which is really funny coming from him, but . . . I don't know, it could be good."

"It might be," I hedged. "I need to work on my builds before Friday's practicum. I went through some combos on paper in class, but I think I messed stuff up because **[Quick-Time Change]** and **[Bit-Part Barrage]** are both Flamboyance."

"I'm so glad I only have one build to deal with," Fursona said. "I'll go get some dinner. We can eat in tonight."

"Thanks!" I gave Fursona a quick hug after checking for glitter bombs, then got to work while she changed out of her fursuit.

My Magical Girl Understudy build needed a lot of work. **[Quick-Time Change]** was the first major addition. A speedy switch between costumes took away a lot of the risk of transforming, even if I only got one use per Act. It also opened up cross-Costume combos.

Equipping it also opened up a power I'd previously thought was a trap. **[I-Frame Transform]** was a Grit power I'd gotten last semester. It was supposed to make me invincible for a couple of seconds after transforming, but it took so long to change that I couldn't use it to avoid damage the way it was meant to. **[Quick-Time Change]** fixed that—plus, it was possible that triggered powers worked with **[Power-Weaving]**. If it did, I had a Flamboyance-to-Grit link between costumes now.

I was, of course, assuming a lot. Like that they wouldn't have some way to simulate **[Power-Weaving]** and that we'd *actually* gain it as a power. But if we did, I'd get a huge power spike compared to my little-league competition—and I could use it. Vigilant Vow was running Shorts. A lot of Shorts.

[Quick-Time Change] only got that one use, so I couldn't rely on it as a combo piece. I needed a Badass or Cunning power with some kick, or even better, another power slot like the minor leaguers, but there just weren't enough slots for Understudy to run combos by itself right now. I ended up with a generalist build that could *almost* do everything I wanted it to.

[Alias - Understudy] [Archetype - Magical Girl] [Community Rank - 348/523]
[HP 8/8]
[Styles and Skills]
►Archetype Skill - Transformation Sequence
►Badass (46)
►Cunning (48)
►Drama (1)
►Stellar Ray 1
►Bit-Part Barrage 1
►Flamboyance (14)
►Signature Skill - Adaptive Armoire
►Stored Costumes: (Rainy Day, Copy Cat)
►Quick-Time Change
►Starwave Sail 1
►Grit (16)
►I-Frame Transform 1

Lab Assistant Panic had started as a grab bag of Professor Panic's powers, but with **[Science Has Rules?]** and **[TA-1LZ Size Boost]**, it finally had an identity as a lunatic engineer working on her attack bot!

It turned out that the answer to **[Science Has Rules?]** was *Yes*. As I'd seen in the Series Finale, any changes to Tails while she was TA-1LZ stayed when she turned back, but the new parts wouldn't remain. So if I ripped out some wiring to attach a new weapon or tool, she'd be missing stuffing on the other side, and she wouldn't keep the improvised weapon for long. She also wasn't very big; she'd been able to carry a Gatling taser during the finale, but couldn't have fit much else.

The **[TA-1LZ Size Boost]** fixed that limitation. Now, with enough junk and spare parts, I could engineer up all sorts of cool TA-1LZ add-ons—at least temporarily. It also gave hope for more TA-1LZ powers in the future; permanent upgrades beat **[Science Has Rules?]** every time.

[Costume - Lab Assistant Panic]
[HP 8/8]
[Styles and Skills]
►Archetype Skill - Transformation Sequence
►Badass
►Cunning
►Speed-Hacker 0
►Check the Script 1

▶Drama
▶Science Has Rules? 0
▶Flamboyance
▶Signature Skill - Adaptive Armoire 1
▶Stored Costumes: (Understudy)
▶Maniacal Reveal 0
▶Grit
▶TA-1LZ Size Boost 0

[Thunderhead] was the stand-out new move for Magical Girl Rainy Day, but it once again left me frustrated with my lack of Cunning and Badass skills. I set up the tween terror's build to support a single combo: **[Spotlight Strike]** into **[Check the Script]** into **[Thunderhead]**, with **[Ride the Lightning]** as its finisher.

I hated using **[Check the Script]** as a combo-enabler. Something about it felt cheap, and for the first time, I realized just how *limiting* six power slots—five, once **[Adaptive Armoire]** took up a spot—really was. It wasn't enough to have well-rounded builds, and I couldn't maintain the utility I wanted *and* run viable combos for Friday's practicum. It was so *frustrating*; there had to be a workaround somehow.

[Costume - Magical Girl Rainy Day]
[HP 8/8]
[Styles and Skills]
▶Archetype Skill - Transformation Sequence
▶Badass
▶Cunning
▶Check the Script 1
▶Drama
▶Thunderhead 1
▶Flamboyance
▶Signature Skill - Adaptive Armoire 1
▶Stored Costumes: (Understudy)
▶Starwave Sail 1
▶Ride the Lightning 0
▶Spotlight Strike
▶Grit

Finally, I had Copy Cat. Fursona's Costume was practically perfect the way it was, but I had a power I wanted to experiment with, and the Bruiser Costume didn't look like it was designed for combos. At least, not the **[Power-Weaving]** kind. It had the best power synergy out of my builds right now, though with a few *useful* Cunning powers, any of the others would beat it easily.

I took out [**Spotlight Strike**] in favor of [**Doom Ball**], imagining leaping onto an enemy, kicking and scratching the shit out of them, and then getting away with [**Hometown Heroine**]. It'd be a solid Bruiser. At least, I hoped so. I'd never *been* a Bruiser before.

[Costume - Copy Cat]
[HP 8/8]
[Styles and Skills]
▶Archetype Skill - Transformation Sequence
▶Badass
▶Leaping Leopards 0
▶Doom Ball 0
▶Cunning
▶Drama
▶Cat-Scratch Fever 0
▶Hometown Heroine 1
▶Flamboyance
▶Signature Skill - Adaptive Armoire 1
▶Stored Costumes: (Understudy)
▶Grit
▶Fursonal Furcefield 0

I left Lab Assistant Panic behind. Tele-Portal wanted firepower, and for the first time in my career, I felt like I had enough of that. Rainy Day and Costume-switching would carry me through the first day of Combat Style Practicum.

9

Combat Style Practicum

FRIDAY, JANUARY 9

"This is . . . the TU Practice Room." Dr. Mindstorm pointed through the plexiglass at a small arena—perhaps seventy feet to a side, with a roof thirty feet high—below us. We were once again somewhere below the ruins of the Mister Felsic statue. This time, the professors and Underdelver had led us down three flights of stairs and into the hidden arena. We stood around near a few seats overlooking the soon-to-be battlefield.

"Before we start, you should all receive a Style System message . . . now," Dr. Mindstorm said.

[Attention: You have been selected for the Junior Minor Leaguers' Child Stars Program. Members of the Child Stars Program gain access to a new power. They also accept the risks associated with minor-league Episodes. Accept Risk? Yes/No]

I pressed Yes, obviously.

[New Skill! Power-Weaving! Use powers from different Styles, then finish on your starting Style for extra damage and Style Points]

"Dr. Mindstorm? This doesn't say it's for a specific Style," I said.

Mindstorm stood by the window. "No. None of the three different powers you may get has . . . a Style. It's similar to your [Archetype Skill]. This is a [Combo Skill]."

Dr. Tennyson had been quiet up until now. He cleared his throat and clapped his hands. "Right. This is the Practice Room. It's a little different from a full-on practice arena like some super teams have. Ours doesn't have infinite customization, and it's nowhere near the size of an augmented reality facility. However, it does have a couple of unique features. First, please put these wristbands on."

The bright green bands clashed brutally against my costume. I could almost feel myself losing Flamboyance Points. Or gaining them; it was hard to tell which.

"These give you damage reduction while in the arena. It's not total, but about half of the damage coming your way will be negated. We'll practice as if you're each taking full damage, so please . . . inform us of your total superhero damage before you enter the arena," Dr. Mindstorm said.

Dr. Tennyson said, "Now, rules. Thanks to the wristbands, we can use almost any power for sparring. If your attack can damage the building through reinforced walls and the observation room's windows, please use discretion in how you aim. Your goal is to defeat your opponent, who may be a hero or villain. Later, we may practice escort simulations, point defenses, or multihero capture-the-flag fights, but today, we're keeping things simple. You'll have one minute to spar today to get used to the arena, so we expect a lot of draws."

"Our first . . . pairing . . . is Fursona and Magical Girl Candi Crush."

"My superhero damage is at nine," Candi said.

"I'm at seven." Fursona looked worried, but I gave her a thumbs-up.

"Head down the stairs and stand inside the starting circles. We'll stop the . . . fight when one of you drops below five and four Hit Points, respectively," Dr. Mindstorm said. "The rest of you may . . . watch . . . from up here."

I took a seat, almost wishing I had some popcorn. Was that a nice thing to think about while watching my girlfriend fight someone? Probably not. Did I think it anyway? Yes. A screen flickered to life on the window, displaying each combatant's superhero damage as hearts.

The two combatants stepped out into the arena and stood in matching circles. Candi stood sideways, almost leaning on her hammer-shaped wand. Fursona bounced on the balls of her feet, kicked the air once, and nodded up at me.

"Begin." Dr. Mindstorm's voice echoed on an intercom.

"[**Big-Rock Candi**]!" Candi yelled, swinging her wand through the air in a complex, four-beat pattern as Fursona catapulted toward her. The Magical Girl's blue dress suddenly shimmered and whirled, and she grew almost a foot taller as her outfit took on a riotous mix of colors. Her wand extended, forming into a gigantic lollipop shaped like a hammer.

Fursona leaped into Candi Crush feetfirst a moment later, and both heroes slammed into the arena's wall. As I watched, they kicked and punched, unable to get the distance they needed to be effective. "Come on, Fursona!" I said.

"They . . . can't hear you." Dr. Mindstorm rolled her eyes.

"Oh, right." I lowered my voice and whispered, "Come on, Fursona."

Both combatants separated enough to get some breathing room. "[**Hard-Candy Hound**]!" Candi called. A German Shepard, but one seemingly made from various peppermints, candy corns, and butterscotch started forming.

"Why do Magical Girls call their moves?" Gourmet asked, poking me in the side.

"It's just what we do. We don't have to, and there's no reason for it—except for a good show," I replied.

Before the dog could form fully, Fursona threw a vicious [**Double-Kick**] at Candi Crush. The blow landed, knocking her across the room. Another Hit Point flew off the scoreboard.

Fursona leaped again, springboarding forward. This time, Candi was ready for it. She set her feet and swung her hammer wand.

Crunch!

It smashed into Fursona's side, knocking her off-balance. A second blow followed, then a third, and for a moment, I thought Fursona would lose.

Then she ducked inside the hammer's arc and started kicking and punching.

"Time." Tennyson held up his hand as he spoke into the intercom. "Draw. Next is Magical Girl Understudy and Gourmet."

For a moment, I didn't understand the announcement. Fursona had been winning, and I knew precisely what Candi Crush's problem was. She took too long to set up. I imagined that if she could get the hammer and the hound, she'd be pretty formidable as a pseudo-Bruiser, but she used two powers before she was even at full strength. I'd have to change that pattern around.

"Looks like it's you and me, Snack," Gourmet said, standing and stalking over to the professors. "Thirteen super*villain* damage."

"Thirteen? What the hell?" a student muttered behind me as others fidgeted and stared at her. "How's she so powerful?"

It began to sink in. I'd spar with Gourmet, and the last time we'd fought, she'd been able to handle both Fursona *and* me. I shook my head. There was no way I'd win this fight, but I *could* change my goals for it. I didn't need to win. I just needed to try out [**Power-Weaving**] before tomorrow's patrol.

"Eight superhero damage," I said. As I jogged down the stairs, I made a plan. I'd run a safe, low-damage strategy and try to delay the inevitable steamrolling long enough to get through one of my combos. It wasn't about burning, but learning!

I stepped into the circle and waited. Gourmet took almost a full minute to stroll down the stairs. When she finally arrived, chewing on a stick of beef jerky, Mindstorm's voice echoed again. "Begin."

I activated [**Power-Weaving**] and used [**Quick-Time Change**]. Time stopped. The power forced me to complete the dance for "The Itsy Bitsy Spider," but thankfully, a much-shortened version. As I dropped in height and time started again, I felt a turquoise glow cover me for a moment. [**I-Frame Transform**] had activated as I switched Costumes.

[Flashy Fitting-Room! +1 Flamboyance Point]
[Steel Yourself! +1 Grit Point]
[Floating Points: 1 Flamboyance]

Huh. I got points for this. It counted as training.

I barely noticed Gourmet, now sporting two massive horns, barrel into me, chewing on something. She bounced off my momentary immunity to damage, looking shocked, and bit off another chunk of her beef jerky. The horns grew, and she sprouted . . . a nose ring?

The invincibility faded, and I felt suddenly vulnerable. And small. Now it was just her and Magical Girl Rainy Day.

I used [**Thunderhead**]. A small cloud started forming above me, and tiny arcs of lightning crackled across my body. The cloud grew and grew. Soon, it'd—

Wham!

Gourmet's two horns caught me square in the chest. The breath whooshed out of my lungs, and I gasped, then felt the air I'd just breathed in leave again as we slammed into the arena's wall. She stepped back, then stomped. Her first stomp caught me in the stomach, but I rolled clear of her second.

[HP 6/8]

The [**Thunderhead**] finished building. A few raindrops splattered into my face as Gourmet finished the jerky stick. "You planning on fighting back?" she asked, grinning and panting. Her face was flushed red—the lunatic was enjoying herself way too much.

[Pause for Effect! +1 Drama Point]
[Floating Points: 3 Flamboyance, 1 Grit]

The [**Power-Weaving**] combo kept building. I just had one more power to go: the finisher.

She rushed me again. I was stuck in a corner. I had nowhere to dodge. There was only one option.

I [**Rode the Lightning**].

The storm that'd been building broke; electricity filled the room, all surging toward me. It danced across my Rainy Day Costume, building as I spun in the air. The star on my chest glowed and flickered. I stared at Gourmet. Her hair stood on end, and she had a wide-eyed look on her face. She charged, narrowing her eyes in determination. I couldn't contain this much lightning even if I wanted it.

I had to let it go.

[Electric Lightshow! +1 Flamboyance Point]
[Thunderstruck! +1 Drama Point]
[Power-Weaving! +6 Flamboyance, +3 Grit, +1 Drama Point]

Blue-white tendrils of electricity reached out and danced across Gourmet's body, and her determination turned into a wince of pain. For a moment, I thought maybe it'd stop her charge. Maybe I could turn the fight into an Understudy win.

Wham!

[HP 5/8]

The massive form of Gourmet slammed me into the wall. Her hair stood upright, and she had scorch marks on her face, but she still grinned as I hit the ground. Before I could get up or even roll, she threw herself on top of me, pinning me to the ground. "Goodnight, little girl," she said.

Then she headbutted me with her horns.

[HP 4/8]

"Enough." Tennyson's voice echoed around the otherwise-empty room. "Gourmet wins. Next is Waterspout and Crusade."

Gourmet grabbed my hand and pulled me to my feet. I stood, wobbly, as she grabbed another jerky stick from her pocket. "**[Aspect of Links]** is ridiculously strong. I'd have had my chain if you hadn't stopped my first charge. Next time, you're dead."

I decided she was joking. "Next time, there won't be walls to bounce me off of. I almost had you."

"In your dreams." Gourmet headed for the stairs. So did I. This wasn't a win—not in the strictest sense—but I still considered it a victory. The power spike from **[Power-Weaving]** was massive; with a few more skills, I'd definitely be able to leverage this into minor-league-level damage! And I'd pulled off the combo before anyone else had. That had to count for something with the professors, right?

[Training Complete! New Stat Totals!]
►Drama (4)
►Stellar Ray 1
►Bit-Part Barrage 1
►Flamboyance (26)
►Signature Skill - Adaptive Armoire
►Stored Costumes: (Rainy Day, Copy Cat)
►Quick-Time Change
►Starwave Sail 1
►Grit (20)

I'd made a mistake, I realized, as I opened the door. Instead of **[Thunderhead]**, if I'd gone with **[Check the Script]**, I'd probably have enough Cunning points to get a new power. But even with that revelation, I didn't care. This was the best prepatrol preparation I could have asked for. The combo wasn't smooth, but it had worked well even so.

At least, I hoped it had. I stepped through the door back to the observation room. Tennyson said, "Begin," and Waterspout and Crusade started fighting. The water Elementalist seemed super effective against Crusade's Bruiser style of fighting; he set traps, slick areas, and whirlpools all through the room, making it impossible for Crusade to get to him.

"Hey, I got a new power," Fursona said. I could almost hear her grin under the fursuit's head. "And you were only two points from beating Gourmet. Nice combo."

"Thanks." I smiled. "You did well, too. You were totally going to win."

We chatted for a while about the different fights. By the time class ended, I felt ready for tomorrow's long patrol.

10

Long Patrol

SATURDAY, JANUARY 10

I woke up excited—and nervous. I'd only done one patrol, and both a crisis on campus and Tele-Portal's exhaustion had cut it short. This time, we'd do an entire patrol in the freezing cold. I headed for the monorail station below the Student Union Building; the one below the TUEAS Building was still closed for repairs. Today's patrol was going to be something special, I was certain.

Sure enough, a chrome camera drone met me at the bottom of my elevator. I jogged through the tunnels below campus, texting Tele-Portal.

<Hey. Confluence Park, 9:00, right - Understudy 7:42>
<Yes. Don't b l8 - Tele-Portal 7:43>

I was *not* excited about stomping through a winter wonderland, but Confluence Park had a winter festival today, and The Triad needed to make an appearance. Since the other two heroes were both booked, it fell on Tele-Portal. While I rode the train, I thought through my goals for the patrol, from most to least important.

One: Public relations. If I could solve a few problems, plug *Heroics 101* as *the* show to watch, and generally schmooze up to the unpowered folks at the park, that'd be a massive victory on the way to the minor leagues. Drawing eyes to my show would help make it more marketable than Vigilant Vow's.

Two: Keep Tele-Portal happy. If Fursona and I could keep earning Style Points every Friday in Combat Style Practicum, this was less important. We wanted the specialized Triad training room to practice "real" Episodes, though. Plus, patrols *could* turn into Episodes. This was an excellent opportunity, and I didn't want to lose it.

Three: Climb the community rankings. It'd be nice to find an Episode and win it while I was out, but the other goals were more long-term planning. Climbing the ranks would come. I just had to stay diligent.

After almost an hour of riding, we arrived near the park, and I hopped onto **[Starwave Sail's]** windsurfer. The bitterly cold air stung my cheeks, and my eyes watered as I rode the blue-and-pink streaks between skyscrapers, but I arrived above Confluence Park just before nine. The winter festival was already heating up, so to speak; the smell of cinnamon and hot chocolate wafted through the air, a few dozen vendors had set up walled tents with space heaters inside them, and people walked from one to the next while music—thankfully not Christmas music—played on a sound system.

But the river caught my eye almost immediately. Below a waterfall, a few brave people had put on ice skates and skated back and forth along the frozen bank. They'd cleared the snow to make an impromptu ice-skating rink, and Tele-Portal stood nearby on her stilts, chatting with a couple of unpowered folks.

I dipped down, landing beside her and spinning to bleed off the speed. Then I waved. "Hiya, Tele-Portal. It's . . ." I checked my phone.

"8:57. You're on time," Tele-Portal said. She shivered a little. "The sun is out, the winter festival is happening, so let's finish up here, get some cider, and patrol for a while. Mr. Nesbit, you were saying something about the East Thornton district having trouble?"

"Yep. 3V1L is moving in, and our resident heroes are too busy with the last D-wolvers." The man looked to be in his sixties, with graying hair around the edges of his head. He squinted at me, nodded, then turned to Tele-Portal. "They're mostly minor leaguers, but they're a real pain in the ass, and they're bringing chaos to East Thornton. Any chance you can spare some time for us? Or tell us who to get in touch with?"

"The Triad's schedule is packed, unfortunately," Tele-Portal said. She pointed at me. "There's a chance that some of Tokyexico University's heroes could help, but it'd be on their schedule, and the spring semester is usually pretty busy. Have you talked to the Council of Heroes?"

"Yes. They're sending someone in a week or two when things calm down. That's not fast enough."

Tele-Portal nodded sagely. "I understand. I may have a little pull, but no promises. If I found someone to help, it wouldn't solve the villain problem. All he'd be able to do is a holding action until the Council has free heroes. You could reach out to the Mutual Assistance League, but you're out of their zone, and their hands are full with 3V1L and Sister Sly."

"I'd do it," I volunteered. "I have time next weekend. If I convinced a few TUSSA heroes to help, we could make a strong team to fight against 3V1L. Or we could do a patrol there the next time you have a day off."

I saw the grin flick across Tele-Portal's face, and I knew she'd say no, but that she was happy I'd volunteered. A learning opportunity was coming, and I suppressed a groan. "You're not ready to fight 3V1L yet, Understudy. Speaking of you, though, this is my part-time sidekick, Magical Girl Understudy. She's a Tokyexico University freshman and a little-league heroine."

"For now. I'm moving up in the world."

"That's great," Mr. Nesbit said. His heart wasn't in it, and I understood. I'd be frustrated, too, if I needed help and it wasn't coming. "I'll be seeing you around, Tele-Portal."

"Have a good day," Tele-Portal said.

We turned back toward the sheltered booths. "Volunteering your time is a noble move, Understudy, but the Extras can usually wait. Your job isn't always to solve problems. Sometimes, it's just to reassure folks that a hero is listening. Mr. Nesbit doesn't actually need a solution."

"He doesn't?"

"Two ciders with cinnamon sticks. Nonalcoholic. We're both on duty. Thanks," Tele-Portal said. Then she turned back to me, speaking quietly. "Nope. Thornton always has a 'crime problem,' which usually solves itself in-district. It's bad right now because of the slow pre–Power War ramp-up and the Man vs. Nature, but I'd bet over half of it isn't even supervillains. Understanding what superheroes are and are *not* responsible for is critical to our jobs."

"Ah," I said noncommittally. It sounded a little like Tele-Portal didn't *want* to help. I mulled it over in my head, trying to figure it out.

We chatted with the Extras at the booths for a while. I signed a few autographs for kids who'd been *Small Town Super* fans and told plenty of people about *Heroics 101*, but I didn't get any hard commitments to watch it. That . . . sucked, but most of the unpowered people at the festival weren't there to talk to me. I made the most of the festival and patrol, though, and even though the conversations were awkward, I felt like I'd found some new fans.

Tele-Portal and I were explaining how heroes were necessary to a skeptical-looking guy with a real belligerent attitude when it happened.

Someone screamed from the river.

"Hold on one moment," Tele-Portal said to the guy, who looked ready to argue. "You get to see why we're necessary right now. Understudy, hang on!"

Before I could ask what I was hanging on to, Tele-Portal grabbed me with one hand. She opened a portal below our feet, then one on the river's far bank. Our ciders lay on the ground where we'd both dropped them, abandoned and forgotten. We instantly traveled through, popping out next to the frozen river.

Only it wasn't frozen anymore.

Huge cracks had opened across the cleared river, and skaters flailed around, clinging desperately to the ruined ice as they slipped farther and farther into the frigid water. One woman lost her grip, and the river pushed her away mercilessly. Her head disappeared under the still-solid ice downstream a moment later.

[Casting Call: Winter is Coming: PG-13]

"[Starwave Sail]!" I didn't bother to read the [Casting Call]. I just accepted it. That woman needed my help, and whatever the Episode was, I'd deal with it.

[Winter is Coming: Act One in Progress]

"Save her! I've got the others!" Tele-Portal yelled. I nodded and took off down the iced-over river.

The woman was hard to spot under the thick ice, but I saw a dark-colored blob moving down the river after a few seconds. A thinner dark spot—maybe her arm— pounded against the ice. "[Stellar Ray]!" I shouted, waving my wand. The bright pink beam hit like a boxer's punch, shattering the ice in a small area above the woman. She clung to the ice for a moment, but the river grabbed her again.

I needed a bigger hole.

I guided the sailboard forward, feet over the frozen river. If I fell in, I'd have a few seconds to get a new [Starwave Sail], but I wasn't dressed to be cold *and* wet. Twenty feet ahead of the woman, I stopped. [Bit-Part Barrage] activated, the sail- board disappeared, and I hung midair a few feet over the river.

[Show-Stopping Plan! +1 Drama Point]
[Good Thinking! +1 Cunning Point]

The salvo of [Stellar Rays] crashed across the river's width, breaking the ice just as the woman surfaced in the newly cleared space. She grabbed a bit of ice and tried to drag herself out again, gasping for breath.

I was too busy falling to help her much right that second.

I plummeted toward the frigid water below as I resummoned the [Starwave Sail]. I pulled up, lowering a hand *into* the literally ice-cold water as the sailboard's edge caught ripples and rocked back and forth. My fingers brushed against the wom- an's down jacket. I tightened my grip and pulled up, popping the sailboard almost straight up.

[Dramatic Rescue! +1 Drama Point]

The woman shivered uncontrollably in my grip as I angled back toward the warm, heated booths at the winter festival. Her skin was blue-tinted, and she kept trying to say something, but she couldn't get the words out between shivers and coughing up water. "Don't worry. I've got you. I'm Magical Girl Understudy, and you're safe now."

Tele-Portal stood outside the nearest hut. She'd saved *everyone* else with her portal cannon; if I didn't know better, I'd have thought she was showing off. I landed, holding the woman in my arms to keep her from falling onto the trampled snow below my feet.

[Show-off! +1 Flamboyance Point]

"Thanks, we'll take it from here," a woman in an EMT outfit said. "You did a great job of saving her, though."

"Understudy, over here," Tele-Portal said. She'd lost interest in the ice-skaters as soon as they were safe. I thought about what she'd said a couple of months back, during our first patrol—after a while, you realize an Episode could start anytime, and it's easier to forget Extras are people. Those people were just props to her. That seemed a lot like what Su-Bin's parents had said at Christmas dinner about how supers were just playing a game.

Still, I was sidekicking with her, so I stomped through the snow back to the riverbank. Tele-Portal knelt by the edge, near one of the bigger ice cracks. She dipped her hand into the water before dunking her arm elbow-deep. "This ice is too thick to have broken from a few skaters. I checked it myself when I saw them out there and again just now. It was safe."

"Then what's happening?"

"I'm not sure, but you got a [**Casting Call**] and accepted it. Check it."

[Casting Call]
[**Episode: Winter is Coming - PG-13**]
[**Role: Snow Angel! Role Accepted**]
[**Role Focus: Drama + Flamboyance**]

"Snow Angel? Really?" I rolled my eyes.

"Shut up and listen," Tele-Portal said. She sounded stressed, but not angry. She closed her eyes. "I was hoping for an Episode, but if it's the villain I think it is, we'll both need to be on our A game. I'm built as a pure support for Man vs. Nature combat. What do you have?"

I rattled off my builds. "Understudy is a ranged attacker. My other two Costumes are Magical Girl Rainy Day, a one-trick-pony combo piece, and Copy Cat, a melee powerhouse. At least, I think she is. I haven't tried her out yet, though. I'm not built for much utility, but Rainy Day has a Cunning skill we could use to get started."

Tele-Portal nodded slowly, yawning. "Okay, switch over. We'll start here and work our way upriver. If we get to the waterfall, we'll turn around and go the other way."

I ran through my transformation sequence into Rainy Day—the slow one, not a [**Quick-Time Change**]. Once I was four feet, eight inches, or whatever height I'd been in sixth grade, I looked upriver and used [**Check the Script**]. But as we searched near the waterfall, the power highlighted something odd. Strange tracks, almost too big to be a person's, led back up the hill. I started following them; the script had pointed them out, so they had to be a clue. "Hey, these tracks lead toward the winter festival."

[Good Thinking! +1 Cunning Point]

[End of Act One! Act Two in Five Minutes!]

[Alias - Understudy] [Archetype - Magical Girl] [Community Rank - 348/523]

[HP 8/8]

[Styles and Skills]

►Archetype Skill - Transformation Sequence

►Combo Skill - Power-Weaving

►Badass (46)

►Cunning (50) (Skill Roll Available)

►Drama (6) (Skill Roll Available)

►Stellar Ray 1

►Bit-Part Barrage 1

►Flamboyance (27)

►Signature Skill - Adaptive Armoire

►Stored Costumes: (Rainy Day, Copy Cat)

►Starwave Sail 1

►Quick-Time Change 1

►Grit (21)

►I-Frame Transform 1

11

The Winter Festival

As we followed the tracks back toward the winter festival, I felt a warm, fuzzy feeling in my chest. I'd done a lot of superheroics over the last few months, but I couldn't remember if I'd *saved* anyone since Riverside. If you didn't count sending Fursona to rescue TUSSA from the villains' clutches or telling Avan and his friends to leave before Professor Panic's TERROR Mech arrived, I didn't think I'd done any good old-fashioned rescuing since the fight with LABRAT. And, honestly, that was a shame—especially given how it made me feel.

I had four Costumes now, and that meant four builds. I *had* to have enough cool powers geared toward rescue and mobility to play at lifesaving. Something *had* to be possible . . . right? If not, I could still be more unpowered-oriented. The people of Tokyexico needed my help, and I'd spent a semester fighting villains. Important? Yes, villains needed to be stopped.

But it didn't create the same warm fuzzies.

"Hey, focus up," Tele-Portal said. She pointed to the rows of vendors and the ever-growing crowd of people. "The villain is probably Polar Vortex or Black Ice. If it's Black Ice, we've got it made. She's a lower-powered minor-league villain who's been trying to move up since we were rivals. She's no threat to us. If it's Polar Vortex, everyone in the area's in danger. And if it's neither, I'll eat my stilts. They're two of the most active winter-themed vils, and King Cold is on turbo-buffalo duty today."

"So which one is most likely?"

"That's the trick. They've got similar costumes, similar powersets, and they use near-identical strategies. The big prints were probably snowshoes, but that doesn't narrow it down much."

"What are their costumes?"

"You're not gonna believe this. Snowsuits."

I burst out laughing as we walked down the row of vendors. "A snowsuit? Everyone here's in a snowsuit except for us."

"Yep. That's why this is gonna be tough. If it's Polar Vortex, we need to find him before he causes a **[Deep Freeze]** event. He's getting stronger fast, and in November, it shut down a large section of the University and Poudre Districts."

I did a double take at the mention of November. I'd been on a sushi date with Bianca during a massive snowstorm. "Wait. Did he cause that storm? If it's him, he's going down! It's personal now!"

"Okay, slow down. What happened?" Tele-Portal sounded bored.

"He ruined my date!" I transformed back to the Understudy costume and rolled my new Cunning skill.

[50 Cunning Credits Used. Rolling Skill!]

[New Skill: Audition Notes! Every Extra brings something to the table. Check their notes to find out what]

[Winter is Coming: Act Two in Progress]

Well, *that* power was vague. Still, I didn't *need* [**Starwave Sail**] to run a combo, and I *did* need everything else. I made the switch and started searching for Polar Vortex. The camera drone hovered fifty feet up, high enough that most people didn't notice it—not that it mattered since everyone knew Tele-Portal and I were here.

I turned a corner and arrived at the cider stand. The smell of cinnamon and apples was intoxicating, and I got in line. As the queue inched toward the man serving drinks, someone in front of me fidgeted with the gloves on their snowsuit. I wished I had [**Check the Script**]. Then I had an idea. An awful idea.

Maybe I could use [**Audition Notes**] to figure out whether this guy was the villain. I gave it a try.

[Informed! +1 Cunning Point]

[**Audition Notes for John Deer: This Extra has realized that the winter festival is moments from becoming a super showdown. He's not sure what to do with you behind him and someone he suspects may be a villain nearby. Does he run? Does he hide? Or does he try to play it cool? He doesn't know. Poor John Deer.**]

I looked around, trying to be surreptitious. Who was the villain? Were they at this stall, or the s'mores stand next door? I couldn't help but glance over my shoulder. Still, [**Audition Notes**] *did* give me the information I needed. Some of it, at least.

Three of the nearby festivalgoers had snowsuits on; with the hoods up, I couldn't tell which were men and which were women, so I couldn't narrow down Polar Vortex that way.

I took a leap of faith and tapped one on the shoulder. "Excuse me."

A handful of snow slammed into my face, blinding me. Then, someone shoved me onto the hard-packed snow. I landed awkwardly; my ankle would have sprained or broken if it wasn't for superhero damage.

[HP 7/8]

As it was, I rolled, wiping snow off my face and tears from my eyes. I wasn't hurt, but by the time I'd recovered, all I could see was a red snowsuit turning the corner.

I pushed myself off the snow and took off after the villain. Or at least, who I hoped was the villain. If it was Polar Vortex, I had to stop him before he disappeared into a crowd or started using his powers for real.

I gained steadily on the red-suited figure, and by the time they turned again, I'd almost gotten close enough to try tackling them. But as I rounded the corner after them, I realized I was too late. They'd vanished.

Not blended into a group of Extras—there were a few red snowsuits, but none with hoods. Not hidden in a stall—none of the tents opened to this side. The villain had just . . . vanished. I hadn't caught him, but at least I'd found something useful. I stopped running and texted Tele-Portal.

<Red snowsuit with a hood - Understudy 10:15>
<k - Tele-Portal 10:15>
<omw 2 u - Tele-Portal 10:15>

I barely had time to start texting my location when the speedskater-suit-wearing heroine blooped through a portal and landed beside me on her stilts. "Did Red Suit use any powers? Anything we can use to ID them?" Tele-Portal was all business, without even a check to see if I was alright.

"They threw a snowball in my face. I'm not even sure it was a power, so it *could* have just been an Extra. But why would someone *do* that?"

"No idea. That doesn't give us a lot to go on. Both Polar Vortex and Black Ice use misdirection and try to hide. It does eliminate King Cold and a few other minor leaguers, but I didn't expect any of them," Tele-Portal said.

I shrugged. "It's definitely Polar Vortex. He'd be the most dramatic villain for the situation. Plus, Black Ice has a black suit, right? It'd make sense."

"Either way, we need to keep looking. Text me if you see Red Suit again. Don't engage this time, just let me know, and we'll beat whoever it is together." Tele-Portal pointed to the abandoned power plant above the half-frozen waterfall. "I'll check there. You stay on patrol down here. Do the patrol stuff, reassure folks that things are under control, and if you see Red Suit—"

"Text you. I got it." I turned and walked back into the vendors' tent rows. Behind me, Tele-Portal vanished.

"If I were Polar Vortex, where would I have gone?" I asked myself. I was starting to really get why supers worked in teams of three or four. Even with so many Costumes, I didn't have the powers to be an investigator. I thought for a minute as I strolled through the stands and talked mindlessly with a few unpowered people—I didn't want to get in the habit of calling them Extras. I wouldn't stick around if a major-league villain was after me. But then again, Polar Vortex had a goal with the winter festival. I wouldn't want to give up on that just because of a minor setback.

Tele-Portal wasn't exactly a minor setback, though. She could bring her whole team over instantly: Bud Lightbeam, the self-replicating, laser-shooting Elementalist, and Underdelver, a Genius who drove a combat mech that put the FEAR and TERROR builds Professor Panic had made to shame.

I decided it all depended on how much Polar Vortex needed whatever he was doing here, and on how prepared he was.

I caught a flash of red moving away from me, but when I started jogging after it, I relaxed, laughing to myself. It was just a kid. The snowsuit wasn't even the same shade of red; it was a bright apple-red, while the villain's had been burgundy.

<any luck? - Tele-Portal 10:34>
<It's been 5 minutes. No - Understudy 10:34>
<There was a kid in a red suit - Understudy 10:35>
<Keep ur Is peeled - Tele-Portal 10:35>

I rolled my eyes once I figured out what she meant. Of *course* I was keeping my eyes peeled. *She* was the one who'd buzzed off to go look at the old abandoned power plant. I kept searching as snow began to fall.

Come to think of it, how had it already started snowing? I'd only been here an hour and a half—less, even—and the last time I'd noticed, the sun was out.

<It started snowing - Understudy 10:39>

Tele-Portal didn't respond.

I thought about going after the superheroine. She was up there, and I'd need her to fight Polar Vortex. Instead, I kept up the search. As the snowfall increased and it got harder and harder to see, I checked the river again. It was already freezing up again, and the cold bit at my cheeks, but there was no sign of a villain. "Screw this. I'm going to get a cider," I muttered to myself. I'd been cheated out of so much as a taste so far, and if I couldn't find the villain, at least I'd have a warm drink while looking.

As I got back in line, the woman serving ciders looked at me nervously. Something tickled the back of my mind, and I tensed. Hadn't the server been a man just ten minutes ago? Where had he gone? I took a closer look, checking the woman's **[Audition Notes]**.

[Good Thinking! +1 Cunning Point]
[Audition Notes for Jane Doe: This Extra has a secret. The secret may impact the Episode greatly, but what could it be? Do you want to spend the time digging, or would it be better to stick to the script? There's only one way to find out; Jane Doe certainly isn't telling.]

I looked the woman over again. She had a faux-fur-lined, dark gray puffer coat and a balaclava that covered almost her entire face. Her eyes locked with mine for a moment before she looked down at the cups. "Small, medium, or large?" she asked, a slight shake to her voice. Her mitten-clad hand bumped into the sample cups, knocking them over.

My mind whirled as she swore under her breath and ducked to recover the cups. I *knew* that the villain I'd seen was taller than the woman standing in front of me. And Polar Vortex was a guy, so this couldn't possibly be the same villain. But the guy who'd run the stand before had bare hands; he'd kept them in his pocket to keep warm and only pulled them out to handle the money, cups, and cider dispenser.

I took a deep breath. Then, I took a bold guess. "I'll take a small, Black Ice."

12

Black Ice

"Sorry, who?" the woman asked. She straightened, still on her knees in the snow. Her eyes met mine. Then she shook her head. "The supervillain? I like her show, but I'm definitely not her. Besides, the hero who fights her is better."

I almost bought it. The apology was halfway out of my mouth when her lip twitched just the tiniest bit. I looked down at her hands as she stood the rest of the way up. She'd crushed one of the cups in her grip—and tiny tendrils of ice were forming on the outside.

I'd guessed right! I struggled not to let on that I'd noticed. "Uh, my mistake. But yeah, a small would be great." My heart plummeted as she went through the charade of filling my cup. I *still* wouldn't get any cider!

I pulled out my cell phone and sent a quick series of texts.

<Tele-Portal, both are here – Understudy 10:47>
<Talking with Black Ice now – Understudy 10:47>
<Dont drink the cider. Somethings fishy – Understudy 10:48>

I wasn't sure what about the cider bothered me. But it wasn't wise to accept if a supervillain offered a hero a drink during an Episode. When Black Ice handed me the cup, I shoved my phone in my pocket, pretended to fumble with the drink, and knocked it onto the slushy snow at her feet. "Sorry. Butterfingers," I lied.

"It's fine," Black Ice said through gritted teeth. She reached up to flip a sign from Open to Closed. "I need to get going. My shift's almost over."

Something was about to happen. Something bad. I could feel it even without [Inkling]. I used [Power-Weaving]. "But you've only just started—"

Before I could finish, Black Ice upended the whole tank of cider at me. The warm, golden-brown juice sloshed toward me, crystallizing instantly into needle-sharp icicles that surged straight toward my head.

"[Quick-Time Change]!" I shouted a moment before the spikes would have hit me. This time, the dance simulator pushed me through some half-sexy catlike dance, complete with goofy, cutesy claw motions. When it ended, my face burned under the Copy Cat Costume's plushie fur.

Time unfroze. **[I-Frame Transform]** activated.

[Flashy Fitting-Room! +1 Flamboyance Point]
[Steel Yourself! +1 Grit Point]
[Floating Points: 1 Flamboyance]

A moment later, the cider spikes slammed into me, shattering instead of piercing my fur. I'd chosen Copy Cat for one reason and one reason only. I could run down anyone with this build.

At least, I hoped I could. If not, I was catgirling around for nothing.

Black Ice crashed through the back of the cider stand's tent, with me just a step behind. The flap hit me in the face; I tore through it a moment later and burst out into the next tent behind her. The vendor, inexplicably selling fresh vegetables mid-winter, screamed and leaped out of the way.

"I'm a **[Hometown Heroine]** meow!" I said. The camera drone caught it all. Tails was in my head, and I couldn't get her out, even when chasing down a super-villain. The blue nimbus formed around me, making my plushie fur stand on end, and I took off after the retreating villain.

She reached back, pulled a cart over, and then froze the path in front of her. Her boots clung to the ice with little spikes. Somehow, she was able to run full speed across the slick surface.

I skidded to a stop. Then I took a step back and used **[Leaping Leopards]**. My running pounce took me across most of the ice; I slammed into Black Ice, who twisted and fell. We skidded across the ice.

[Badass Takedown! +1 Badass Point]
[Floating Points: 3 Flamboyance, 1 Grit]

I was almost to a combo. All I had to do was finish it off. I activated—

"No, you don't!" An icicle formed in Black Ice's hand, and she stabbed it at my throat. I coughed and reeled back as the ice shattered, the **[Cat-Scratch Fever]** I'd been starting up falling away. It didn't hurt. I didn't take any superhero damage. What happened was worse.

[Combo Broken! Floating Points Lost. Power Lost.]

"What the hell?" I asked no one in particular. She'd broken my combo. I'd have to ask the professors or Tele-Portal about that later.

Black Ice struggled to her feet and ran a few more steps toward the ice's edge. "First time weaving in the minors? You're just a baby super, aren't you?" she taunted, waggling a finger. Another icicle formed in her hand, and she flourished it like a sword. Then she bowed theatrically in her snowsuit and started sprinting again.

I followed, shakily at first, then more quickly. My phone buzzed in my pocket, but I ignored it. Tele-Portal would just have to figure it out herself.

The screaming, running Extras would give her plenty of clues if she was nearby.

Black Ice whirled around a corner, with me in hot purr-suit. Then she dipped through another stall. I barreled through it behind her, sprinting furiously even as **[Hometown Heroine]** faded.

I skidded to a stop. The camera drone hovered overhead and then zoomed in.

Not ten feet away, Black Ice held her icicle against an Extra's neck. "Freeze, or I'll put him on ice!"

<You'd better do what she says,> Tails's voice echoed in my mind. *<Maybe we can talk her down. Try getting her talking and comfortable.>*

How could that possibly work? I took a closer look at the Extra—John Deer, the man who'd been nervous in line before. I shook my head slightly; that guy was having a *bad* day.

<You don't have to stop her right meow. You just have to stall until Tele-Portal shows up.>

Okay. That made sense. "What do you want?" I said. I was shouting. Why was I shouting? That wasn't how you de-escalated a hostage situation. I'd done this before, though always with Peter, or occasionally LABRAT.

"Who the hell are you?"

"I'm Magical Girl Understudy. You probably haven't heard of me, but I'm on my way up, and I'm going to tear your plan down." I tried to project confidence while toning down my voice a little. My phone buzzed again, but with Black Ice's eyes locked on me, I couldn't answer it to tell Tele-Portal my location.

"You're right. I've never heard of you. And your gimmick is that you turn into a cat? That's pretty stupid. Now, here's what's going to happen. You're going to go back through the tent and count to ten. When you finish, you're going to come out. I'll be gone; this guy will be on the ground right here, and you can save him. If you come out early, he's taking an icicle to the face."

"Extras have protection," I bluffed.

"Not enough to save him from being in the wrong place at the wrong time." Black Ice's voice cut like a knife; she was so tense I could see the icicle shaking. "You can save him. Just back. Off."

"I want to know something in return," I said. I needed to stall, and what villain would pass up the chance to monologue? "What are you getting out of all this?"

[Dramatic Setup! +1 Drama Point]

Black Ice laughed, and I knew I had her, at least for a few seconds. "Me? I'm getting paid. But Polar Vortex? He's got a plan. I can't say much since he never lets lieutenants in on the gimmick, but the winter festival needs to go for his plan to succeed, so he hired me to help him ruin it. I'm saving lives, baby!"

My phone buzzed yet again. Hopefully, Tele-Portal was close. If not, I'd need to do something drastic to save the Extra's life. I took a step toward the half-torn tent flap I'd torn through. "Okay, Black Ice. I'm going to go in there and transform. I'm trusting you to leave your hostage behind. Can I trust you?"

"Of course." Black Ice grinned; the smile felt misplaced—a mix of feral maliciousness and genuine glee. "I'm *nothing* if not trustwort—"

A portal opened in the tent flap next to her. One of Tele-Portal's hands reached through and grabbed John Deer the Extra, yanking him through before Black Ice could react. She screamed and threw her icicle sword toward the portal, which closed.

<Go, go, go! Right meow! Get her!> Tails screamed in my mind. She sounded more aggressive than I'd ever heard her. Fortunately, I agreed.

I used [**Leaping Leopards**] again, flying through the air as Black Ice stood dumbfounded. Once again, I pounced on the supervillain, and we skidded across the packed snow and slush.

[**Badass Takedown! +1 Badass Point**]

She might've been off guard, but Black Ice recovered like a champion. The ground under us grew slick with a thin layer of clear, perfectly smooth ice. Neither of us was totally helpless; she dug her crampons into the ground, giving her some leverage, and I had my claws. We scratched, stabbed, and slashed at each other for a moment, struggling to gain an advantage.

All I *had* to do was hold out. But I didn't want to hold out. I wanted to *win*. One scratch found purchase, and I flipped around so my clawed hands and feet faced the supervillain. Then I used [**Doom Ball**].

[**Badass Damage! +1 Badass Point**]
[**Badass Damage! +1 Badass Point**]
[**Badass Damage! +1 Badass Point**]
[**Badass Damage! +1 Badass Point**]

My claws, all four limbs' worth of them, ripped into Black Ice's snowsuit. She barely noticed at first, but by the time all the damage had piled up, I could see I'd drawn blood. Thin tears sliced through her snowsuit; long, delicate-looking cuts scored her skin.

I expected her to summon a gigantic icicle and stab at me. I did *not* expect her to fall through the ground and into the air a few feet away. The portal under her closed before she could fall back through, and she landed with an audible "Oof!"

Tele-Portal walked up; her portal cannon trained on Black Ice. "We need to work on your communication, Understudy," she said.

"I can't exactly check my texts during a hostage crisis, Tele-Portal," I snapped back, picking myself up off the ground. "Surrender, Miss Ice?"

"I did my job, so sure, why not?" the supervillain said. She started to stand, then stopped as Tele-Portal gestured with her gigantic portal cannon. "We still win, and you still lose. I beat a major leaguer! Ahahahaha!"

"What do you mean?" I asked, glaring.

To my surprise, Tele-Portal answered, "Polar Vortex is planning on climbing to the major leagues. It's been his goal for a while, but he needs a big stinger of an Episode to gain the ranking. It's not unlike your situation. You're looking to rank up. That's why you want my training facility and suddenly care about patrolling."

"Yeah." There wasn't much point in hiding it. Tele-Portal was a veteran; she'd been doing this a long time, and I probably wasn't her first sidekick.

"Go on, guess! Guess!" Black Ice hissed from the ground. I transformed back to Understudy.

"I'm not playing your game, Miss Ice," Tele-Portal said, sniffing at the villain. "Understudy, have you seen Polar Vortex?"

Before I could answer, Black Ice burst out laughing. I braced myself for a **[Maniacal Reveal]**, and sure enough, it happened. "You fools! You total fools! I was bait the whole time! The actual Episode isn't taking place at this festival! It's happening—"

Behind us, the ground shook, and the air filled with the horrific, nails-on-chalkboard sound of rusted steel screeching on steel. Tele-Portal and I whirled as a cloud of white mist belched from every smokestack and window in the brick building above the river.

"—at the power plant!"

[Good Thinking! +1 Cunning Point]
[End of Act Two! Act Three in Five Minutes!]
[Alias - Understudy] [Archetype - Magical Girl] [Community Rank - 348/523]
[HP 8/8]
[Styles and Skills]
►Archetype Skill - Transformation Sequence
►Badass (52) (Skill Roll Available)
►Cunning (3)
►Drama (7)
►Stellar Ray 1
►Bit-Part Barrage 1
►Flamboyance (28)
►Signature Skill - Adaptive Armoire
►Stored Costumes: (Rainy Day, Copy Cat)
►Starwave Sail 1
►Quick-Time Change 1

▶Grit (22)

▶I-Frame Transform 1

[50 Badass Credits Used. Rolling Skill!]

[New Skill! TA-1LZ New Head-Cannon: A variable-ammunition cannon that scales depending on the Episode's rating]

13

Power Plant

"You know more than you're saying." Tele-Portal glared at Black Ice. "People's lives are in danger. Talk."

"People's lives are *always* in danger, but the only time you heroes ever notice is if the threat's costumed and cowled. An Extra could get hit by a bus in the next five minutes, and you two wouldn't even blink. It's not until someone tries to better themselves that you get involved. But that changes soon. Soon, Tokyexico—no, the world! Soon, the world will be under new management, and Polar Vortex, King Cold, and I will see that everyone who's kept us down gets left out in the cold." The supervillain sure could monologue—the Student Supervillain Society president could probably learn a thing or two.

"Fine. Have it your way." Tele-Portal dragged the villain into a tent, then placed a portal on the ceiling and another on the snow below her. She started falling through them. "That should hold her until the police show up."

"That's gotta be torture. Are we allowed to do that?" I asked as a camera drone hovered nearby. The villain fell faster and faster, occasionally screaming. Her black snowsuit was a blur.

"Yes." Tele-Portal shut the tent flap. She looked at me critically. "You want to keep Extras safe? Don't give the villains a second chance in the same Episode. You can't save them all unless you beat the villain and stop the Episode, and it doesn't matter what you do to make that happen."

"Oh." That didn't sound like the "We don't interrogate our enemies—that's vil shit" that TUSSA lived by.

We started toward the power plant. Tele-Portal strode ahead on her stilts, heading for the snow-spewing building. She carried her portal gun, and she looked exhausted again. I jogged through the snow to keep up.

[Winter is Coming: Act Three in Progress]

"How long have you been a superhero?" I asked Tele-Portal.

"A decade." She pointed at the power plant's main door as we got closer. It hung open. "I got inside before shit hit the fan back at the festival. It's an ice maze in there. Black Ice and Polar Vortex were *busy*. Good job, by the way. You might actually have beaten her without me."

"I might have. I had a plan, and when you pulled the Extra out, I could have attacked her. I was waiting because I couldn't let her hurt him."

"Yeah. You get used to it."

"When? I've been doing this for five years." But then I thought back to the Episode at the end of summer. I'd left Extras in a bind before when taking out the villain was more important, and they weren't in immediate danger.

"Shhh. We're going in. Keep your eyes open; the ice is tricky, and I can't use my portals until the police have Black Ice. We don't want her getting free. Sometimes they reengage. They're not supposed to, but then again, they are villains."

We stepped through the door into the old, abandoned power plant. As soon as we did, the roaring sound of machinery filled my ears. Tele-Portal shrugged and pointed to the end of the long hall in front of us, then started walking. I couldn't hear what she said, but the message was clear: this way, follow me. Shimmering windows made of ice allowed us a view down at the plant's massive turbines, which spun and squealed ominously.

Tele-Portal pointed to the double doors on the end and made a flicking motion with her finger. She said something, then repeated it. I couldn't hear over the machinery. Kick in the door? That seemed aggressive, careless, and very much the style of a superheroine who always had a "get out of jail free" card. I took a deep breath. Then I ran up to it, jammed my foot into the handle, and kicked as hard as possible.

[Explosive Entry! +1 Badass Point]

Tele-Portal rushed through the door. A moment later, I joined her just in time to see a flash of red in the ice blocking our way forward. It disappeared around a corner as I shouted, "**[Stellar Ray]**!" The beam barely scratched the ice, and Tele-Portal shook her head. She pointed down a hall that met ours at a T-junction. Then she started jogging toward a sign labeled Break Room.

I followed her, moving quickly. But as I did, a massive spike of ice shot out of the jet-black ice sheet covering the hallway. It crashed into Tele-Portal, pinning her to the wall.

I fired another **[Stellar Ray]** at the blurry red figure as it ducked away again. Then I turned to Tele-Portal.

She was good and stuck. The spike had pinned her to the wall, but her superhero damage had kept it from being catastrophic. I tried to move it, but she shook her head and pointed at the portal gun she'd dropped. I grabbed it and pulled the trigger.

Nothing happened.

I pulled the trigger again—still nothing. Tele-Portal slammed the wall with her free arm, rolling her eyes, and then squeezed them shut in concentration. A weak, wavery portal shimmered slowly into existence behind her. Another appeared on the wall as sweat broke out on Tele-Portal's face. Her fist clenched, and she fell backward through the portal, out of the ceiling, and onto the floor.

I could hear her grunt of pain over the machinery howling.

I helped her up, slinging her arm over my shoulder, and half-dragged her to the break room. Inside, a few dust-covered chairs sat around a table; the rest had long since fallen apart or were covered in frost.

"Give me the cannon," Tele-Portal groaned. She collapsed into a chair as I handed it to her. "Shit, that takes a lot out of me."

"I thought you needed the cannon to make the portals. Aren't you a Genius?" I asked.

"Ha. No. Elementalist." Tele-Portal coughed. Whatever she'd had to do to make the portal had taken a ton out of her. "Underdelver's the Genius. He came up with the rig back in high school; it channels my power, strengthens it. I can only make two or three a day without the stilt/cannon combo. He didn't want me fading off as we moved to the minors, so he built it for me. God, I'm exhausted. I need a few minutes."

Sure enough, the bags under her eyes looked much darker than they had just a moment ago. She suppressed a yawn. "I'll be right behind you, Understudy. But you've gotta track down Polar Vortex. If you can get him in a straight fight, you have a chance, but don't let him play his game. He's an ambusher. Try to shut down the power plant if you can. I'm not sure what they're up to, but this place is important to them."

"How do you know so much about all these villains?" I asked.

"Over a decade of experience. Six years full-time as a minor and major. Now go." Tele-Portal waved at the door, but she swore again as my hand closed on its handle. "Shit. Black Ice may be free, too. I'll be as close behind you as I can. Go!"

I sprinted out of the room, stomach lurching. This was supposed to be a simple patrol, not a fight against two minor-league villains at the same time! I'd need to be smart, but I'd left my smartest Costume behind.

The screech and rumble of the turbines filled my ears again. I steeled myself and crept down a set of rusted steel stairs. Pipes, some as wide as I was tall, crisscrossed the lower floor, and the sound of running water echoed through them. Occasionally, a machine belched sooty, acrid smog as it started up or clattered to a stop. Somewhere down there, the villain lurked. I just knew it.

I wished I still had [**Inkling**]. Its half-second of precognition once or twice in a fight like this would be invaluable.

As I reached the bottom of the stairs, I stopped to take stock. A maze of ice walls and piping filled the room. The control room for the whole plant sat on the far side, covered in snowdrifts and ice. And inside, for just a moment, I thought I saw a red blur.

I had Understudy's ranged attacks, but [**Stellar Ray**] couldn't break the ice walls. Copy Cat might have the firepower, and it'd be warmer than this outfit. And Rainy Day . . .

Rainy Day might be the way to win here. If the power plant was active, I might get a truly massive combo. Maybe I could preload some of it and set a trap for the trap-setter himself. I could—

CRASH!

An ice spike, just like the one that'd taken out Tele-Portal, smashed free from an ice wall. The impact spun me off-balance, and I took a moment to rebalance. Then I started running into the generator room's maze.

[HP 6/8]
[**Gritty Recovery! +1 Grit Point**]

Ice exploded around me as I ran. The villain seemed only a few steps ahead of me, almost tauntingly close. I fired a [**Stellar Ray**] into another wall of ice; this one shattered, filling the entire section of the maze with snowy powder and making it impossible to see. The machines' whine rose in pitch momentarily. Then, a deafening cough filled the air as it backfired before whining more.

[**Dramatic Turn of Events! +1 Drama Point**]

I couldn't see; the snow blocked my vision. I couldn't hear; the generator room was far too loud. A trio of icicles filled the hallway behind me. The only way through was forward, so I plunged into the snow, feeling my way along. Hopefully, Polar Vortex couldn't see me in here, either.

The snow started slowly falling toward the ground. I took one breath. Then another. As the path in front of me grew gradually clearer, I used [**Power-Weaving**] and threw myself toward another ice wall.

I had a plan.

This one exploded as another massive spike zoomed toward me. I used [**Quick-Time Change**], pausing the world, and did the Itsy Bitsy Spider. The tip hit me dead in the chest, but instead of pain, I felt a tickle—and an opportunity.

I looked down at the spike. "Oh no. I've been impaled," I said. Then, I casually walked off the icicle and jumped through the hole in the ice wall.

[**Flashy Fitting Room! +1 Flamboyance Point**]
[**Steel Yourself! +1 Grit Point**]
[**Floating Points: 1 Flamboyance**]
[**Stylish Quote! +1 Flamboyance Point**]

I skidded to a stop just feet from a figure in a red snowsuit. "Polar Vortex, stop!" I shouted, barely audible over the giant turbine howling behind him. Sparks shot off it—I couldn't tell if they were from the grinding parts or a building electrical charge. But I had to take a chance, and I had to do it right now.

I used [**Thunderhead**] just as another ice spike slammed into me. This one caught me, shoving me back and pinning me to a wall.

[HP 4/8]
[Pause for Effect! +1 Drama Point]
[Floating Points: 3 Flamboyance, 1 Grit]

I screamed as it hit me, then again as I tried—and failed—to wriggle free. But my power was working; the storm cloud mixed with the machines' smog cloud and Polar Vortex's snow cloud. Like my fight with Gourmet in the training room, I had to hold out for a moment. And I had to hope Polar Vortex couldn't disrupt my combo like Black Ice.

The villain stalked toward me, getting too close before shouting at me, the only way to be heard over the generator's turbine. "Tele-Portal sent a little kid to do her dirty work? What the hell is this?"

I stopped wiggling, feet an inch or two off the ground, and glared right back. "I'm the best person for the job. What are you trying to do here anyway?"

"I'm glad you asked!" Polar Vortex said. The camera drone dipped in close, the microphone practically in our faces. "A power surge from a single plant running in overdrive at peak hours could easily overtax Tokyexico's fragile grid. We'll plunge the city into darkness, then take over easily tonight. The heroes won't have a choice but to let us rule on a throne of ice."

"That sounds like Power Wars crap," I said, mustering all the sarcasm of a sixth-grader. But he was right; this plan wasn't anywhere near as ridiculous as taking over the sewage treatment plant, and *that* would have left Riverside helpless. I steeled myself as the [**Thunderhead**] above the generator grew and grew. I only had one move that would save Tokyexico—and *might* get me out of this. "Is this power plant connected?"

"Not yet! We're maxing it out, *then* flipping the switch! But you and Tele-Portal won't be around for that." The villain formed a gigantic icicle in his hand. He grinned at me. "Goodbye, little heroine."

I nodded. "Goodbye. [**Ride the Lightning**]!"

14

Ride the Lightning

My plan had worked perfectly. It was pretty simple.

One: I'd been building my combo since I entered the maze. I needed a target to **[Power-Weave]**, but I could cause massive damage using the generators if I got the whole combo off. Since I'd built Rainy Day specifically for this, she was my go-to.

Two: As Polar Vortex monologued for the camera drone, I realized he wouldn't see a combo coming. He was too wrapped up in his project, unlike his lieutenant, Black Ice. But I needed time for **[Thunderhead]**, so I stalled.

Three: Polar Vortex wasn't the real threat. The real danger was letting the power plant stay running. With Black Ice potentially free, we had an uncontained villain who could shut down the power to the whole city.

I only had one option.

As **[Ride the Lightning]** siphoned power from the generator and **[Thunderhead]**, I felt it build inside me. The energy was unimaginable. I couldn't hold it, so I let it go. Tendrils of blue-white lightning picked me up and danced across Polar Vortex's red snowsuit, but most of the electric fury went in one direction.

Straight back at the generator.

[Electric Lightshow! +1 Flamboyance Point]
[Environmental Combo! +1 Cunning Point]
[Thunderstruck! +1 Drama Point]
[Power-Weaving! +6 Flamboyance, +3 Grit, +1 Drama Point]
[Feedback 1]
[HP 2/8]
[Combo Collapse]

The whole machine lit up like a Tesla coil; sparks filled the air over our heads, and both my hair and Polar Vortex's stood upright. Then flames licked across it, rapidly melting the icy maze I'd navigated through. It didn't explode, but the turbine started ripping itself apart as it spun faster and faster.

It wouldn't be generating power—not enough for a power surge, even if Black Ice or Polar Vortex connected it to the grid.

"You little monster! I'll kill you!" Polar Vortex screamed. His face twisted in rage, and he launched another ice spike my way. It rammed into a pipe—one of the big ones as tall as Rainy Day, then shot back toward the villain as the water started spraying out in a frigid blast.

I pulled myself free and ran.

Quickly.

But I couldn't run quickly enough. Polar Vortex practically surfed across the incoming water, freezing it beneath his feet, and I didn't have the speed to keep up with that. He summoned another icicle, then another, and dipped down toward me. I didn't have the superhero damage to tank those hits.

A portal opened below me, dropping me through the floor. I fell out of the ceiling somewhere else inside the maze and hit the ground hard.

[HP 1/8]

"Switch Costumes!" Tele-Portal yelled. She'd broken out a window overlooking the generator room. She waved her portal cannon at me.

I glanced at Polar Vortex—or where I'd last seen him. Mist from the broken pipe mixed with smoke from the ruined generator, and it was hard to be sure, but I thought I had a moment or two to switch.

"Transform meow!"

<Transform meow!>

[Rejuvenation Activated! HP 4/8]

I shifted back into Copy Cat, feeling Tails's mind merge with mine. *<Good to be back. Let's hunt some villains,>* the plushie cat said in my head.

"We won't have to hunt. He'll come to us." I waved up at Tele-Portal. "You coming?"

"Nope! I'm built for support. Like it or not, I'm not set up to help directly." The superheroine's voice sounded strained, and I couldn't tell if it was from exhaustion, worrying about me, or both.

I didn't have time to find out. Polar Vortex ducked around the corner and launched another icicle, but Tele-Portal couldn't move fast enough to drop me to safety this time. It hit me, shattering on my **[Fursonal Furcefield]**. Tails's promise that she was my fursuit seemed to be true.

[True Grit! +1 Grit Point]

I used **[Leaping Leopards]** and pounced toward Polar Vortex, but the villain was ready for it. He raised a sheet of jet-black ice in front of him.

I hurdled toward it, unable to stop my pounce, but a portal opened in its center, and a moment later, I was back on track, pouncing toward Polar Vortex from behind. I slammed into the surprised supervillain, bowling him over and sending his icicles crashing to the ground.

[Badass Takedown! +1 Badass Point]

He rolled, but I'd landed on top of him, and I used **[Cat-Scratch Fever]**. My . . . Tails's . . . paw lashed out and ripped across the man's face, leaving a trio of scratch marks that quickly grew red and started leaking puss.

[Dramatic Damage! +1 Drama Point]

"Goddamn pussy! Where the hell did the girl go? I'm gonna kill her!" Polar Vortex shouted, an edge of pain in his voice. He summoned a gigantic snowball and hurled it at me. This close, it smashed me a moment before the portal appeared, shoving me through it and onto the floor right next to the collapsing generator.

[HP 2/8]

"This is working!" Tele-Portal shouted from above. "You're trading well! Switch again!"

I transformed back to Understudy. Lab Assistant would have been perfect in this environment; I could have harassed the injured, inaccurate Polar Vortex with TA-1LZ. But I didn't have her equipped. Instead, I went with Understudy—my hardest-hitting ranged damage.

The villain staggered through the maze of pipes. Every ice wall he touched let him pass cleanly through it. Water lapped at his calves and mine as another rusted pipe ruptured. The generator room was filling with water!

I didn't waste any time trying for a combo—I didn't have a **[Quick-Time Change]**, and without it, I didn't have the pieces to make it happen. Instead, I used **[Bit-Part Barrage]**, firing it almost point-blank at the villain.

[Dramatic Damage! +1 Drama Point]
[Dramatic Damage! +1 Drama Point]
[Dramatic Damage! +1 Drama Point]

That should have been the end, but a portal opened on a pipe, and the missed **[Stellar Rays]** rocketed back at Polar Vortex, one slamming into him from behind.

[Dramatic Damage! +1 Drama Point]

I'd gotten some good hits in, but the villain was *right* there. He formed a massive icicle and swung it like a club, smashing it into the side of my head. "How many heroes *are* there?" he shouted.

[HP 1/8]

I only half-heard him. My ears rang, and I saw stars even through the superhero damage. I watched him backswing for another blow through the pinprick where I could still see clearly.

It never landed.

Instead, the floor opened under him, and he fell, screaming, through a portal in the ceiling on the other side of the room. He rolled before Tele-Portal could trap him in a loop and started running toward me, firing icicles right at my head.

I ducked. An icicle flew overhead as I waved my wand. "**[Stellar Ray]**!"

[Dramatic Damage! +1 Drama Point]

It wasn't going to be enough. I fired another **[Stellar Ray]**.

[Dramatic Damage! +1 Drama Point]

The villain kept charging, wading through the ever-deepening water. The scratches on his face looked terrible; they practically pulsed red, and his eyes looked bloodshot and puffy. I dodged an awkwardly thrown icicle, then leaped into another portal. "Thanks, Tele-Portal!"

"No problem. Keep it up, he's almost—"

[Dramatic Damage! +1 Drama Point]
[Anticlimactic! -2 Drama Points]

"Shit. I think it's over," I said. "I lost points somehow. Anticlimactic."

"Well, find him. He's in here somewhere, and we're *not* leaving him to drown. That's bad business," Tele-Portal said. "Did you use poison or something? That's a good way to win, but it's bad TV. Next time, try to finish the villain off in direct combat. I'm going to start draining the plant. You'll like this."

"Got it." I sloshed through the frigid water.

It didn't take long to find the villain. He leaned against a pipe that hadn't burst yet, groaning and clutching his face. He cracked one eye as I approached, my wand out. The other had practically swollen shut. "The hell was *that* shit?" he grumbled at me.

"Magical Girl Understudy, reporting in!" I said to the camera drone as I struggled to pull the man to his feet. His snowsuit hadn't fared well in the water; it was soaked and probably weighed thirty pounds. I grunted as I yanked on his arm. "It's . . . it's time for the villains to exit stage left!"

[Episode Finished!]
[Episode: Winter is Coming - PG-13]
[Penalties: N/A]
[Episode Finished! +5 of each Style Point]
[Winner Winner! +2 of each Style Point]
[Role Focus: Drama + Flamboyance - Goal Met! +10 of Each Focused Style]
[Alias - Understudy] [Archetype - Magical Girl] [Community Rank - 315/523]
[HP 1/8]
[Styles and Skills]
▶Archetype Skill - Transformation Sequence
▶Badass (11)
▶Cunning (11)
▶Drama (32) (Skill Roll Available)
▶Stellar Ray 1
▶Bit-Part Barrage 1
▶Flamboyance (58) (Skill Roll Available)
▶Signature Skill - Adaptive Armoire
▶Stored Costumes: (Rainy Day, Copy Cat)
▶Starwave Sail 1
▶Quick-Time Change 1
▶Grit (41)
▶I-Frame Transform 1

I grinned breathlessly as Tele-Portal fired her cannon at Polar Vortex and me. She missed, sending it down into the water. Not that it would matter much for us if it had hit; the other end wasn't set up, so we couldn't have gotten through. I groaned. "Guess I'm taking the stairs."

"Guess so," Tele-Portal said. She yawned. "Keep an eye on your prisoner. Don't let him try anything funny. Black Ice must've decided not to make a run for it since the Episode ended. I'll meet you outside."

While I trudged up the stairs and out the door, I rolled both of my new skills.

[50 Drama Credits Used. Rolling Skill!]
[50 Flamboyance Credits Used. Rolling Skill!]
[Rank-Up! Stellar Ray 2: The beam hits much harder, dealing environmental damage and punching through heavier armor]

[New Skill! Hog the Limelight! Draw attention to yourself, redirecting the next hostile attack away from allies and toward you]

The rank-up was huge; I hadn't gotten many yet, and any power increase to something I used was welcome. But I wasn't sure about **[Hog the Limelight]**. It seemed pretty risky. Maybe I could combine it with a Grit-focused Copy Cat build or something. But I wasn't excited about it, not when I routinely paired up with heroes with more superhero damage than me.

Then, suddenly, I realized what it was for. This was the rescue power I'd asked for. With it, I could run escort for Extras and *guarantee* the villain couldn't hurt them. My weariness faded as I dumped a shivering Polar Vortex on the ground. Without his superhero damage shield, the **[Cat-Scratch Fever]** and the soaking-wet snowsuit worked against him, and he looked blue. "We'll get you someplace warm soon. Like prison."

"Come look at this," Tele-Portal called from the river's edge. I hurried toward the icy-cold mist that filled the air behind her. Arcing out of the building's side was a jet of water. She'd placed a portal on the building, and the power plant was draining. I didn't see how it'd fix the flooding, but at least it wasn't getting worse.

"Good job, kid," the superheroine said to me. She looked terrible; the bags under her eyes were dark, and she definitely needed some sleep. "I called Edgar. He's going to pick us up and get you back to TU. He'll be here in five or so."

"That's fast. There's no time for a PR plug back down at the winter festival?" I asked, disappointed.

Tele-Portal sighed. "Fine. Hurry. But you're explaining why you care so much on the ride back. Then we're getting you back on campus. You have studying to do."

PART THREE

15

Clubbing

"I'm not sure why I'm even in this class," Su-Bin muttered as we pored over the Child Psychology notes from Dr. Roberts's lecture. The professor wasn't boring, that was for sure. She scared us too much to be boring. She said everything with such seriousness that I couldn't believe she'd been an elementary counselor for a decade before teaching. And worse, she did weekly quizzes on Tuesdays about the previous week's material.

So Su-Bin and I sat on my apartment floor, trying to study the hierarchy of needs.

"You need a psych class to get a degree, and this one's got real-life use. It's a solid choice. At least, that's what my advisor said when we filled out my schedule. Now, where does theater fall on the hierarchy?" I asked.

"Probably under self-actualization for you, nerd," Su-Bin teased. "I'm not sure for me, though. It's fun to *watch*, but it's not something I need to *do*. But yeah, no, I'm not going to use Child Psych. I'm not having kids, I'm not working with kids, and if I'm in a life-or-death situation where I need to know how a six-year-old thinks, I'll just die."

"Ooookay." I sighed. I wrote 'theater' up by self-actualization. "How's your roommate doing?"

"Oh, she's *fine*. She's got a new boyfriend, though. I had to draw some lines with her. Now she spends most of her time at his place instead, which is great for me. I'm filling my physiological need for sleep much better now." She wrote 'getting rid of the roommate' under physiological needs.

I furrowed my brow. "Does she go to classes?"

"Who cares? She's only back one or two nights a week now. Is sex a physiological need or a love and belonging need?"

I reddened slightly. "I'm not sure. I'm going to call it . . . both? Because, uh, sex itself is physiological, but the closeness and intimacy is love and belonging."

"Makes sense." Su-Bin scribbled 'my roommate's loud lovemaking' under both. "How about cafeteria food? Not the food court with the burritos and *good* pizza, but the cafeteria itself?"

"Doesn't even make the list." The Student Union Building's cafeteria had emptied out. The quality had plummeted over break. No one wanted *yet another* greasy slice of pizza or overcooked hamburger—not after home cooking—and even the enticement of "free" food wasn't enough to bring people in.

Su-Bin laughed, not quite snorting her extra-large soda out of her nose. "What'd you do this weekend?"

"Oh, I went to the winter festival at Confluence Park. Just me, though. Bianca had other plans." None of that was a lie. I *had* been at the winter festival, and Bee spent most of the morning as Fursona, coordinating with the radio show host about our roundtable discussion.

Surprisingly, Su-Bin narrowed her eyes. "Didn't some supers ruin the whole festival and blow up the old power plant?"

"Not . . . exactly. A pair of supervillains attacked the festival's river skating, and Tele-Portal and some other heroine saved a bunch of people. Then they chased down the villains and kept the festival safe. It wasn't a big deal."

"It sounds like a big deal to me. I heard one of the villains said something about trying to take over the city. Dad thinks we're heading for another Power War in the next year. It'll be a total mess this time, too. Supers keep getting more and more powerful, and Extras like us aren't any safer."

I did *not* want to have this conversation right now. "Yeah . . . anyway, the festival had some great ice skating, and I got to try some delicious cider. I liked it so much I came back for four helpings. There were some art booths and a few people selling skis, snowshoes, and ice skates, but I only stayed for a few hours. What did *you* do yesterday?"

"I signed up for a couple clubs." Su-Bin shrugged. "You'd hate the first one. Theorems and Theses. It's a pseudo-role-playing club where we work through historical math and engineering problems for fun. There are races to solve the most or to solve problems the fastest. One guy's been working on solving the Riemann hypothesis, but that's *impossible*, and everyone else knows it. But, yeah, it's a cool club, and I'm already meeting a lot of neat people in it."

"That sounds . . . great," I said, hedging. I did *not* want an invitation; thankfully, one wasn't forthcoming. "How about the other club?"

"You'd get a lot out of it. It's a really great group of people. We're united under the banner of making the world a better place, and the vice president has a really driving vision for its future. It's called APPEAL."

Something about the name sounded familiar, but I couldn't place it. "Appeal? Is it a fashion-focused club? You don't strike me as particularly fashion-conscious, Su-Bin."

"Ouch." Su-Bin pointed dramatically to her gray sweatshirt and sweatpants. "That'd hurt more if it wasn't true. No, APPEAL is the Anti-Power Protestors' and Extras' Advancement League. We're the Tokyexico University chapter."

Shit. I'd looked it up but forgotten all about it. Bianca had even mentioned that APPEAL was part of the roundtable radio shot. And *of course*, Su-Bin was part of it. Her parents had been antisuper, and she'd said that she didn't really like supers last semester. I tried to find a way out before she could nail me down. My brain was in overdrive.

But it wasn't fast enough. "We're having a meeting tomorrow evening. Free pizza—the good, off-campus kind—and drinks. You should come."

Double shit. "Uh, I don't know, Bianca and I have plans to—"

"She can come too. The more we are, the more powerful we become, like a bundle of sticks. It's the only way to stand up to the supers." Then, before I could "maybe" my way out of it, she dropped the hammer. "Plus, I'm the vice president!"

Triple shit. I closed my eyes and blew out a long sigh. There wasn't a good way out of this. I had no excuses lined up—not really—and *not* showing up would be letting Su-Bin down. Still, I had to try. "Su-Bin, you know I *like* superheroes, right?"

"Well, yeah, Annie. *Everyone* likes superheroes until they knock down your house or fumigate your school or something. But society post–Launch Day is so structured around supers that you'd never know how things used to be. I'm offering you a chance to see past the shiny suits and flashy powers—to realize how dangerous even a little-league hero is!" Su-Bin took a deep breath, flustered. She squeezed her eyes shut. "I'm off-script so bad right now. Just . . . just come to the meeting tomorrow? Seven o'clock, the Alder Building, Meeting Room 237."

I relented. "Fine. I'll be there."

"Thank you. Now, where does the city's wall fit in on the hierarchy?"

"You did *what*?" Bianca half shouted.

"I agreed to go to her stupid meeting, okay?" I said. We sat on my apartment couch. Well, *I* sat. Bianca stood, hands on her hips, glaring at me. I flinched under her glare.

The moment Su-Bin left, I'd texted Bianca and told her to come over as soon as she could. I kind of regretted not telling her *why*, though. She'd walked through the door in such a good mood, and I'd dropped the bomb that we had dinner with an antisuper club tomorrow.

"No, I get what you did, I just . . . I don't understand why." Bianca's face was flushed, and the scent of apples competed with the much-less-pleasant stink of nervous sweat. "You know you're talking with one of their members—probably their president—in ten days, right? If whoever it is recognizes Understudy as Annie, it'll blow up in Su-Bin's face, not ours."

"Oh, don't worry. No one's going to recognize me. I'm a master of disguise."

Bianca laughed, and I started relaxing, but her expression soured again a moment later. She spoke, her voice somehow both soft and severe. "Annie, I think you're awesome, and you're a ton of fun to do superhero stuff with, but you're not subtle. You're not subtle at all. I figured you out in like ten minutes, remember?"

I flushed and looked down. "You're special. Most people won't see it."

"The Crumb and Flare caught you spying without even trying."

"We'll be fine. This is a great opportunity to get a leg up for the radio roundtable."

"I think this is a terrible idea, Annie. There's no way it doesn't go badly for Su-Bin, us, or everyone."

"I'm making a decision as team leader, Bianca. We've got a chance to figure out the talking points for one of the roundtable participants. I'm taking that chance. You're the one who's big on preparation. I'm preparing!" I half shouted and stood up.

"You're being stupid!" Bee shouted back. "You're going to get caught, and I bet APPEAL would *love* to expose the hero who blew up the engineering building."

"I'm not being stupid. I'm being realistic!" I took a deep breath and forced myself to sit back down. Peter and I had fought like this sometimes. Once, we'd had a full-on screaming match in Riverside High's halls that devolved into an Episode later that day. I didn't want that with Bee. I took another breath. "Look, we're committed, so I need your help. Maybe I can wear a goofy mustache disguise or something. We can make me unrecognizable for one night, right?"

"I don't think *Pataki* could make you unrecognizable."

"Thanks. I'm pretty awesome. But seriously, we have this afternoon to plan, then we're going in. Or I am if you won't come with me."

Bianca deflated. Or maybe she just didn't want to fight anymore, either. Her eyes still burned, and she still seemed pissed, but she sat down next to me and snuggled up against me. I wrapped an arm around her and kept talking. "I'm a lot better with you than I am alone, Bianca. I need your help."

"Okay." She relaxed in my arms. Not much—she was still pissed—but a little. "But we're gonna have to reverse roles for this one. You've gotta be the sidekick because you need to be invisible. I'll draw attention. I'm always in my fursuit as a hero anyway, so it won't matter if I'm recognizable."

"Fine. You're the hero, and I'm the sidekick. What's your first order, boss-lady?" I asked, rolling my eyes.

"You need . . . a script."

"A script, huh?" I *was* an actress. I could do a script.

"Yep. You're the weak link since you have no idea how to maintain a secret identity. So we're going to make a script for you. You're going to be on that script all evening because if you're not, and you blow your cover, I'll never forgive you. Got it?" Her voice cut like a knife; she was deadly serious.

"Got it."

"Good, now let's start with what you *can't* say. You're not allowed to talk about superhero Episodes. If anyone asks about the TUEAS Building, you don't know anything, but it's a tragedy that it collapsed, and you hope it gets rebuilt soon. Do *not* mention Understudy or Fursona. And try to keep any conversations you have with people who aren't me to a minimum," Bianca instructed.

I gulped. "You're keeping me on a short leash here, huh?"

"Damn right, I am. If I'm risking my identity, too, you're gonna play by the rules." She stood up, grabbed a paper and pencil, and sat back down. "I've got homework, so we've got an hour to plan this spy mission."

16

Spy Mission

TUESDAY, JANUARY 13

Bianca and I stood outside the Alder Building. The weather had been surprisingly warm, but now it was pitch-black out, and I suppressed a shiver. Part of that was the cold, but mostly, I just felt scummy. Like I was betraying a friend.

Which was, in fact, what I was about to do.

"Are you sure this is a good idea? We could back out," I mumbled.

"No. *You* got us committed to this. *You're* going to see it through." Bianca clearly hadn't entirely forgiven me for getting us into this mess. Her glare softened. "I know she's your friend. I know you feel like you're about to stab her in the back. But that doesn't matter. You go in there, and you stick to the script. We'll be better positioned for that minor-league spot if you do. And that's what you want, right?"

I gulped. "Right."

"Good. Let's *go.* We have five minutes."

As we walked through the Alder Building's sterile halls, I kept fidgeting with my hair. "Stop that. You look nervous," Bianca said.

"I *am* nervous."

"Don't be. Just remember your training."

"I haven't had any training," I muttered. "An hour of prep figuring out what to talk about doesn't count, especially because you pretty much told me to shut up and look pretty. I bet Tele-Portal—"

"No superhero names. And you *do* look pretty, so shut up once we're in there."

"Right. I bet my mentor would have some advice on surviving a club meeting you're not sure about joining. She knows a ton about the law business, and it's gotta be similar, right?"

Su-Bin stood outside Meeting Room 237, talking animatedly with an older-looking guy. She waved. "Erik, these are the two new members I told you about."

"Uh, *possible* new members," Erik said, winking. "We don't push our thinking on others here, unlike *some people.*"

"Yeah, *possible* members. Anika, Bianca, meet Erik. He's APPEAL's president."

We said our pleasantries and shook hands; his squeeze felt looser than it needed to be, almost like shaking with a dead fish. He laughed as Bianca tried switching hands on him, then pointed through the doors. "We bought enough from Mario's for everyone to have three slices, and there's soda inside, too. Make yourselves at home. We'll start the actual meeting in fifteen minutes."

I nodded, thanked him, and entered the metaphorical lion's den.

Meeting Room 237 was enormous—the size of a lecture hall, but without the terraced seating and long, curving desks. Instead, a gigantic table stood in the room's center, with a projector aimed so most people could see the screen and comfy-looking office chairs lining it. If it were smaller, it would've felt like a boardroom. As it was, it felt almost *too* big. But only almost, because as empty of furniture as the room was, it was packed full of students. Most looked like they were here for the free pizza, but not all.

I recognized one—or more accurately, he recognized me before I could do much about it. "Annie! Annie from Post–Launch Day History! And you brought your girlfriend. I guess that means you're still not taking me up on coffee?" Avan winked at me. Bee narrowed her eyes just slightly. "Oh. Not in a joking mood?"

"Not at all, Avan," Bianca said, a touch of coldness in her voice. She'd never liked Avan, the few times we'd run into each other on the elevator.

I'd last seen Avan running for his life from the TERROR Mech while Professor Panic and I got ready to fight by the Mister Felsic statue. Before that, I'd run into him on the elevator after our history final. "I'll get in line for pizza," I said.

"Sure. See you in a few." Bee planted a kiss on my cheek that wasn't for *my* benefit—or hers. "Why do you flirt with Annie all the time? She's mine."

I didn't stick around for the rest of their conversation. The pizza line only took a minute or two, but it was enough time to formulate a strategy—or as much of one as possible. I loaded up the plates; a mix of different toppings for Bee and plain cheese for me. Then I returned to the upset-looking Bianca. "You're cranky tonight, Bee. Have some food."

"Thanks." Food was the only way I could think of to keep Bee happy sometimes, and free food was even better.

As she dug in, I turned to Avan. "So, what made you interested in APPEAL?"

"Oh, I'm not. I reached out to them about showing up on my radio show, though. I'm having a couple of supers on for a roundtable, and I thought an antisuper perspective might spice things up."

I couldn't think of much to say, but luckily, Bianca saved me. "Are you getting a hero and a villain? Who are they? I bet they're not even top-rate supers."

"Actually, they're both very much in the public eye. One hero, one villain, though if you talked to APPEAL, there's no difference. Plus, the villain's been more heroic than the hero recently, according to Erik. I plan on discussing that at the roundtable, but I can't say much about it. If I spoil it all, you won't tune in."

"I won't tune in no matter what," Bianca said around a bit of sausage pizza.

"I might. I've always been curious about, uh, public perceptions about specific supers," I started.

"Oh, you'll be a great fit for the club," Erik interrupted. He had a slice of pizza and a red cup filled with a bubbly blue drink. "We keep a running record of TUSSA and the SSS and how the rest of campus perceives their actions. I'm working on my capstone project for superpower law, and I'm focusing my research on how public perceptions impact regulations and rules for supers and how the community pushes back."

I stared, flummoxed for a moment. "I'm looking at superpower law as a career," I finally said half-heartedly.

Bianca glared and tried kicking me surreptitiously, but the damage was already done. Erik took the hook. "Oh? Most students focus on regulations or super rights, but I think there's a lot of unlitigated space in repealing the Third Ilneat Compact and restricting superpowered activity to only a few cities, with willing Extras."

"You mean the New Gotham Accords?" Avan said. "I've been doing my research before the roundtable and for some of my other shows. It's all fascinating stuff."

"Yeah. The New Gotham Accords would be a good start, but I'm thinking bigger," Erik said. "Su-Bin will have more details on our plans at your roundtable, though."

I relaxed slightly as he left to go fiddle with a laptop. Things would get better once the meeting started.

Things didn't get better.

I tossed my last slice of pizza in the trash—my appetite had vanished—and found a seat around the long, skinny table as Su-Bin and Erik formally started the meeting. Avan being the host was bad enough. We'd spent time together, but I felt confident my Magical Girl Understudy costume would hold up to casual inspection. Besides, a villain would be there, too. Hopefully, it'd be someone flashy; Tearjerker, maybe, or Monologue if he didn't [**Monologue**]. Either would draw plenty of attention.

But Su-Bin was my friend, and if she was anything like her parents, she wouldn't hold back on the radio. Could I deal with having a friend badmouth me personally, to my face? I wasn't sure; I'd never had anything like this happen to me. And she *would* say some pretty horrible things. I wasn't 100% sure what Erik's list looked like, but if I had to guess, Magical Girl Understudy was pretty far down it. The incident at the TUEAS Building alone would have done it, but the Mister Felsic statue fight hadn't helped, either.

Bianca kicked me again, this time under the table. "Script," she mouthed at me.

Right. I needed to stay on script, and I hadn't done a great job so far. It was only Erik's chill interest in superhero law that'd let my faux pas slide. Or maybe . . .

maybe they just didn't care. Erik and Su-Bin probably dealt with recruits constantly, and some might have mixed feelings about supers. He probably had a script of his own for that.

He sure did for running the meeting. "Hello, and welcome to Anti-Power Protestors' and Extras' League's first meeting of the new year. We have a packed agenda tonight, so let's run through the big points. We don't need any surprises, right?"

He gave Su-Bin a thumbs-up. She clicked the remote, and the projector sprung to life, displaying their agenda.

One: Fundraising for APPEAL Shirts/Stickers
Two: Recent Superhero Disasters
Three: Round Table 1/22
Four: Open Floor for Discussion

Su-Bin cleared her throat. "We're working on a fundraiser to replenish our coffers and maybe even buy some APPEAL swag. Some of you have official stuff from the larger League, but we'd like some TU-focused shirts and stickers. We're looking for ideas on how to raise that money and shirt designs, so we'll have an in-club contest. The winner gets a free shirt when we make them."

She launched into a tedious explanation of the club's finances and the process for getting official TU/APPEAL shirts and stickers made. I sort of tuned it out. Well, I tuned it out a *lot*. Math majors liked that stuff, not me.

Then Erik talked about the Episodes over the last week that'd made headlines for destruction, danger, and general bad vibes. Somehow, "Winter is Coming" made the list, which was *ridiculous*. Neither Tele-Portal nor I had done anything wrong there. We'd executed well, but my name came up anyway. How was *that* fair?

"So, with that Episode fresh in our heads, and with "Haze-Matt's Escape from Almhurst!" and "Absent-Hearted Professor" fresh in our minds, let's move on to talking about our chance to strike back against some supers," Erik said. "Avan, also known as DJ Smooth, contacted us about participating in a radio roundtable on his show. We accepted, of course, and tonight's main focus is on our strategy for talking with a hero and villain and making our case directly to the people who keep us down—and to the audience, of course. Su-Bin Pak is our chosen representative. She'll take it from here."

"Thanks, Erik. I have big plans, but putting our heads together is more powerful than me trying to solo-plan a whole roundtable discussion. So, there are three major points I want to make. First, crime on campus is going wild, especially superpowered crime. Second, the heroes aren't keeping us safe from the villains. They're more focused on their shows and games and less on people. Third, what have supers ever done for us? Do those seem pretty reasonable to you all?"

I almost said something right there. But Bianca squeezed my hand meaningfully. The message was clear: I know you're pissed, but this is why we came here. Stick to the script. I gritted my teeth and prepared to tough it out.

The rest of her audience felt like her points were fine. Objectively, I felt the last one was weak, but I couldn't place why. I needed someone to talk to about all this. Maybe Tele-Portal, if I could get some time with her preroundtable.

"Great. The other part of this is tone. I want to come out swinging and really pressure the hero. The villain will likely sit back and laugh, although he's been involved in Man vs. Nature stuff for a while, so he might get prickly about some of that."

I grinned. The villain had to be Theseus. If it was, Su-Bin was in for a rude awakening. The limb-replacing villain might not look brilliant, but he was a hard worker. His preparations for the roundtable probably looked more intense than mine.

"I think we might be able to break the hero on-air, though. Magical Girl Understudy's gotten some horrible publicity recently, especially on campus, and she's gotta be frustrated about that."

I shot a stunned look at Bianca. She glanced back at me, the same look mirrored on her face—a look that said she was reevaluating our roundtable strategy. Then she leaned in close and whispered in my ear, "Stick to the script."

17

Stick to the Script

Back in the green room, when Bianca gave me my script, she'd been very, *very* clear about this part. The small talk was the highest risk because I'd have to talk, but the meeting might be the most *useful* for figuring out APPEAL's plans. Sure enough, everything Su-Bin said qualified as either important, very important, or critical. So I gritted my teeth behind a—hopefully—bored expression and stuck to the script.

The script said, "Shut up and listen."

So I did my best. It shouldn't have been this hard, but hearing that not only was my friend on the roundtable but that she planned on attacking me—or more accurately, my superhero persona—deliberately? My blood boiled.

Still, the best plan was to follow the script. So I shut up and listened.

"Our main goal is to make listeners realize that Magical Girl Understudy and Theseus are two sides of the same superproblematic coin. In fact, we could even argue there's been a total role reversal. Theseus, for all he's a supervillain, participates in the Man vs. Nature fights," Su-Bin said.

"But couldn't we handle Man vs. Nature without supers at all?" someone said. I didn't catch their name.

Su-Bin nodded. "We could. It'd go a long way toward our cause if unpowered people took over fighting our own battles for a change. We used to have an army. We could probably rebuild it—then we wouldn't need supers anymore."

"Getting ahead of yourself, Su-Bin," Erik said.

"Right. Today, TU, tomorrow, the world!" That sounded like a slogan to me, but Su-Bin pressed on after sucking on a soda straw. "If we can get Understudy to lose her cool, we can expose her as the force of destruction both heroes and villains are."

"Just like the Pherris Report," someone said.

"Yeah, or Alpha Strike. But the point is, we know what supers do. We have to get the rest of the public to figure it out, and maybe this will be a start. Anyway, that's my basic strategy." Su-Bin grinned. "Any helpful critiques?"

"Understudy's the one that blew up the engineering building, right?"

"No, Professor Panic did that," I did not say.

"It was a real tragedy, and I hope it gets rebuilt soon," I said, sticking to the script. Bee suppressed an eye-roll, but barely.

"That bitch."

"Hey, we don't swear. APPEAL is a polite, law-abiding organization, and we're not going to personally attack anyone, not even heroes and villains. What we're going to do is hold them accountable." Erik glared at the offending student until she nodded slightly. This time, *I* struggled not to roll my eyes. The whole thing was so ridiculous; we heroes weren't doing anything *wrong*. But APPEAL honestly thought we were.

Pointers about how to do a roundtable rolled in, and Su-Bin sat at the laptop to jot down notes. I really wished this was an Episode; then I'd have a camera drone, and Rocko could replay the meeting for me so we didn't miss anything. But I followed the script, sat down, shut up, and listened.

Eventually, Su-Bin nodded thoughtfully. "Look at the time. We're going to open it up for general discussion now, so new members, don't feel obligated to stick around the whole time. I know you've got classes tomorrow. And Annie, I'll see you on Wednesday in Child Psych." She grinned at me.

"You got it, Su-Bin." I grinned back. "I'll see you later."

Bianca and I headed for the door before she could say much else. Neither of us said anything until we'd left the Alder Building far behind us. Then, we both broke into nervous giggles.

"Holy shit," Bee said, glaring at me but unable to keep her relieved laughter down. "You almost blew it twice in there. New people don't talk at meetings, and you shouldn't have said anything about superpower law."

"I know, but it all worked out." The laughter faded quickly, and the weight of what was about to happen hit me. "I'm going to have to defend myself against her attacks somehow. Holy crap, this is insane. Should we back out? I feel like we should—"

"No. You've got a huge advantage here. We know what APPEAL's plan is. We just need to figure out how to disrupt it. Let's head to your place."

Half an hour into breaking down the meeting, I flopped back onto the chaise lounge, fully in cat mode except for the cat Costume. "This is pointless. I have no idea how to win a PR campaign against this."

"Annie, you've got all the advantages. Now scoot." Bianca waited until I sat up, then sat down and rested her head on my leg. It was my turn to play with her hair. "You know what she's going to try, *and* you have public sentiment as a superhero. Most people will forgive a little destruction one way or another."

"Yeah, but our code of ethics doesn't make it look good. We should have figured out if she knew what it said."

"And how would you have done that? We learned a ton even without that, and they didn't suspect a thing," Bee said confidently. "If you want, we can assume they know our code and plan accordingly."

"We've been planning for half an hour, and we have nothing."

"Fine. I admit we're not equipped to solve this problem. Why don't you talk to Mindstorm? She's gotta be an expert on solving bad PR problems."

I rolled my eyes. "I doubt it. She had her lawyer army, and besides, why would she care about a bad reputation?"

"Yeah, she wouldn't give a damn, would she?" Bee shivered as I scratched her scalp. "How about Tele-Portal? The Triad has to have trouble with public relations."

"Sure. Let's try it." I reached for my phone, making Bee growl in annoyance, and sent a quick text.

<Hey. How do you deal w/ bad pr? - Understudy 8:15>

"She probably won't text back for a while," I said as my phone buzzed.

<Ive been xpecting this txt 4 a bit - Tele-Portal 8:15>
<Gonna vidchat u in 5 - Tele-Portal 8:15>
<Sure. We'll be ready. Fursona is here - Understudy 8:16>
<k. Got ur email already - Tele-Portal 8:16>

"Costume up," I said, pushing Bianca off my lap. She groaned but hurried off to the bathroom to change.

While I went through my song and dance, I thought *yet again* about Su-Bin. The relief of getting away with our spy mission warred with a sense of betrayal, and betrayal won. Part of me knew it wasn't rational to feel this way, but a much larger part felt angry—really *angry*—that Su-Bin hated me so much. I finished my transformation and got the screen ready for Tele-Portal. Fursona joined me on the couch, and thirty seconds later, the video chat program rang.

"So, you've got a PR problem." It wasn't a question. "You blew up a couple buildings—" Tele-Portal said by way of greeting.

"We didn't do it," Fursona interrupted.

"Doesn't matter. Plenty of people won't care. You need an angle on this. Gotta give it some spin. I'd recommend a lawyer. Edgar handles all of my PR issues, and The Triad has a half-dozen on retainer. We're practically villains, we have so many. But you're two college kids in real life and little-league heroes, so lawyers might be a bit beyond your usual needs."

"Ouch, but true. So, here's the situation." I laid it all out; the whole story behind the TUEAS fights and the Mister Felsic statue; the fallout on campus from it, including my ban from Episodes at TU, and the situation with Su-Bin and APPEAL. She knew a ton of it, but I said it all anyway. "So, that's what's up."

"APPEAL, huh? They've got a branch in Tokyexico City, but it's mostly conspiracy theorists and people who've lost stuff directly to Episodes. They're persistent, though. They must smell blood in the water with you. So, I'd break your whole strategy into a few chunks. First, spinning the TUEAS Building issue. Your Series Finale played already, right?"

"Right. Rocko ran it as soon as they finished the edits."

"Great. As long as it doesn't show anything implicating you, you can argue that you were trying to stop a villain. That puts the responsibility back on your nemesis and gives you deniability." Tele-Portal paused, fidgeting with her hair. Despite the later hour, her eyes didn't carry the same exhaustion they had after "Winter is Coming." "I have to ask, but I think I already know the answer. You had nothing to do with blowing up the building or statue, right?"

"Right." Technically, it was true.

"Good. The one thing you don't want to do is lie. You lose a ton of credibility if you're not an honest superhero. The second thing you want is to redirect. You've got a villain there, too?"

"Theseus," I said. "I'm pretty sure it's Theseus."

"Perfect. Try getting the host to put this Theseus on the spot. You shift the spotlight onto him, and you'll get some breathing room. If your friend is a typical APPEAL type, she'll attack-dog at the easiest target once she's worked up. You need to let Theseus be that target, but that'll be harder because she wants to fight *you*, not him."

"I don't think that'll work," Fursona hedged. "The host didn't say much, but he's interested in making his show popular. He'll get more buzz from a spicy show than something that follows the typical 'villains equal bad' script."

"Then you need to get Theseus in the public spotlight before your radio show. That'll be easiest if he starts something and you get involved, even if he stomps you."

"Shit. I'm banned from Episodes on campus since 'Absent-Hearted Professor,'" I said. "That's not going to work."

"I'll make it work," Fursona said. "I can fight him."

"He'll kick your ass solo."

"Sure will, but that's okay. It might be even better if I lose. Gotta show him as a problem villain."

"That's point two. There's one more thing you can do, but it's longer-term, and that's invest in some solo patrol time. You want to build your rep? Showing up and stopping low-level crime is the best way, especially if you're visible. You can get around your ban that way, too. Just go to the Poudre Districts; the heroes there needed help at your job fair, and I doubt that's changed."

I thought about it. That was a great idea, but it wouldn't help me *now*, and I didn't have time for long-term planning. "Thanks, Tele-Portal. I appreciate it."

"No problem, kid. And look, it's probably best to keep your head down on campus other than semiscripted appearances. Sometimes, heroes get bad PR—Underdelver's usually the one who needs damage control on The Triad. We have him stay home for a couple of Episodes, make some charity appearances, and generally show he's a good guy. That's all it takes. Just be a good guy for a while." Tele-Portal grinned. "Anything else?"

"Yeah. When can we get into The Triad training room?"

"As per the contract you signed, next month, if you do your patrols. Talk to you later."

Once the screen blanked off and we'd both changed out of our super-suits, Bianca grabbed the pen. Next to the 'PR' circle on her gigantic plan, she wrote another one connected to the KRTU bubble. The new circle included two bullet points: 'Redirection' and 'Fursona Solo Episode!'

18

Fursona Solo Episode!

THURSDAY, JANUARY 15

I gave Bianca one last kiss—it still felt weird kissing her as a kangaroo, but I was getting used to it—and buckled her helmet over her head. "Be *careful*, okay?"

"Annie, the whole point is to *not* be careful. I'm signing up to get my ass kicked by Theseus, remember? And to do it in a public, embarrassing way. Luckily, we're up against Theseus here. A different villain might try for an ID reveal against a solo side-kick to punish hubris, or they might go all-out and actually hurt me, but Theseus is a professional, and he knows me. I'll be totally fine."

"The last time you fought, he knocked you out in the weight room."

"Yep. It was great," Fursona lied.

She had *not* thought it was great at the time. I'd had to coach her through losing, and I hated losing almost as much as she did. Bianca was playing the "I'm a tough girl" role, and she played it well, but I was an actress—and I could see right through her charade. She was terrified. She *had* to be.

I gave her one last hug. "You've got this. I'll be watching the whole time."

"I know." Fursona hopped to the elevator door. "See you soon."

As the elevator descended, I stepped through the door to my own destination.

[Welcome to Rocko's Backstage. System Disabled. Now arriving at Costuming.]

"Aaaaaay! This is the stupidest goddamn idea you two have pulled, and you've pulled a *lot* of stupid ideas, DuPont. You're intentionally throwing an Episode—and for what?"

"Not now, Rocko," I muttered, throwing myself into a chair. "Pull up the drone feed for Fursona. I'm not allowed to play, but I'm going to watch."

"Fine. Be my guest, DuPont. You know, you could be out there chasing down Shorts. You *should* be out there chasing down Shorts. Vigilant Vow is pulling ahead, and that ain't a good sign." The Ilneat climbed into a chair beside me and fiddled with the remote. Then, they pointed to an ice mountain stuffed full of water bottles. "Help yourself, kid."

I grabbed a bottle and sipped gratefully. The shorts and spaghetti-strap tank top that had felt frigid in the green room weren't doing enough to keep me cool in Rocko's studio.

Fursona appeared on the camera. She lurked outside the robotics lab—it'd taken us two days of digging and pulling strings to figure out Theseus's next play. The villain wanted something there, and Fursona, being the hero, would try to stop him. Only, instead of playing it smart and grabbing a buddy, like Milo or Springlock, she'd made the rookie mistake of going in solo.

I couldn't help her. I'd get expelled from TU. But still, it was a bold move for a fresh little leaguer, even one who'd grown like she had, to go up against a minor-league villain solo. Rocko seemed pissed.

"DuPont, I need an explanation. You're sending her on a suicide mission here."

"No, I'm not!" I snapped. I really didn't need Rocko being pissy with me right now. "Look, I know what it looks like, but the play here is to get people watching *Heroics 101*. They won't *do* that if this radio roundtable goes sour—it'll be all over the net, and you Ilneats will get a hold of it somehow. It'll drive ratings down when we need the good PR. We're taking a fall here so that Theseus is the obvious villain on-air. It's theater and misdirection."

"That's the dumbest thing I've ever heard in a while. You're gonna lose to make yourselves look good?"

"No. We're going to lose to make Theseus look evil."

The camera drone flicked as Rocko fiddled with the remote again, this time over to Theseus. Sure enough, he looked frustrated—annoyed, even—at the presence of a hero. But as he peered into the twilight and saw Fursona hopping closer, he grinned. "Pushover incoming. Are they . . . solo?"

"Yep," I said, grinning my own predatorial grin. "She's solo. No one's coming to save her. Just take the bait and make it splashy."

We'd developed the plan as soon as we knew Theseus's target. It was pretty simple. Fursona wouldn't fight to win. Instead, she'd fight to position Theseus so he destroyed as much of the lab as possible. She wouldn't break a single calculator, but every last bit of destruction would be on both the camera drones and the hidden one we'd slipped into Fursona's pouch. Then we'd leak Fursona's footage.

It *was* a suicide mission, like Rocko said. But it was the best way to discredit a villain we could think of on short notice. And Theseus was chill. He'd crush Fursona, but she'd be fine. I hoped.

"Alright, Wombat, where are you?" Theseus asked. Fursona's camera drone hovered in the lab's center, next to a long arm ending in two clawed grippers. Theseus groaned, popped his arm off, and left it on the table. He installed his brand-new robot arm, then stalked into the shadows—the same shadows Fursona *had* to be hiding in.

I braced myself, but she didn't attack. "What are you *doing*? Get him!"

But she still didn't spring out of the shadows. Seconds ticked by. Minutes dragged on. The lab sprawled out on the screen; students' projects littered every table, most with tape labeling them inoperable or unpowered, some still in pieces. Theseus found a second arm, this one less impressively powerful but much more precise—a tool, not an experiment. Then he turned and started walking toward the exit.

"Well, if you're not going to stop me, I'll be leaving now. Efficiency is important in a good lieutenant, and I need the reputation since I'm springboarding up the rankings to the majors. I talked about that in class, remember? Do things efficiently. But you and that Understudy wouldn't listen. Besides, you're probably worried about— Oh, come on! What the fuck, Fursona?"

The camera zoomed in, and I laughed. His arm—his *real* arm—wasn't on the table. She'd stolen his goddamned arm.

"Goddammit!" Theseus lost it. His face flushed, and he flexed his metal arms. "You're making this personal."

"Am I? Oops. Guess you want me to *hand* this over, then?" Fursona finally made her appearance. She waggled Theseus's detached arm at him from the lab's far side almost scoldingly. "I'll make a deal with you. If you put your new arms back and leave, I'll give both of these back to you."

"You've only got one," Theseus yelled. I'd never seen him this pissed, ever. Not when the group backfired. Not when we'd tried to stop his "arms deal" during "Whey Too Few Leg Days" last semester. Not ever.

"Not for long." The lab was dark. Fursona couldn't see how angry Theseus was. How close to losing control. She shoved the arm into her pocket and bounded forward, ducking past Theseus's new arm as it smashed into a workbench.

"Ooooh, she's got a chance at getting that arm," Rocko said. They puffed on their cigar as I stared incredulously at them. "Oh, like you didn't know this was coming— Marino's teasy. Fursona's usually such a serious superhero, but it's because she wants to win. Without a chance at victory, she's letting herself loosen up."

I huffed and turned back to the screen. Rocko was right. Fursona was a serious-minded, competitive superhero. But Fursona wasn't driving right now. *Bianca* was. That made a difference in how she'd fight Theseus.

And somehow, I realized, that also made a difference to me.

My stomach churned as Theseus crashed after the Marsupial of Justice, destroyed lab equipment flying in his wake. I'd overestimated the villain's patience. Or I'd underestimated his pent-up fury. Either way, we'd made a mistake. Suddenly, I didn't want Bianca out there.

"Can we call this off? There's gotta be a way to call this off, right?"

"Nope. You asked for this, and it's gonna happen one way or another, DuPont. We can pull the drones, but that's just taking a ratings hit, and you *don't* want that right now, do you?"

"No." But I *did* want that right now. Fursona was one thing, but Bee?

Bianca got to the second arm a full second before Theseus did. She scooped it up and pocketed it. Then a table hit her. She flew across the room and caromed into a glass wall, which shattered around her.

As she picked herself up, Theseus pounced. He grabbed the kangaroo fursuit by the throat and squeezed—the suit's eyes bugged out theatrically, but Bianca was fine inside. At least, she was *probably* fine.

Hopefully. My fingernails dug into my palms as I tightened my fists.

"Relax, kid. Pataki and I do this all the time, and it always turns out just fine."

The villain struggled to control himself. "I've gotta *hand* it to you. You disarmed me at first. But I need you to get a grip on reality. You can't win this."

"Come on, let me go, and you can chase me around for the arm again. I'll give you a *head* start!" Bianca kicked out, landing a blow to Theseus's temple. He winced and rocked backward, but the robo-arm didn't let go.

"Enough." Theseus held the struggling marsupial in the air with his weaker robo-arm, reeled back with the stronger one, and punched Bianca in the face. At the same time, he let go, and she flew across the lab, landing in a tangle of robot parts and schematics.

"Well, almost always. Sometimes you gotta pick up the pieces after, but that's just showbiz."

"Rocko! Please."

Theseus pushed through the rubble toward Bianca, who found her feet and started hopping away from the villain. "Dodge left!" I squeaked. Rocko looked at me and shrugged, but Bianca dodged left.

Then she turned and kicked out at the onrushing villain. Theseus's robo-arms blocked it, picked her up, and tossed her through another glass wall into a brand-new lab. "That's the best you've got? I should have sent Gourmet. She'd have had fun with you! But now it's personal."

He followed Fursona through the glass. One of his arms lay on the floor, and a trail of broken glass led through the room. He leaned down, picked up his detached arm, and smiled. "One down, one to go. Or maybe two. Maybe I'll borrow one of yours, too."

But the heroic kangaroo was nowhere to be found. "Dammit, come out and fight me!" Theseus screamed into the dark lab. He smashed another table with his big arm.

"I don't think so," Bianca quipped from somewhere in the shadows. I couldn't find her anywhere, and neither could Theseus.

Rocko flipped to the drone following the Marsupial of Justice. Then the Ilneat snorted. "Now *that's* clever."

Bianca stood on an open closet door, using her legs to shove it against the wall so it wouldn't move, while one hand held Theseus's arm against the ceiling. She balanced like that in the dark lab, just a few feet above the villain. The villain's robotic hand almost brushed her foot, which she lifted carefully into the air.

"Seriously, give it back! I need it for classes tomorrow!" Theseus stuck his head in the closet, searching.

Bianca couldn't resist. "I'll *finger* 'bout it."

Theseus pulled back, looking around the room. Rocko rewound the feed, playing the next few moments twice while I shot a glare his way. From Theseus's camera drone's angle, he'd seen Bianca's clever hiding place. But from Bianca's, it seemed like the spot was still working.

"Fursona. I'm going to shut my eyes and count to three. The arm will be sitting in front of me, and you will be gone. If it's not there when I open my eyes, I'm going to take that very . . . personally. We were friends in class. If not friends, then at least not enemies. Hell, we argued the same points *against* your girlfriend more than once. So make this easy on yourself." Theseus almost sounded like he was pleading. Almost. But I knew the end was coming.

"Give him the damn arm, Bee," I whispered. "You've won. It's all on camera. Just walk away."

"She can't hear you, DuPont!"

"One." Theseus closed his eyes. Bianca wavered on the edge of the door.

I wavered on the edge of my chair. "Just do it. It's not worth continuing this."

"Two." Theseus slammed the door shut, and Bianca crashed down on top of Theseus. They hit the ground in a tangle of limbs—human, kangaroo, robotic, and detached!

"Three. Time's up."

19

Time's Up

"And then he kicked in my fursuit's teeth and pulled my arm out of its socket!" Bianca grinned from a cushion inside her secret lair. "It was awesome! And it was my first solo!"

"I saw." I *didn't* think it was awesome. She'd gotten her ass handed to her in the final thirty seconds of the fight, and while her arm wasn't broken, she'd be in a sling for a couple days. Luckily, according to Rocko, supers healed quickly, so she'd be back in business by the end of next week. The Ilneat had also given her something to speed up the process.

"Battered, bruised Bianca," I said, forcing a grin. She'd dragged herself back to my lair, and from there, we'd gone to the hospital. She hadn't thought it was awesome then. She'd been pissed about making the sacrifice play. We had to make up some bullshit—neither of us wanted to do the "I fell down the stairs" routine—and then the nurse made me leave the room for a minute. They'd gotten me less than thirty seconds later, apologizing, and then jammed Bee's arm back into place. She'd screamed a lot.

"Oh, shut up. The things I do for you, I swear to god." Bee winked. Then she got another grin, this one wicked—no, scheming. "While I'm recovering from my terrible injury, you'll have to help me with everything! You can type my homework up, make me PB and Js, and even rub my shoulder when it's sore. Also, you owe me. You owe me a ton."

"I'd do that last one anyway." I got up and started massaging her. Then I stopped. "Green apple again? Really?"

"You know you love it. Keep going."

"I do." As I pushed gently on Bee's shoulders, I looked around. I'd never been in Fursona's secret base, which she'd jokingly named Outback Stakeout Zone. She'd gone completely chairless, which didn't surprise me, given how inconvenient sitting was with her animatronic tail. Instead, pillows and cushions lay scattered in the corners, some facing the ubiquitous TV screens tuned to Tokyexico's news. One blared on and on about the turbo-buffalo herd and its migration away from the city, as well as the lack of D-wolver attacks.

"Sounds like the Man vs. Nature is wrapping up," I said.

"Sure is. It's about time, too. I missed home." Bianca leaned back into me, pressing her ponytail against my stomach. She shivered as I moved my massage up onto her neck, lowering her head to let me rub. "We might actually get a Spring Break. Thought about what you're gonna do?"

"I'm going home. Back to Riverside. I miss my parents a lot."

Bee looked crestfallen, and I felt her suppress a shiver. Then she dropped her head onto her unslung arm and sobbed; if it weren't her, it'd look melodramatic. But I knew enough about her body language to take her seriously. "I can't get home. It won't be enough time to be worth the ticket."

"You're a superhero. Rocko's paying you royalties, right?" I got a small cut of *Heroics 101* and *Small Town Super*'s profits. It wasn't enough to buy a plane, but it'd be more than enough to buy a plane ticket.

"Mom and Dad would know something was up. It's a thousand dollars to fly, and I'm a 'broke' college student." Bianca rubbed an eye, then leaned back into me again. I wrapped my arms around her waist.

"So you need somewhere to go? No problem. You can come to Riverside with me. It'll be boring, but you can meet my mom and dad." I paused. "We should sign up for a ride-share soon, though. Two people are harder to fit in than one, and it'll be busy. Some students came from the desert cities, and if they're not flying, they'll definitely ride-share with each other."

"That'd be great. What's there to do in Riverside?"

I stopped to consider. "Well, there's movies, and the river, but it'll be too cold for that in March. We could see the mountains, though, and if you want to suit up, we could hunt some megafauna out in the desert west of town. But mostly, we just hang out—"

"Ow!" Bee adjusted so her hurt shoulder wasn't jammed against mine. I loosened my grip while she got comfortable again. "Yeah, that sounds slow. But nice. And honestly, our superhero lives are fast enough. I'm fine with slow time with you."

We sat there for a while, my arms around Bee's waist, and I sniffed her green apple and light sweat smell. I kissed the back of her neck, and she gently moved my hands up a bit higher. I smiled sheepishly; I'd been letting them stray.

"So, show me the rest of your place?" I asked.

I felt her stiffen in my arms. "I'd rather not. It's not . . . I haven't cleaned in a while."

"Bee, I've seen how you leave my place. Clothes everywhere, make-up open on my sink, and black hair in my shower. Nothing there's going to surprise me."

"You'd be surprised how surprised you'd be," Bee muttered. I moved to stand up, but she grabbed my wrist and pulled me back around her. "You put a boundary on me snooping for the present, and I'm putting one on you checking out my dorm room. Deal?"

"Deal."

"Good. Now I can let you go. Let's head to your place. We do our best planning in the green room, and all our notes are there."

"Okay, type in *super watch* on your phone. Tap the third link, then click 'Tell me about exciting new watches,'" Bianca said from the couch. "Enter your email—not the super one, but your personal—and then hit 'Accept All Cookies' and 'Accept All Promotions.' There should be a pop-up. Hit Decline. It'll boot you back to the main page, but this time, you'll have a new watch in the seventh spot. Click the new watch."

"Seriously? How does anyone find this shit?" The Super Watch site didn't sell watches. You could add them to your cart, but you'd just get an email that your choice was sold out or discontinued if you tried to buy. Super Watch had another purpose. "And how did you find this site?"

"Research. You became a superhero as a kid. You were molded by it. By the time you knew how to look for stuff, you knew everything, or thought you did. I was eighteen. I merely adopted the suit. So I had to do some digging. One of my sources led me to Super Watch."

"And what, exactly, is Super Watch?"

"It's a fan site, but well-hidden and 'dark.' What gets on here isn't policed by the Ilneats, although anything juicy gets out. Lots of speculation about hero identities, villains' next moves, and the leaderboard. Hand me the phone; I'll get logged in. I've got a reputation for knowing things, so me finding a video of Fursona in action? That'll be big."

"Then why are we using my phone?"

"Security. Deniability. And, most importantly, this whole scheme has been your idea, so your device is the one Theseus will find if he has a Genius backtrack this. That's also why we're doing it from *your* secret base. That way I have deniability."

"Okay, that's fair. Theseus was pretty pissed at you." I handed the phone over and plugged in the drive we'd loaded our slightly doctored video onto. We'd cut out most of the audio, leaving just the video and a few half-garbled lines to tell the tale. Rocko had offered to help us, especially once they saw how butchered the recording was getting, but the whole *point* was to look like amateurs.

We tinkered with the post itself; it had to be just right to grab attention, but not *too* much. We wanted it all over the fan site's forums, but *not* leaked right away. Eventually, though, we had the following post.

Raw, Slightly Corupted Bodycam footage: Fursona vs. Theseus Round Two: The REVENGENING

Hey, I dont think the episode is out yet, but I have some amazing footaage. Th e fight in the wight room last year was amazing, but this ones even better. I found this after itwas all over. It was on a button camera, and I think Fursona wore it into battle. Might be something new for Heroics101, but its all mine now.

Theres limited sound. When I downloaded it, the sound messed up, so I've only got a few lines in there, and they're garbled. Still, scoop of the year, right? And it's only January.

<u>*Theseus Destroys Fursona in Epic Battle.mp4*</u>

"Good enough. Posting it now," Bianca said.

"Doesn't that video name sound a little . . . lewd?"

Bianca laughed. "Well, yeah. It'll catch more eyes that way. Now, let's talk over-all strategy. Hopefully this will make the rounds and get to either APPEAL or DJ Smooth before the roundtable. That'll put Theseus under the spotlight. Either way, we need a defense for your actions in the Series Finale—and I don't think 'It was a Series Finale' is gonna cut it."

She was right. I needed a better defense than that for sure. Luckily, I had one. I'd been working on it while Bianca spent the night in the hospital. "I'm sorry for what happened, but in both cases, I did what was necessary to stop a greater threat to Tokyexico University and the city at large. Professor Panic is the one at fault. He built his robot factory under the TUEAS Building, *and* rigged it to blow. He even set the timer on his explosives.

"And then, when I stopped him, he moved into a Student Supervillain Lair inside the Student Union Building and kept plotting. He knocked down Mister Felsic, he left tasers all across campus, and why? Because he couldn't get over a relationship that wasn't working. Meanwhile, I tried to evacuate the people under the statue, including *you*, DJ Smooth."

Bianca thought for a minute. "That's not bad, but let's work on the ending. We need you to be more compelling as a hero than as a force of destruction, and that appeal to—ugh, Avan—might work, but we need more than that. You put Professor Panic in Almhurst, right?"

"Yeah. There's a low-security wing for temporary holds and rehabilitation cases, and since the Man vs. Nature was on, no one wanted to try moving him to Riverside. Even his lawyers agreed—they wouldn't make the drive either."

"Perfect. Mention that he's in Almhurst right now. That'll drive sympathy."

It took another twenty minutes to build the rest of the plan. Most of it was right there, but we planned contingencies for anything Theseus or Su-Bin could throw at me. Then we pulled up the Tokyexico Community Rankings, and I groaned. I was still 315th on the list, which made sense. I hadn't actually done anything since last weekend, and if I wasn't pulling Episodes, I wasn't moving up. That'd change after the roundtable, though.

But clearly, Vigilant Vow hadn't stopped. If anything, he was speeding up. When I went to find him, his rank sat at 272.

Bianca noticed my anxiety and gave me a side-hug. "Don't worry about him. You can't rush Episodes. The last time we tried that, we ended up at Tottergarten struggling for *something* to get you that Sara-N-Dipity gig. It was fun, but we don't need a repeat. I'll find you something—just focus on classes."

20

Focus on Classes

MONDAY, JANUARY 19

"How many of you went out and tried Episodes with your *phenomenal new powers* in the last two weeks?" Dr. Mindstorm asked. Almost every super-student's hand went up. Fursona's nonslung paw did, too; her ass-kicking at Theseus's hands counted.

"Great. And how many of you . . . got your combo to work successfully?"

Fewer hands this time. Mine stayed up. Fursona's went down. No surprise there. Theseus had all the minor-league powers, not just [**Power-Chaining**]. He'd done exactly what Black Ice had done to me—either that or Fursona hadn't even tried for a [**Power-Chain**] of her own.

"And, finally, how many of you had your combos broken?"

My hand went up, but Fursona's stayed down. Gourmet's went up, too, and so did Flare's. The two villains had been active, and they'd been stomped down by minor leaguers, then.

"Every year, junior minor leaguers get their combo power, and every year, they run off to find a minor-league fight. And, inevitably, they lose. The biggest difference between little-league fighting and minor-league fighting is the cat-and-mouse game that happens. Since combos are so strong, fights revolve around rock/paper/scissors," Dr. Tennyson said.

He clapped his hands. "An example, if you'll indulge me. Dr. Mindstorm was a combo player in her *very* brief appearance in the minor leagues. She'd easily beat any hero who wasn't on the lookout for her favorite [**Power-Chain**], because its finisher was already overwhelming. So, Mindstorm's goal in combat revolved around safely launching that finisher. Mindstorm and other combo players are scissors.

"Her rival, Mister Felsic, came to power at the same time. He quickly learned to recognize and disrupt her combo's steps with [**Combo-Breaker**]. Mister Felsic, when combo-breaking, is rock."

"And . . . all the heroes who tried to fight me without studying my most power-ful combo, or who ran across me on the street and took a shot at . . . the fastest-rising minor-league supervillain ever . . . they were paper. If they weren't ready for me, they lost. A properly executed combo can end fights, sometimes before your opponent's even fully set up." Mindstorm smiled. "So, today, we're going to pair up—hero to villain—and discuss each other's preferred combos. Find the best place to disrupt your classmate's move. But . . . only do it on paper. No fighting in the classroom."

Fursona shrugged, grabbed Flare by the neck, and dragged him to a desk. Mindstorm snapped her head around to look at them. "I said *no fighting*."

"Sorry," Fursona said. "Just ready to hop to it."

Gourmet sat down heavily across from me, biting a piece of jerky and chewing furiously. I raised a hand in greeting, and she returned the gesture. "Hi, Snack. Let's start with yours since you've used [**Power-Weaving**] successfully."

Something felt off. This wasn't the goofing-around Gourmet I'd known last semester. She seemed almost professional. Almost . . . Theseus-like. On the other hand, that meant we'd get something done. I pondered for a moment, shrugged it off, and talked her through one of my combos. *Not* the one I'd used on her and Polar Vortex, though; that one was too good to spoil completely.

Instead, I described my all–Rainy Day combo. "[**Spotlight Strike**] to [**Check the Script**], then [**Thunderhead**] and [**Ride the Lightning**]. It drops a pretty powerful finisher, especially in the right environments."

"Easy. You used [**Thunderhead**] and [**Ride the Lightning**] on me. I can disrupt it without a combo-breaker. I just need some blue raspberry sour candies."

"What—no, don't say anything. Let me guess. Blue raspberry sours give you electrical resistance? That seems like cheating to me."

"It's not. The instructions were to disrupt your combo. It's disrupted if it doesn't deal damage." Gourmet grinned and chewed on her jerky. "But if you insist, I'd put a combo-breaker in between [**Check the Script**] and [**Thunderhead**]. I'm not gonna stop the [**Thunderhead**] damage bonus, but I could mess up your [**Check the Script**] since you're using it as filler for the combo."

I shook my head slowly. "Yeah, that's the best spot to stop it. Enough commitment that it'd be hard to recover, forcing me to decide between starting over or finishing with a weakened combo."

"And it's hard for you to out-damage me without a full combo," Gourmet said. "Now, mine is [**Snap Into a Jerky**] into [**Bull Rush**] into [**Stampede Stomp**] into [**Furious Strike**]. Nice and simple. Just try and stop that."

"I did. If I time it right, I can [**Quick-Time Change**] and [**I-Frame Transform**] your [**Bull Rush**]." And what kind of power was [**Snap Into a Jerky**] anyway? Did it just change based on what she was eating?

"That didn't actually stop my combo," Gourmet interrupted. "I disrupted it myself when I backed off and took another [**Snap**]. That reset the whole damn thing, but I was one move away from combo-ing during our practice when they stopped us. You'd have been dead."

I stuck out my tongue. "Okay, I'd put the combo-breaker right after the [**Bull Rush**]. It cuts the most damage off. I'm starting to think the middle of the combo is the place for disruptions. But that doesn't make sense because Black Ice broke my combo after my third move. I'm not sure what's optimal."

"Stopping the combo is optimal," Underdelver said from behind me. "Anything else is a bonus. It's possible your opponent didn't recognize the combo coming or didn't feel threatened by it, so she let it go longer than she should have. But in the minors, The Triad followed a pattern. For Weavers, break early in the combo—around power use one or two. For Chainers, three or four is better. And for Geniuses with our [**Systematic Chaos**] bullshit, try to break if you get an opportunity. We don't play fair, and it's hard to see combos coming from us."

Armed with our newfound knowledge, Gourmet and I went through several different mock fights, using different powers and trying different disruption points—all on paper, of course. By the end, I thought I knew how to stop her—and I'd kept a few of my powers back, so maybe I'd have the advantage if we fought again in the training room or in real life.

Class dismissed, and Gourmet grinned at me. "See you on Thursday, Snack."

"See you on Thursday," I said. The big girl hustled out the door, and I thought momentarily. "Wait. Combat Style Practicum isn't until Friday."

"Maybe she's going to be at the roundtable like me," Fursona suggested. "I'm going to wait outside the studio, and she's Theseus's friend. She could just be supporting him."

"Yeah, that's probably it," I said, nodding. Then I hurried out, Fursona in my wake. I had studying to do for Child Psych.

TUESDAY, JANUARY 20

"So, by six months, a baby should recognize faces, be starting to reach for toys, and should be sitting without support. Unlike newborns, they're a lot more interactive," Dr. Roberts said. "And yes, the entire newborn and infant stages will be on next Tuesday's quiz. I strongly recommend you look through the chapters on both stages and work through the hierarchy of needs for a child at each stage, since you'll need to classify different activities on a model hierarchy to pass the quiz."

Su-Bin groaned; she hated this class more than I'd hated Algebra last semester, and I wasn't good enough at this to pay her back for all her help in passing math. Dr. Roberts dismissed the class, and I stood up. "I'll ask Bianca to help us later. She's taken these classes before. Lunch, Su-Bin?"

My strategy for making our friendship survive this Thursday was simple. Annie and Magical Girl Understudy were separate people, and Su-Bin and Vice President Pak were different people, too. If Annie didn't interact with Vice President Pak much, and Understudy avoided Su-Bin, we'd stay friends. Hopefully. But I had a feeling Vice President Pak planned to make that difficult, even if it was by accident.

"Sure. I've got some work to do for Thursday, but I can plan and eat at the same time. As long as it's not cafeteria food."

"Agreed." The cafeteria's quality had *really* taken a nosedive after Christmas.

We walked through the frigid campus; the icy air burned my nose, and my freshly washed hair had frozen when I'd left home this morning. I tried to keep the conversation on anything but the impending roundtable. We talked about her roommate—she was okay, especially since she'd practically moved in with her new boyfriend, which gave Su-Bin space to just . . . exist and relax for the first time since she left home. She mentioned that her parents wanted her to move back in but that her work with APPEAL was too important.

"What about your classes? Wouldn't living on the other side of Tokyexico impact them, too?" I asked.

"Well, yes. But right now, the priority is on making the campus safer." Her voice lowered to a whisper. "The supers are *always* a danger to Extras—I hate that term so much—and we need to get things under our control again. I was digging around, and they didn't even expel Magical Girl Understudy for blowing up the TUEAS building. Unbelievable. Either way, I can stay if I can prove to Mom and Dad that TU is getting safer. Otherwise, they'll pull me out of the dorms, and I *don't* want that."

"I could see that," I said. I took a deep breath and decided to leave the script for a bit. Bee wasn't around to enforce it, after all. "I heard a rumor that Understudy got banned from superhero stuff on campus."

"Yeah, I knew about that. It's not enough, though. You know she cost the school—"

Twenty-eight million dollars in damages and another five hundred thousand in tuition for make-up classes because of the tools Professor Panic destroyed. I didn't *say* that, of course, but I *knew* it.

"—Thirty million. Any Extra who did that would be expelled instantly."

We arrived at the Student Union Building, and the giant vents washed hot, vaguely sterile air over us just before the smell of "food" hit us. I wrinkled my nose and pointed toward the burrito restaurant. Su-Bin nodded. We stood in line. I ordered a veggie burrito, Su-Bin ordered a sausage burrito and a large soda, and we found an empty table.

"Okay, so what do we do about this upcoming quiz?" I asked, trying to find a topic to pull Su-Bin off the roundtable and APPEAL.

"I think we should study for it on Friday or Saturday, Annie. There's no way I can deal with it right now. I've got so much on my plate prepping for this roundtable." And off she went again on another tangent about Extras' rights and crime rates on campus.

I didn't see any of it. Yeah, the Series Finale had been bad, but neither the Tokyexico University Student Superhero Association nor the Student Supervillain

Society had acted up since winter break. I hadn't heard of a single on-campus Episode other than Theseus and Fursona, in fact. That alone was weird, especially after Ikenga's New Year's Eve speech about how things would get worse soon.

I filed that away for later, though. Instead, I focused on supporting my friend—and, honestly, on some good old-fashioned spy work. I didn't want to crush her hopes and dreams on Thursday since she clearly cared so much about this roundtable. And I got *that* part, at least. As a freshman *and* a leader in APPEAL, she needed to prove she could handle it. Or at least, she felt she did. It felt a lot like me trying minor-league Episodes. I needed to prove I could win them.

After an hour, Su-Bin stood up to head to her next class. I had an hour, so I texted Bianca.

<We need a strategy adjustment. Going to push it all on Theseus - Understudy 12:45>

<Also, Gourmet will be there. Suit up for sure. Bring Tails with you - Understudy 12:46>

21

Bring Tails with You

THURSDAY, JANUARY 22

Ilneat One, my language class, ended on time, and I hurried out of the classroom to find a tunnel entrance, transformed, and took to the sky. According to a text she'd sent fifteen minutes ago, Fursona was already at the Student Union Building, and so was Theseus.

The KRTU radio station was comprised of a small glass booth, a larger waiting room with a couch and a couple of armchairs, and a closet. Avan poked his head out of the closet, then emerged with an armful of recording equipment. "Hello, Magical Girl Understudy. Avan, though you'll be calling me DJ Smooth. A pleasure to meet you in slower times," he said, referring to the Finale from last semester. He adjusted the equipment and stuck a hand out. I shook it.

"Come on in; find a seat. Your villainous coguest is already here. I'll get set up. Su-Bin from APPEAL said she was running late—something about a last-minute talking point—so you'll have time to catch up. The villains say they know you two, and your friend and Theseus are *not* happy with each other."

"Uh, thanks, Avan," I said. *DJ Smooth* was a dumb name, and I couldn't call him that. Not until I had to. I disappeared behind the glass and found Fursona waiting on the couch. I handed her Tails, who she tucked into her pocket. Theseus and Gourmet each had an armchair, and Theseus glared at a defiant-looking Fursona. "You realize that shit could have outed me? Having to show up for a class with the wrong arms? It'd be a goddamn disaster, and I had tests the next day."

"Sounds like you shouldn't let yourself be disarmed so easily," Fursona quipped back.

Theseus breathed in. "Actually, I should thank you. You put your finger on a serious weakness, which I intend to patch up. I'll keep a better hand-le on my limbs in the future. You can count on that."

Okay. He was making puns. That either meant we were settling into the Superpower Ethics roles we'd been comfortable with last semester, *or* he was about to kick our asses. No **[Casting Call]** popped up, though, which was good, because I couldn't agree to one except in self-defense. "So, you put Fursona in the hospital, you know that?"

"Is this about the fight in the robotics building?" Su-Bin asked from the door. She stood awkwardly, arms crossed over her chest, but her stance felt like she'd go on the attack at any moment. "Haven't you supers done enough to the engineering department?"

"Nope. I didn't target anyone, and it's not my fault some of their equipment is perfect for me." Theseus seemed smug. He sat straight in his chair, clearly more comfortable sparring with Fursona than trading verbal barbs with Su-Bin. "You can check. Everything I did was strictly by the book; I even got Dr. Mindstorm to check it before I started, just in case it came up today. I didn't think it would, but then Fursona here jumped in."

"Yep. Wombat does that." Gourmet grinned. "They're *aggressively* stupid that way."

"Hey now, Gourmet, we're all friends here," I said, holding up my hands appealingly. I could *not* let this go south. If it did, I'd have to back off and let Fursona take whatever beating came her way. Even worse, Su-Bin would get all sorts of ammunition against us. Neither of those outcomes worked for me. "Let's save it for the radio. That's when we'll discuss these points like heroes and villains."

"With our fists?" Gourmet asked.

"Please don't," Avan said. He swung a boom microphone over the couch and placed another in front of each armchair. "This stuff's expensive. We're ready and on-air in two minutes. Please wait downstairs if you're not part of the roundtable."

Fursona stood, gave me a quick high-five, and said, "You've got this. Stick to the script." Then, before I could stop her, she left.

Tails's head bounced up and down as Fursona hopped away. *<You be careful. We'll be here to support you if you need us.>*

Gourmet stood as well, smiled menacingly at me, and nodded. "Have fun in there, Snack!"

"Thanks, guys."

"Seriously. *Break a leg,*" Gourmet replied. Then she was gone, and it was showtime.

Avan sat in the vacated armchair, leaving a spot on the couch for Su-Bin. She sat next to me, pointedly not looking at me or even saying hello. I took a deep breath and remembered that she wasn't Su-Bin, and I wasn't Annie. We were Vice President Pak and Magical Girl Understudy.

"We're live in ten. Nine. Eight . . ."

"Three, two, one. And we're back. That was Flying Donkeys with 'Outside Your Eyes,' and before that, we heard from Metal Aeroplane and The Belief Cycle," Avan rattled off. His whole personality had . . . well, not shifted, but tweaked. His smarm felt more in character now; his confidence and easygoing attitude fit perfectly as a radio host.

"Now, we've got a very special set of guests for this week's interview. A few weeks ago, I received an on-air call from a superhero named Fursona. They wanted to know if I'd be willing to host their fellow superhero for an interview. Naturally, my gears started turning. I said yes and pitched the idea of a roundtable discussion. Getting my guests in the same room without starting a fight has been challenging, but listeners, I'm happy to present the latest installment of 'Smooth Talk with DJ Smooth.'"

He pointed at me. "My first guest is a superhero and freshman at Tokyexico University. She recently had a pair of . . . explosive . . . Episodes to wrap up her show, *Small Town Super*, and she's here to explain what happened in them, some behind-the-scenes of how superhero work . . . well, works, and to pitch her new show, *Heroics 101*. It's Magical Girl Understudy." He pressed an applause button, filling the waiting room with canned clapping. This looked like it'd be quite a production.

"Thank you for having me," I said. Keep it polite and brief. Don't draw attention.

"You're very welcome. My second guest is a little more villainous, but arguably more important to the safety of students on campus. Theseus is a villain—but not only that, he's been fighting against the D-wolvers' incursions onto our campus. He's going to talk about villainy, why it works, why he's necessary, and about Man vs. Nature. Please give him a warm welcome and your wallets!" Avan pressed the applause button again.

Theseus nodded. "Thanks."

"It'd be an unfair roundtable with only super perspectives, though, so we have a special third guest this afternoon. As part of the Anti-Power Protestors' and Extras' Advancement League, Su-Bin Pak believes that superpowers should be banned, restricted, or regulated much more heavily than they are right now. Her ideas put her and APPEAL as an organization at odds with heroes, villains, and Ilneats, but do her points have merit?" A third round of applause filled the air.

"Thank you. Let's get into it." Vice President Pak pulled out a bottle of soda and glared at me. At me!

"I agree. Let's get into it. We're opening the lines for questions in a few minutes, but for now, I'd like to start with a game of Mad Libs. I'm going to read a sentence. You'll each fill in the blank with a word at the same time, then explain your word. Here's the first sentence. 'Superheroes on campus are a . . .'"

"Threat."

"Bunch of punching bags."

"Necessary to stop villains," I said. I recognized Su-Bin's plan, but Theseus almost seemed to be making light of the whole thing. What *was* his strategy?

"Interesting. Let's go to Theseus first. You said, 'Bunch of punching bags.' Care to elaborate?"

"Yes." Theseus smirked at me. "I'm a freshman on campus, and I've been in a few Episodes on campus. All four times, the heroes who tried to stop me failed. Not only that, but I destroyed them. I expected better when I came here. It's good that the learning opportunities outweigh the fights, or I'd ask for my money back."

"But there *are* advantages to being a villain on campus, correct?"

"Like I said, I'm learning a lot, which advances my goals. And since the university studio pays for damages, I don't have to worry about being in my villain persona on campus. My debts get paid, my guilt gets washed away, and I can attend superpower classes as a vil instead of a disguised vigilante."

"I see." Avan nodded, seemingly thoughtful. "Speaking of damages, Miss Pak, you said superheroes on campus were a threat. What do you mean by that?"

That was a softball setup if I'd ever seen one, but I stuck to my script and held my tongue while Su-Bin answered. "In the last three months, we've had multiple superpowered fights break out at the Engineering and Applied Sciences building, all due to the same superheroine—the same one joining us for this roundtable. The total damages are close to thirty-five million dollars, not including the time students lost on their projects and the tuition value lost by students repeating part of a semester. More importantly, these fights haven't been safe for students. Destroying buildings, trashing weight rooms, and wrecking public spaces all put unpowered students at risk while supers play their games."

"I see. And how would you respond to that, Magical Girl Understudy? Why, in light of that, are superheroes necessary on campus?"

Su-Bin was inflating the numbers, but I couldn't let that get to me. I took a deep breath to steady myself. "Miss Pak thinks superheroics on campus are a threat. I agree that there's a threat to student safety, but I believe it's the villains causing it. My nemesis, Professor Panic, took over the TUEAS Building she referenced, using a Student Supervillain Society lair in its basement to create a robot army. Who knows what kind of damage he'd have caused without me stopping him? Then, when I beat him, he destroyed the whole building to escape. As Theseus can confirm, my sidekick and I were buried in the rubble and had to fight past a D-wolver to escape.

"Speaking of Theseus, he's proven to be almost as damaging as my fight with Professor Panic—who's in Almhurst now, by the way—but with strictly self-motivated goals. He's defaced art from Roth Arena, destroyed the robotics department's labs, and more—all with the goal of becoming a lieutenant for some villain. Who knows what else he'd destroy without heroes to hold him accountable." That was more than I'd intended to say, but Bianca couldn't be mad; my whole speech followed the script perfectly.

"I can tell we're in for a feisty roundtable today, ladies and gentlemen. Let's take a moment to dig deeper into this one before we complete another sentence." Avan smiled and pointed at Su-Bin. "Miss Pak, you argue that superheroes cause more destruction than villains?"

"Not exactly. My argument is that villains and heroes cause the most destruction and crime together. By letting them not only live on campus but *funding* their activities, paying for their damages, and providing them with lairs, Tokyexico University tacitly approves of their dominance in Earth's society and the illegal activities they're responsible for."

"I see. And, Magical Girl Understudy, your response?"

Avan wanted to play us against each other, I realized. He *wanted* me to melt down about my Episodes on air. That's why he'd bounced right to me. I didn't have to play his game, though. "I'd like a world without supervillains, too, Miss Pak, but that's not the world we live in. Right now, I don't know any Extras—sorry, unpowered people—who can stand up to a minor-league villain, much less a big shot like Haze-Matt or Lord Destructo. So it makes sense for Tokyexico University to finance heroes."

"But not villains. They shouldn't be subsidizing powered students over *Extras*"—Su-Bin insisted on using the term, highlighting my self-correction—"to begin with, and they subsidize both heroes and villains. The amount of scholarship money that flows into superpowered students' coffers from the school is astronomical."

Avan cleared his throat. "Thank you both for clarifying. We'll have more questions about the money later since it's usually all about money, right? But for now, let's fill in another blank. 'Legally speaking, heroes and villains should be more . . .'"

"Accountable. Especially villains."

"Regulated."

"Free."

And on and on it went. My neck stiffened, and my hands got sweaty as Su-Bin alternated between attacking supers in general and attacking me. Theseus was unapologetically villainous, but the time wasn't right to bring up the video we'd posted. Not yet, at least. And I tried to play the we're-necessary angle, but I couldn't tell if it was landing or not.

Finally, after nearly ten minutes of back-and-forth built on the fill-in-the-blank game, Avan cleared his throat. "Alright, we've had a good start to our conversation, but I'd like to take things a little off-script. We're opening up the phone lines for listener questions!"

22

Listener Questions

"Keep to the script," Bianca had told me repeatedly. And, up until now, I'd done an excellent job of it, but we hadn't gotten a good read on *DJ Smooth*'s audience. I didn't know if they loved superheroes or if they'd rather see APPEAL get their way. I couldn't tell the audience turnout because Avan hadn't done a superhero interview since we'd talked to him.

I grit my teeth and clenched my fists, waiting for hardball call-ins from Su-Bin's friends with APPEAL. But that's not what happened, at least not at first.

"Su-Bin, you're a member of APPEAL, right? How do you explain the crime rates from before Launch Day compared to the lower overall rates right now?"

Su-Bin took a minute to think. "Well, that's a great question. I can't speak for people like the Pherris Report, but when the TU branch of APPEAL talks about crime rates, we're not referring to bike theft or white-collar crimes. We're specifically talking about violent or flashy crimes, like stealing the arms off a famous weightlifter's poster or blowing up a building."

"Sounds like you're cherry-picking," Theseus interrupted.

"Hey now, this question's for Miss Pak only," I said, thinking fast. The questioner *had* found a weak point in APPEAL's rhetoric. And I *could* exploit it the same way Theseus wanted to. But my position wasn't any less precarious, and questions might come my way. I needed the protection that keeping questions focused on their answerers afforded more than I needed Su-Bin to lose here.

Also, she was my friend. I didn't want her to lose badly. I just wanted to come out of this looking good myself.

"Thank you for interrupting, both of you," Avan said. He didn't look put out either way. "Some questions *will* be for more than one responder, but that one *was* aimed at Miss Pak specifically. Here's one for Magical Girl Understudy and Theseus.

"I did some research and learned you both follow a similar code of ethics. How can heroes and villains share the same codes? Doesn't that lend itself to the argument that there's no real difference between heroes and villains and that they're all just playing the same game?"

Theseus held up his hand before I could respond. I saw him smile before he answered. "I'll open, and the *hero* can follow up. For my most recent heist, I attacked a robotics lab, as has been mentioned. It would have been easiest to blow up a wall, waltz in, and finish my arms deal while the cops surrounded the building, then fight my way out. I'm *very* good at fighting. But our code of ethics forbids vils from hurting Extras without justification, so I broke in quietly instead. It would have been a clean heist if it weren't for Fursona's interference, too."

Damn. Theseus was much too clever for a supposed meathead Bruiser. He'd maneuvered me into a trap, and I didn't have a way out. I couldn't drop the video reveal here because it'd feel like Fursona had caused the destruction—he'd preemptively defended himself. And I couldn't contradict him on our code of conduct because he hadn't said anything untrue. I didn't have a choice but to defend him here.

"It's true. We developed our code of ethics over a semester of watching superheroes and villains behaving irresponsibly in Episodes that aired edited and ones that were never broadcast. Our Superpower Ethics class is literally designed to get hero and villain behavior under control in a voluntary way, without needing something like the New Gotham Accords to regulate supers. We took the experiences of other heroes and villains, learned from them, and wrote a code of ethics that addressed as many of the problems we'd seen as possible without being impossible to use."

Theseus interrupted. "Magical Girl Understudy and I were on the same team. We worked hard to keep the process fair to both heroes, villains, and the studios we're contracted to. Does that mean villains still do bad things? Absolutely. But a villain with a good code of conduct doesn't hurt people *intentionally*, at least not without purpose. So, to answer your question, there is a difference, and it's written into our code of conduct."

"Besides, the code of ethics is meant to be something to keep both heroes and villains in line. The *real* threats are villains who don't have one, or who don't follow it," I finished.

Avan clapped his hands once, sounding like Professor Tennyson for a moment. "We'll ask for that code of ethics and see if we can get it posted to the 'Smooth Talk with DJ Smooth' website after our show. And now, our next question, for Magical Girl Understudy."

"Are you ashamed of having your personal drama leak into your superhero life? The last moments of 'Absent-Hearted Professor' laid bare your relationship with Professor Panic, which seems wildly unprofessional."

My jaw dropped. I hadn't thought *that* would come up. It seemed so minor compared to everything else, but now I realized it was a wound—a very pokeable wound. Of course someone would give it a jab eventually. I steadied myself as I tried to think of what to say. Then I cleared my throat.

"This . . . being a superhero doesn't give many opportunities to find a partner you can be totally honest with. If a super dates an Extra, there's always that *one thing* you can't tell them. It's not a healthy place for a relationship. Professor Panic was the only person in my small town who *got* me for a long time, and over months of fighting, we grew closer due to this shared secret. That doesn't excuse what happened, and it wouldn't have happened if he and I hadn't been seeing each other, but that's not something I can change."

I paused for a moment, holding up a hand to signal I wasn't finished. "What I can say is that when the time came for Professor Panic to face justice, I didn't try to shield him. He's in Almhurst, and I hope he gets the rehabilitation he needs, and can start atoning for what he did in response to our relationship falling apart. And I hope I've learned something from this as well. Villains might be, in some regards, coworkers, but they're not personal friends or possible partners."

"I see," Avan said. "And our next question goes to Miss Pak."

I relaxed as the caller asked her about joining APPEAL. It was an obvious setup question designed to pitch the club, but at least I could chill out for a minute. Catch my breath. Gain my composure again. Su-Bin prattled on for a bit about the TU branch and the wider, world-spanning organization. Then it was my turn again.

"How do you justify Lab Assistant Panic?"

"I . . . Look, not all heroes are perfect bastions of justice and truth. I live up to that standard as best I can with the costumes I use, but Lab Assistant Panic has some powers I can't get elsewhere. That costume has some serious drawbacks—I'm sure you're talking about the end of 'Grant Building Dogpile.' But I justify it by using her *sparingly*, accessing the skills I need while I have control, and then switching back. Lab Assistant Panic is part of the toolkit, not a defining aspect of me as a hero."

"She's still a villain, and you've lost control of her twice," Su-Bin interrupted.

"Hey, that wasn't your question, Miss Pak," Avan said, and I grinned internally. One more win for Understudy!

"Any last words before we end the show? Miss Pak?" Avan asked.

"Yes, a reminder that APPEAL's TU branch is accepting new members. If you want to make a difference and take back our world, APPEAL may be for you."

"And Theseus?"

"No. I said what I said."

"Ooookay. And finally, Magical Girl Understudy?"

"Yes. Don't forget that you have the superpowers of kindness, love, and respect for each other. And, not to shamelessly plug, but check out *Heroics 101*! It's my studio's new show, and it's been a blast so far!" I said, squeezing in that last-minute pitch.

"Got it! I'm sure many of us will tune in," Avan said. He clapped his hands once. "This has been 'Smooth Talk with DJ Smooth.' Tune in next week when we'll talk to the school's gymnastics coach about TU's athletic legacy, injuries, and performance enhancement use on campus."

He pushed a button on his equipment and relaxed in his armchair. "And that's a wrap. Thank you all for coming and for such an interesting conversation. It seemed like you each had goals, and I hope you all accomplished them."

I nodded slowly and stood up, the adrenaline burning off as I headed for the door. My feet moved methodically down the stairs toward where Fursona waited. But when I got there, she was nowhere to be found. I checked my phone.

<Hey. Flare Short. Be by your place after. Tails w/ me - Fursona 3:56>
<Hope it went well - Fursona 3:57>
<Thanks. Went fine. Good luck w/ Flare - Understudy 4:05>

It *had* gone fine. Not perfectly, no. But with Theseus and Su-Bin there and with audience questions, perfection was never an option. I sat in the Student Union Building's atrium to get my bearings and decide what to do next.

"Well, Snack, you didn't break any legs? Disappointing," Gourmet said. She sat down across the little table from me.

"Hi to you too, Gourmet. What do you want?" With the adrenaline gone, I didn't have the energy for this. I needed her to spit it out.

"I got rid of Fursona for a bit, and Theseus won't be around." Gourmet looked from side to side anyway, a paranoid, unsure feeling to her movements. "I want to collaborate on another Episode, just like last semester. But this time, it might turn into an ongoing *thing*, so I don't want Theseus or Fursona involved," Gourmet said seriously. "It's got potential, and we wouldn't need to fight each other, which is good for you. I know you can't afford the losses right now, and neither can I."

"What's with the attitude change?" I asked. Gourmet had always been a goof last semester; her whole thing was that she'd never be minor-league material, but I couldn't figure out if she'd meant her weight, appearance, or power set. She'd been off in our last Combat Style Forum, too. I'd shoved her out of my mind for a while, but clearly, something had happened.

Gourmet sighed and seemed to deflate in her seat. "I don't want to talk about it, but life comes at you pretty fast, and I'm gonna need some money. I could smash and grab with Theseus, but he's drawing the wrong kind of attention to himself. He wants a career. I just want to run a couple of quick, cheesy Episodes to meet some upcoming expenses—something low-key and safely repeatable. It'll be this semester sometime. You in?"

I nodded. My line about villains not being good friend candidates was bullshit, and I knew it now. "What do I need to do?"

"Not much." Gourmet tore off a bit of her costume and handed it to me. I whistled, impressed. She'd done her research. "Just take the scrap to your producer, get the costume built, and wait. Don't use it in an Episode. Get used to the powers, but if you use it to fight, the deal's off. It's an alternative build I've been working on. Oh, and it's a loaner. I'm gonna want the scrap back when we're done."

"Got it. Uh, nothing too illegal, right?"

"Having second thoughts? No. Short-term kidnapping, maybe a little extortion, vandalism, and airwave theft. No big deal, right?"

"Uh, right." I took the sleeve scrap. I didn't *have* to accept the Episode when it happened. I could always back out if it felt wrong, or turn the tables on Gourmet if it went off the rails halfway through. "I've got studying to do. See you around."

"Good luck, and thanks."

I waited in the green room for Fursona to return, staring at her whiteboard. The marker was right there, so I crossed out 'KRTU' under 'PR.' I'd had enough of that— the backstabbing, the spying, and the politicking on-air—and I needed a break to run some Episodes and get my community rank up. I checked the calendar; Spring Break was still months away.

23

Chef Ramsey Fieri

TUESDAY, FEBRUARY 10

"We have options," I announced after reading the physical sign-up posted on the Student Union Building's wall. "But they're not all great ones. We can leave on March 21. That's Saturday, but the driver's only going halfway. He's got a girlfriend in some tiny town between here and Riverside. I don't know if Mom has the day off, so she might not pick us up until Sunday. And we'd need to—"

"Sounds like too much work for everyone," Bee interrupted. "Next?"

"Friday morning. I'd miss, uh, Creative Writing and Ilneat Politics, and I can't afford to miss either. And you'd miss . . . ?"

"Biomes, which I can totally miss, and Fencing Two, which I can't." We'd *really* miss Combat Style Practicum, which was a scary thought.

When you got down to it, the ride-share system at TU was downright archaic. Sign up for classes? Website. Joining a club? Online. Want to form a study group or get tickets for a Rams game? The university's page had you covered. But ride-share for Spring Break? Write down your name, car, license plate, and destination on a sheet of paper taped to the SUB's wall, then hope the right people sign up on the *same* paper. It wasn't even an official-looking list; every time it filled up, the student government just taped another sheet to the bottom like a scroll.

And no one wanted to head west.

"Well, that's what we've got, Bee. Miss classes or inconvenience my mom and maybe get stuck in the middle of nowhere. Can you check and see if there's a hotel in Basalt Point?"

"Yes, but they're probably pretty pricey, and most could be closed down for the season," Bee replied. "Let's just sign up for the Friday one and . . . see if we can figure something else out, I guess?"

I scribbled 'Anika DuPont and Bianca Marino' under the ride-share, but I didn't like it. Missing Combat Style Practicum could put me hopelessly behind; I'd been winning half my practice bouts, and the Style Points were a much-needed boost that, in theory, would let me hold my own against minor-league opponents *without* Tele-Portal's help. But missing it meant missing the best training I'd get that week.

"It'll be fine," Bee said as we left toward my apartment. "We can work hard over Spring Break and make up the difference."

"How? There aren't any villains in Riverside. Not anymore."

"We'll . . . think of something," Bee said. She poked me in the side, and I squealed. "Either that, or we can use it as a time to relax and *not* do the super thing for a bit. That way, you can hit it really hard in April and catch up without giving Vigilant Vow time to respond. Either way, though, let's head back to your place."

February clouds sat overhead much like January's had; the winters in Tokyexico were one long slog. My most recent patrol with Tele-Portal had been focused on investigation, though—we'd hunted for any sign of Polar Vortex or Black Ice trying for the electric grid again, and found nothing. So, I felt pretty confident that this wasn't another freak November storm.

Which didn't make me any warmer. Bee, despite being a Tortuga West girl, seemed more comfortable in the ice and snow than me! It wasn't fair; I should be used to this crap, but when we got to my apartment, it was me snuggling into Bianca for warmth every day.

"I'm so excited!" Bianca squeaked as soon as the door shut. "Your parents are probably totally awesome, and I want to meet Collidus! I bet he's got all sorts of stories from being your sidekick. You might as well tell me them now and save yourself the embarrassment later."

"I'm pretty excited, too," I said. And I was. It'd been far too long; August was the last time I'd seen Mom and Dad in person. Had it really been that long? I shivered a little, either from being sad or being cold. Spring Break was still a month away, but I'd made it five months already. I could survive one more. Plus, the Man vs. Nature was officially over. The Triad had dug the last D-wolver out from its lair near the wall, and the turbo-buffalo herd was long gone.

I was ready to go home.

But, like I said, that was a month away. "Got homework?"

"Yep," Bianca said, opening her overstuffed backpack and pulling out an E.O. Wilson book. "I'm studying ants and their hive structures in different environments, as well as super-colonies."

I grabbed my laptop and headed for the bedroom. "That sounds way more interesting than what I'm working on."

"Oh? What's that?" Bianca asked as she threw herself onto my bed and lay on her back, flipping through her book to find her place.

"'Local' power structures in Ilneat Politics. I have to write an essay on the pseudo-feudal system in the systems near Earth and how it impacts Ilneat/Earth relations. The problem is that I don't see *any* of that at play with Rocko. I think Dr. Quailman is full of shit, and there's a guest lecturer this Friday night. I'm going to ask a real

Ilneat some questions and see if I can trap my professor in some mistruths. But I need to turn this essay in first."

"Alright. Lay down and get to work." Bianca patted her stomach, and I rested my head on her and my laptop on my legs. It was precarious—especially when she turned a page in her book—but comfy.

The principles of rulership on Ilneat frontier planets are simple. Rather than directly interfering with local politics, Ilneats generally make deals that gradually give them increased power over the local population. They rarely abuse this power, though. Instead, they seem content to siphon off resources or a product from the locals, generally allowing culture and politics to continue unhindered.

"I give up!" I screamed. I'd been working on this stupid essay for an hour. It wasn't even *due* until Friday. I shut my laptop and rolled my head off Bee's stomach—I'd just woken her up, and the light up-and-down of her breathing had been replaced with tense muscles. "This is all just bullshit. It's probably not even how any of it works."

"Show me," Bee said, sitting up. I opened the laptop again, and she skimmed what I'd written. "That sounds like the movie studios and Launch Day, right? They moved in, set up a deal to rebuild Earth in exchange for the whole studio world thing, and haven't done much else. The product is superhero movies and TV shows. In other words, us."

"Huh." That *did* make more sense. "I guess when you're caught up in it your whole life, you don't really see it. I don't think it's as nefarious as Dr. Quailman says it is, either. But I can't know for sure. He wrote the damn book."

"Take a break. Something else is on your mind. You can talk to me about it—I'm all ears."

I sighed. Bee knew something was up. I hadn't told her about Gourmet's special request or the Gourmet Costume, but maybe now was the time—at least for half of it. "I got a new Costume after the KRTU roundtable."

"Really! Tell me about it! Is it Monologue? I bet Avan's actually Monologue. It'd be such a great disguise. I thought Su-Bin might be Gourmet for a while since she's always got a soda and Gourmet's whole thing is food, but they've been in the same place at the same time, so it can't be her. But Avan as Monologue makes so much sense."

"It's not Monologue, and Avan's a freshman. He can't be Monologue, since he's been running the SSS for years." I narrowed my eyes at Bee jokingly. "Hey, you said you weren't the type to dig into secret identities."

"Well, I can *speculate*. As long as I don't try to prove anything, guessing is fun!" Bianca blushed. She'd known my identity instantly last semester, and I jokingly reminded her about it all the time now.

"Anyway, it's not Monologue. It's Gourmet, and it's . . . probably the weirdest Costume I've ever gotten."

"Let me see!"

I nodded slowly. "Go get me a snack. I need a snack to make it work. Then meet me in the green room. I'll show you the Costume, then tell you about its powers."

She nodded and headed for the kitchen while I grabbed Tails and went through my transformation sequence. The new outfit still felt strange; I'd been in my classic look for five years, and the new one felt luxurious and glamorous, especially the gold highlights.

Bee came in with an apple. "Really?" I asked, but I bit down into it anyway. It tasted crisp, fresh, and . . . wrong. I tossed it aside and spun around, brow wrinkled and a look of faux disgust plastered on my face. "You didn't fucking *cook* this. It's *raw*!"

Bee opened her mouth for a retort, but the smell of garlic and oregano filled the air. A kitchen knife with a star on its pommel appeared in my hand in place of my wand, and an apron rolled down over my dress. The finishing touch was a chef's hat far too big for me; I'd complained to Pataki about it, but they didn't seem to care.

The weird thing about the Magical Girl Ramsey Fieri Costume wasn't the food theme or the star-and-moon apron. It wasn't even the silly chef's hat or the obvious reference to old-time celebrity chefs. I'd expected something dumb like that, given what Gourmet had said about it being based on one of her experimental builds. No, that wasn't the weird thing. It was the powers themselves. They had basically no combat applications.

[Costume - Magical Girl Ramsey Fieri]
[HP 8/8]
[Styles and Skills]
►Archetype Skill - Transformation Sequence
►Badass
►Cunning
►Just a Pinch of Spice 0
►Drama
►Speed-Plating 0
►Hometown Heroine 1
►Flamboyance
►Signature Skill - Adaptive Armoire 1
►Stored Costumes: (Understudy)
►Spotlight Strike 1
►Grit
►Iron Stomach 0

"Okay, this is the Gourmet costume," I said. "It's Magical Girl Ramsey Fieri, and it's . . . not a villain costume, somehow. But it's also not a hero. I think the best descriptor would be vigilante, but that doesn't fit perfectly. It's got three powers, but I haven't been able to try them out. The first is Cunning. **[Just a Pinch of Spice]**. It, and I quote, 'lets me measure out the perfect amount of any ingredient, for *anything*."

"Anything, huh?" Bianca asked. "Like, gunpowder for a bomb or poison for a meal?"

"Food. It's about food. Especially because the second new power is **[Speed-Plating]**. It's a presentation-focused ability that lets me quickly arrange small objects to be aesthetically pleasing. I'd imagine that as I powered it up, it'd let me arrange bigger and bigger things, but at Level 0, it covers a couple plates at a time."

"Level 0? I never get Level 0 powers."

"Yeah, that's a quirk of my **[Signature Skill]**. The powers on my Costumes are always weak. Can we hurry this up? I'm starving." My Costumes all had quirks, whether Lab Assistant Panic's evil streak, Rainy Day's age change, or Copy Cat's personality merge with Tails. Ramsey Fieri was judgmental about food and was hungry. All. The. Time. Was this what Gourmet felt like?

"Sure. Sorry." Bianca sat down on the couch. "What else do you have in that toolkit?"

"**[Iron Stomach]**. I can eat whatever I want. I can't benefit from different types of food at this low level, but this is Gourmet's **[Signature Skill]**. It's how she powers up. Remember when she ate the—"

"—Yes, the wrestling singlet. So gross."

"Yeah, well, I can do that now."

"Disgusting. Switch back, please," Bee said.

I did. "Anyway, Gourmet didn't give this to me out of the goodness of her heart. I'm supposed to do an Episode with her sometime soon. She claims it shouldn't be a big deal, and I'll be in this Costume the whole time, so I should be untraceable back to Understudy. But I need to talk to Rocko so the Episode doesn't get run on Earth if I get caught."

"Fine. I'm going too. Let me know when the Episode is, and I'll be there to make sure she's not plotting something with Theseus," Bianca said, standing up. "I bet she is."

"I don't think so. She seemed upset about something and said she needed the money from a couple of quick Episodes. I'm not sure why she trusted me, though."

"Clearly, she wants to kick your ass and ambush you. You'll have to ask her about it at practicum."

"Yeah," I said. I wasn't looking forward to another fight with Gourmet.

PART FOUR

24

Something Different

FRIDAY, FEBRUARY 13

We'd just finished lunch—bacon, lettuce, tomato, and avocado wraps, made by me—when Rocko called.

"You've got clean-up," I told Bianca. She groaned, stood up, and wandered into the kitchen with our two plates. We hadn't eaten at the Student Union Building since my Magical Girl Ramsey Fieri Costume reveal, which made Bianca happy. I had mixed feelings about it; cooking anything up to Fieri's standard took *forever*, and I couldn't half-ass it either. But the food *was* better. I needed to figure out a way to have some friends over for a dinner party without giving away my secret identity. Either that, or they had to be superheroes.

My phone buzzed again, and I stared at it for a moment. Then I hung up. It'd just be Rocko snapping again, like the end of last semester, and ordering Bianca and me over to the studio. I'd just as soon miss that step. "Bee, change of plans. We're paying Rocko a visit."

"You got it, Annie." Bianca stopped scrubbing the cast-iron pan and walked into our—my—bedroom to change into her summer outfit. I followed her. Neither of us needed that kind of heat.

"This is just a quick business visit. I've got homework, and we both have practicum in two hours. Let's get in, let them lecture us on how we're not climbing the rankings, and get out." I pulled my shirt off and grabbed a tank top, then dropped my jeans to trade them out for shorts. Bianca whistled, and I blushed and turned.

"I can bring the whiteboard." Bianca meant The Plan, which we'd covered in crossed-out words and arrows linking one part to another. We'd actually gotten quite a bit done, including getting Tele-Portal to open up her training arena. But the one thing that hadn't moved much was my community ranking, which was . . . a problem.

"Nah. We'll explain what we have to, but Rocko doesn't need the visual aids. Let's rock." We shivered even in the heated apartment and quickly headed for my secret base and Rocko's door.

[Welcome to Rocko's Studio. System Disabled. Now arriving Backstage.]

The heat and humidity hit me like a brick wall.

"DuPont. You are *aware* of the situation, right?" Rocko's hands were empty. They sat at their desk, staring at a TV screen showing the Tokyexico Community Rankings. I sat at 315 still, while Vigilant Vow had jumped to almost 280—well within minor-league range.

"Yep. Doesn't look good, does it?"

"Doesn't look good? No, it looks *terrible*. Cartman's messaging me *constantly* about when you two are gonna get your butts in gear, and I have to say 'They're working on it' every time. So I need you two to get your butts in gear. Seriously."

"We are, Rocko. This is all part of the plan, just like the 'Fursona Solo' Episode and the radio show," Bianca said.

"I don't— No. No, there's no way that's all gonna work. On a long enough timeline, sure. But you have three months. We ain't getting this minor-league slot at the rate you're going." Rocko glared at me. I glared right back. Then their expression shifted, and they ran a pair of hands through their otter-like fur. "Look, I appreciate that you've got a plan. But I *also* appreciate that you've run two Episodes since your Finale."

I seethed. Rocko *knew* why I couldn't run Episodes all the time. **[Casting Calls]** popped up all the time on campus these days, and I had to ignore them all. It'd been worth it then, but if I had a do-over, I'd probably have laid low and tried to let Professor Panic make a mistake. It'd have been easier than this restriction. "Rocko, I *can't*—"

"Don't give me that. You searched for a week to find the perfect Episode after Gourmet and Theseus wrecked you last year. You need to pound the pavement and find *something*," Rocko said. They stood up, walked over, climbed the chair, and touched my shoulder. The scent of cigar smoke hung heavily around them, even though they weren't smoking anything. "The stakes are higher than you know. *Heroics 101* needs some Episodes to stay afloat. Give me *something* here."

"Fine. We'll have an Episode for you by tonight," I said. "Tomorrow, for sure."

"For sure?" Rocko asked. Bianca opened her mouth but thought better of saying anything when I squeezed her hand slightly.

"For sure," I said.

"Good, because if you don't, we're gonna have problems, you and me. *Financial* problems, and neither of us can afford that." Rocko climbed down from the chair. "Now, how's that new Costume treating you?"

"I love it!" Bianca said.

"It's fine, but it's not villainous or heroic, and it's not great in a fight. Listen, Rocko, we have homework and class in a bit. We need to get going. We'll go hunting tonight."

The second we walked back into my green room, Bianca started whining.

"Annie, it's not fair! We were gonna watch some Episodes tomorrow, and you were cooking spaghetti. If we're hunting an Episode all night, that's not gonna happen."

"Shit," I said. Bianca was right. Tomorrow was the fourteenth, and that meant Valentine's Day. And I'd promised her the shows and dinner; somehow, I knew being stuck in her fursuit wouldn't fly. "So, we have to find something tonight. This feels disgustingly like deja vu."

"Not quite. This time, there's a lot more riding on it," Bianca said. She wrapped her arms around my waist, as much to capitalize on my body heat as to hug me. Shorts and a T-shirt didn't work for mid-February. "And this time, I'm with you to the end of the line."

"Thanks, Bee." I gave her a quick, stressed-out kiss on the forehead, then untangled myself and opened the door to my apartment. "To the covers. Study and snuggle time!"

Bianca grabbed her science book, we both found our computers and without changing into anything warmer, we crawled under the blankets to get to work. Tails watched, as she always did, from between our heads.

Ilneat Politics, for once, didn't require Quailman's book. In addition, it didn't look like he'd actually *read* the article he'd linked, which Magister Fenton had written and Dr. Rogers had translated. The first was an Ilneat name, for sure, and the content in the article reflected that. It contradicted most of Quailman's book in just a few sentences.

While at its highest levels, Ilneat politics revolves around a caste system similar to that on Earth prior to 1600 Local Year, the realities of the Ilnean Empire are that inter-caste movement happens frequently. In fact, that movement has made all but the highest ranks of Ilneat politics essentially homogeneous in the last four hundred cycles. This transformation has created massive tremors in—

"Ow!" I squealed as something pinched the meaty part of my thigh through my leggings. Bianca giggled and pulled her hand away from my leg. I glared, she shrugged and winked, and I returned to reading.

—massive tremors in the political landscape.
The largest of these changes is the rise of new political entities. Many of the "lower" caste groups have banded together to carve out voting blocs within system-local governing bodies, and the old systems in these systems seem to be falling out of favor. In their place,

corporations and cooperatives seem to be taking more and more control politically. Indeed, the Ilneat Empire appears to be heading toward an Ilneat Corpocracy or Plutocracy.

I argue that these shifts are largely negative for the Ilneats in the upper castes and the local species populating resource systems. To better protect—

I let a hand stray under the covers, looking for revenge.

—both Ilneat interests and long-term viability for resource planets, I believe that protections must be codified to prevent these corporations and cooperatives from gaining too much control and compromising the system we've spent countless cycles creating, and that benefits both Ilneats and other species.

Something about that last line . . . rubbed me the wrong way, and I stopped reading, shut my computer, and rolled over. "Hey, Bee, do you think we're weaker than the Ilneats?"

"I've never thought about it, but . . . probably."

"Huh. I've never thought about it either." They'd *always* been around, in the background and then in person in the form of Rocko and Pataki, so I'd never thought about our place in their system. I'd just kind of . . . done what I needed to.

And their presence *had* saved the world. I pushed it out of my head. If I wanted to *really* dig into humanity's relationship with the Ilneat Empire, I'd have paid more attention last semester. And honestly, the world *was* better with the Ilneats around, even if Su-Bin disagreed.

So, instead of finishing my homework, I lay around, played on my phone, and watched Bee work on her chemistry or whatever. It all looked way too mathy for me, but she seemed lost in it—so much, in fact, that I decided *not* to get revenge for her pinch. Instead, I flopped an arm over her shoulder and just snuggled. She rolled her eyes. Many of our snuggle study sessions ended up like this, either on her part or on mine.

And then, finally, it was time to get ready for Combat Style Practicum.

Bianca stepped into the Fursona suit. "Hey, help me out here. Buckles, helmet, the works." She held her arms out and wiggled her hands.

I tightened straps, looped loops, and checked that Fursona's suit fit snugly. Then I transformed, and we rode the elevator down into the tunnels. We'd made it halfway down when Gourmet appeared from around a corner. I waved. "Hey, Gorgonzola."

"Snack. Wombat."

"Fursona!" Fursona said.

As we walked toward the training room, Gourmet cleared her throat. "I'm aiming for late March, Snack. After Spring Break. Be ready."

"You got it, Gourmet. I'll be there." My mind was on class. Last time, we'd done multisuper fights, with three heroes against three villains. What kind of crazy stuff would Mindstorm and Tennyson have for us today?

She nodded. "Good. Ready for class. I heard from the SSS that it's hostages. The villains defend them, and the heroes try to rescue them without getting any of them 'killed.' I'm ready to eat some heroes for breakfast."

Fursona snorted. "The only thing you'll be eating for breakfast is our dust when we get to the hostages first. And how'd the SSS know all that, anyway?"

"Oh, you know, they've *taken the class*. Monologue told us everything. A bunch of the villains even changed their builds for it, but not me. I don't need a special build to mop up you two or to keep you from getting to the hostages."

"It's not because your other build is worthless in combat?" Fursona asked. I glared at her; I'd told Gourmet I'd keep the Ramsey Fieri Costume secret.

"I knew you'd tell Wombat, Snack. It's fine. Just be ready to lose in there."

I laughed. "Oh, I don't think so. I'm here to upstage the villains!"

25

Upstage the Villains

"Today's . . . practicum will allow you to put our discussion about hostage rescue to the test from both a villain's and hero's perspective," Dr. Mindstorm said as we looked at the absolute maze of an obstacle course that filled TU's training room. "From a villain's perspective, keeping hostages alive and out of the heroes' hands increases the likelihood your . . . polite requests will be met. Therefore, you'll want to defend each hostage intensely."

"Right." Dr. Tennyson cleared his throat. "And from the heroes' point of view, the most important thing is that the hostages survive, followed by safe rescues, with the villains' defeat last in importance. We've discussed all this, though, so here are the rules."

I peered down into the maze. Drs. Jackson and Mays, as well as Underdelver outside of his mech suit, stared back up from a small room in its center. They each sat on a folding chair, a single loop of used Christmas tinsel "tying" them in place, with a placard on their chests reading Hostage: Do Not Kill. Underdelver raised a hand and waved at us, showing that the so-called hostages weren't *really* prisoners.

Dr. Tennyson clapped his hands. "We'll divide you into teams of three, with a mix of villains, heroes, and vigilantes on each when possible. Team One will play the villains first, and Team Two the heroes. Then they'll switch. The goal is to rescue all three hostages as fast as possible. For each villain your team defeats, we'll take a minute off your time. For each hostage that the *heroes* hit with a power, we'll add three minutes. If a hostage gets hit by a villain *during a rescue attempt only*, we'll add a minute. So, speed, safe passage for the hostages, and defeating the villains."

"This is a no-holds-barred practice. Superhero damage is at 50% of normal, and if you drop below half your [HP], you're considered unconscious. Heroes, you can make up thirty seconds by saving an unconscious hero. The fight ends when all hostages and unconscious heroes are safe or when fifteen minutes is up," Mindstorm said. "Team One is Gourmet, Candi Crush, and Understudy. Team Two is Waterspout, Flare, and Grapple. Team Three is Punch, The Crumb, and Fursona. Team Four is . . ."

I didn't listen to the rest. Gourmet and Understudy, teaming up? The battle was as good as won if we could avoid killing each other. The food-powered villain and Magical Girl Candi Crush seemed like a weird pair, though. I wondered for a moment if Gourmet could power up from eating Candi's dog. Then we headed into the maze, a blinking line of LED lights guiding us.

"Hey, here's the plan, Snack," Gourmet said. "We'll all go Bruiser and try to gun down Flare fast, then get back to the hostages. We can defend a three-versus-two fight forever. They'll lose for sure."

That sounded shockingly reasonable. Sure, Underdelver was shaking his head, but Candi seemed all-in. She changed from the diminutive blue-dressed form into her hulking form with the candy cane mace, then summoned her dog. I shifted into Copy Cat, letting Tails merge with my mind.

<Oh, hunting Flare today? How fun,> the plushie cat said.

"Begin." Mindstorm's voice echoed over the intercom.

Gourmet started running through the maze, Candi, the **[Hard-Candy Hound]**, and I following in her wake. The heroes hadn't had time for a better plan, so surely they'd still be talking through their assault. They wouldn't expect a raid. They *couldn't* expect an attack.

But by the time we maneuvered our way out of the maze, they were nowhere to be seen.

"Spread out. If you find one, shout. We'll beat them together!" Gourmet shouted. It felt weird listening to *her* orders, of all people, but I dutifully dove back into the maze. Twists, turns, and empty rooms were all I could find.

Then Candi Crush shouted, "I've got one! East side!" I looked toward the windows far above; they were west, so I'd go the other way, and I'd find her. I ran faster and faster through the maze, Tails urging me on. I turned a corner, and there she was, the ridiculously buff girl swinging her candy mace for all she was worth. But she hadn't cornered Flare. She'd caught the absolute worst of the heroes for our plan.

The candy mace smashed against Waterspout, then through his arm, which turned to water for a moment before solidifying again. We'd caught Team Two's Tank, not their Speedster.

As if to drive the point home, a bell rang. "That's one rescue." Mindstorm's voice echoed.

I growled in frustration, used **[Cat-Scratch Fever]** and **[Leaping Leopards]**, and jumped through the air. We needed Waterspout *down* so we could focus on stopping the rescues. I crashed into the watery warrior, scratching for all I was worth. But even though a jagged cut opened on the hero's ebbing skin, it hadn't accomplished my goal. The poisonous fever washed straight through him instead.

[Badass Damage! +1 Badass Point]
[Poison Negated! -1 Drama Point: No Drama Points Available]

Candi used my distraction to pull her mace free while the [**Hard-Candy Hound**] harassed Waterspout. For his part, he pressed the attack against Candi Crush, slamming her with watery tendrils.

The bell rang a second time.

"Change of plans," I said, dashing for the door. "We gotta go, or we'll lose!"

Candi Crush nodded. "Right behind you."

But as we reached the door, a shimmering liquid barrier covered it. "Water you running away for?" Waterspout asked. He *slid* toward us, leaving puddles behind. We'd have to beat him to get out. Candi and I both nodded and ran toward the hero. I used [**Doom Ball**], my most potent move as Copy Cat, and scratched and clawed the hero.

[Badass Damage! +1 Badass Point]
[Badass Damage! +1 Badass Point]
[Badass Damage! +1 Badass Point]
[Badass Damage! +1 Badass Point]

A gong sounded. Mindstorm's voice cut through the fighting and shouting. "A hero is down!"

I stared at Waterspout. "That you?"

"Nope. You nearly scratched my armor, though!" He surged backward away from us. We hadn't broken free yet!

[Badass Damage! +1 Badass Point]
[Stylish Assist! +1 Flamboyance Point]
[Badass Damage! +1 Badass Point]
[HP 7/8]

As we fought back and forth, slowly wearing Waterspout down, the bell sounded. "The downed hero has been rescued!"

Then, finally, after what seemed like an eternity, I heard another sound from the intercom. But it wasn't the gong I'd hoped for. Instead, the bell rang again. "Enough. The last hostage has been saved. Final time: Five minutes, thirteen seconds. Switch sides. Superhero damage and powers are reset," Mindstorm said.

The room shimmered. So did Candi Crush. When she stopped, she'd returned to her small blue form, and I knew I was Understudy again. We stomped our way back to the heroes' rally point, passing the professors on their way back to the hostage room.

When we got there, Gourmet was livid. "What the hell happened? I took down Flare as planned, by myself, but you left me in a two-against-one. Is it because I'm a vil?"

"No, it's because Waterspout is a *problem*. He's ridiculously strong," I said.

"Oh really? How much damage did he do to you two?"

"Two points." Candi Crush looked ashamed.

"One point," I said. "But he locked down the whole room, and he takes barely any damage. He might be able to fight all three of us without losing for five minutes. We need a plan to take him down."

"Yeah, we do. What've you got?" Gourmet asked.

"How about I stay Understudy and try landing a [**Ride the Lightning**] combo? He might have a natural weakness to lightning. He's gotta be weak to *something*, right?"

"Right," Candi said. "Gourmet can push hard and try to stomp Flare again, and I'll attack the hostage room from the flanks because I can summon [**Hard-Candy Hound**]."

"It's aggressive. I like it." Gourmet grinned and snapped off a bite of jerky to grow her horns.

"Begin," Mindstorm said over the intercom, and I started jogging into the maze. Gourmet smashed *through* a wall ahead of me while I turned toward the same room Waterspout had trapped me in before.

Behind me, Candi Crush shouted, "It's not *working*! [**Big-Rock Candi**]! [**Hard-Candy Hound**]! Something, come on!"

I poked my head back around the corner. Candi stood there, face red and eyes squeezed shut from concentration, still small and still dressed in her blue dress, not the candy colossus she needed to be. Frustrated tears ran down her cheeks. Something felt . . . off. Really off. But I couldn't place it.

She definitely wasn't faking, though. I'd been an actress, and I knew acting, and you *couldn't* act this well on a dime. "Dr. Mindstorm, something's wrong! We're tapping out!" I shouted up to the glass.

A buzzer sounded. "Enough. Team One forfeits their attempt."

Gourmet was *pissed*.

The whole way up the stairs, she screamed and shouted. I wasn't sure why she was so upset, since she'd never been like this last semester, but something had her more worked up than a power malfunction should have. She would *not* leave Candi Crush alone, though, so finally, I'd had enough.

"Gourmet! Enough! Holy shit, enough! It's not her fault," I snapped. "She wanted to win as much as you, got it!"

"Really? You screwed up the villain run, then botched the hero side completely. I'm not sure you two know how to win."

Mindstorm cleared her throat from the stair door. "Enough. Candi, you're with me. If you give me permission, we can find out what's going wrong quickly. Just step into the . . . hall with me. Gourmet, Understudy . . . wait here."

Candi nodded slowly, tears in her eyes. She was already talking before she even got to the observation room. "I can usually summon [**Hard-Candy Hound**] anywhere, even if I'm not in [**Big-Rock Candi**] form. I couldn't do either. Then I tried [**Flavor Ray**] or even getting my wand to change. It felt . . ." her voice faded away as the door shut.

Professor Tennyson clapped his hands. "Teams Three and Four, head down. We'll start your runs in three minutes. Remember, three-minute penalty if you hit a hostage, heroes. Villains, you can take advantage of that. Do so."

Fursona shot me a look; I couldn't see it through her kangaroo head, but I could picture the mix of concern and confidence. She was going to kick Team Four's butt on time, but her thoughts had to be on Team One. She wanted to know why we'd bailed. At least, I told myself she did.

"Begin," Tennyson said a few minutes later, and I watched as Fursona and her team defended the hostages. Unlike us, they'd opted to all stay nearby but spread out. It seemed to work better than our aggressive, all-in strategy had, but then again, Team Four didn't have an area-denial Tank like Team Two had.

I wasn't sure what had happened to Candi Crush, but I couldn't take my eyes off Fursona. What if it happened to her, too? If it was a classmate's power I didn't know about, that was bad. But worse, what if it was a System problem? If it was, it could happen to anyone!

To distract myself, I reevaluated Waterspout's power level. He'd barely gotten a functional combo together the first day of Combat Style Practicum, but his power wasn't in damage. If he used it right, he'd be a fantastic teammate, even if he never landed a blow.

Candi came back, somehow more distraught than before. Mindstorm had asked for permission; she'd probably been inside the Magical Girl's head. I put an arm around her shoulder, commiserating. I'd felt bad after registration last semester, and I'd been in a good mood before. Mindstorm herself whispered something to Tennyson, who shook his head.

Eventually, Fursona finished her two runs: eight minutes, thirty-one seconds as villains and six minutes, nineteen seconds as heroes, with no power malfunctions. The moment Teams Three and Four reached the observation room, accompanied by the "hostages," Mindstorm cleared her throat, looking worried.

"We'll have Teams Five and Six run on Monday. Meet us here for practicum instead of in the classrooms," Mindstorm said. "Class dismissed. And Understudy, we have a meeting next Wednesday right after Ilneat Politics."

"That seemed abrupt," Fursona said as we exited the observation room. I nodded. It *was* abrupt. And the meeting with Mindstorm weighed on me. That wasn't our regularly scheduled meeting time.

Then Gourmet shoved past me and hurried down the hall, a set of keys jingling from her hand.

Car keys.

26

Car Keys

"Are we gonna talk about Candi?" Fursona asked as we hurried down the hall. "That was wild. I've never seen powers fail except with Jackson, and this wasn't Jackson, or it'd be everyone, so what happened?"

"I have no idea. Mindstorm seemed worked up about it, though. I don't think it's a common issue." Candi's transformational dysfunction wasn't my main concern. I only had eyes for Gourmet. What was she doing? A lot of students had cars, but she'd have to be pretty stupid to get in hers as a supervillain unless . . .

Unless the car was Gourmet's, not her alter ego's. In which case, she probably wasn't cruising for fun. She had a plan, and if Gourmet had a plan, maybe that meant an Episode. "Want to see what she's up to?" I asked.

Fursona nodded. "Just be careful. No Episodes on campus, remember?"

I gritted my teeth. That rule was going to get me in trouble one of these days. "I know."

The tunnel ended at the Mister Felsic ramp, and Gourmet hurried out. We waited ten seconds, then pushed the doors open. It wasn't like she'd be hard to find; she was probably the least subtle villain on campus, and she routinely spent time in costume on campus. I remembered when I'd had to feed her in the dining hall, and we'd all eaten as supers—how awkward had *that* been?

The moment we stepped out of the doors below the repaired and renovated Mister Felsic, we got our [**Casting Calls**]. I hesitated, thinking about my on campus Episode ban, then shrugged. I just wouldn't report it, and wouldn't do anything until I was off campus. It'd be like it never happened.

[Casting Call]
[Episode: Braking and Entering - PG-13]
[Role: Flag Girl! Do you accept the role? (Yes/No)]
[Role Focus: Flamboyance + Badass]

"Minor league," I muttered, frowning. I wasn't so sure about this. We could *probably* handle Gourmet. We might even be able to fight two vs. one against Theseus.

But the minor leagues weren't the friendliest, and we could easily run into a real loose-cannon villain.

On the other hand, dealing with a minor-league Episode without help from Tele-Portal would do wonders for my community ranking. Fursona accepted. I waited; the longer I could put it off, the more deniability I'd have if TU's administration got upset.

As we tailed Gourmet, careful to keep our distance even though she didn't seem focused on checking for followers, Fursona cleared her throat. "I mean, it didn't happen to anyone else, right? You could still use your powers, and Gourmet had no problems. So it's gotta be a Candi Crush issue."

"Yeah." I ducked around a scooter, stepping off into the snow-covered grass to avoid it. Its clattering wheels faded into the distance, and I cursed myself for not buying one from Walmart when they were on sale. "Whatever it was, hopefully it's a one-off problem. It'd be awful if that happened to her in a real Episode and not training."

"I hadn't even thought of that. Getting cut off from your powers would suck in an Episode."

"It happened to me once," I replied. Gourmet angled toward the massive parking structure on TU's east side. While Bianca had parking near her dorm, most students ended up in the parking garage. Honestly, I thought they had it better than Bee since they didn't have to make their girlfriends scrape the windows. Bee disagreed, but her butt wasn't out there scraping. I'd never gotten my license, and I didn't have a car even if I had. She drove, and I scraped, and I only complained a little.

"It did, huh?"

"Yep. Orientation Episode. I didn't have Tails when it started because Peter couldn't fit her into my backpack. But I didn't know that, so I accepted the role, went to transform in the bathroom, and couldn't. The waitress at the No More Mr. Rice Guy? She was in the bathroom when it happened. She probably still thinks of me as Toilet Girl." I tried not to look embarrassed.

Gourmet dipped inside the towering parking garage. I paused. If we followed her in, we could have our fight right here. But in that case, we wouldn't figure out the rest of the Episode, and it wasn't a Short. The only way we'd be able to figure out the plot was if we followed her in her car, and I doubted Fursona could keep up.

However, I had a terrible idea. "Want to go plain clothes for the first part of this one?" I asked.

"What are you thinking?"

I told her. She was *not* happy. But after some back-and-forth, she nodded. "I don't like it, and I don't think it's the best strategy, but I'll do it. Just be careful, and stay in touch." She hopped away, back toward her dorm, and I knew why she wasn't happy. I usually did it for her, but this time, I wouldn't be there to scrape her car!

I'd never been more jealous. How did a villain score *that* as their getaway vehicle, and why didn't I have one of my own? Not that I could drive, but it was the principle of the matter.

The Mustang was, in fact, cherry red with sparkly paint and two white racing stripes, immaculately clean, with not even a smidgen of dust on it. Gourmet's arm stuck out the window, tapping lightly on the car's side as she pulled out of her spot. It purred as Gourmet slowly drove it through the parking garage and out the exit—two floors below my perch.

Then she pulled out onto University Drive.

<Got her. old Mustang, cherry red, extra-loud engine - Understudy 3:42>
<West on University. License plate 378-XLG - Understudy 3:42>
<On it. Gonna tail. Im the gray civic - Fursona 3:43>
<I know lol - Understudy 3:43>
<Shut up - Fursona 3:43>

By the time I'd finished texting Bee, Gourmet was halfway down the block and stopped at a red light. "[Starwave Sail]," I said, stepping off the parking garage and into thin air. My sailboard caught me, and I rocketed up until I circled overhead, even with the twelfth-story windows. She probably wouldn't notice me here. Probably. I accepted the [Casting Call] and flew off campus. Total time in-Episode on TU grounds? Three seconds. That didn't count, right?

[Braking and Entering: Act One in Progress]
[Good Thinking! +1 Cunning Point]

Bee's gray Civic pulled onto University Drive a few blocks back, and I sent her one more text.

<Hey. After I get her location, change back - Understudy 3:45>
<You got it boss-lady - Fursona 3:45>

The lights changed from red to green one after the other, with only a second between each. Bee crept forward behind a semi, but Gourmet floored it the second a space opened up in the traffic. I quickly learned that the woman was a speed freak; my sailboard's sail shook and rattled as I dove to keep up.

And worse, as she swerved between a pair of Extras and slid through a red light, I realized she wasn't just fast—she was a menace. Bee's Civic wouldn't be able to keep up, and without her costume, she'd be out of the fight anyway. I took a deep breath and plunged downward; it was up to me to stop her.

With the extra speed from the dive, I caught up—but that wouldn't last. I had to slow Gourmet's hot rod down somehow, or I'd lose her. As she whipped left around a delivery truck, I angled so I'd pass it on the right, just a few feet above a busy sidewalk. The Mustang cut in front of the semi, I ducked in the other way on my sailboard, and I let go of my steering bar with one hand.

"[Stellar Ray!]"
[Dramatic Damage! +1 Drama Point]

The beam punched through Gourmet's open window, catching the villain on her shoulder, and the Mustang wobbled back and forth for a moment before correcting. The window started rolling up, and I tried for one more shot. The [Stellar Ray] crashed into the passenger-side window, leaving a ripple of cracks across it.

[Dramatic Damage! +1 Drama Point]

I got points for damaging Gourmet's car? That hadn't happened during either of the Jumper Episodes last year. I fired off one more ray, which dissipated harmlessly on the car's cherry-red door.

Then Gourmet turned off University and onto the narrow, two-lane Lincoln Street. I bit back a curse; Lincoln was tight, with overhanging fire escapes, lots of stop lights, and an ancient overpass-turned-walking park. Gourmet would have to drive slower, yes, but she'd have plenty of obstacles to shake me on.

It'd be like the Trench Run in *Star Wars*, especially if she could shoot back.

I dove into the oncoming traffic, trying to get on her left side this time. The shattered passenger window had to be blocking her vision—if I could knock out her driver's side, it'd—

"Shit!"

I dove for the sidewalk, barely avoiding the balcony that loomed out in front of me. As I hit the ground, I rolled once, scraping my legs and shoulders on the cracks in the cement. "[Starwave Sail]!"

[HP 7/8]
[Dashing Dodge! +1 Flamboyance Point]
[Gritty Recovery! +1 Grit Point]

I didn't feel dashing as I ducked between street signs and dumpsters. I felt out of control, on the edge, and behind. Gourmet's tail lights flashed at a red light, and she pulled into an alley. I raced to catch up, eyes tearing up from the cold air. If I could stop her, maybe she'd tell me what was *really* going on. We were friends, after all. Kind of.

WHAM!

[HP 6/8]

A white ball slammed into me, sending me into a spin. As I recovered just inches above the dirt alley, I saw Gourmet's left arm reeling back to toss another softball at me. Her mouth chewed furiously on something, and I doubted it was jerky. I pointed my wand. **"[Stellar Ray]!"**

[Dramatic Damage! +1 Drama Point]
[HP 5/8]

The sailboard vanished as I slammed into the ground. I'd scored a hit, but so had Gourmet. I couldn't trade damage like this! She was too tough.

Then her brakes flashed at the end of the alley. A car blocked the way—a gray Civic.

Bianca screamed dramatically, opened her driver-side door, and ran for a nearby monorail station.

"What the fuck?" Gourmet yelled. Her door opened, too, and she got out. The Civic was still running, and she headed straight for the open door.

I couldn't let her get there. She'd *steal* Bee's car! And even if she didn't, she'd move it and carry on with this crazy car chase.

And I couldn't use **[Bit-Part Barrage]**. Sure, I'd probably hit Gourmet a *lot*, but any misses would wreck the old Civic.

I **[Checked the Script]**. There was only one good choice. So as Gourmet clambered into the Civic's driver's seat, I rushed into the Mustang's. She started driving, and I honked the hot rod's horn. "Hey, Gourmet, going somewhere?"

[Good Thinking! +1 Cunning Point]

The Civic stopped. Gourmet got out and stomped toward her Mustang. I'd rarely seen her truly angry, but from the furrows on her brow and her clenched fists and jaw, I'd succeeded in getting her there twice today.

Yay me.

I pushed the door lock down and started rolling up the window, but before I could, her arm shot through and grabbed my neck. As her fingers tightened, I aimed my wand, but not at her. Instead, I pointed it down, next to my feet. "I'll . . . I'll fry your engine. I just . . . just want to talk." I coughed.

[HP 4/8]
[Gritty Sacrifice! +1 Grit Point]

Her grip tightened again. What had she *eaten*? I waggled the wand meaningfully, and she let go, slamming me into the seat. "Fine. Neutral Field. Right here, right now."

"Terms?" I coughed again as air rushed into my lungs.

"I don't mess with the Extra's car, you get out of mine, and we don't kill each other until we're done talking," Gourmet said. "Best deal you're going to get."

"Agreed." I opened the door. "You were so easy to please last semester. Now you're a race-car-driving hardcore villainess. What's with the hot rod?"

[Cool Under Pressure! +1 Drama Point]
[End of Act One! Act Two in Five Minutes!]
[Alias - Understudy] [Archetype - Magical Girl] [Community Rank - 315/523]
[HP 4/8]
[Styles and Skills]
▶Archetype Skill - Transformation Sequence
▶Badass (11)
▶Cunning (13)
▶Drama (36)
▶Stellar Ray 1
▶Bit-Part Barrage 1
▶Flamboyance (1)
▶Signature Skill - Adaptive Armoire
▶Stored Costumes: (Rainy Day, Copy Cat)
▶Starwave Sail 1
▶Quick-Time Change 1
▶Grit (43)
▶I-Frame Transform 1

27

What's the Rush?

"Nothing's wrong. Everything's great. Just fucking peachy," Gourmet said as Fursona hopped up, ready to fight. I waved her down as the supervillain continued. "You're messing up everything, though. Roadrage is gonna be pissed, and I need the win."

"You need the win?" I asked, incredulous. But her expression had shifted. Veins still bulged on her forehead, and her throat was still tight, but her eyes had changed. Instead of burning anger, I saw pain. A lot of pain. "Okay, you need the win, but so do I. We've both got goals here, and—"

"It'd be better for both of us if you backed off, Snack." Gourmet crossed her arms over her chest. It felt like part of her wanted me to, but the rest wanted me to stay.

"I can't do that. I need a win tonight," I said, putting my hands on my hips.

"My mom's sick." It came out as a whisper. "She's sick, and I need the payday."

"Shit." I hadn't thought about something like that, but Gourmet's attitude change suddenly made sense. Her determination—her anger—none of that had been there last semester because her life had been fine. Now, it wasn't. I felt for her. I didn't know what I'd do if Mom or Dad got sick, but running Episodes could be an excellent way to get paid, especially as a villain.

Still, I couldn't see a way for us to win this Episode *and* let her get the payday. What *was* the payday, anyway? It had something to do with this Roadrage villain. But who was he? I needed more information.

"So, your mom's sick, and you're doing villain stuff to pay for treatments or something?" I asked. "Roadrage, whoever he is, is going to, what? Rob an armored truck? Come on, tell me, and maybe we can work something out."

"Close. A prison bus. His henches did something dumb, and now he's gotta get them out of jail. They broke the rules, so henchman protections didn't apply."

"So you're not getting paid for what you loot?" Fursona asked.

Gourmet shook her head and reached for a jerky. "Just on whether or not we win."

"Well, we can't back down, but if we win, I'll give it my all for whatever Episode you want my help with later," I said. "I swear on justice, love, and all those things."

"Hold on. Why are you telling us Roadrage's plan?" Fursona asked.

"I get paid extra if there's an actual fight, so if you won't back off, you might push less hard if you know what's at stake for me. Since you're here, and you won't back off, you can show up instead. Corner of Washington and Jefferson. Five minutes. That's where it'll go down." Gourmet climbed into her Mustang and threw it into reverse. She sounded more like Gourmet than she had for most of our conversation. "So long, Snack. See you soon, Wombat."

"It's Fursona! Fursona!" The kangaroo hero was hopping mad but powerless to do anything as Gourmet left the Neutral Field. "Washington and Jefferson? That's what? Three blocks away? We can get there in five minutes."

[Braking and Entering: Act Two in Progress]

"I have an idea, but we need to test it before the fighting starts." I grinned. "And I don't think you'll like it much."

"Aaaaaaaah!" Fursona screamed as we wobbled through the air on my **[Starwave Sail]**. "Put us down! Put us down!"

I already regretted this brilliant idea, but I couldn't back down now. The kangaroo superhero had wrapped her paws around the steering bar, and I had to struggle against her on every turn. My sailboard wanted to dive; it wasn't built for two, and the extra weight pushed it down, so I had to constantly pull it up into little dips and dives.

We were *not* using **[Starwave Sail]** as intended. But I didn't care because the vast, brick-covered roundabout at the intersection of Washington and Jefferson loomed below us, and it'd only take two minutes.

"Seriously, Understudy! Put me down!" Her panic pushed through the voice modulator's monotone, and I dove for the roundabout's center. Off to the side, I could see Gourmet. She sat on her Mustang's hood, staring at us. And somewhere north of us, I could hear the loud song of an overtuned engine.

That *had* to be Roadrage.

"Don't puke, Fursona. You'll get more comfortable in the air," I said.

She started to retort, but Roadrage's vehicle appeared before she could. The semitruck glowed neon from every surface; even the cab's windshield glowed a bright green. It vomited smog that reflected the riot of colors below it, and on its wide, flat trailer, I could see a swarm of minions waving weapons and readying what looked like two massive turrets, each with glowing spears attached to chains.

"Roadrage, I'm Magical Girl Understudy, and it's time to exit stage left!" I shouted. I couldn't tell if he heard me, though. Instead, the eighteen-wheeler accelerated, heading straight for us. It slammed into the roundabout's curb and hopped into the air, then crushed bricks as metal screeched against concrete. Fursona dodged left, I ducked right, and the air filled with diesel fumes, smog, and reddish brick dust.

[Cool Catchphrase! +1 Flamboyance Point]

When it cleared, the eighteen-wheeler sat high-sided in the middle of the roundabout, the trailer's spiked wheels still spinning in ruts they'd dug in the soft, decorative bricks. A swarm of minions clambered down—at least a dozen shouting, weapon-brandishing henchmen in motorcycle helmets, carrying wrenches, lugnut removers, and other mechanics' tools—but my attention was glued to the cab, which had tipped to its side. The passenger door flew open, and Roadrage pulled himself out.

Roadrage's Costume looked like something from an old TV car show if you covered it in neon tubes and painted it black. His racing helmet's visor glowed a red so bright it was almost white, and his leather racing suit featured glowing red-and-yellow neon threads that formed patterns across his arms and chest. He pointed a jet-black glove at Fursona, then silently waved his minions forward.

Then he pointed at the eighteen-wheeler, and the semitruck's cab shimmered and vanished. In its place sat a motorcycle, but one with no wheels. Instead, a trio of small jet engines sat where the tires should have been. He hopped on and pressed a button, and a cannon sprouted from the windshield, facing forward. Before I could stop him, he catapulted into the air and started strafing Fursona, who had her paws full fighting the minions.

"[Starwave Sail]!" I shouted. If the villain wanted an air campaign, I'd show him an air campaign!

I'd done this before, of course, with LABRAT and the Panic Pals. I'd never tried it against a villain like Roadrage, though. As the speeder bike and my sailboard circled the roundabout far below, both of us looking for opportunities to attack, I watched him maneuver. He turned quickly, but his weapon was fixed; he'd need to face me to fire it, and I could probably keep out from in front of him.

We traded a few shots—lasers from him, [Stellar Rays] from me—but neither of us could hit from this range. We'd have to close the gap somehow.

I cut in first. The sailboard's sail dipped as I tightened my turn, dashing through the sky toward the villain, who turned in a second later. My wand pointed right at him as we passed like two charging bulls. "[Stellar Ray]!"

[Dramatic Damage! +1 Drama Point]

His laser seared a hole in my pink-and-blue sail a second later. He arced through the air, just like LABRAT had, but then turned on a dime and ducked behind me.

[A Vigilante is Joining the Fight]

The message popped up out of nowhere, disappearing as I blinked it away. I didn't have time to deal with a vigilante right now! I juked left, dodging a laser barrage, then right. But no matter what I did, I couldn't shake him! His bike stuck to my sailboard like glue, and it was only a matter of time before—

PEW!

The laser slammed into my side as I jerked the handle an instant too late, burning a hole through my Understudy Costume and scalding my skin. Out of control, I rolled through the air, the sailboard disappearing from underneath me.

[HP 3/8]

The ground grew closer and closer as I flailed for something that wasn't there. A second from landing, I twisted around and used the first power that came to mind. **[Bit-Part Barrage]** froze me in midair, and I aimed at the first target I saw: the big rig's trailer.

Specifically, one of the harpoon launchers.

[**Dramatic Damage! +1 Drama Point**]
[**Dramatic Damage! +1 Drama Point**]
[**Dramatic Damage! +1 Drama Point**]

BOOM!

The turret exploded as beam after beam slammed into it, hundreds of pounds of compressed air ripping free from the massive tank that launched the harpoon. The giant spear shot forward a dozen feet before gouging into the roundabout's bricks.

A moment later, I resumed my fall—but only for a second. Then I cratered into the bricks. I'd said they were soft before, but it didn't feel like it now. The air whooshed from my lungs, and I coughed to try resetting my breathing.

[HP 2/8]

As I picked myself up, lasers slammed into the bricks around me. I used **[Quick-Time Change]**, did the Itsy Bitsy Spider, and **[I-Frame Transformed]** a pair of laser shots, cursing myself that I hadn't thought to start a combo. I'd have to deal with Roadrage the old-fashioned way.

And the villain certainly wasn't interested in fighting me on even footing. He strafed back and forth, shooting as I dodged right and left, punching henchmen with **[Spotlight Strike]** where I could. I *had* a combo I could use with just Rainy Day, but no good windows to use it in.

[Stylish Strike! +1 Flamboyance Point]
[Stylish Strike! +1 Flamboyance Point]

Suddenly, the lasers stopped, and the henchmen ran toward the trailer and the last harpoon launcher. It spun around ponderously, engine whining, then lowered until it aimed straight down Washington Street.

Straight at the bus barreling toward the intersection.

The navy-blue bus, so dark it almost looked black, featured a golden star in a circle and the words *Lewisville Henchman Penitentiary Work Crew* under the picture. It revved its engine, the sound almost as deep and loud as Roadrage's big rig, and accelerated into the roundabout.

TWUNG!

The last harpoon launcher fired. I watched as the massive bolt sliced into the bus, just below the rows of seats. It pulled taut a moment later, jerking the prison bus to a halt. The engine revved, but an even more high-pitched sound filled the air as the harpoon launcher wound its chain tighter and tighter. It dragged the bus back, even though, by the cloud of rubber smoke, the pedal was to the metal.

"Can you stop it?" Fursona shouted.

"Yes!" I shouted. I didn't know if I could. "Just get me closer!"

I used **[Thunderhead]**, casting a shadow over the intersection as clouds rolled in and the anvil-like shape of a storm formed. The air grew electric. Fursona charged the remaining henchmen, kicking, punching, and smashing minions with her cybernetic, animatronic tail. And I ran into the gap she'd made.

PEW! PEW!

Two lasers slammed into the ground next to me, missing by inches, and Roadrage's bike roared overhead. My hair practically stood on end. Another three steps. Two. I **[Rode the Lightning]**.

[Electric Lightshow! +1 Flamboyance Point]
[Thunderstruck! +1 Drama Point]

BOOM!

The remaining harpoon launcher's tank blew as lightning ripped across it and the minion behind the controls. The whole semitrailer tipped this time, tossing henchmen into the air. The bus pulled forward, dragging it closer and closer to us—and to the downed henchmen Fursona and I had taken out.

Then the chain gave with a crack, and the bus lurched. It stood on two wheels for a moment, then crashed to its side in a spray of glass. Tires spun in the air, and Roadrage landed on the overturned bus. He wrenched the bus's door open with a metal screech.

I ran toward him, trying to get in range for **[Spotlight Strike]**, but he dragged two henches onto his bike before I could. Others pulled themselves through the door and started running every which way while Roadrage took to the air.

As they ran, I caught a glimpse of Gourmet's car. But Gourmet was missing. Where the hell had she been? With her in the fight, Roadrage would have won for sure.

I pulled up the System message I'd ignored just as a half-dozen animals ran toward the downed bus, a boy in a white hoodie and multicolored plaid scarf right behind them.

[A Vigilante is Joining the Fight]
[Name: Vigilant Vow]
[Shifting Alliances: Multiple factions of heroes. Choose your relationship]
[Ally] [Neutral] [Enemy] [Rival]

28

Rival

I recognized Stella-Lunar's owl, two pastel cats belonging to Magical Girls Sugar and Chili Powder, and a weasel I couldn't place. The familiars vomited beams of light and magical attacks into the fleeing former prisoners, going wherever Vigilant Vow pointed. **[Moon Rays]** exploded against traffic barriers, the two cats pounced on a henchman who hadn't surrendered or been knocked out, and the weasel chased down a man, tripped him, and leaped on his back.

Vigilant Vow tapped another crystal, and a gigantic rubber ducky appeared. The thing was easily four feet tall, and it faced the few henchmen we hadn't beaten yet. The vigilante cleared his throat. "I swear to clean up crime in this town. We won't stop until we've flip-flopped the villains, combed the city for criminals, and brushed off our enemies. I'm quick, clean, and ready to wash the scene."

The moment he finished his vow, the ducky inhaled, inflating until it looked ready to pop, and let out a stream of pinkish bubbles—just like Rainy Day's **[Stellar Ray]**, but much bigger. Henchmen flew through the air and crashed against the overturned trailer or shattered bricks as they popped.

I thought for a moment. An alliance would help both of us. We'd be able to take down Roadrage and win the Episode. But he had the lead on the community rankings. Fursona and I couldn't work with him. No way! I chose **[Rival]**.

[Magical Boy Vigilant Vow Has Chosen Rival]
[Magical Girl Understudy Has Chosen Rival]
[Fursona Has Chosen Neutral. Choice Overridden by Majority]
[Community Ranking and Role Focus Points will be divided based on contribution.]

Shit, I thought.

"Magical Girl Understudy, I presume?" Vigilant Vow said. Dark shadows played across his white hoodie, imitating Stella-Lunar's Star Form. He ignored his familiars as they bubbled, tripped, clawed, and energy-beamed minions and escaping prisoners all around us. "How about we split up the Episode? You hunt down the cons, I'll chase down Roadrage, and we'll get this done."

Something about his smarmy attitude and perfectly wrapped plaid scarf rubbed me the wrong way. I decided right away that I didn't like him, and not just because he was my [Rival] now. "No, we're taking down Roadrage. If you want the minions, go for it, but we've got him." I started transforming back to Magical Girl Understudy.

[Rejuvenation Activated: HP 6/8]

"A race, then," Vigilant Vow laughed. "Come on, Iyago. Let's go, Sprinkles and Frosting. Bubble-Bill, we have villains to destroy."

One by one, the familiars either vanished into their crystals—which floated near Vigilant Vow's head—or, in Iyago's case, flapped over to land on his shoulder. Once he'd assembled his team, he nodded. "See you later, haters!"

"Not if we see you first! Fursona, get ready to fly!"

"Really, Understudy?" Fursona complained, but she hopped over, letting me position her so the board wouldn't overbalance immediately. It'd be a bumpy ride no matter what, but we couldn't let Vigilant Vow get too far ahead, and I didn't know if he'd attack us to win the Episode. Our best chance was speed.

As we took off, sailboard wobbling and dipping, Fursona cleared her throat. "We should catch any prisoners we come across. It'll help pad our ratings in case Vigilant Vow beats Roadrage without us."

"Sure. We'll bomb them," I said.

"Bomb them?"

"You'll see," I said. *You won't like it, though*, I didn't say.

Fursona screamed the whole first bombing run.

She screamed as we dove toward the fleeing henchman. She screamed when I pulled up on the steering bar and pushed her off the sailboard. And she kept screaming until she slammed feet-first into the fleeing minion. Then she finally stopped. "Hey, that's worth a *ton* of Style Points!"

[Badass Bomber! +1 Badass Point]
[Dramatic Assist! +1 Drama Point]
[Clever Plan! +1 Cunning Point]

"Yeah, it is! Get back on here, and let's do it again!" I shouted as I landed near her. The henchman groaned underneath the kangaroo-sized weight that'd smashed him into the sidewalk, cursing, while Fursona climbed off him. He wasn't going anywhere, but a casual inspection showed that his point of superhero damage had taken the hit. Most of it, at least.

Could I have used [**Stellar Ray**] instead? Absolutely. But I wanted to see if the drop-kangaroo plan would work because even at Rank Two, [**Stellar Ray**] lacked the punch I needed for bigger fights. Besides, splitting up right now seemed like a bad idea. We'd find Roadrage faster, but we'd be split up against a minor-league villain when we did. Playing it safe would be better since I doubted Vigilant Vow could solo Roadrage. Of course, *something* had happened to Gourmet, and I wasn't sure what.

I heard shouting and fighting sounds from the next block over and took off, Fursona searching for another target. "Get a little lower this time. I'll jump instead of you pushing! I don't like it when you push!" she shouted over the wind.

"Got it!"

But as we soared around the skyscrapers and down Franklin Street, we realized another bombing run wasn't in the cards. Vigilant Vow had his whole familiar swarm out, and though a few henches fought on, they wouldn't last much longer. Fursona shook a paw angrily. "He's stealing our Style Points," she muttered.

"Yeah. We have to find Roadrage. He's the key to the Episode." The last of the henchmen threw his hands up as Iyago, Sprinkles, and Bubble-Bill cornered him. I turned my sailboard away. Wherever Roadrage had gone, we'd just gotten the jump on Vigilant Vow.

[End of Act Two! Act Three in Five Minutes!]
[Alias - Understudy] [Archetype - Magical Girl] [Community Rank - 315/523]
[HP 6/8]
[Styles and Skills]
▶Archetype Skill - Transformation Sequence
▶Badass (12)
▶Cunning (14)
▶Drama (42)
▶Stellar Ray 1
▶Bit-Part Barrage 1
▶Flamboyance (5)
▶Signature Skill - Adaptive Armoire
▶Stored Costumes: (Rainy Day, Copy Cat)
▶Starwave Sail 1
▶Quick-Time Change 1
▶Grit (43)
▶I-Frame Transform 1

[Braking and Entering: Act Three in Progress]

I shouldn't have worried about finding Roadrage. The villains I'd fought before had all been at least a little subtle, though. Theseus had used Gourmet as a distraction. Jumper didn't even want to fight. Even the Anti-Naptime League had maneuvered the Playpen Patrol around before their final confrontations.

By contrast, Roadrage's neon speeder bike stuck out like a sore thumb over the Lincoln Park district. The moment we whipped around an apartment tower, he dove. I expected the villain to make a run for it; he had what he wanted, and it didn't make much sense to stand and fight.

But Roadrage wasn't a subtle one. He landed in the middle of Roosevelt Avenue.

"We're gonna bomb him!" I shouted. His henchmen hopped off the bike as the wind whipped around us. I squinted against the frigid air as the smell of chemicals and diesel filled my nose. "Three! Two! One!"

Fursona jumped, screaming the whole way down but tackling a henchman and quickly punching him unconscious as I skimmed the asphalt. She turned toward the other one, but Roadrage beat her to the punch. He pointed his finger, and the speeder bike disappeared a moment later. In its place sat . . . a sphere.

A glowing red sphere, with another smaller glowing green sphere inside. Roadrage and the remaining henchman sat inside in a pair of comfortable-looking chairs, a joystick between them. I couldn't see a single weapon on the . . . whatever the thing was, but Roadrage looked like he planned on a fight.

Still . . . we had the advantage. He couldn't hit us from range, and we could hit him.

"Hang on! Don't jump!" I shouted, diving toward him. The second I let go of the steering bar to use my wand, the whole sailboard overbalanced, and I had to pull a hard left to stay in the air. Roadrage pointed at me, then ran a thumb across his neck. The ball surged forward, spinning silently in contrast to his deafening semitruck or howling speeder bike. Then it popped into the air right beneath us. The force smashed the magical sailboard apart, and all four of us—the two sphere riders, Fursona, and I—crashed to the ground.

[HP 5/8]
[**Gritty Recovery! +1 Grit Point**]

I hit the ground and rolled just as the neon sphere zipped by, turned, and charged at me like a bull. Roadrage stared at me momentarily, his passenger hanging on to a pair of grips with white knuckles. Then I fired a **[Stellar Ray]** at the neon-tinted, transparent pod. Nothing seemed to happen, but I got a Style Point message, so I must have hit *something*.

[**Dramatic Damage! +1 Drama Point**]

The sphere turned and charged at me, intent on running me down. I started sprinting, but it only rolled faster, the inside somehow offering a smooth ride even as the outside's neon flashed faster and faster. Fursona tried to knock it off-course with a **[Double-Kick]**, but it zipped past her feet. It was going to hit. I couldn't stop it.

A massive white lance of energy shoved Roadrage's orb to the side. It slammed into an apartment building, shattering windows as it rolled almost a story up. I stared at my rival and the two-headed white owl familiar; Vigilant Vow had saved me.

"I swear to defend Tokyexico in starlight and under new moon. To stand against evil and corruption. And, above all, to remain true to what's right and just. So witness star, so witness moon." The words were Stella-Lunar's, but the voice was Vigilant Vow's.

But the vigilante didn't speak to me. He barely acknowledged I existed. His silhouette glowed a brilliant orange around his otherwise-black body. Miniature solar flares arced across his glowing aura, and the shadows bent wildly all along the street. I recognized that look; he was in Stella-Lunar's Eclipse Form. He summoned the giant rubber ducky, which squeaked and started spraying bubbles across the battlefield. The two cats joined it a moment later.

Roadrage flipped the bird at Vigilant Vow and floored it right at the vigilante. Part of me wanted to let him get hit, but realistically, he'd help win the Episode. We needed to box him out once we'd cracked Roadrage's egg. "Roadrage! Duck!" I used **[Bit-Part Barrage]**, filling the night with **[Stellar Rays]**. He couldn't duck.

[Dramatic Damage! +1 Drama Point]
[Dramatic Damage! +1 Drama Point]
[Dramatic Damage! +1 Drama Point]

I hit three times, which felt low. On the other hand, those three rays pushed Roadrage off-course and into the bubble slick Bubble-Bill had laid out. The globe lost control, spinning wildly and shaking the riders inside. It slammed into the rubber ducky a moment later, which disappeared with a long, mournful squeak.

Fursona got a good kick in before Roadrage got moving again, but much as I hated to admit it, Eclipse Form Vigilant Vow's swarm of familiars were the stars of the show. Rays, beams, and a golden-red lasso lashed out at the villain's ride. Vigilant Vow *had* to be ahead on the community rankings for this one. Worse, I'd just used my most powerful move short of a combo. How much longer would Eclipse Form last? Stella-Lunar's forms rotated, and Eclipse lasted the shortest. Maybe we could get control of the fight again once it faded.

Or maybe the play was to get control now.

The sphere rolled toward me, flattening a familiar, which vanished. "Roadkill," the henchman laughed.

I planted my feet, activated **[Power-Weaving]**, and waved for Roadrage to bring it on. As the sphere flashed toward me, I used **[Quick-Time Change]** to switch to

Rainy Day, activating [**I-Frame Transform**]. The ball still ran over me, but I popped right back up, unharmed.

[**Flashy Fitting Room!** +1 Flamboyance Point]
[**Steel Yourself!** +1 Grit Point]
[**Floating Points: 1 Flamboyance**]

I used [**Thunderhead**] as Roadrage flipped around, but Stella-Lunar's familiar took another Eclipse-empowered shot as the clouds built. The [**Moon Ray**] tore across the battlefield, engulfing the orb in crackling white energy, then slopping over it and onto me. The light burned at my skin; the same solar flares that'd leaped across the vigilante's golden-orange aura sparked back and forth over me.

[**HP 1/8**]

My eyes narrowed, and my throat tightened even as the beam finally stopped. Vigilant Vow had shot me on purpose. It'd look like friendly fire on the TV, but he'd planned it. I started to say something, but his Eclipse Form ended before I could. I'd deal with him later; Fursona and I had to press the advantage and win the Episode.

[**Pause for Effect!** +1 Drama Point]
[**Floating Points: 3 Flamboyance, 1 Grit**]

The clouds finished forming, and I turned my attention to Roadrage's neon ball. [**Ride the Lightning's**] lightning tendrils crashed into it, and between that and the Eclipsed [**Moon Ray**], the ball shattered and vanished.

[**Electric Lightshow!** +1 Flamboyance Point]
[**Thunderstruck!** +1 Drama Point]
[**Power-Weaving!** +6 Flamboyance, +3 Grit, +1 Drama Point]

Without his ride, Roadrage would be vulnerable. Fursona, Vigilant Vow, his familiar army, and I all dashed toward the vehicle-less villain, but just as we got close, Vigilant Vow skidded to a stop. He held a hand to his ear momentarily, then turned without a word and disappeared down the same alley he'd come from.

"You two are on your own now," the henchman said, grinning menacingly as Roadrage summoned a brand-new, ethereally glowing eighteen-wheeler. "Your friend must've gotten a flat tire."

29

Flat Tire

What. The. Fuck.

Vigilant Vow had abandoned the fight in what should have been our moment of triumph—or his. Part of me wanted to hunt him down and figure out why, but Roadrage—and the key to winning the Episode—stood right in front of us. I took a step toward him and his henchman.

The air shimmered as he pointed with a gloved hand, and the sphere vanished. A second later, the whole street filled with shimmering neon steel. He'd brought back his eighteen-wheeler! The semitruck's diesel exhaust choked the air, and the asphalt rumbled as the engine idled.

But Roadrage himself didn't take the wheel. Just before the big rig started moving, I saw that his henchman sat in the driver's seat while he rode shotgun. He racked an actual shotgun with an unpleasant chunking sound.

I gulped. This Episode kept getting more and more dangerous.

The truck rolled away, slowly at first, then picking up steam as it pulled off Pine and roared toward the overpasses. I could either finish Roadrage or hunt down Vigilant Vow—not both.

"**[Starwave Sail]**!" I shouted. I did a loop over Pine Street and dipped low, grabbing Fursona and pulling her onto the board, which wobbled and nearly hit the ground before I pulled up. She screamed into her voice modulator while I pushed her into a balanced position.

[Flashy Pickup! +1 Flamboyance Point]

"How much superhero damage do you have left?" I asked. I was tapped out, and we needed a plan to take out the big rig and, hopefully, finish off Roadrage.

"Four! What are you thinking?"

"Bombing run! Get on the trailer, and I'll support you from the air! If I see a chance, I'll try to land and help out, too, but I'm almost out of the fight!" The wind howled past us, and the glowing neon semitruck rumbled up the on-ramp onto I-25 and plowed north, ignoring the cars in its way. "Gotta do it now!"

"Fine!" Fursona snapped. She tensed, ready to jump, and I dove.

My eyes stung, but I couldn't close them. Goosebumps covered my skin from the frigid wind. As we descended, the trailer grew faster and faster, its empty flatbed a perfect landing strip. "Now!" I shouted, hitting Fursona's shoulder. She jumped a moment later and rolled onto the flat steel bed.

[Badass Bomber! +1 Badass Point]

"You good?" I shouted. Fursona flashed me a thumbs-up and started hopping toward the semi's cab. I nodded and pulled up. The lighter sailboard rocketed ahead of Roadrage's semi, leaving a blue-and-pink trail over the neon red-and-green eighteen-wheeler.

BAM!

Roadrage's shotgun blasted into the air, tearing off his passenger-side mirror. Pellets filled the air, but the few pellets that went my way slammed harmlessly into the sailboard's bottom. I looked back to see the villain pulling his gun back inside. "**[Stellar Ray]**!" The beam caught his arm, and the shotgun clattered to the road. Ten thousand pounds of semitrailer crushed it a second later.

[Dramatic Damage! +1 Drama Point]
[Smart Shooting! +1 Cunning Point]

Then the semi door opened, and Roadrage swung out. He grabbed a steel handle on the truck's side, thumped against its body, and reached for another near the smoke-belching exhaust. Then he jumped and landed on the trailer—right in front of Fursona.

I could only watch as the villain and my sidekick traded blows, rolling and grappling on the semitruck's bed. Fursona looked like she was winning, but as she reeled her feet back for a **[Double Kick]** that'd shove the villain off the trailer, he slammed a fist into his watch, and walls, a roof, and a pair of open back doors shimmered into existence. Just before they solidified, she kicked, and he rolled. Two roo-foot-sized dents appeared in the trailer's wall.

Then I lost sight of them. I fired a **[Stellar Ray]** into the trailer's wall, but though it also left a solid dent, it didn't break through. When I circled to check the back, the doors slammed shut. Fursona was on her own.

I couldn't help my sidekick, but I *could* stop the semi. I looped around to the front. The driver's hand flashed out of the window, his middle finger extended, and the green safety glass rolled up.

Maybe I could wreck the semi just like I had Jumper's van? "**[Stellar Ray]**!" The beam fired off toward the truck's grill but didn't penetrate. Instead, a black burn mark appeared on the red-hot chrome.

I had one more move. Roadrage's rig shoved a city bus to the side, blocking traffic behind us. Not a single car on the road could stand up to the neon big rig's weight and armor, but the Poudre Canyon Bridge arced over the river ahead of us; if I could break up the windshield like I had Gourmet's window, the hench would have to stop or risk driving into the water below. Surely, he wouldn't be crazy enough to keep going with that kind of danger.

I'd used my [**Bit-Part Barrage**] and [**Quick-Time Change**] combo, so it was a race. Could I bust enough of the windshield to stop the rig before he got to the other side? I fired one [**Stellar Ray**] after another into the windshield. On the third, it finally started to shatter—only for a flamethrower to shimmer into reality on the semi's hood. It filled the air with fire, and I fell back. Had I done enough damage to stop Roadrage's big rig?

[**Dramatic Damage! +1 Drama Point**]

No.

The truck hopped the median, the trailer bouncing up into the air. Both doors flew open, though Fursona and Roadrage managed to stay inside. I could only imagine how beat up they both were from that.

The semi accelerated, and I raced up and fired another [**Stellar Ray**] into the windshield. I had to stop it before it killed someone!

[**Dramatic Damage! +1 Drama Point**]

Cars pulled out of the way or were shoved aside as the neon semi barreled across the bridge in the wrong lane. It weaved back and forth, and a tire blew. I saw the windshield just before the flamethrower turned on again—it shattered completely. Then the air filled with heat, and I pulled up, looping around.

Only to see a tanker truck screaming toward Roadrage's. Its brakes screeched, but I could already tell it wouldn't be enough to stop.

I needed to make sure Bee was fine. Then I could save the Extra driving the tanker. And if I had time, I'd get to the henchman. No one had died on a Magical Girl Understudy Episode yet, and I didn't want to change that today. I'd try, I decided. I'd try *really* hard.

As Roadrage's semi and the oncoming tanker truck closed in on each other, the Poudre River far below, I dove toward them. The trailer doors opened, and Roadrage and Fursona tumbled onto the highway, kicking and punching. Fursona grappled with the villain, trying not to let him touch his watch again. I relaxed just the tiniest bit. Bee was safe. Well, safe-ish.

The tanker truck driver, though? He jammed on his horn, trying to get Roadrage's eighteen-wheeler out of his lane. Then he tried to dodge, but the neon semi was out of control. I poured on the speed, accelerating past the glowing trailer, the driver's side door, and into the rapidly closing space between the two big rigs.

The Extra trucker's door opened, and he threw himself out—off the bridge and two hundred feet down toward the frigid Poudre River. I dove, sail snapping back and forth like a whip.

Ten feet. Five.

[Dramatic Rescue! +1 Drama Point Pending]

I grabbed the Extra's hand and pulled out of my dive. I still had time. I could still get the henchman. A big rig's horn screamed behind me, and I whipped around in time to see the two semis collide.

The cabs crunched first, collapsing like soda cans with a horrible crumpling sound and screaming steel. Then, a moment later, Roadrage's trailer folded in on itself. I watched the shockwave ripple across it almost in slow motion. Sparks flew, brakes squealed, and both semis folded until they were virtually unrecognizable.

And then the tanker's tank blew.

There wasn't a roar. It didn't sound like any explosion I'd heard before. Instead, a flat *Whump!* filled the air. The fireball lit up the Poudre River—and half of Tokyexico City. Air whooshed out of my lungs as the shockwave rolled over the Extra and me, shoving us down toward the water. I fled the expanding fireball.

[Don't Look At Explosions! +1 Badass Point Pending]
[HP 0/8]

After an eternity, it stopped and faded into smoke, the crackling of fire, and the stink of burning gas. I looped around, dropping the shaking, sweating Extra off a safe distance away on the bridge. Despite the explosion, it looked more or less stable, and I had business on the bridge.

I landed next to Fursona and Roadrage; the kangaroo had somehow pinned the helmeted villain so he couldn't get to his watch—which meant he couldn't summon another vehicle and keep the chase going. As I dashed up, the villain relaxed and stopped pounding his free fist on Fursona's fursuit. The Episode was over, except for the sign-off.

"You take this one," I said to Fursona. I had a sinking feeling, and I ran toward the tanker truck's burning wreckage—the neon eighteen-wheeler vanished right in front of me.

Leaving an unmoving body on the ground.

[Episode Finished!]
[Episode: Braking and Entering - PG-13]
[Penalties: N/A]
[Episode Finished! +5 of each Style Point]

[Winner Winner! +2 of each Style Point]

[Rival: Vigilant Vow Contributed 20% to Victory! -20% Role Focus and Rank]

[Role Focus: Flamboyance + Badass - Goal Partially Met! +8 Flamboyance Points]

[Alias - Understudy] [Archetype - Magical Girl] [Community Rank - 299/523]

[HP 0/8]

[Styles and Skills]

▶Archetype Skill - Transformation Sequence

▶Badass (21)

▶Cunning (22)

▶Drama (60) (Skill Roll Available)

▶Stellar Ray 2

▶Bit-Part Barrage 1

▶Flamboyance (33)

▶Signature Skill - Adaptive Armoire

▶Stored Costumes: (Rainy Day, Copy Cat)

▶Starwave Sail 1

▶Quick-Time Change 1

▶Grit (48) (Skill Roll Available)

▶I-Frame Transform 1

[50 Drama Credits Used. Rolling Skill!]

I rolled my skill, dashing to the battered, mangled henchman lying on the asphalt. The one point of superhero damage hadn't been enough, but he was still alive. I covered up his wounds, packing them with his jacket and trying to keep pressure on the worst ones. Every time I dealt with something, a new problem came up.

[Rank-Up! Hometown Heroine 2: Keep up the pace for longer]

<Leave him,> Tails said in my mind. I ignored her, fighting to keep him alive, then fighting the EMTs who tried to get past me. I blinked. *<It's okay, they've got him. You can go.>*

I blinked again. Flashing red-and-blue lights filled the evening sky on the Poudre Canyon Bridge, and sirens screamed. A pair of police officers wrestled Roadrage into a squad car while another held up his watch and dropped it into an evidence bag. Another looked at me, clearly unwilling to confront me but under orders to do so. "Miss, I'm supposed to get your statement about what happened. As ranking super on the case, it's TPD policy to get your statement as evidence. Not that we'll prosecute the guy. His lawyers will have him out tomorrow."

"Of . . . of course." I was still shell-shocked, and I stared back at the hench-man as the medics strapped him onto a stretcher and shoved an oxygen mask over his face. "I'll tell you everything I know. Just make sure I know if he lives, okay?"

"You got it. Soon as we know, we'll be in touch."

30

We'll Be in Touch

SATURDAY, FEBRUARY 14

The phone rang for the first time while I was doing my make-up.

It was Valentine's Day, and I'd told Bee I was cooking, then we'd watch an Episode or two. Neither of us needed a night out, and Magical Girl Ramsey Fieri could out-cook most restaurant chefs. And since we'd successfully beaten Roadrage, we had the time.

Not that the victory had been bloodless.

When my phone rang, my first thought was the police. I'd asked them to call me as soon as they knew the henchman's status. I hadn't slept much last night; if he died, he'd be the first Extra whose death I was responsible for. I didn't know how to feel about that. On one hand, he'd been henching, so he wasn't technically an Extra. On the other hand, I kept running scenarios for how I could beat Roadrage without the explosion, the rescue, or having to watch the EMTs cart him away.

I picked up the phone without looking. "How is he?"

"Aaaaay! You really came through, DuPont, you know that?" Rocko's voice filled my ears and blared from the speaker. I winced. "Minor-league wins look good for *Heroics 101*, even if they take a *lot* more editing. And you beat out Vigilant Vow! Solid performance, lots of drama at the end with the flying catch and the explosion. The drones loved it. Loved it!"

Rocko never called after Episodes. Something was up, but they'd tell me soon enough. "Thanks. I told you I'd do it."

"You did, you did, but I didn't quite believe you—and I'll be honest, when Vow fried you with that [**Moon Ray**], I thought you were gonna lose for sure. Now listen, I didn't call to chit-chat about the Episode. Something went down at Cartman's Studio last night while we were filming. I only heard about it an hour ago, but Stella's producer seemed pissed. They had it out, a full-on screaming match in the Hot Zone, then ducked into Cartman's for more. That was, uh, ten minutes before Vigilant Vow left."

"What does that mean?" I'd assumed Vigilant Vow was being a coward, leaving as Eclipse Form faded, but what if he'd been called off? What did that mean for our race? Surely Cartman wanted him to win; they wouldn't pull him out of an Episode where he had a good chance of victory for nothing. Something was up, but I couldn't think of what.

"I don't know. I wasn't there to see the fight, but if you get an Episode in the next couple of days, take it. Do every Episode you've got a chance of winning. We could build up a lead if Cartman's gets shut down temporarily. Now's our chance to go, go, go!"

My phone buzzed. This *had* to be the call I'd been waiting for. "Will do. Gotta take this other call, Rocko."

"No problem. Push hard, DuPont!"

The second Rocko hung up, I answered the phone, my make-up half finished. "Magical Girl Understudy!"

"Detective Rathburn, TCPD. Miss, you asked for a status update on a hospitalized henchman, correct?"

"Yes." My heart pounded. Was he okay? Had he lived? I held my breath as Detective Rathburn shuffled some papers, my mascara temporarily forgotten.

"According to the doctors, it's still pretty touch and go. He's in intensive care, and he'll be there for a while. The explosion hit him way harder than Extras' and henches' protections could handle."

"That's it?" I asked. That couldn't be it. Alive, but in the ICU—that wasn't any better than not knowing.

"Miss, is this your first near-death?" Detective Rathburn asked.

"Yes."

"Call the Tokyexico Council of Heroes, kid. They've got programs for first-timers to work through it. You're not the first to get in over your head and not be able to save everyone. I've had to shoot a few times myself, and I've lost people because I couldn't get there fast enough or I missed a clue on an investigation. You're not alone." His voice had shifted; it felt less formal and much more like he was talking to a teammate or comrade.

Then he continued, and the formality was right back in his voice. "I'll keep you updated until we're sure he's going to survive, but understand there are things I can't tell you. Confidentiality applies to suspects and patients. Goodbye, MG Understudy."

I didn't say anything. The phone beeped as Detective Rathburn hung up. Of *course* there'd be resources out there for this. The Council of Heroes wouldn't just let their supers go through someone dying on their watch—I couldn't bring myself to think "killing someone"—on their own. I made a mental note to call them on Monday. That'd be soon enough to schedule support. And honestly, the idea that someone *had* thought about this, even if I hadn't, helped. I reached for my make-up brushes.

The phone rang just as I finished the mascara and started applying bright red lipstick.

"Holy shit," I muttered. My phone never blew up like this. I didn't recognize the number, but the area code matched Su-Bin's—a Tokyexico City number. I pressed the Answer button and held it to my ear. "Yes?"

"Magical Girl Understudy, this is Vigilant Vow."

I froze up. How had he gotten my number? I certainly hadn't given it to him! And why was he calling me? What was going on here?!

He kept speaking, voice cold as he monologued at me. "I know you're there, so I'll say what I called to say. My time messing around here is over. I'm dropping from my soccer and trivia teams on Monday. That'll free me up to *really* push. You won't be able to compete if last night's the best you've got. I'm pretty consistently winning minor-league fights solo."

"You shouldn't play sports as a super, cheater. Why are you telling me this?" I asked, throat tight. This was moving too fast. He sounded like Theseus or Monologue, not like a vigilante.

"To get you to quit. The kid gloves are coming off."

Something about that comment upset me, and before I knew it, I was shouting into the phone. "Kid gloves? What are you playing at? You're like sixteen! All you *have* are kid gloves! We've got you beat; you just haven't realized it yet. And your producer's in trouble, huh?"

He went silent for a moment. I laughed. "That's what I thought. This feels like a last-ditch effort to get me out of the way. There's no other competition, is there? If you push *Heroics 101* out of the race, it won't matter how messed up your schedule gets or if *Vowsworn* goes on hiatus. You'll win. Well, I've got bad news for you. I'm not done. Last night went badly after you left, but Fursona and I still got the win."

Bee chose that moment to open the green room's door, saw me on the phone, and raised an eyebrow. I mouthed "VV" at her while the vigilante went off about how he hadn't used close to his full strength and how some setback he wouldn't name couldn't slow him down.

"Hang up on him," Bee mouthed.

I nodded and pressed the button just as he threatened to, and I quote, "Leave me as powerless as an Extra."

"What. A. Jerk," I muttered. My phone buzzed.

<Im coming for your Episodes, MGUS - VV 3:14>
<Watch yourself. Dont make an enemy you cant handle - VV 3:14>

I showed Bee, forcing a smile. The text felt like one more dose of threat on top of everything else, and it worried me, but today wasn't about Vigilant Vow. It was about spoiling Bee. There was only one thing I could send back that'd work *and* give her a laugh before I blocked him.

<Meh - Understudy 3:16>

Bee finished slurping her spaghetti, and I laughed. Her face and shirt were covered with sauce splatters, and her cup had spaghetti lip stains on its rim. "You've got to figure out your manners, Bianca."

She paused, then wiped her mouth on her sleeve. "Nah. That was great. What's next?"

"Cleanup. Magical Girl Ramsey Fieri cooks, and Bianca Marino cleans. That's the deal."

"Really? On Valentine's Day?"

I nodded seriously, watched as she pouted, walked toward the kitchen, and then laughed. "Get your butt back here. All this will keep until later."

"Nope, I've gotta clean up," Bee snarked. "That's the deal."

I put my hands on my hips. "Bianca, couch, now. There's supposed to be a new Stella-Lunar Episode tonight, and I'm not missing that to watch you put dishes in the dishwasher. Supposedly, she's fighting a whole rogue's gallery of lower-powered majors and high minors as she attacks 3V1L's lair. It'll be wild."

Bianca pretended to waffle, and I rolled my eyes. Then, I sweetened the deal. "It's a live Episode, too. Stella-Lunar POV mixed with camera drone footage, thirty-second delay, the works."

"Ooh, fun!" She abandoned the stack of plates on the counter, hurrying to the couch and patting it. "Come on, Annie. We're supposed to watch the Stella-Lunar Episode tonight. It's live!"

I rolled my eyes again and settled down, arm around Bee. Usually, I wouldn't have bothered with actual TV, not when streaming older Episodes worked so well, but even major leaguers only did live Episodes a few times a year. I could learn something from the rawness that I couldn't after a producer's studio sanitized it. Plus, Stella-Lunar's fighting pattern worked well against a single, powerful opponent. It'd be fun to see her fight against a group instead.

The TV blared a theme song. Bee was very distracting, and it took me a moment to realize that the music wasn't right. Stella's kept a certain liveliness that came with the Magical Girl territory, almost like a pop song, but this one felt darker . . . more operatic. I stared at the screen as a male voice read words off it.

"Due to unforeseen circumstances relating to her personal life, Magical Girl Stella-Lunar is canceled. Golden Goose has graciously agreed to shoot the Episode, excluding point-of-view filming and with a five-minute delay. Stella-Lunar thanks you for your understanding."

I groaned. "We might as well go do the dishes. Golden Goose with a five-minute delay isn't the right mood for the night. She's got a bitter aftertaste, and that's not what I'm looking for."

"Not even with a drinky-drink?" Bee asked. She got up and ducked to the kitchen, where a bottle of something stronger than wine sat under the counter. She pulled it out and hurried back, just in time to watch Golden Goose land with a shockwave outside 3V1L's lair.

It wasn't how I'd have attacked a hornet's nest of villains. And it certainly wasn't how Stella-Lunar would have done it. She'd have scouted it out, tried to fight only a few of 3V1L's rogue's gallery at a time, and kept things under control, more or less. But by the time Golden Goose kicked in the door to 3V1L's inner sanctum and pushed through their combined power, I was too busy cuddling with Bee, drinking vodka by the shot, and trying not to fall off the couch to care.

PART FIVE

31

Ride-Share

FRIDAY, MARCH 20

I'd fought six different villains in the month since "Braking and Entering," and Grandmaster had been the hardest to track down. He'd always felt like he knew my next move, and even though he wasn't as fast as Jumper, he started moving so much earlier than she did that it felt the same. But I had him now. If I could get him before—

—No. Before I could reach him, he slammed a door in my face. A moment later, I heard something crash inside. I ripped the door open. Fursona sat on top of him, paws ready to punch him in the face. I breathed a sigh of relief. The Episode was as good as over.

As Grandmaster's hands went up, I paused for a moment. The villain had an illustrious career ahead of him; his **[En Passante]** power and the ability to predict his opponents' every move would make him a major-league threat in time, but luckily for Fursona and me, his lack of henchmen or lieutenants had made this the least combat-oriented Episode in our little-league marathon.

And not once in over a month had Vigilant Vow shown his face.

I grabbed the chess-themed villain's wrist, stared at the drone, and said, "Evil may be thinking three moves ahead, but Grandmaster's board just got flipped!"

[Episode Finished!]
[Episode: Castle King's Side! - PG]
[Penalties: N/A]
[Episode Finished! +5 of each Style Point]
[Winner Winner! +2 of each Style Point]
[Role Focus: Badass + Cunning - Goal Unmet]
[Alias - Understudy] [Archetype - Magical Girl] [Community Rank - 254/523]
[HP 3/9]
[Styles and Skills]
▶Archetype Skill - Transformation Sequence

►Combo Skills - Power-Weaving
►Badass (31)
►Cunning (8)
►Drama (49)
►Stellar Ray 2
►Bit-Part Barrage 1
►Flamboyance (53) (Skill Roll Available)
►Signature Skill - Adaptive Armoire 2
►Stored Costumes: (Rainy Day, Copy Cat)
►Starwave Sail 1
►Quick-Time Change 1
►Grit (15)
►I-Frame Transform 1
[50 Flamboyance Credits Used. Rolling Skill!]
[Rank-Up! Quick-Time Change 2: Switch between costumes twice per Act]

As the police bundled Grandmaster into a squad car, I could already see the lawyers circling like sharks. But I didn't care; that win put me only one point behind Vigilant Vow on the community ranking list. Between that and the workouts with Grapple and his shockingly weak brother, Punch, I was feeling pretty confident!

More importantly, I'd gotten rank-ups in **[Speed-Hacker]**, **[Ride the Lightning]**, **[I-Frame Transform]**, and **[Rejuvenation]**, plus two new skills. **[Diva Dive-Bomb]** felt like it'd fit for Copy Cat or an aggressive, melee-focused Understudy, but I didn't have space in either build. But the second, **[Virga]**, completely changed Magical Girl Rainy Day's role.

She was still a combo superhero, but instead of using **[Check the Script]** as a filler, I could run **[Virga]**. The healing rain healed everyone, which was a drawback in some ways, but it'd usually be more effective in combat than the filler Cunning power had been. More importantly, it healed *everyone*, including injured Extras and henchmen. I'd finally gotten the rescue power I'd wanted back in January. Despite all my new powers and upgrades, Rainy Day was the only Costume I'd changed much on.

I changed more now; **[Quick-Time Change's]** Rank Two upgrade meant switches from Understudy to my other Costumes, then back to Understudy, were possible in-combat now. I could take advantage of that with **[Rejuvenation]**, which had ranked up, and the new Rainy Day looked like a mix between combo-superhero and rescue/support.

[Costume - Magical Girl Rainy Day]
[HP 3/9]
[Styles and Skills]

▶Archetype Skill - Transformation Sequence
▶Badass
▶Cunning
▶Virga 0
▶Drama
▶Thunderhead 0
▶Flamboyance
▶Signature Skill - Adaptive Armoire 2
▶Stored Costumes: (Understudy)
▶Ride the Lightning 0
▶Quick-Time Change 2
▶Grit
▶Rejuvenation 2

I flew us back to Walnut Tower on my sailboard. Fursona had gotten a lot better at it, leaning *with* me instead of standing stiff in the middle of the board, and occasionally even letting go of the steering rail. I still had to push her a little on our dive-bombs, but she'd gotten a power that benefited from her speed on impact—something Collidus had in his starting build but new to Fursona. It made the bombing runs much more effective, even if she hated the flights.

The moment we landed and ducked inside, Fursona's head came off. "Where the hell is Viggy V?" Bianca asked, annoyed that he hadn't followed through on his threat yet.

I felt much the same way. I'd gotten enough power-ups that the Understudy Costume felt ready for more minor-league Episodes, and the three **[Adaptive Armoire]** builds were only getting more synergistic. I was confident we'd be able to outcompete even Vigilant Vow's familiar army now. But the vigilante had only run one Episode since "Braking and Entering," and he hadn't pushed himself much.

"No idea. We're all caught up, though, and just in time. We won't get much action during Spring Break."

"I intend to get a little one way or another," Bee said, winking.

I grinned back but shook my head. "The double-wide is a little small for that. Mom and Dad sleep on the far side, but even so, let's take it easy and enjoy my parents and the great outdoors."

"Awwww."

Subject: Ride-Share Problems
Anika DuPont and Bianca Marino,
Hey, my car's in the shop. Someone busted up the engine with a bat or something, and it'll be a week or two before it's up and running. I've gotta back out of the ride-share deal. Sorry.

I hope you can find a way home,
Bradley Jamison

"Shit," Bianca said. She lay on the chaise lounge, half in and half out of her fursuit, scrolling on her phone. "Think there's another option?"

"This late? No way," I said, throat tightening. I pushed down my sadness, but I just wanted to cry for a bit. It'd been months since I'd made it across the mountains, and the video chats weren't doing it anymore. I missed my parents. "Unless you want to drive?"

"I don't trust the Civic, sorry. I'll be right back. I'm gonna go check," Bianca said. I helped her out of her suit, and she disappeared out my front door, heading for the Student Union Building and the sign-up sheet.

I held it together until she left, but the moment the door closed, I flopped down on my bed and started tearing up.

<Hey Dad. Ride-share canceled. Working on it, but may not be home - Annie 4:45>

I didn't expect him to text me back right away. D.A.C. Drillworks had struggled during Peter's extended sick leave, and everyone hoped their boy genius of a programmer would come back soon. The fabrication crew had to pull overtime consistently, and Dad was probably busy. At this time of day, Mom wouldn't even be worth texting. The diner hopped between five-ish and seven, and she wouldn't have time to check her phone, either.

But the message was sent. All I could do was wait for a response and take the ten minutes before Bee returned to mope. And I fully intended to take advantage of every second.

So it was honestly a bummer when my phone went off, telling me I had a new email. All the same, I rolled over and opened it.

Subject: Call to Duty
Magical Girl Understudy,
I am Crossbow, current speaker for the Tokyexico Council of Heroes. The city needs your help, and you've been called to assist.
As you know, the TCoH helps run Almhurst Penitentiary, where your former rival is incarcerated. His attitude toward revenge has shifted, and though he refuses all attempts at rehabilitation into a hero or vigilante role, we believe he's safe to release. Further, with Man vs. Nature ending, we have no legal justification to keep him locked up. His lawyers request his return to Riverside within ninety-six hours.
Usually, escort duty would be carried out by one of our minor-league heroes, such as Gatecrash. However, as a college student needing passage to Riverside yourself, you and your sidekick are perfect escorts.

Here is our offer. The escort will happen tomorrow at 9:00 AM, outside of Almhurst. You and Fursona will ride escort in our van until you arrive at the Riverside Police Department. Professor Panic will be in a sealed chamber and will not know who his escorts are. When you arrive, you'll hand him off to his lawyers under the supervision of the town's current hero, Collidus. In return, the van will wait until Sunday, March 29, before departing to give you time in your hometown.

Please let us know if this arrangement works for you and your sidekick,
Crossbow
Speaker, Tokyexico Council of Heroes

Every instinct screamed at me to say no. I was done with Peter; I'd told him that when we broke up and again when I'd beaten the TERROR Mech. The Council of Heroes couldn't know the details of our relationship, but they *had* to know something. This was a setup, but whether it was Rocko's, the Council's, or someone else's, I couldn't tell.

What I did know, though, was that this stupid idea was my only way home.

When Bianca returned, she had two burritos in her hands and a glum look on her face. She tossed one my way and pouted. "There's nothing. I looked through all nineteen pages, and every car heading west is full. We're screwed."

I kept typing my response email, ignoring the bacon-and-egg goodness inches from my nose. I ignored Bee, too, which I knew drove her crazy, but I had to get this right. When I finally finished, I unwrapped the burrito. "Look this over. Read theirs first, then read my response."

RE: Call to Duty
Crossbow,
I have some reservations about this job, and I need help with a few things.

First, I need to know how Professor Panic's equipment will be transported. If it's in the same vehicle, that dramatically increases the danger.

Second, your schedule has me missing two classes, one of which I really can't have absences in. What can you do to make sure those get excused?

Third, and most important, I need help. I'm pushing for a minor-league spot, but I can't participate in on campus Episodes due to fallout from my Series Finale. I'd gladly run an escort for Professor Panic if you can pull any strings to get that ban lifted.

Thanks,
Magical Girl Understudy

"Oooh, a chance to have Spring Break." Bianca read over both parts. Then she nodded. "Send it. Even if they say no, we should take the chance."

"I agree," I said. I *really* missed home, and Professor Panic wasn't a threat to me. I'd grown more powerful than he could imagine—or at least more powerful than he could have in jail. I pressed Send.

The response came within thirty seconds. I'd never met Crossbow—heck, I'd never even heard of him—but it seemed he didn't have much to do except check his emails.

> *RE: Call to Duty*
> *Magical Girl Understudy,*
> *First, the arrangement is to transport Professor Panic, not his inventions or tools.*
> *Second, your Superpower Studies professors will be informed, and your other absences will be excused. That's routine business for us.*
> *Third, I'll see what I can do.*
> *Crossbow,*
> *Speaker, Tokyexico Council of Heroes*

I looked at Bianca, raising an eyebrow. This wasn't the email I'd hoped for. I needed the Council to lift this ban; that'd put me in a prime position to take the lead in my race against Vigilant Vow. "You should say yes," she said, and I saw the hunger in her eyes. She needed a vacation, and so did I.

"Alright." I typed a quick response, pressed Send, and squeezed her against my side. "We're going to Riverside."

32

To Riverside

Bee didn't trust the Civic over the mountains, but it got us to the visitor parking lot outside of Almhurst Penitentiary just fine. The prison's walls loomed over the Cherry Creek district, searchlights panning along its gray face. It felt out of place in Tokyexico, like something from a pre–Launch movie, and I shivered. There wasn't a prison with higher security in North America—equal, yes, but not more. And Peter had been in there for three months.

After a night to think about it, the whole offer felt suspicious. Bradley's car hadn't broken down; it'd been attacked. And then, conveniently, an escort job *happened* to be available, moving Professor Panic? That stretched belief. And how had the Council of Heroes and this Crossbow known we wanted to go home? I'd never even heard of Crossbow. Either the hero was ridiculously discreet—which didn't fit in with the Ilneats' TV-centric model—or he'd done a lot of scrubbing to erase his footprint before I was old enough to care about heroes. Either way, something about the whole mess gave me the heebie-jeebies. I wanted to go home, though, so I'd have to play ball.

I pushed down the nervous shake, but the supervillain supermax was my real worry. Somewhere in its depths, Professor Panic was being discharged. Crossbow had said that my villainous ex wouldn't know we were there, but I doubted that. Peter probably knew exactly what was going on.

"You good?" Bee asked as she parked her car and shut off the engine. It clunked and hissed.

"Yeah. Yeah, I'm good. Let's do this," I lied. I grabbed my bags, Bee grabbed hers—drowning under the sheer bulk of her overpacking—and we headed in to change and transform.

Almhurst's entrance smelled like disinfectant. A sign on the door pointed Bee and me toward a pair of changing stalls. "All superheroes must be in Costume beyond this point. Unpowered visitors may use the main entrance" it read, with an arrow pointing to a yellow line on the floor. I slipped into one and started my [**Transformation Sequence**].

It was too late to back out now, even if I wanted to. And I did want to—kind of. As far as I was concerned, the Professor Panic/*Small Town Super* arc had ended when I walked away from the squad car. I wanted nothing to do with him, but life, the Ilneats' plots, or fate kept shoving him at me. I gritted my teeth; if I had to deal with Peter to go home, then I'd deal with Peter.

The light show died down. I mumbled, "Villains, exit stage left," and a door opened on the changing room's far side. Through it, I saw a lobby.

Just a lobby, nothing special. Plastic chairs, fake plants, Muzak played softly over the intercom, and more of the disinfectant smell—this time mixed with something I could only describe as "industrial oranges." A sense of pressure lay over the room's tile floor. It felt like every dentist's office I'd ever been in, but without the cheer.

Behind a counter sat a superhero in a green cape and goggles. He looked up from his monitor and nodded slowly. "Name and reason for visit?"

Fursona hopped up behind me as I cleared my throat. "Magical Girl Understudy and Fursona. We're here as escort heroes for Professor Panic, who's being released today."

He handed me a small plastic-and-metal box with a screen displaying an arrow. "Parking garage. Three lefts, through the security door, and one right. The arrow will guide you, and the remote's your key card. It'll only get you through that door, so don't try anything else. Sergeant Alvetti is prepping the van now. He'll walk you through the job."

"Thanks," I said.

The superhero looked at me, nodded slowly, and returned to his monitors. I shook my head and headed into the belly of the beast, or at least Almhurst Penitentiary.

I'd expected something like the Lewisville Penitentiary bus. Something armored, with on-board weapons to defend against megafauna or supervillainous rescue attempts. Or at least something that had room for several villains.

Of course, I'd also expected Sergeant Alvetti to be a hero, so I was wrong twice.

"Welcome aboard," he said, adjusting his uniform under the lightly armored vest he wore. The dark-haired man could have been Bee's grandpa; he was slightly over-weight, his uniform was a little crumpled, and he'd balded quite a bit. And, more importantly, he wasn't a hero. He pulled himself out from the stock-looking sprinter van's back doors and grinned as we shook hands. His had oil and engine grime on them.

"Alright, heroes, here's the deal. I used to run skiers over the mountains before Launch Day, and I know the road like the back of my hand." Alvetti stared at his hand, looking momentarily confused, then laughed. When we didn't, he frowned. "Lighten up, kids. This is a simple run. The perp's not even a major threat, especially without his toys. I could handle it solo. I'll give you the tour since we've got a few minutes."

He waved us forward, and I took a quick breath. The last thing I wanted was to look uncertain. The van's back included a single seat, buckle, and, shockingly, a TV screen and remote. I raised an eyebrow.

Fursona cleared her throat and spoke through her modulator. "That's pretty posh for Professor Panic."

"Yeah, when we transport rehab vils, they get some luxuries. Plus, the guy's a little leaguer. Supposedly, he was only in here because they couldn't get him home or something. So, this is the holding tank. Professor Panic will be back here." Alvetti pointed to a black barrier behind the TV screen. "The TV is mostly there so he's not bored, but it also encourages him to face forward so he's easier to keep an eye on. The whole wall's a one-way screen. Come around to the other side. I'll show you."

"I have a concern," I said as we opened the passenger doors. "Professor Panic is a tech Genius. Should we be giving him a screen and remote?"

"Sure, I get that. The profile says he's a slow operator. He builds stuff, tests it, iterates, finds a design he likes, tests it, and so on. We've got a six-hour run here, and he takes days." That was true, but it still felt weird letting him chill in the back.

I climbed into the back seat. Alvetti nodded. "You two can check on the perp whenever you want. I'll be up front with the monitoring equipment."

Sure enough, the passenger side front seat was gone. In its place, whoever built this van had installed a full computer setup. It dominated the space where someone could have ridden shotgun, and I winced at the *thought* of trying to see the right side mirror through the maze of wires and screens. Before I could say anything, though, a voice echoed on the intercom. "Attention. Prisoner entering the garage for transport in one minute!" The voice repeated, then cut off.

Alvetti grinned. "Sorry, but we're going to cut the tour off here. Hop in—sorry, roo—and find a seat. Sorry, roo again. There's a removable pad that fits some tails but not all of them. I'll put your bags in the frunk. Don't accept the [**Casting Call**]."

I buckled in, Fursona hopped to the other side, and we shut our doors. Fursona slipped a paw into my hand. "Here we go. No turning back now."

I opened my mouth to say "We've been committed to this for the last half hour," but before I could, a loud buzzing noise filled the air. I peered through the van's windows as a door opened on the garage's far side. Two heroes stepped out, escorting a short, thin man in a lab coat and goggles. My heart dropped.

Professor Panic had arrived.

[Casting Call]
[Episode: Orange is the New Evil - R]
[Role: Prison Guard! Do you accept the role? (Yes/No)]
[Role Focus: Grit + Badass]

The mad professor stalked to the van and climbed in without being ordered; as he did, both heroes moved as if to stop him, then relaxed when he flopped insolently into the chair and turned on the TV. It stayed muted while the heroes and Alvetti ran through a long list of rules Professor Panic was supposed to follow, but he wasn't paying attention. Instead, it seemed like he was staring forward.

Right at me.

Should I say something? Roll the window down? Ignore him? I didn't know what to do, and my stomach rolled.

It took me a minute—and Fursona's hand squeeze—to remember he couldn't see me. He was watching the on-drive movie, not staring at me intently. He had no idea I was here; even if he did, it wouldn't matter. We were done. I'd told him we were done. We'd had *Episodes* about being done—two of them! This was just a job—and a way to get home. I turned around and forced myself to relax in my seat.

Alvetti spent almost ten minutes talking with the two heroes. Then they turned and headed back for the gate. Alvetti slammed the back door shut, climbed into the driver's seat, and turned the key. The van started with a roar and shook slightly as he gently stepped on the gas; the vehicle's power reminded me of the Roadrage Episode, and I shook my head to clear it.

The van didn't pull onto the main road. Instead, it dropped into a tunnel and rocketed forward, then out a massive door that opened onto the highway outside Tokyexico City. I stared out the window in shock.

I'd been asleep across most of the plains and foothills when Mom and Dad dropped me off in September, but I remembered grass, fields, and trees. Instead, the ground was churned, pitted, and bare. Something had torn up the earth, chewed the grass to the roots, then turned its attention to the trees; not a single branch lower than ten feet had a leaf, bud, or pine needle, and some trees had been uprooted. Battle scars covered Tokyexico City's walls, and MIRACLE repair crews patched dozens of holes in the city's defenses.

The Man vs. Nature had taken its toll on Tokyexico.

"Yeah, it's pretty bad," Sergeant Alvetti said. "Not as bad as Four, though. The Bear Lord broke in and devastated Thornton. It took three dozen heroes plus the top five villains to stop him from devouring the whole city, and Thornton never recovered."

"I haven't seen that Episode," I hedged.

"Never aired. Too brutal for TV, but the repair crews learned a lot from it. We've never had a significant breach since."

"A D-wolver got into the university's rail station in November," I said.

Alvetti laughed. "A single D-wolver isn't significant. You'd need a whole herd of turbo-buffalo or five or six Kudzu-Zilla-level threats to match The Bear Lord. We're talking city-enders, stuff Golden Goose couldn't handle solo if she came down from Yorkston. A real challenge for you hero types."

"Ah," Fursona said. She yawned. "If it's all the same to you, I'm going to sleep."

"Sure," Alvetti said. "I've seen perps like Professor Panic before. He's done. He won't try anything, and if he does, you're both right there. As long as one of you stays awake, that'll be plenty."

"Okay. Wake me up in two hours so you can nap," Fursona said. She leaned against me and started snoring. I envied how quickly she could do that.

As the van zoomed up the twisting road into the mountains, I turned around to look at Peter. At Professor Panic. He sat quietly, staring out the windows at the turbo-buffalos' aftermath. My old nemesis seemed just as disturbed by it as I had, but as the van turned a corner and the plains disappeared behind a pine-covered mountain, he turned to face me. His goggles locked on my eyes momentarily, and I . . . panicked. Then he turned the TV on, pulled on a pair of headphones, and started watching TV.

He couldn't see me. But I couldn't help but wonder how long that'd last. When we got to Riverside, would he want to fight? I'd outgrown him in every way, but I really didn't want to spend the time rehashing old battles. I had plans. Plans like introducing Fursona to Collidus, taking Bee to my old movie theater job, and letting her meet my parents.

33

Parents

The van hissed to a stop on Carver Street, next to the Riverside Police Department. "Alright, let's get him out, hand him over, and call this good. I'll be back to pick you up on Sunday," Alvetti said. He shut off the van and stretched, then eased himself out.

I opened my door to a small welcoming committee. Mayor Ambrose stood there, along with Sheriff Harris. But they weren't the ones that caught my eye.

Instead, a trio of men in suits and sunglasses stood outside the police station. As Sergeant Alvetti nodded at the sheriff and the two started talking, one of them stepped toward me. I recognized them—Professor Panic's legal team—and nodded but didn't say anything.

"Our client is inside, correct?" he asked.

"Yes. He should be fine back there. If you'll excuse me, I've got business in Riverside," I said.

"No, not yet. We must ensure Professor Panic was treated well during his stay in Almhurst and the subsequent trip across the mountains, especially since you served as his escort. Release him to our custody, fill out some paperwork, and then you can go do whatever it is you're planning on doing." The lawyer grinned a sharklike grin. Did he smell blood in the water, or did lawyers always act like this? Had Tele-Portal's lawyer been this predatory? I wasn't sure, but I didn't think so.

"Fine," Fursona said, interrupting my thoughts. "We'll fill out the paperwork, but if Professor Panic starts anything, he'll have an ass-kicking coming his way."

I groaned. Fursona—no, Bianca—had gotten prickly about Avan at the APPEAL meeting. If she did the same thing here, it could be a lot worse than a little verbal spat. I put a hand on her shoulder. "No, we're not going to fight anyone. Let's see the paperwork."

I was so busy signing, initialing, and dating blank spaces that I didn't realize Sergeant Alvetti had released Professor Panic until I heard his voice. "Mr. Riviera, thank you for arranging this. We'll be back in business in no time. I trust the lab's been kept up in my absence?"

"There was one incident with the superhero Collidus breaking in, but that happened before your arrest and incarceration, Professor," the lawyer said. I turned reflexively and met eyes with Professor Panic for a split second. That was enough. I physically couldn't look at him, and my stomach churned.

He clearly felt the same way, from the look of disgust on his face. He turned to stare at his attorney. "We're leaving in one minute, then."

"What about—" Fursona started. I turned to glare at her, but it was too late.

Professor Panic cleared his throat, still not looking at me. "No. Thank you for bringing me home, but no. I want nothing more to do with you, Magical Girl Understudy. I'm over this. Just leave me alone." Without another word, he climbed into his lawyer's car and slammed the door.

<Hey dad. Were here. 5 minutes - Annie 4:56>

I felt a whirlwind of emotions as Fursona and I windsurfed into the woods and sat down next to the Winter River.

Relief, for sure. Professor Panic was many things, but he'd rarely lied to me. If he said he wanted to be done, he was done, and that was what I'd wanted, wasn't it?

I wasn't sure. I'd expected more from him somehow. It seemed unbelievable that he wouldn't want vengeance for his defeat at Tokyexico University. Had his time in Almhurst really changed him that much? I wanted it to be over, but at the same time, it felt wrong to leave my long-time nemesis behind like this—like I'd lost something I couldn't get back, even if I didn't want it anymore.

But mostly, I felt nervous about something I hadn't even thought about. "How do you want me to introduce you?" I asked Bianca as she pulled the Fursona head off and shoved it into her backpack.

"Girlfriend, obviously," Bee said.

I laughed. "Well, duh, but I mean your secret identity. My parents aren't stupid—I used to think they were, but they've known I was Magical Girl Understudy for years, and Professor Panic's return will definitely make the news. If they see me with a strange superhero, then they see me with my college girlfriend, they'll know who you are."

"Oh. I hadn't thought about that. Do you think I can trust them? They're not going to tell anyone, are they? Maybe this whole thing was—"

I cut her off. "They've known for six years, and they didn't even tell *me*. You can trust them."

"I'm just not sure. I really don't . . ." Bianca zipped up her backpack. "Let's just play it by ear, okay?"

"Sure." I untransformed into the street clothes I'd worn to Almhurst this morning, and we walked through the trailer park.

I opened the squeaky gate and walked past Mom's station wagon. I hadn't thought about it, but in a lot of ways, it made Bianca's Civic look good. Then I knocked on the front door. No one was home, and I knew that; Mom had said she'd be working until at least eight, and Dad didn't get off until five. "It's fine, I know where the spare is. Third flowerpot on the left, two inches into the soil."

"Which parent smokes?" Bee asked as she dug through the cigarette butts and topsoil, fished out the key, and dropped it into my hand.

"Mom." I opened the door and stepped back into my home. "Here we are."

The double-wide looked exactly like I'd left it, right down to the garbage that needed to be taken out and the spot on the wall where Dad had painted over my childhood doodles in not-quite-right paint. I led Bianca to my bedroom. "Brace yourself," I said, and opened the door.

I'd never invited anyone over to my house during high school except for Peter. He'd understood. The pink bedding still covered my bed, and the bright purple mirror reflected Bee's face back at me, so I didn't have to turn to see her reaction. The Tele-Portal poster still hung unsigned on my wall next to the other supers' pictures, and my *Midsummer Night's Dream* cast photo sat on my nightstand—with just a hint of dust on it. I dug through my backpack and tossed Tails onto my pillow. She stared back at me with her star-button eyes.

"Now I get it," Bee said. She pointed at the posters, then stepped inside. The room smelled a little stale, and when she flopped onto my bed, dust flew up. My parents probably hadn't opened the room since I left. "This is *exactly* the room I'd imagine a Magical Girl having. It's like the archetype was made for you."

"Sure was," I replied, grinning. "So, it'll be tight on the bed. If that doesn't work for you, I'll take the floor."

"I'm good at sharing."

"Oh, I know." I winked.

The front door opened, and Dad's voice echoed through the double-wide. "Dot, you in there? Mom's on her way home. I got your text, and she shuffled some shifts around to get the evening off. She's bringing burgers."

Mom did, in fact, bring burgers from the diner. She also brought buttery corn, a paperish bucket of mashed potatoes, and coleslaw—a staple meal from my childhood. I introduced Bee to them and we talked about school. Mom raised her eyebrow a bit when I mentioned Bee and I were dating, but honestly? We had *aliens*. Most people weren't worried about who you spent time with anymore. They didn't even make a stink about us sharing my bedroom, which shocked me after how they'd handled Peter and me.

Mom, however, was not most people. She was a lot like Bianca in that she liked snooping, but unlike my girlfriend, she was almost a professional snoop. She knew *exactly* who Bee was, and she clearly didn't feel like being subtle. As we cleared our plates and Dad started the sink to do dishes, she cleared her throat. "So Bianca, what's your superpower?"

Bianca flushed and choked on one last bite of coleslaw. I laughed. "Yeah, not much fun figuring out that you're not as sneaky as you thought, is it?"

"No." She stared at her empty plate for a minute, trying to decide how to explain Fursona. I could tell she'd never had to deal with this before, and she fiddled with her last few bites of potato instead of talking.

Eventually, I saved her. "It's better to watch. You'll get to see all my ridiculousness too."

Mom and Dad finished cleaning while I found the Episode I wanted and made sure it was loaded up. Then my parents took the couch, leaving Bee and me to fight for the armchair. I lost and sat down in front of her with my head on her knees. Then I hit Play.

"Ivory Keys" wasn't our finest work, but after a relatively uneventful first and second act spent investigating The Piano Man's plot and waiting for him to appear at the Arcadia Theater, he finally struck with his mind-controlling music. Fortunately, Fursona and I had prepped for that with headphones and earplugs, and equally luckily, we were friends with Springlock and Milo. They'd taught us a few very basic signs.

So, instead of the Episode ending right there and The Piano Man's newly mind-controlled henches robbing each other and piling the loot up for the supervillain, I did crowd control while my sidekick hopped toward the stage and interrupted The Piano Man. Feet flew, the music crescendoed, and in the end, the mind control broke. So did the grand piano The Piano Man had been playing.

He tried to run, but Fursona's hybrid Speedster/Bruiser build was too fast, and she got the capture—and the sign-off at the Episode's end.

Dad cleared his throat. "So, her power is that she's a kangaroo?"

Bianca kept staring at the floor, so I had to save her again. "Kind of. When she puts on the kangaroo suit, she gets a bunch of kangaroo-themed powers. Double-kicks, fast hopping, and a cool cybernetic tail or something. I'm not sure how it works."

Dad nodded, but Mom was deep in thought. As the credits rolled, she asked a question I couldn't believe we'd never thought of. "Could she get different powers from other suits?"

If I thought I looked shocked, Bee's face must've been a mirror to mine. "I've never tried it, but I suppose it's possible. I'd have to ask the studio, and Pataki would probably insist I supply the suit, but wouldn't that be cool? It'd be a lot like your power, Annie."

"Yeah, it would," I said. And it would be. What if Fursona could be a bird or a bear and get flight or claws or something? It'd be a huge power spike for her. But it was also *my* gimmick, not hers.

I thought about it the rest of the evening and into the night, as Mom and Dad interrogated Bianca about her family, her ambitions, and what she liked to do for fun. Eventually, they went to bed, leaving Bianca and me to fight for space on my twin bed. Even once she'd gotten comfortable and fallen asleep, I thought about it, and by the time I was ready for sleep, I'd come to a conclusion. It might be my gimmick, but this was my childhood bed, and if I could share that, I could share anything.

Just before I fell asleep, I asked myself a question. If I were Bianca, what would I want to do on Spring Break?

34

Spring Break

TUESDAY, MARCH 24

<Im bored and its your fault. Fix it - Collidus 9:13>
<Come take a hike - Collidus 9:14>
<plz -Collidus 9:14>

Collidus wasn't the only bored superhero.

Clearly, Bianca had never been in a small town. By Monday, we'd gone to the movies, explored Carver Street, and even hit up the pizza place, plus flown over the school and done the obligatory make-out session on Flat Top Hill. And as excited as she acted while we were *doing* things, I could tell she needed some excitement. So did I, to be honest, though I *also* enjoyed hanging out with Mom and Dad, playing board games and catching up. We'd finally handed each other the Christmas presents we'd unwrapped over video chat, and it felt good to be home.

But Collidus had offered a chance to check out the sandstone canyons west of town. That almost made up for the fact that he was *clearly* ditching classes, and that he blamed me for being bored.

"Well, we doing it?" Bee asked from the seat in front of the purple mirror. She looked hopeful, like it'd break up some routine we *certainly* didn't have.

I hesitated, mostly because aiding a thirteen-year-old in ditching class wasn't the right thing to do. Then I nodded.

"Yay!" Bianca cheered.

<20 minutes, the trailhead? - Understudy 9:16>
<10. Suit up. Not messing up my identity for your friend - Collidus 9:16>
<Got it - Understudy 9:17>

We disappeared into the woods, suited up, and took off. The trailhead was ten miles west of town, up an old dirt road, and it led into the pinyon-juniper forest and canyon country. By the time we arrived, Collidus looked half asleep; he leaned against a post in his speed suit. But the moment I landed, he grinned.

"What?" I asked.

"Nothing. But seriously, a kangaroo?"

"Yep," Fursona said. "Gives me all sorts of cool powers. I'd be dumb to turn it down."

"Well, you look dumb in it," Collidus said.

I groaned and introduced them. "Fursona, this is Collidus, my sidekick on *Small Town Super*. Collidus, Fursona, my *Heroics 101* sidekick."

The two sidekicks glowered at each other. I facepalmed. "Are we *really* having an ego competition? And how is it my fault you're bored?"

"Yes," Fursona said.

"Uh-huh. You took away the only villain in town for months, and now he's back, and he won't fight me while you're here. You owe me. Let's go," Collidus said.

"Okay. What's the hike?" I had to change subjects, or these two would bicker and boast the whole hike.

"We're going into Dolores Canyon. There's a spring back there that's pretty cool, and if you two are fast enough, we can see an arch. No superpowers, though," Collidus said. "My new producer gets upset if I use them too much outside of Episodes, and I already ran for five minutes to get here."

"So, why are we all suited up?" I asked. I didn't feel like strolling through the woods in my skirt and tights, and even in the cool spring air, Fursona had to be overheating.

"Because, uh, I'm not giving up my secret identity," Collidus said again. "Look, let's get going."

The temperature dropped again as we walked into a red, orange, and tan canyon until it felt like my January Episode. I shivered, but Collidus jogged slowly, forcing Fursona and me to sprint to keep up. As even Fursona left me behind, I decided I hated Speedsters, and Collidus was cheating. He *had* to be using a power.

"So, Understudy, you're racing for a minor-league spot? How's that going?" Collidus asked.

"How'd you know about that?" We ran past a splintered pinyon tree whose branches lay across the trail and whose bark bore deep gashes.

"What? You think just because I'm not sidekicking for you, I don't follow you? I watch your show weekly, and it's all over the introduction. Plus, I keep track of the rankings in Tokyexico."

"Then you know we're close, but Rocko will keep our noses to the grindstone if we're not in front. He needs the win here; he paid out too many favors to clear a path for us to finish the *Small Town Super* Series Finale, and now he's gotta pay them all back."

Collidus grinned. "Then he's going to love me."

"What?" Fursona asked.

"You'll see."

A few moments later, we stopped in a wide spot in the canyon, where an alcove caught the sun. I rubbed my gloved hands together, trying to warm up, and looked around. I'd been so focused on the trail and keeping up with my faster sidekicks that I hadn't seen where we were going. But all around us, every tree's bark had been shredded. Branches clogged the little creek in the canyon bottom, and a towering pile of deer bones sat inside the alcove.

Collidus cleared his throat. "Welcome to a special crossover event."

[Casting Call]
[Episode: Short: Small Town Speedster x Heroics 101 versus Snagglemaw - PG-13]
[Role: Huntress! Do you accept the role? (Yes/No)]
[Role Focus: Badass + Cunning]

Fursona looked almost furious, even through her fursuit. "This was a trick? A trick to get us in on one of your Episodes? I can't believe this—"

I cut her off. "You should have told us, Collidus. What's your game here?"

"Background first. Three weeks ago, someone's dog went missing up here. I investigated and found we have a megafauna problem."

I saw Fursona stiffen just before I flashbacked to the caves underneath the Grant Building and the subway station. To the musky smell of the D-wolver and how hard we'd fought just to get it to leave. I'd gained a lot of power since then—we both had—but out here, it probably wasn't a D-wolver. "Is it snakes?" I asked. Collidus and I had fought snakes before. But I already knew it wasn't before he answered. Snakes didn't tear trees apart.

"Snakes don't tear trees apart," he said. "It's a scythetooth. I've fought with him a couple times; I can get away, so I wanted to see if I could whittle him down. I couldn't even touch him. He's not fast, but he's old, and this isn't the first time he's fought supers. So, I got the sheriff to close Dolores Canyon to Extras, worked on keeping him stuck in here, and hoped The Huntsman would make it out here. But you two got here first."

"Okay. You've got an Episode you can't handle, but you think the three of us together can?" Fursona asked.

"Yeah. And I'll sweeten the deal. If we run this as a *Small Town Speedster* Episode, you'll have another chance to grab some crossover audience."

"Deal," I said immediately. I accepted the **[Casting Call]**. Fursona did, too. "Where is he?"

[STS x H101 vs. Snagglemaw: Act One in Progress]

"Nearby. This is his lair. He'll come in from his morning hunt soon."

I didn't know if mountain lions usually kept a lair, but scythetooths definitely weren't normal mountain lions. I sighed and settled in to wait, the cool spring air blowing down-canyon and keeping us cold but on our toes.

We didn't need to wait long. In less than fifteen minutes, the morning stillness split as a bone-chilling yowl filled the air. I hadn't realized how loud the alcove was—how many bugs were flying, how many birds sang—until the scythetooth's scream silenced it all. It took almost ten seconds for the birds to peep again. Then, another howl echoed down the canyon, then a third.

I shivered. Anything that loud had to be massive.

It took almost five minutes of periodic yowls for Snagglemaw to arrive. His dun-and-tan hide was covered with the wounds of hundreds of fights, and a scar ripped from an empty eye socket to a missing fang. Small mercies, I thought, but not enough. The other fang was a good eight inches long, and the lion's paws were each the size of my head. He dragged a bloodied deer carcass along behind him.

"You want us to fight that?" Fursona whispered.

The lion's eye snapped toward us, narrowing as he dropped the deer at the creek's edge with a thud. He yowled, then coiled up. For a moment, the canyon was perfectly still.

Then Collidus slammed into the giant lion like a cannonball, knocking him off his feet. "Weeeeeeooooo!" the superhero yelled. And just like that, the battle was joined.

In another fight against a supervillain, I'd hold my best moves for a clean shot, but here, we needed to do enough damage fast enough to slow it down. Plus, the lion couldn't interrupt a combo. I used **[Power-Weaving]**, then **[Quick-Time Change]** into **[I-Frame Transform]** while the lion chased Collidus around. I was going for my standard lightning combo. The megafauna's paw slammed into my former side-kick, sending him flying, but he bounced off a canyon wall and cannonballed right back into the creek.

[Flashy Fitting-Room! +1 Flamboyance Point]
[Steel Yourself! +1 Grit Point]
[Floating Points: 1 Flamboyance]

While I charged **[Thunderhead]**, Fursona joined the fight. She leaped into battle feet-first, delivering a massive kick to the lion's side. Any normal animal would have been flattened, but the scythetooth wasn't normal. He yowled and wobbled but spun, drawing three huge gashes across the kangaroo's chest.

"I've got you!" Collidus shouted as the lion closed in on Fursona. The two side-kicks battered the monstrous cat back and forth, but though he could barely keep his feet, it didn't seem like they'd caused much damage. I had to change that.

[Pause for Effect! +1 Drama Point]
[Floating Points: 3 Flamboyance, 1 Grit]

The battle went back and forth, and both sidekicks had taken hits. Collidus looked to be in much better shape than Fursona. His speed and power kept him out of danger while she relied on her armor and [**Fursonal Furcefield**]. But the time had come to [**Ride the Lightning**]. "Clear! Get clear!" I shouted.

Both sidekicks ran. A moment later, the storm broke.

[**Electric Lightshow! +1 Flamboyance Point**]
[**Thunderstruck! +1 Drama Point**]
[**Power-Weaving! +6 Flamboyance, +3 Grit, +1 Drama Point**]

As lightning filled the canyon and ripped into Snagglemaw, I wished I'd waited for the lion to set foot in the water. The smell of lion musk mixed with that of burning fur as the storm raged on and on. And then, before I could react, Snagglemaw leaped through the air, lightning trailing behind him, and landed on me!

[**HP 9/9**]
[**HP 7/9**]
[**HP 6/9**]

Claws ripped into my arms as I tried to shield my face, hurting even through the superhero damage shield. Magical Girl Rainy Day didn't have any escapes except [**Quick-Time Change**], and I wasn't done with the Costume yet, but if the lion didn't give me a moment, I'd have no choice. I punched and kicked feebly against the massive cat, but my sixth-grade body couldn't do anything.

Then, suddenly, the cat went flying.

I looked up, and a somewhat beat-up Fursona stood over me, her feet glowing red. "New power?" I asked, climbing to my feet.

"New power," she confirmed.

"Me too." The [**Thunderhead**] clouds hadn't yet dispersed, and I leaped into the air below them and spun slowly. Rain covered the battlefield, and the big cat's wounds were stitched back together wherever the drops landed. But so did Fursona's suit and Collidus's bruises—and equally importantly, so did my jagged-looking scratches.

[**Medic! +3 Cunning Points**]
[**HP 7/9**]
[**Doctors Without Borders! -1 Cunning Point**]

I winced. [**Virga's**] mechanics made sense. I earned one Cunning point for every friend it healed but lost one for every enemy. That could hurt, especially against a swarm of henchmen. I pondered for a moment whether surrendered henches counted.

But only for a moment. The lion swiped at me with both front paws as I descended, scoring a pair of scratches across me. My [**HP**] seesawed as, just a moment later,

I used my second [**Quick-Time Change**] and spun to the light show. A moment later, I was Magical Girl Understudy again.

[HP 5/9]
[Flashy Fitting-Room! +1 Flamboyance Point]
[Steel Yourself! +1 Grit Point]
[HP 9/9]

I grinned and leaped into battle as Understudy. Fists and feet flashed through the air, Collidus slammed into the monstrous cat, and I launched [**Stellar Rays**] into the fight. I wanted to [**Bit-Part Barrage**], but with two melee sidekicks, I couldn't get a clear shot before—

The lion roared. He had yowled or screamed before, but this time, his roar echoed up and down the canyon, shaking loose boulders down and stunning us like a Monologue speech. He grabbed his deer dinner and dashed off up the canyon.

The moment the stun faded, Collidus started shouting. "He's heading for the spring! Let's go!" He disappeared after the lion in a cloud of dust, Fursona sprinting for all she was worth to keep up.

I sighed, summoned my [**Starwave Sail**], and took off after my too-reckless sidekicks.

35

Too-Reckless Sidekicks

Even flying above the canyon's wall, it wasn't hard to see where Collidus, Fursona, and Snagglemaw fought. The canyon walls closed off right above the spring, and there wasn't anywhere else for the big cat to go.

Not that I could see the fighting through the gigantic dust cloud as the Speedster and kangaroo dashed back and forth, trying their best to avoid Snagglemaw's claws. I cursed under my breath as I dove. Collidus had said the damn thing wasn't fast, but I'd forgotten that compared to him, only a few things *were*.

I set down, running to bleed off speed as the sailboard disappeared below me. My wand was already up, and both sidekicks were clear momentarily. I jumped, skirt spinning behind me as I rotated, and used [**Bit-Part Barrage**]. [**Stellar Ray**] beams filled the air, surging toward the big cat.

Which started dodging.

[**Dramatic Damage! +2 Drama Points**]

He weaved back and forth between the rays. A few hit, but most sizzled harmlessly into the sand. A moment later, Collidus collided with the cat, knocking both of them into the canyon wall. The sandstone shattered, fragments filling the air like shrapnel as the spring erupted in a surge of water that sprayed across the canyon and splashed against the far wall.

I fired a [**Stellar Ray**] at the two, but even as the beam hit, Snagglemaw pinned Collidus beneath one massive paw. I screamed and ran toward him, wand firing as fast as I could use [**Stellar Ray**].

If he couldn't move, Collidus's best defense did nothing.

[**Dramatic Damage! +1 Drama Point**]

I couldn't get there fast enough. The other paw came down over and over in a series of swipes, each of which shook the ground. Then the big cat grabbed Collidus in his fanged mouth.

Fursona kicked as the cat whirled to escape with its new prey, and Collidus went flying. He crumpled to the ground below the spring, water gushing over him, and Snagglemaw turned his attention toward my newer sidekick.

I didn't have the juice to do meaningful damage as Understudy, and switching to Rainy Day would leave me vulnerable if the cat decided I was the right victim. I only had one possible move.

"Transform meow!" I said, waiting for Tails to repeat the line.

Nothing happened for a heart-stopping moment, and I felt my stomach drop. Was whatever had happened to Magical Girl Candi Crush happening to me?

Then, as if she hadn't missed a beat, the plushie cat's voice echoed in my head. *<Transform meow!>*

And just like that, I was Copy Cat, at full **[HP]**, with all the Costume's moves. *<There's only room for one cat in Riverside!>* Tails said in my mind.

I used **[Leaping Leopards]** to close the gap and landed directly on Snagglemaw's back. The big cat reacted immediately, whirling in place and rearing up, his massive claws looming over me. I quickly used **[Cat-Scratch Fever]**, ripping my claws across his back, then let go. The force of his spin slammed me into a wall, but **[Fursonal Furcefield]** took most of the hit, leaving me shaken.

[Gutsy Move! +1 Badass Point]
[True Grit! +1 Grit Point]

Had I broken skin? If I had, the fever would set in, slowing down the massive cat—and leaving his sight weakened while he slowly dropped from the disease.

But I couldn't be sure. His thick, gnarled skin was tough, and his fur covered any wound I might've created. I took a deep breath as he turned toward me; I'd have to fight him like I hadn't landed the debuff.

I used **[Hometown Heroine]**. The move would give me Speedster speed—at least for a moment—but it wouldn't be enough on its own. I needed to get in close enough to use **[Doom Ball]**. It was my last powerful move outside of Rainy Day.

But the cat didn't want to let me close. He almost fought like a supervillain, adapting as the fight changed around him. That didn't make any sense. Something else had to explain it.

He leaped toward Collidus, who'd just gotten to his feet, and grabbed him again. Then the cat bounded back down the canyon toward his alcove lair, shaking Collidus as he ran. I relaxed; yeah, it looked terrible, but Fursona and I would be there in no time, and as long as Collidus was moving, he'd be hard to injure.

The cat slammed into the canyon wall shoulder-first, yowling in pain, and disappeared.

[Dramatic Damage! +1 Drama Point]

Even as we chased them, I grinned, blue nimbus flaring in the sun. [**Cat-Scratch Fever**] had broken skin. Sure, it wasn't much damage, and I remembered how many powers we'd hit the D-wolver with before it left the battle, but if we could keep the fight going long enough, we'd win.

Snagglemaw hadn't stopped at the alcove.

A fresh trail of destruction matching the old claw scars and broken limbs led further down the canyon, back toward the trailhead. I didn't know where the cat had gone, but he hadn't gone there gracefully. The fever was setting in. I'd gotten two more Drama Points during the chase.

But we had problems of our own.

Fursona was exhausted, and I was out of [**Hometown Heroine**] uses. Neither of us had the juice to finish the fight—not if we had to run the rest of the way. Fursona groaned. "Dammit. Damn, damn, damn. Fine, Understudy. We'll fly."

I smiled back at her and transformed back into Understudy. All I had left was [**Ride the Lightning**]. Nothing else had any stopping power. But if we could help the [**Cat-Scratch Fever**] damage a little, we could win and save Collidus.

Fursona hopped over to me, I summoned [**Starwave Sail**], and we took off. The board wobbled, and Fursona laughed nervously. "Less cafeteria pizza for both of us, I think."

"Yeah, the Freshman Fifteen is really adding up," I quipped back.

Even with the weight of two superheroes, though, the board was still faster than Snagglemaw's now-staggering run. The scythetooth had clawed his way up a cliff face and onto the flats beyond, but every time he tried to get up to speed, he slammed into a pinyon or juniper. The trees couldn't stop him, but they acted like speed bumps—as long as he couldn't see them, the cat couldn't outrun us.

"Fuck! Drop me!" Fursona shouted as the wind rushed past our ears.

"What?"

"You have to drop me. I can stop him!"

"Fine. We're going in!"

We dove, the air howling past our ears. Below us, the big cat sprinted; he'd reached an open field with nothing but sagebrush to slow its stride, and it dragged Collidus through them. "Three! Two! One! Go!" I shouted in Fursona's ear.

She jumped from the speeding sailboard, knocking my arm as she went. I dipped even lower, almost matching her free fall.

She slammed into the lion's back, and she, Collidus, and the cat skidded to a stop on the clearing's far side. None of them moved.

[Badass Bomber! +1 Badass Point]
[Dramatic Assist! +1 Drama Point]

I didn't have time to see more. **[Starwave Sail]** spun back and forth, wobbling in the air as I dropped far too quickly. It crashed into the ground, throwing me toward a juniper, which disintegrated as I bounced off it. Branches and evergreen needles flew everywhere, some going down my collar and scratching my back. But I hardly noticed them.

[HP 6/9]

I'd hit hard enough to lose a third of my superhero damage! And worse, the scythetooth pushed himself to his feet. His jaws weren't wrapped around Collidus anymore. They weren't wrapped around anything. He panted, his eye staring at me. I would have felt his hatred for me if he had been human. As it was, I knew exactly what he was thinking.

If he couldn't escape from the Speedsters or me on **[Starwave Sail]**, he'd have to fight his way out.

[Dramatic Damage! +1 Drama Point]

The debuff was still active. Collidus picked himself up, wincing and looking at a leg that would have been broken or torn off without his powers and superhero damage, but as it was, it probably had a nasty sprain. Fursona limped, too, her hops less than half the distance they should have been.

"Fuck." However this went down, none of us had anything left in the tank. How had we all spent so much? My wand went up as the scythetooth moved. "**[Stellar Ray]**!"

The blast caught Snagglemaw in the shoulder, right where he'd crashed into the canyon wall earlier. He screamed an almost human scream and hobbled toward me.

[Dramatic Damage! +1 Drama Point]

"Dammit! Ow!" Collidus got up to speed despite his ankle—I *knew* his superhero damage was dropping with every step, and he couldn't have much left, even with all his Grit points. But he still hit fast enough to knock the cat off his feet.

Then Fursona was there, slamming her glowing back paws directly into his face. He growled and swiped, bowling her over as her feet made contact. She hit the ground with a thud fifteen feet away.

But the balance of power had shifted. Snagglemaw struggled for purchase in the sand, trying to get to his feet so he could finish one of us off. It'd probably be Fursona. She still hadn't gotten up, but she was far enough away to be safe if the cat couldn't rise.

"The itsy bitsy spider went up the waterspout!" I shouted, throat dry. "Down came the rain and washed the spider out!"

Collidus hit the gigantic mountain lion again, tossing him back into the dust, but he went flying, bouncing across the field and into a pinyon, where he stayed.

"Out came the sun and dried up all the rain!"

[Dramatic Damage! +1 Drama Point]

Snagglemaw got to his feet again and dragged himself toward Fursona. She tried to scrabble away but didn't have a chance if he caught up.

"And the itsy bitsy spider went up the spout again! [Ride the Lightning]!"

The air filled with lightning as I transformed and vomited electricity at the cat. His fur stood on end and crackled for a split second. Then he fell to the ground mid-clearing, his single eye closed and ragged breaths escaping his mouth.

[Electric Lightshow! +1 Flamboyance Point]

Snagglemaw wasn't dead. We'd won, though. Collidus picked himself up and poked at the unconscious mountain lion with a foot. Then he nodded. "I'll call Riverside Animal Control to relocate him into the desert west of here. Hopefully, he won't be back. If he returns, though, he'll remember that we defend Riverside."

[Episode Finished!]
[Episode: Short: Small Town Speedster x Heroics 101 versus Snagglemaw - PG-13]
[Penalties: N/A]
[Short Finished! +3 of each Style Point]
[Winner Winner! +2 of each Style Point]
[Role Focus: Badass + Cunning - Goal Unmet]
[Alias - Understudy] [Archetype - Magical Girl] [Community Rank - 250/523]
[HP 6/9]
[Styles and Skills]
▶Archetype Skill - Transformation Sequence
▶Combo Skills - Power-Weaving
▶Badass (38)
▶Cunning (16)
▶Drama (16)
▶Stellar Ray 2
▶Bit-Part Barrage 1
▶Flamboyance (18)
▶Signature Skill - Adaptive Armoire 2
▶Stored Costumes: (Rainy Day, Copy Cat)
▶Starwave Sail 1
▶Quick-Time Change 2

▶Grit (26)
▶I-Frame Transform 1

We limped our way back toward the trailhead. It'd be a long walk or flight back home, and Collidus couldn't put enough weight on his ankle to run. "We really pushed our luck there, you know?" Fursona said.

"Yeah, we could have been cat food. But I knew you two had it the whole time," Collidus said, and I realized that a camera drone was still hovering overhead. He waved at it. "The girls from *Heroics 101* are on fire, and you should absolutely tune in to their show!"

I winced. It was the most shameless plug I'd heard since "Smooth Talk with DJ Smooth." But if it drove ratings toward us, I'd take it.

My phone buzzed as we walked past the trailhead. I stared at it for a moment. Then I picked it up. "Hello, Rocko. You're on speaker with Collidus, Fursona, and me."

"You passed him, DuPont!" Rocko yelled. I winced—the Ilneat hadn't bothered hiding my identity, but everyone here knew it already. "You're in the lead. Keep the pace up, and we'll be on the home stretch!"

36

Home Stretch

FRIDAY, MARCH 27

Dinner felt tense, and I couldn't figure out why.

Mom kept wanting to know more about the race between Vigilant Vow and me. I'd already told her everything I knew, but she seemed overly interested in Vigilant Vow's producer, Cartman. No matter how I switched the conversation, it kept returning to them.

Finally, in desperation, I tried to turn things around with one last ploy. I looked her in the eye over my plate of boneless chicken wings. "Mom, remember how you said you were antisuper?"

"Yeah." She took another bite of Minute Rice, acting casual. I wasn't fooled. "What about it?"

"Why?"

Mom sat there for a minute, eyes closed and body tense. Dad stopped eating for a moment to look at her worriedly. Then she set her fork down and stared at me. "If you're sure you want to have this conversation with company over?"

I nodded, and she took a deep breath. "I was on my way to following my sister to college when Launch Day hit. Junior year of high school, grades good enough to get scholarships and a chance at cheerleading money, too. I was going to make it out of Delta—after Launch Day, it became Riverside—and go to the big city for college."

"Suddenly, the TV and my phone started screaming about nuclear war. Delta wasn't a big town, and there wasn't anything worth targeting nearby, but panic hit the family hard anyway. We could *see* missiles going overhead, heading for Denver. And then suddenly, we were on a spaceship somewhere."

Bianca cleared her throat. "So you made it, though. Shouldn't that have made you happy about the Ilneats and their deal?"

"Yes. It should have," Mom said. "And it did, at first. They cleaned up the Denver Wasteland and got the walls around Tokyexico put in before realizing that people needed those jobs. I was back in school in three weeks—that was the soonest they could clean up Riverside and get basic infrastructure stuff working. And then, I had two months of pushing hard in my classes and trying out for the girls tennis team."

"So, if Launch Day was fine for you, why did you hate supers?" I asked. My food sat forgotten on the table. Mom had never told me any of this story. Of course, I'd only known she'd been antisuper for a few months.

"Dot, Bianca, what your mom's about to tell you is a secret. You can't tell anyone. Understood?" Dad's usual joking tone had vanished entirely. "Something happened to your mom, and she couldn't forgive the Ilneats after."

My mind immediately went to the worst things possible. Had a super killed a family member? I couldn't remember meeting my grandpa on her side, but that didn't mean he'd died in a superhero battle. Or maybe someone she cared about had been contracted. I tried to think about how I'd have taken Peter being Professor Panic if I weren't a hero—or Bee being Fursona. Either way, it would have been devastating and confusing. "I'm sorry, Mom," I said before she'd even started to explain.

"Anika, I haven't even told you yet." Mom rolled her eyes, and I couldn't blame her. Before I could apologize again, she continued. "Two weeks after I turned seventeen, in the summer between my junior and senior years, the Style System contracted me."

My brain stopped. I couldn't think. Luckily, Bee saved me. "Wait, what? You were a superhero?"

"No. I was *supposed* to be Madame Shockwave, Terror of Riverside. Cartman was *supposed* to be my producer, and they needed a villain in the Riverside area. I got Style System access, superpowers—my signature move was a shockwave with actual electricity on top of the force that countered our local hero—and even a Costume. It's still in my closet, like some ridiculous prom dress. And, Anika, believe me, that Costume ruined my life."

Mom stood up, abandoning the dinner table. She headed to their bedroom, and I could hear her rooting around in the closet. Dad cleared his throat. "This story is why Mom wants you to have a backup career, Dot. And you should have one too, Bianca. It's a dangerous world out there, and what you're doing is viable long-term—but only until or unless something goes wrong. For Claire, it went wrong early."

Mom returned, carrying a spandex outfit. Even though it wasn't stretched out, Mom would never fit into it. Its yellow-and-green color scheme screamed fashion disaster, and it had poofed-up shoulders and heels. I groaned, and I could tell Fursona agreed. Heels were so hard to fight in.

"This was my Madame Shockwave outfit—only worn once while using powers, good as new." Mom laughed bitterly. "Once to try it on so Cartman's Costume designer could make sure it fit right, and once in my only Episode, then a few times after. My first Episode went sour. And when the dust cleared, I realized I couldn't take the pressure of being a villain. They get blamed whenever anything goes wrong, and yeah, I had legal protection, but I didn't *do* anything wrong."

"Claire, your fist," Dad said, putting an arm around her shoulder.

"Right." Mom unclenched her fist. "That was my only Episode. I tried to switch sides or resign that day, but Cartman wouldn't have it, so I just stopped. He wouldn't let me stop being powered, but I refused to use them. I didn't feel right cheering or playing tennis as a super, and it all weighed on me so much that my grades slipped. Those scholarships disappeared, and I couldn't do anything about it, so I started to hate powered people. After all, their bosses had ruined my life."

My mind whirled at the implications. Mom had been a villain. That alone seemed impossible to wrap my head around. But to find out that she'd, what? Killed someone? Blew up a building? Endangered children? Worse? Dad was right. This *did* explain why Mom cared so much about my superpower law classes. She'd felt like accountability failed in her only Episode and wanted me to have a solid career.

But one thing was missing. "So, that explains you through high school, but that was, what? 2019? I wasn't born until 2023. What about those four years? How long were you antipower?"

"I really think that's enough, Dot," Dad said, looking at Mom's face. She looked pale and exhausted.

"No, Garret, it's fine. She needs to know." Mom took another bite of Minute Rice and chased it with water. The Madame Shockwave Costume sat abandoned on the floor. For a moment, I thought about taking it to access my mom's powers—something she could do would open new doors. I decided I'd ask her after dinner. She knew how my **[Signature Skill]** worked, so she'd surely let me have it.

"I joined APPEAL the week after losing my ninth Episode by not showing up. I was sick of hiding from my costume, and I figured if APPEAL had a super on their side, that could amplify their voice. I only wanted to have the life I *should* have had. So, just like you at Riverside High, I made PSA videos, only mine were for antipower causes. I explained, as best I could, the legal dubiousness of superheroes and villains and how this would never have been acceptable in pre–Launch Day society. And they even gave me an alter ego so I could be a regular person in interviews and talk about how superpowers had ruined my life."

"And you did that for four years?" Bee asked.

"Three. I met Garret, and he convinced me to come home. I still did some digital work for APPEAL until I started showing with Annie, then I retired as their spokesvillain. But I kept in touch with them for another thirteen years after that."

"What made you stop?" Bee asked. She was full of questions, but I already knew the answer.

"I got my powers," I said.

Bee and I lay in bed, not moving. The little twin mattress had just enough space for us both to watch an Episode on Bee's phone if I wrapped my arm around her waist and didn't mind eating her curly black hair. She searched away, looking for the only Madame Shockwave Episode ever screened.

I'd decided I didn't need Mom's Costume. I already had a solid Elementalist in Rainy Day; if she wanted me to have it, it'd be there as a gift. Even so, I couldn't help but feel like she'd held out on me, and I wanted to know what her powers *did*.

"Do you think Mom was right?" I asked Bee.

She rolled slightly to look at me. "I don't know. What if you'd been blamed for the Grant Building disaster?"

"I *was* blamed for the Grant Building disaster," I said.

"You know what I mean. Like, legally. You were only involved in it, and there's a difference."

Yeah, that was true. "I don't know. I'm not sure how I'd have felt. Plus, this was her first Episode."

"I've got it."

Bee pressed play on her phone, we shoved headphones into our ears, and I watched my mom be a supervillain. She'd attacked a bank—what was with villains and banks? By the time the camera drone started rolling, the building's power was out, the safe-deposit boxes littered the floor just like Professor Panic's bank Episode, and she'd filled several bags with ill-gotten gains. The whole scene had me torn; part of me wanted to root for the incoming hero. But the rest of me, the part whose mom was on the screen, wanted her to win.

The hero tore through a wall with a pair of mechanized tentacles that looked like a squid's. His power level was beyond Mom's, and even though she fought hard, it only took a handful of seconds before the Episode's outcome was preordained. The hero was *going* to win.

At least, he was until Madame Shockwave used her [**Signature Skill**].

It looked like a LABRAT airburst, but it went in all directions, and blue-white lightning rode along as it blasted through the bank. As the air crackled, both of the hero's squid arms sparked and crashed to the ground, then dragged behind the hero uselessly. It looked like the tables had turned.

Then the bank blew up.

I jerked backward, rolling off the bed and dragging Bee with me. The explosion came out of nowhere, and there were Extras inside. Had something Mom did caused it?

"Come on, Annie. You knew it was coming," Bee started. Then she stopped. "Oh shit."

Words popped over the screen. "Both the hero and villain went unconscious due to the explosion. Eight Extras were hospitalized, and one later died. The Episode ended here, and Madame Shockwave's lawyers agreed to pay restitution from her future earnings. Unfortunately, she retired a few months later, and within four years, she had completely disappeared from the public eye."

"Oh shit, Annie," Bee repeated. "Your mom killed someone."

I flashed back to the Poudre Canyon Bridge—to that henchman who, as far as I knew, was still in the hospital. I'd been talking with a few superheroes about what happened, and they'd convinced me that even though I hadn't done everything right, I hadn't done anything wrong. I'd done my best to stop the henchman and saved the Extra. It wasn't my fault.

But Mom hadn't had that kind of support, and she'd been given minor-league powers in a little-league body and mentality. Before the first Power War, the leagues hadn't been established, and the Ilneats ran their shows like the Wild West. The mismatch between powers and personality had destroyed her career—and her dreams.

I tapped the Off button on Bee's phone. She glared at me until she saw my face. "Roll over, Annie," she said.

I did, and she held me for a while. I didn't say anything for a long time. Then, just when I was about to sleep, my eyes sprung open. "We missed something about APPEAL, Bee. They're crazy, and their plans would just give villains free reign over the world, but there's a reason they think like they do, and I want to figure out what it is. Mom might know, but I pushed her hard enough tonight."

"So what do you wanna do about it?" Bee's words slurred. I'd woken her up, and I wasn't sorry.

"I need to talk to Su-Bin. Something feels off."

37

Something Feels Off

SUNDAY, MARCH 29

I didn't get a chance to call Su-Bin on Saturday.

My parents dragged Bee and me out to the Mesa—not Flat Top Hill, but the Mesa that rose behind it. We explored the woods, then visited a fake pioneer town that'd been old before Launch Day. Back then, they'd had sheriffs and cattle rustlers, not superheroes and villains, but the world hadn't been any safer. If anything, it was safer now. At least, I thought so.

Then we ate lunch and headed home. Mom disappeared for a few hours while we went bowling with Dad. By the time we finished, it was late, and everyone crashed.

So now, while I said my goodbyes, I felt a weird combination of sadness and relief. Sadness because I was leaving home again, and relief because Mom hadn't been the same since her confession. We hadn't told her we'd looked up the Episode, but she knew. She had to know.

I hugged her. "Goodbye, Mom. I'll be back as soon as summer rolls around."

"Bye, Anika. Goodbye, Bianca. Take care of our daughter for us, and don't let her do anything dumb."

"How can I stop her? She has *too much* dumb," Bee joked. I punched her on the shoulder playfully, and she winced and made a big deal about it. "But yeah, Mrs. DuPont, I'll make sure I do."

"For the last time, it's Claire. Garret, say your goodbyes."

I hugged Dad, and he messed up my hair. Then Bee and I walked out the front door, disappeared into the woods, and changed into our Costumes. Sergeant Alvetti awaited, and we hurried to meet him and his van.

The moment we got inside and started moving, I asked a super-important question. "Is everything we say in here confidential?"

"Yeah, kids, I don't talk about what happens in the van. As long as it's not illegal, you're okay. I'll turn the radio on, and you can push a button that'll raise a barrier."

"Great. I need to make a phone call as my secret identity, and I'd rather not let any more people know who I am." Bianca pressed buttons until the barrier raised, Alvetti's cheesy oldies filled the front cab and faded even through the new wall between us, and I called Su-Bin.

The moment she picked up, I set the phone on the van seat between Fursona and me. "Hi, you're on speaker with Bee and me."

"Hey, Annie! How was your break? Sounds like you're on your way back."

"Yeah. I'm curious about something, though. I met some people here who used to be antipower, which got me thinking. They had reasons to hate supers, so what's your family's reason?"

Su-Bin hesitated. "Well, crime's up, especially superhero-related crime, and a lot of police systems rely on supers to resolve even nonpowered crime. It feels like—"

"No, those are the points you talked about on the radio and your APPEAL meeting. What's your real reason for not liking supers?"

"I don't . . ." Su-Bin faded off, and I thought we'd lost her for a second as we drove into the mountains, but then she continued. "I don't want to talk about this, Annie. Not right now. Something happened, and it was horrible. My parents won't tell me the details, so I can't talk more about it. But supers aren't good for anyone, Annie. Not long-term."

"I see. Thanks." She wasn't being honest, but I also couldn't pick at any of it. I hesitated, then cleared my throat. "Do you want to grab dinner tonight?"

"No thanks, Annie. I'm with my parents for one more night. Maybe sometime this week, though?"

"Sure. Bye." I hung up and looked at Bee. "Think she was telling the truth?"

Bee closed her eyes and sighed. "Probably. It wouldn't surprise me if a lot of people were pretty frustrated by superheroes. For every person helping to rebuild the Grant Building, a student missed class time."

"Please stop bringing up the Grant Building."

"Right, sorry. Sore spot. The point is, I could see people being over this. It's not how life was before. But."

"But it's not about how life was before. This is life now," I finished. It didn't matter what the world was like before. What mattered was how life was now, and that we made the best of what we had. If Bee and I were to quit superheroing, a new hero would step up, or a villain would win unopposed. According to Su-Bin, we were an evil. But even in that worldview, we had to be a necessary one.

As the van rocketed toward Tokyexico, we talked about Mom for a while before I successfully shifted the conversation to Bee's parents. She called them and spent almost an hour talking despite dropping the call repeatedly as we crossed the mountains. Then, as Tokyexico came into view, I got a text.

<You ready? Tuesday evening. TU parking garage. Be in new costume - Gourmet 2:36>

I nodded slowly. "It's time for the Gourmet Episode, Bee."

"Yeah?" Fursona grabbed my phone. "Tuesday evening. Got it. I'll make sure my schedule's clear and stay nearby in case it's a trap."

"I don't think it's a trap. She needs the win, especially because we messed up her Episode with Roadrage. But I do appreciate it. I'll text you the plan as soon as she tells me what we're doing."

<Yeah. I'll be there in Magical Girl Fieri. You be ready too - Understudy 2:38>

<You bet. Bring your A game - Gourmet 2:39>

<We're going to be live on Earth TV the whole time - Gourmet 2:39>

"What the hell? Earth TV?" I hadn't signed up for that. I mean, I had. But live shows had different pressures than prerecorded ones like the Ilneats usually did. A five-minute delay meant there'd be no editing, like the Golden Goose Episode on Valentine's Day. I'd need to watch it with Gourmet.

"Understudy, Spring Break is supposed to be about relaxing. Now chill out. When we get to school, you can do some work."

She was right. I'd been way too focused on figuring out Su-Bin, and now the Gourmet Episode loomed before me, but I had a few precious hours to relax, and I was going to enjoy them.

My precious hours flew by far too quickly.

When we got back to campus, Bee conveniently remembered some homework she had to finish, and she disappeared to her room. I didn't mind; as long as she was there, I'd be focused on her, and I had my own questions to answer.

Now that Gourmet's Episode had a date, I needed to reevaluate the Magical Girl Ramsey Fieri Costume. I'd previously decided that its powers had no combat applications, but was that true?

[Just a Pinch of Spice] could be useful if I could prep weapons in advance. Maybe I could build gas bombs or something. But Gourmet didn't want to tell me about her plans, so I couldn't set up right. I tried one more time.

<Whats your plan? - Understudy 6:32>

<Youll see. Ive got a good show cooking - Gourmet 6:33>

"Dammit. She's having too much fun teasing the answer," I muttered. "Tails, what do you think?"

My plushie cat didn't respond.

"Uh, Tails?" It was pretty strange for her not to be around, but then again, she'd spent the whole day traveling. I shrugged. She'd probably fallen asleep on my bed.

Instead, I started thinking about [**Speed-Plating**]. That power felt useless at first glance, but maybe instead of the aesthetics of a plate, I could use it to set traps. I was really at a loss on this one.

I didn't have any ideas for [**Iron Stomach**]. It felt like Gourmet had given me a noncombat Costume, which didn't bode well for the Episode. How could she keep a fight from breaking out? Did she have deals with other heroes not to interfere?

I couldn't figure it out, so in the end, I gave up.

"Tails, it's bedtime." It was only seven thirty, but I hadn't slept well sharing a twin with Bee, and the floor hadn't been an option.

That damn cat still didn't respond.

"Tails? Where are you?" I dug through my bags; maybe she'd gotten packed and couldn't get out. But that didn't explain why she wasn't talking in my head. Sure enough, all I found was clothing, though I did find *one* outfit that I knew I hadn't packed. Mom had carefully folded her old Madame Shockwave costume into the bottom of my duffel, and she'd pinned a note to it.

Anika,

Dad and I talked about this after you and Bee went to bed, and we agreed you should have this. I'd prefer it if you didn't use it, but I have no delusions about how your Signature Skill works. I don't believe superhero work is a long-term solution. Cartman planned to use me as a villain so his hero could make it big, not so I could benefit from my powers. I don't doubt Rocko means the same for you.

Rocko wasn't perfect, that was for sure, but he'd never used me like that before, and he was supporting my goals of getting to the minor leagues. I read on.

However, I want you to know I support you. Madame Shockwave is a minor-league-level villain. Her Signature Skill overloads electronics in a pretty explosive way. I've only used it once.

Seriously!? Mom had the perfect counter to Professor Panic the entire time!? And she hadn't shared it with me!

I know you'll be tempted to use this suit, and perhaps mad at me for not sharing it with you, but I ask that you don't use it until you're a minor-league superhero. The electric overload is extreme, and I believe it caused a horrible accident that ended my career before it began. You likely know what I'm talking about, but you can look up the Episode "Breaking the Bank" if you need to learn more.

Anika, I'm with you. You're not on the path I want you to be, but it's your chosen path. There's a lot going on behind the scenes you might not see. I know I didn't for years. Just be careful.

Love,

Mom

I held up the spandex super-suit, all worries about Tails forgotten. It looked like it'd fit me, more or less, and it was the entire suit, not a part. Would [**Adaptive Armoire**] work on it without Pataki's involvement? I had to find out.

I stripped to my underwear and wrestled my way into the far-too-tight suit. I'd been half right; it wasn't that it didn't fit. It just didn't fit comfortably. And when I went to look in the green room's mirror, I didn't see me.

No. I saw my mom. She'd been smaller than me at seventeen. The yellow-and-green spandex seemed to blur and spark, and her domino mask painted a permanent smug look on my face. I shuddered and changed out of it without transforming. I didn't want to know what Mom's powers did. I didn't even want to see if it'd work. She didn't want me using it yet, and I could respect that.

The moment it was off, I collapsed into my bed and pulled the covers up. Tails sat there on the pillow, right in her usual spot. I'd checked there, but I was too tired to question it. And I had other stuff on my mind. For all that Lab Assistant Panic had been a villain's Costume, this one would be worse. Much, much worse. And I wasn't ready to keep it under control.

At least, not yet.

PART SIX

38

Academic Check-In

TUESDAY, MARCH 31

I climbed the Beaumont Administrative Building's stairs like a prisoner on their way to the guillotine, but in reality, I was just a super student heading to meet with my advisor.

When your advisor was Mindstorm, it felt the same.

It should have been a standard meeting; we'd been having them every couple of weeks, and they'd . . . I didn't want to think they'd helped, but for the most part, they'd kept me focused on my classes. They *were* annoying, though.

Tuesday wasn't our usual day, but Mindstorm insisted, and since I'd just missed her class—and ignored her warning about missing too many on purpose—I opened the door and slipped into her dark office. She'd once again ordered lunch for us. This time, she pushed an apple salad my way as I sat. "Thank you for . . . agreeing to meet today, Anika," she said the second the door closed.

"Yep," I said. I was trying to be peppy, not annoyed or worried. Her use of my real name bothered me—it felt like a power play, and our relationship as student and professor already had too much imbalance. "What's going on?"

"I wanted to get your read on how your classes are going."

"Oh." She hadn't asked my opinion in a couple of weeks. "Prop Design is super cool. I didn't like shop class in high school, but power tools are fun. We're working on the castle for *Young Frankenstein* and designing the stables the horses stay in. I've got the lead on the stables, which is pretty awesome."

"And Ilneat One and Ilneat Politics? How is . . . Dr. Quailman doing?"

Was she being derisive? "Honestly, he's not thrilling, and I think he's wrong about most of what he's teaching. The Ilneat sources we read don't match his lectures, and neither match what he said in Ilneat Relations. He's got this idea that the Ilneats are running some sort of feudalism thing, but that doesn't match other sources. It's all very confusing. Language is fun, but I'm not sure how, uh, relevant it is with translator devices."

"That's what I hoped you'd say." Mindstorm popped her neck and leaned forward. "You owe Dr. Quailman and me make-up assignments. I contacted him to ask about a few different students who missed class in the last three weeks as a . . . cover . . . for you. He would like you to attend a lecture by a certain Eustace Bagges, a renowned Ilneat historian, on April 17. It's a reschedule. Eustace had a conflict for the February date. Clear your schedule. You must attend."

"The seventeenth? I don't think I have anything that far out," I said. "I guess if I have to. What time?"

"7:30 p.m."

"Got it."

"Good. I think you'll like Professor Bagges. I've seen a few of his lectures—and disrupted one or two in Episodes—and they're very . . . insightful. The lecture may also shed some light on why Ilneat sources contradict Dr. Quailman. Now, your other classes. You've been carrying your . . . friend through Child Psychology, correct? Tell me what that's like."

She was referring to Su-Bin. "We're learning about the six-to-twelve age bracket. Su-Bin hates kids. I think her parents signed her up for the class or something, but I don't know. It doesn't matter. She helped me a lot in Algebra with tutoring and stuff, so I'm returning the favor. It's felt pretty good to pay that back."

I stopped talking and fidgeted with my salad. I only had one class left, and Mindstorm always saved hers for last.

"That leaves Combat Style Practicum with me. I am . . . not in the habit of listening to the Tokyexico Council of Heroes. When they contacted me to let me know they'd excused your absence, my first thought was to throw a fit. Do you know what my fits are like, Anika?"

I had a guess—she'd been the top villain in Tokyexico City, after all. "No."

"Liar." Mindstorm didn't seem to mind my fib. The accusation was almost casual. "Luckily, I had a long break to cool down and . . . do some minor-league Episodes. As part of my retirement, I have a couple of alter egos. One you may have met is Felicia Fire from the . . . Anti-Naptime League. The Narrator keeps our egos in line. But I have another for when I feel more serious. So by the time I'd solidified my plans to destroy the Council's tower again, I no longer wanted to."

I started responding, but Mindstorm held up a hand, and I fell silent. She felt deadly serious, a far cry from her usual bored personality. "However, that leaves the problem of your make-up assignment."

"Can't you just let it slide?" I asked, not expecting a positive response but hoping for one. "It's not like I wasn't doing superhero work or anything, and it was the day before break."

"No, I can't. For one thing . . . Superpower Slacking. I warned you not to ditch classes in favor of superhero work, and then you ditched *my* class for it. That puts you not only on the school's naughty list—though not for much longer if the Council of Heroes has any sway—but on *mine*. And second, if I allowed you to . . . avoid consequences, other students would try similar shenanigans. I have my reputation as a terrifying . . . teacher and villain to consider.

"Therefore, you and Fursona will report to our training Room half an hour before class. Tennyson will set up the arena, and you will face a true challenge for the first time."

"Who is it?" I asked, a sinking feeling in my gut. Mindstorm said she'd cooled down and wasn't interested in taking revenge on the Council of Heroes for interfering in her classroom, but she hadn't said anything about us.

"Me."

Shit. There had to be another option. Fursona and I couldn't beat Mindstorm—no way—and my absence was excused, not ditching. I imagined us getting flattened by Mindstorm, then having to turn around and fight Gourmet and Waterspout. Two brutal practice losses in one day felt like too much punishment for taking our only chance at a Spring Break.

But this was *Mindstorm*. Not Tennyson or Jackson, who'd probably be reasonable, but *Mindstorm*. I started to nod slowly, resigned to our practice bout.

Then I stopped. Why *not* try? The worst she could say was no. "Are there any other options? Something else we could do to make up the assignment? This seems wildly unfair."

Mindstorm grinned. It wasn't a friendly grin. "If you're planning on the minor leagues, you'll have to get used to wildly unfair fights. That's what the practice you missed was about, and major leaguers play down all the time . . . in fact, Tele-Portal was in a minor-league Episode with you two months ago, correct? Nevertheless, I'll think about it. We'll be in touch."

Bee had the whiteboard going again.

"So, given what Gourmet's told you so far, I've narrowed down her likely targets to a handful of studios in Mid-Town and one on Tokyexico's outskirts. If it's that one, I don't see how I can cover it and the others, so I'm gambling that it'll be Mid-Town." She wrote 'Mid-Town Studios' on the board.

I'd told her about my meeting with Mindstorm, of course, but she wasn't focused on Friday. She only cared about getting through tonight. I knew she hated the idea of me teaming up with Gourmet; she'd never forgiven the villain for crushing us last semester. And I knew she hated that I wouldn't even be in touch. But I had to do this. I'd messed up Gourmet's get-rich-quick scheme with Roadrage, and she needed the money for . . . whatever was wrong with her mom.

Bee thought she'd need a studio for her scheme. I wasn't sure about that, but we'd both agreed that she couldn't use an Ilneat one. No one *wanted* to go into the Hot Zone—not from outside, at least. As far as I knew, every super visited their producers through doors in their lairs or just being teleported, and most Extras didn't have a reason to see the Ilneats—plus the Compact placed limits on cross-Zone mobility for humans and Ilneats alike. So if Gourmet wanted to be on Earth TV, she'd need a human studio.

Bianca kept writing. "After we figure out where you'll be, I'll hang out nearby. If I tail the car, I can be outside the building a minute after you go in."

"No, don't. You'll need to be Fursona, and I don't think you can drive with the full-on fursuit," I said.

"No, you're right. I wish there were a phone booth nearby."

"A phone booth? Really?"

"Yep. Superheroes used to use them to change all the time."

"Aren't most of them glass-sided?"

"Shut up. So, I'll find a place to change, then wait around for something to go wrong." She wrote 'Something Goes Wrong' on the board right below 'Mid-Town Studios' and then looked at me. "What's going to go wrong?"

"Well, you think Gourmet's setting a trap for me, so it'll probably be Theseus. But if it's him, I can't imagine you'll be able to shift the balance of power. If security's too tight, Gourmet and I won't even make it to the studio, much less do whatever she's got planned." The whole time I talked, Bianca scribbled on the whiteboard. "Of course, Gourmet can probably handle whatever unpowered security the place has. It'll come down to whether they have a superhero on speed dial and *who* their superhero is. If it's Stella-Lunar, even Gourmet will back off."

It felt strange to be conspiring *against* Stella-Lunar. I'd always imagined that we'd be on the same team if I ever appeared in an Episode with her, but with three hero Costumes and two villain ones—three if you counted Madame Shockwave and one if you didn't count Ramsey Fieri—I supposed it was only a matter of chance.

"So, assuming it's a hero, I can't help you," Fursona said. She wrote 'Hero Attack' and 'No Fursona Help.'

"Yeah, I get it. I'll be okay."

"Annie," Bianca said, putting down the marker. "I don't like this. You've got a one-point lead. We should try to extend that, not play around with one of our nemeses."

I paused. "Gourmet's a nemesis? I hadn't really thought of her that way. Fun!"

"Stop, Annie. Take this seriously." Bianca sighed and collapsed onto the chaise lounge, dramatically sprawling out. I couldn't tell if *she* was taking this seriously or not. "At least let me track your phone so I'm sure you're safe. You can keep it in your apron pocket or something. That way, I know."

"I trust Gourmet," I said. "Let me think for a minute."

I *did* trust Gourmet. She'd seemed genuine during "Braking and Entering," and she'd given me part of her costume. She trusted me, so the least I could do was return the favor.

But Bianca didn't.

And right now, that mattered more than my own feelings. Bee still stung from the gym Episode last semester, even though we'd worked with Gourmet and Theseus for months after. Or maybe she just didn't like me going solo—which wasn't fair. She'd gotten to solo Theseus. It didn't matter, though. Letting her track my phone would make her feel better. "Okay, how about this? I'll give you tracking for my phone for tonight. You'll know exactly where I am, and you can make sure I'm safe. But if you do solo Episodes, I get to track yours while you're in the Episode."

"Deal," Bianca said. "You have half an hour. I wish we could have prepped better for this."

"Me too." I turned on Tracking Mode and punched Bianca's number into my phone. Then I hugged her. "I'll be safe, I promise."

"I hope so," she said. "I just *know* Gourmet's cooking up trouble."

39

Cooking up Trouble

"Get in the car, loser. We're going villaining." Gourmet smirked from behind the wheel of her disgustingly cool hot rod. "Quit staring at it and hop in."

I ignored Gourmet's eye-roll and sat down. My chef's hat rubbed against the ceiling, and I pushed it down. As requested, I wore the Magical Girl Ramsey Fieri Costume, but I'd also equipped Lab Assistant Panic for the first time in months, just in case I needed a villainous option with actual combat power. I looked at Gourmet. "What now?"

"Buckle up."

Before I could even grab the seatbelt, Gourmet jammed down on the accelerator, and the candy-apple-red car took off with a roar. The acceleration pressed me back into my seat, and I held the chef's hat down so it wouldn't go flying. She whipped out onto University Drive and started weaving through traffic.

"How come you get a cool hot rod?" I asked. I'd seen her Mustang before. I'd even been *in* it, but now we had time to talk about it.

"Insurance fraud and bribery to stop me from eating buildings," Gourmet replied. "Now that we're alone, here's the deal. This is a *must-win* Episode for me. I need the payout for family reasons. Mom's not doing great, and it'll cost a fortune to get her here, into Tokyexico General, and to the right specialists. Theseus proposed kidnapping them, but I'd still need all the equipment. So instead, we're going to have ourselves a little Episode."

The speed leveled off, and I took a breath, thinking. It wasn't about climbing the rankings. It was about family. I understood; if something happened to my mom, I'd do whatever I could to help her. One thing bugged me, though. "Why didn't you do this weeks ago?"

"You messed up my plan weeks ago, so I had to run my back-up. Look, Snack, if we're gonna make this work, I need two things from you. First, you shut up and do what I say, and we get through this. And second, you follow the plan I've been building this whole time. Got it?" She swerved around a truck and whipped the car toward Mid-Town.

"Got it. What's the plan, then?"

"Glad you asked. We're going on a cooking show."

"What?"

"Yep. I got the idea from Theseus. He said I'd need a brand if I wanted to make some money. And there aren't many superheroes who look like me." Gourmet gestured at her chubby body. "So, after thinking about it, my brand is cooking show vigilantism. All these shows think they're teaching people the right way to make food—"

"They're not?"

"—But I know we can do better. You're not my long-term lieutenant for this, but I needed someone who'd work with me until I can lure the ideal one away from Flare."

"Wait. You want The Crumb? No one *wants* The Crumb."

Gourmet laughed. "Three weeks ago, you'd have been right. But he's not a bad villain. He's just misunderstood and misused. But focus, Chef Girl. Until I get him, I need you. So here's the plan. We're moving fast, hitting hard, and taking over *Cooking with Charlene*. It's one of the only prime-time cooking shows with everything we need. It's got a well-known celebrity chef we can kidnap, tons of ingredients on-set, and most importantly, it's filmed live."

"Why do we care if it's filmed live?" I asked.

"Because my producer isn't 100% on board with this. They think I should focus on getting a lieutenant position with a minor leaguer. But they don't *understand*." Gourmet gritted her teeth, weaved between two cars, then spun the steering wheel until the tires screeched, and I slammed against the locked door. "I'm not doing this for fame or anything. I just need a payout. They're gonna film it, but they might not run it. So we need the live filming to get ourselves out there in case the studios don't love what we do."

Broadway Mall flashed by, its bright lights just a blur. Then Gourmet slammed on the brakes. I jerked forward before my seat belt caught me. A moment later, the stench of burning rubber caught up to us. A police siren whined faintly in the distance.

Gourmet shut off the engine. "Last chance to back out."

I took a deep breath. Then I shook my head. "Where's this being shot?"

"Twenty-fifth floor. Don't worry about the car. She'll take care of herself. Just get to the elevator, break into Studio 2502, and *don't* let the camera crew or Charlene escape. Got it?"

I took a deep breath. Then, I steadied myself. I'd never intentionally been a villain, but how hard could it be? "Got it. Let's do this."

[Casting Call]
[Episode: Pilot: Gourmet's Glutton Hour - PG]
[Role: Celebrity Chef! Do you accept the role? (Yes/No)]
[Role Focus: Cunning + Grit]

The studio definitely wasn't Ilneat. For one thing, it wasn't a hundred degrees. For another, the camera crew and executives standing around weren't aliens. And most tellingly, there wasn't a single powered person on set.

At least, there hadn't been until five seconds ago.

"You can't be in here! Security! Oof!" An executive shouted just before Gourmet punched him in the stomach. He went down with a groan. The other Extras raised their hands in surrender, except the woman behind the camera, who swung it around to face us.

Gourmet gave her a thumbs-up. "Keep that rolling. *Cooking with Charlene* is canceled for the evening. Tonight, we're bringing you a fun change of pace. Welcome, guests, to *Gourmet's Glutton Hour*! I'm your host, Gourmet, and with me is a special guest star, Celebrity Chef Ramsey Fieri. We're going to be cooking up a brand-new recipe for your enjoyment!

"I've been working on perfecting this recipe for years, so tonight, prepare to learn how to make fried shed!"

"Seriously, Gourmet?" I asked

"No, not really. We're doing a taco salad, enchiladas, and sopapillas. It'll be great."

I sighed in relief. The idea of making fried *shed* on camera was too much. "And the Extras?"

"You decide what to do with them. Throw them out a window. Shove them into the elevator. Whatever." Gourmet grabbed Charlene, who'd pulled out a cell phone, and shoved her into a chair behind the counter. She grabbed the phone and tossed it into a pot, where it sparked and hissed before dying. "No phones!"

<You should keep them meow-round, Understudy,> Tails said from inside my apron. *<You could use the taste testers, and hostages could be helpful when the heroes come knocking.>*

I nodded decisively, putting on the villain show for the execs and the camera-woman. "Right. You all sit down and hand over your phones. Don't you move. You're our live studio audience now. No more canned reaction shots—when we ask for it, you give your honest, unbiased opinions. And if we don't *like* that opinion . . ." I pointed to the window meaningfully. I wasn't about to tell Gourmet that *I* had a phone in my pocket or that it was actively recording my location for a hero to track, but the executives didn't need to be talking to anyone.

Gourmet held up a cheese grater. "Cheddar, Monterrey Jack, and Mozzarella, quick. Let's make some god-[**Beep!**] TV!"

And just like that, we started filming the pilot episode of *Gourmet's Glutton Hour*. I scrambled for the cheeses; the studio hadn't been designed to be *useable* as a kitchen. Sure, its restaurant-grade fridge loomed over a corner away from center stage. And yeah, it had cabinets filled with every spice and canned veggie I could imagine. But the set wasn't built for cooking. They'd designed it to look good on camera.

So, instead of things being logical, with a good triangle flow between the fridge, stove, and sink, I felt totally lost in this kitchen. "Whoever built this place should be fired . . . from a cannon!" I complained.

By the time I'd gotten Gourmet her ingredients and she'd shoved them into Charlene's hands to prep, both the show's regular host and the supervillain looked impatient. Charlene turned toward Gourmet. "I *was* showing the audience how to make a pork roast if we want to stick with—"

"No! Taco salad and enchiladas or your doom," Gourmet snapped, and Charlene shut up. "Now, the taco salad's a little on the generic side. Ramsey Fieri, I've sent you the recipe. I'll be prepping the butternut squash for the enchiladas. It's my grandma's recipe, but my mom . . . Mom taught it to me."

"Oh, that's a great backstory for your meal," Charlene said. She just couldn't take a hint—not even when Gourmet glared at her. "Do you want to tell the audience more?"

"No, I don't."

By the time I'd finished plating the taco salad—chips, lettuce, beans, tomatoes, avocado, onions, peppers, cheese, a sprinkle of garlic, cumin, and cayenne pepper; repeat three times—I was thoroughly sick of having a live studio audience.

They refused to sit still, they wouldn't stop trying to escape, and I had serious thoughts about bailing, stepping out into the hall, and returning as Lab Assistant Panic. Surely it'd be worth it to lose my cooking powers in exchange for letting TA-1LZ guard the hostages. But even so, I had enough taco salads plated for each of them.

[Just the Right Flavor! +1 Cunning Point Pending]
[Stunning Plating! +1 Drama Point Pending]

This would be a low-point Episode, but maybe it wouldn't matter. The goal wasn't to earn Style Points, after all.

Gourmet was having a blast, though. While the camera barely lingered on me, even when I plated the salads, it seemed glued to the supervillain and her hostage/host.

"Next, we'll get started on the enchiladas. Everyone rolls their enchiladas, and that's great. But in my grandma's kitchen, we build enchiladas in layers, like onions, ogres, or emo teenagers. Every food is lasagna, after all, and layered enchiladas are just Mexican lasagna. So, Fieri, deliver these salads to our guests. And make *sure* Charlene gets one. I'll get to work on the—"

BAM!

The door burst in, and a Magical Girl wearing a dress made mostly of soap suds crashed through on a tidal wave of water. She landed in her flip-flops, and the water sloshed forward, covering the studio audience in suds. Behind her, a rubber ducky filled the hall. I recognized it as Bubble-Bill, which meant this had to be . . .

"Magical Girl Foamy Flash is here to clean! I'm ready to straighten up the scene!"

Yep. I set the taco salads down safely on the counter, away from where the fight would probably happen. Then, I started to transform into Lab Assistant Panic.

"SHE'LL SAVE THE DAY! SHE'S A GREAT MECHANIC!
EVERYONE CHEER FOR LAB ASSISTANT PANIC!"

I slapped the goggles on my face and spun around. The lab coat formed, whirling around me. This time would be different! This time, Lab Assistant Panic had free reign to do her worst—and her best! "Foamy Flash, you've fallen into my trap!"

TA-1LZ landed on the floor next to me. The robot cat wasn't just a cat-sized robot anymore. She wouldn't hold a candle to Snagglemaw, but she'd grown solidly bobcat-sized thanks to the **[TA-1LZ Size Boost]**. More importantly, her back opened up, and a Gatling taser grew from it, latching onto the back of her head. It revved with a hissing, spitting sound as TA-1LZ started talking. "Calculating a 43% chance of winning this fight without Gourmet. Your evil breakdown percent is 64. Have fun!"

I laughed maniacally but didn't use my **[Maniacal Reveal]**. Not yet. "Ahahahahaha! **[TA-1LZ New Head-Cannon]**: you lose!"

40

New Head-Cannon: You Lose

For the first time since I'd put on Peter's goggles, the Costume felt *right*.

My laughter trailed off as TA-1LZ launched her attack, Gatling taser howling. I ran the other way, putting the hostages between myself and Foamy Flash. I'd always resisted the call of evil as Lab Assistant Panic, but now, I was a villain. Now, I could finally cut loose.

"Hey, Labcoat, win this thing fast! Camera on me, not them!" Gourmet shouted. The camerawoman stopped herself from turning to film our battle and refocused on the supervillain and Charlene. "Win that quickly so you can serve the salads!"

"Got it, boss!"

A small part of me wondered how disappointed Fursona would be to see me going full villain, but most of me knew I needed to crush my enemy. I had to drive her from the studio or get her to surrender; that way, we could get some TV executives crying on camera. So, as TA-1LZ's Gatling prongs bounced off Bubble-Bill and popped Foamy Flash's bubble bath suds, I grabbed a spare camera.

[Familiar Flex! +1 Badass Point]

I needed the camera because I was questioning something. "**[Science Has Rules?]**" I don't think so. If I pop the lens out of this and attach these batteries, then rewire this, I can—"

Pop! Pop! Pop!

A wall of bubbles slammed into me, tossing me to the side. I held on to the camera as I slammed into the set's edge. Foamy Flash started yelling. "Go! Go! Get out of here!"

[HP 8/9]

"My hostages! Quit stealing my hostages!" I needed those—who else would taste test our taco salad? I finished rewiring my newest invention. "Using kinetic electricity circuits, I've developed a brand-new weapon. I call it . . ."

I pulled the trigger and forgot to finish my sentence.

Ka-ROM!

The blast knocked me back, and my weapon whined piteously as it vomited a black hole into the middle of the studio. Suds flew *everywhere*. The shot spun gravity for a quarter-second, showering the set with bubble bath and soaking TA-1LZ, Foamy Flash, and me. Only Bubble-Bill seemed happy with the results. My cannon looked worse for wear, but I'd get another shot with it—maybe even two—before it tore itself apart.

[**Pseudoscientific Mumbo-Jumbo! +1 Drama Point**]

Foamy Flash glared, then winced as more taser hooks slammed into her. Shockingly, her superhero damage seemed to be cutting off the worst of it—either that or she had a Grit power running. She leveled her wand, which looked a lot like a loofah on a stick, and shouted, "[**Bubble Burst**]!" A barrage of bubbles burst from the loofah, filling the air between her and me in seconds. They each popped, leaving soapy spheres of water in the air and cleaning everything in their path.

Including me.

[**HP 7/9**]

I winced and rolled behind a chair to avoid another bubble blast, and my phone buzzed in my lab coat pocket. Whoever wanted my attention, they'd have to wait. I turned and fired the . . . I'd never named it. The Deep Subject Gravity Well Launcher; that would work. I fired the Deep Subject Gravity Well Launcher at Foamy Flash. It ripped through the air, this time tossing Bubble-Bill to the side and covering half the set with soapy water.

Ka-ROM!

[**Pseudoscientific Mumbo-Jumbo! +1 Drama Point**]
[**Gritty Recovery! +1 Grit Point**]

"Hey, watch it, Minion!" Gourmet shouted. "You ruin these enchiladas, and this show is *over*!"

I glared back for a moment. Her counter was covered with butternut squash, half-diced green chilis, and browned chicken breasts. She'd finished the enchilada sauce, and a mix of sour cream, spices, olives, and squash sat in a bowl beside her. "I have something to reveal—Maniacally." Then I stopped. I'd unequipped [**Maniacal Reveal**] to make room for [**Ta-1LZ New Head-Cannon**].

"Never mind. You got it, boss." On further consideration, she was right. If Foamy Flash soaked the counter, this whole thing would be for nothing. I had to press the attack—but my Deep Subject Gravity Well Launcher smoked and sparked.

Even so, I pulled the trigger—just as Foamy Flash leaped into the air. She started yelling something about me not being able to stop her, but the blast caught her mid-speech and threw her toward the ceiling.

Ka-ROM! BOOM!

A different blast caught me.

My cannon ripped apart as the gravity shifted, plates shattering and exploding outward. I catapulted into the counter, and a spice jar full of garlic overturned, pouring down on top of me.

[HP 5/9]

[**Pseudoscientific Mumbo-Jumbo! +1 Drama Point**]

I hurried to my feet as TA-1LZ opened fire, trying to keep Foamy Flash pinned down behind the audience seats. Tasers bounced off chairs, and panicked executives-turned-tasters ran every which way. Some headed to the door and sprinted out. Others took cover; one particularly clueless one crouched between Gourmet and Charlene until the supervillain glared at him. Then he fled.

A taser punched into a jar filled with cayenne pepper, coating half the studio in the spicy . . . spice, including me. I coughed, trying to clear my lungs. Tears ran down my face—I couldn't see. I couldn't breathe. And I certainly couldn't fight.

"It's . . . It's time for a [**Cleaning Cleanse**]!" Foamy Flash shouted between coughs of her own.

Shit, I thought between coughs. Shit, shit, shit. That didn't sound good. Gourmet vaulted over the counter and crashed into the camera—which spun on its hinge, getting a view of the chaos before the camerawoman could get it under control. I was only a step behind her. A huge vortex of soapy water was forming around Magical Girl Foamy Flash. We had to stop it, or the whole meal would be ruined.

"You're too late!" Foamy Flash shouted again. "[**Cleaning Cleanse**], activate!"

The bubble tornado crashed outward like a tidal wave, engulfing the room in its raging, too-clean tide. It scoured cayenne pepper from every surface, Foamy Flash's face, and my eyes. It kept growing, filling the room. The camerawoman leaped from her seat, letting the studio's camera swing freely in the storm. Extras scattered. And through the raging storm and bursting bubbles, I heard Gourmet's scream of anguish.

"You [**Beep!**] My enchiladas!"

The tide fell slowly, and as bubbles popped in a machine-gun staccato, I tried to get control of something—even if that something was myself.

Lab Assistant Panic was running out of options. My [**Science Has Rules?**] cannon had failed. TA-1LZ wasn't responding, so I couldn't rely on her [**Head-Cannon**] for suppression and distraction. And, honestly, most of Lab Assistant Panic's powers relied on my familiar being functional.

I [**Checked the Script**]. My phone buzzed, but I ignored it. My power pointed toward the lights. Could I [**Speed-Hack**] them? I could give it a shot. At the very least, it'd provide Gourmet and me a chance to get control.

[**Good Thinking! +1 Cunning Point**]

I activated [**Speed-Hacker**], letting the world turn to ones and zeros for a few seconds. Foamy Flash was still channeling her power, kind of like when I used [**Bit-Part Barrage**]. She wouldn't be more of a threat than she already had been. The lights flickered, then turned off. Then they flashed on and off, blinked, then turned on—but this time, they glowed pink.

As they continued to flash and pulse, the color shifted. I smiled thinly; I'd accidentally made the studio into a rave, but at least it'd be harder for Foamy Flash to find us. That gave me time to plan my next move.

[**Good Thinking! +1 Cunning Point**]

I needed a base gizmo. I could turn this around if I could get another [**Science Has Rules?**] weapon.

Gourmet screamed again. "I'll kill you! Those were for my mom!" She sounded agonized—barely human. Then I saw her silhouette rise above the fading bubbles, and she took a bite of something. She coughed once. Twice. Three times.

On the third, she coughed fire.

"You'll pay for ruining my meal!" the supervillain shouted. I winced. I'd never been on the receiving end of a truly enraged Gourmet, and I didn't want to start now. As she charged Foamy Flash, Bubble-Bill leaped between them, and I ducked into the kitchen. I needed a weapon.

I grabbed an electric mixer, shoved the spinners into a blender's pitcher, then slammed that all against a toaster. A camera drone hovered nearby, focused on me, while a second one watched Gourmet and Foamy Flash fight it out. I cleared my throat. "Two-Shot Protein-Shake Shotgun. Uh, ammo goes in, spinners activate, and shake-sludge sprays out. Uses, um, Bernoulli Effect Particles to stabilize its ammo for better accuracy."

[**Pseudoscientific Mumbo-Jumbo! +1 Drama Point**]

"That sounds like baloney," Charlene said from beside me. She breathed rapid, shallow breaths, and her perfectly styled hair was askew, only held in place by far too much hairspray, but she had a shit-eating grin plastered on her face—like she was either the world's biggest suck-up or having the time of her life. "Your boss is breathing fire and flapping dragon wings, and all you've got is a MacGyvered gun?"

I aimed the Two-Shot Protein-Shake Shotgun at Foamy Flash, pulled the trigger twice, and grabbed a loaf of bread. "Want to argue with it?"

"Point taken."

[Pseudoscientific Mumbo-Jumbo! +1 Drama Point]

I glanced over the counter at Foamy Flash, who was covered in stinky-smelling pinkish goop. She screamed, pointed her wand at herself, and shouted, "[**Spot-Clean Shower**]!" Water jetted from her wand, lightly spraying her down and cleaning her off. The effect looked a lot like my [**Virga**]. She *had* to be healing, too.

A gout of flame ripped through the momentarily dark studio, colliding with a massive bubble. As the soap burned through, the bubble released air, and the fire flashed, then faded.

Gourmet ducked one bubble burst, then another, but as I reloaded the Protein-Shake Shotgun, she got forced back toward the counter. I tried to cover her, but Bubble-Bill blocked my second volley of shots.

Then Gourmet breathed another fiery breath.

Chairs burst into flame. The sprinklers on the ceiling went off. And worse, an alarm started howling. In the chaos, I ducked out from cover, pumped two more shots toward Foamy Flash, and slid across the floor toward TA-1LZ. "Ahahahaha! I've got you, minion!"

Bubbles filled the air behind me as Bubble-Bill turned in place, squeaking and vomiting soapy water. They started popping and throwing chairs across the room. One slammed into me, then another.

[HP 4/9]
[Gritty Recovery! +1 Grit Point]

I had to get to cover, and then I had to fix TA-1LZ. Without my minion, the Lab Assistant Panic costume just didn't *do* enough, and the robot cat had shorted out. I ran back to the counter. Bubbles popped against it.

"Well, Snack, you got anything?" Gourmet asked. She coughed up a thin, weak fireball. "I'm out of juice. Need something new to chew on."

I glanced at TA-1LZ, but one look told me she wouldn't recover—not in time to help with this fight. I shook my head. "No. I may be a great mechanic, but water's [**Beep!**] on electronics."

[Rating Warning #1! Episode Rating - PG! Censor in Effect]

"Alright. We need a plan, then. That jury-rigged gun any good?" Gourmet reached up and grabbed a handful of scattered, soaked taco salad fixings. She looked mournfully at it, then popped it into her mouth.

"It shoots protein shakes."

"It shoots what?" Gourmet spat the taco salad out. "Hit me."

"What?"

"Hit me! Come on, right in the face, both barrels! This is our chance!" She closed her eyes and opened her mouth. "Can you imagine what a bullet of protein shake will buff me with?"

"I'm not sure I want to," I complained. Then I leveled the [**Science Has Rules?**]-powered gun. "You're sure?"

"Absolutely."

My phone buzzed again. I ignored it. Instead, I shot my supervillain boss in the face.

41

In the Face

Gourmet flopped to the floor from my two-shot smoothie blast. I stared at her in horror; had I knocked her out? She couldn't have lost that much superhero damage, could she?

I didn't have time to find out. Foamy Flash surged forward, this time seeming to surf on a wave of bubble bath water. We'd already lost all our taste testers, and Gourmet would kill me if Foamy Flash liberated Charlene, too. I reloaded and popped over the counter. My Two-Shot Protein-Shake Shotgun smoked and crackled in my hands two shots later. It'd done its best, and it couldn't do any more.

The shots missed, but they forced Foamy Flash to duck behind some chairs for a moment. I spared another glance at Gourmet.

And blinked.

Had she always been so muscle-bound? No. No way. She'd never cared about being in shape. Now, though, she looked like she spent twelve hours a day at the gym. Muscles rippled under her Costume as she breathed. Her eyes opened. And she roared, shaking the glassware in one of the set's cabinets.

Then she grinned and winked at me. "That hit the spot, Snack! Now it's time to get serious."

She stood up and charged, still roaring like a maniac. I winced. Foamy Flash wouldn't stand much of a chance if Gourmet closed the gap, but even her magnificent musculature couldn't catch up to the Magical Girl as she surfed the bubble bath wave again.

I needed to help, but Lab Assistant Panic was officially out of juice—and I had no way of knowing if a villainous breakdown was coming or if I'd already been suffering one. I needed to switch back.

I looked around, grimaced at the remains of the enchilada sauce, and stuck a finger in it. As I sucked my finger clean, I muttered, "You didn't cook this. It's **[Beep!]** raw."

[Rating Warning #2! Episode Rating - PG! Censor in Effect]

A moment later, I stood there in full chef's regalia. Tails spun her star-shaped eyes and squeezed herself. Water poured from the plushie cat like a sponge. *<Wow! What hit me?>*

"No time!" I shouted. I didn't have many great options in the Magical Girl Ramsey Fieri Costume. I could **[Hometown Heroine]**—er, **[Hometown Villainess]**—as a gap-closer and try landing a **[Spotlight Strike]**, but the last thing I wanted was to get in Alpha Gourmet's way. She kept chasing after Foamy Flash, shouting and yelling. I watched Bubble-Bill try to intercept, only to be tossed aside.

No, I'd have to do some creative cooking, I decided. My phone buzzed again. I didn't have time to answer it; Mom or Dad would have to wait.

I grabbed a stack of plates. Charlene looked at me like I'd lost my mind. "What are you going to do with—"

I threw the first one at Foamy Flash. It hit, but not before I had two more in the air. The first two didn't give me any Style Points, but the third caught the Magical Girl on the cheek. She squeaked in pain and fell off her bubble bath wave, crashing to the floor.

[Dramatic Damage! +1 Drama Point]

Before Gourmet could reach her, she shouted, "**[Slip-and-Slide Escape]**!" She slid across the floor. I shook a fist in frustration as the slide turned back into a surf, and she fired a beam of bubbles my way. They exploded, showering the counter with soap and glass—and spices. I wrinkled my nose at the too-intense mix of cumin, green chili powder, and soap.

Then I got an idea. I flung another pair of plates, as much to get them out of my hands as to hit anything, and dashed for the spice cabinet. Then I shoveled as many bottles as I could fit into my apron pocket, burying my phone. I had just enough time to think about what a bad idea this was, then I started cooking.

Sort of.

The goal wasn't to spice anything—at least not properly. Instead, I activated **[Just a Pinch of Spice]** and filled my hand with coriander. I flung it toward the incoming bubbles, which popped as the powdered spice filled the air between them and me.

[Good Thinking! +1 Cunning Point]

That wouldn't be enough, though. I had to actually stop Foamy Flash long enough for Alpha Gourmet to get a hold of her. If she could do that, it'd be over in a heartbeat. But that meant coming out from behind the set's cover. I took a deep breath, inhaling the coriander and letting **[Iron Stomach]** deal with it, and dashed out into the wreckage of the studio audience seating.

[Gritty Meal! +1 Grit Point]

"Eat this!" I lobbed a handful of curry powder at Foamy Flash, then another. The first caught her in the back, and she laughed. "You'll have to do better than t—urk!"

The second covered her face.

[Good Thinking! +1 Cunning Point]

She pawed at her eyes and tried desperately to spit the spice out. But it didn't work. The bubble bath wave collapsed a moment later, dropping her against the studio's wall. Alpha Gourmet leaped toward her, a wall of muscle and hatred, and punched her. Once. Twice. Three times.

[Clever Assist! +1 Cunning Point]
[End of Act One! Act Two in Five Minutes!]
[Alias - Understudy] [Archetype - Magical Girl] [Community Rank - 250/523]
[HP 4/9]
[Styles and Skills]
►**Archetype Skill - Transformation Sequence**
►**Combo Skills - Power-Weaving**
►**Badass (39)**
►**Cunning (43)**
►**Drama (23)**
►**Stellar Ray 2**
►**Bit-Part Barrage 1**
►**Flamboyance (18)**
►**Signature Skill - Adaptive Armoire 2**
►**Stored Costumes: (Rainy Day, Copy Cat)**
►**Starwave Sail 1**
►**Quick-Time Change 2**
►**Grit (29)**
►**I-Frame Transform 2**

Gourmet cleared her throat, fist back for another punch. The studio, which had just felt like a madhouse, now sounded utterly silent. A single bubble popped against the back wall, and powdered spices drifted softly toward the floor. I let go of the double handful of curry I'd held ready in case Foamy Flash escaped.

"What are you two waiting for!? Let's make some fucking television!" Charlene shouted from behind the somewhat worse-for-wear counter. She'd righted a stool and sat staring at the enchilada mix. "This is salvageable!"

"I stuck my hand in it," I protested. What the hell? The hostage was participating? I'd heard of Stockholm Syndrome, but this was too much.

Gourmet grabbed Foamy Flash and carried her unconscious form to the studio door. She cracked it open, yelled, "Oh shit," and threw her out, then slammed the door. "We've got company out there! It's the cops!"

"Just yell that you've got a hostage. That usually gets them to back off on the shows," Charlene said.

Gourmet followed her directions, then stomped over to the counter. While she and Charlene examined the enchiladas' wreckage, I took stock of the room.

Aside from the counter, the entire studio was wrecked. Shattered chairs lay haphazardly in the audience section, and the carpet was soaked. I stepped onto it, letting **[Hometown Heroine]** fall off, and felt water squish up around my boots. What wasn't covered in soap residue was coated with half a dozen different spices. We'd also lost the hostages—all except two. Charlene sat with Gourmet, working through a plan to salvage the enchiladas—or to start over and still have a decent product. And, inexplicably, the camerawoman had returned to her post.

I raised an eyebrow at her, and she shrugged. "I'm nobody to you villains, not worth hurting if I do as I'm told, and this beats another night of *Cooking with Charlene*."

I nodded. "Bosses, am I right?"

"Yeah. You too, huh?"

"Yep. I'm just doing this gig as a favor to Gourmet, but I'd much rather work for myself. She doesn't know how to manage a kitchen for shit."

The camerawoman stared at me for a second, then burst into laughter. I held my serious face briefly, then cracked up, too. We were still laughing when the Episode resumed.

[Gourmet's Glutton Hour: Act Two in Progress]

"Alright, we're starting over, ditching the taco salad and sopapillas and focusing on getting these enchiladas done! Fieri, get the oven preheating, new olives, new sour cream, and check the spice cabinet for backups of garlic, chili powder, cayenne, and cumin. Charlene—"

"Chicken prep, yeah. Your cutting technique is weak," Charlene said. Her eyes shone.

"Yeah, sure," Gourmet said. "I've got the sauce. Go!"

I had no idea how we'd Stockholm Syndromed the two perfect hostages for our cooking show. I didn't know why the camerawoman hadn't fled; her excuse seemed flimsy. I could see why Charlene would stick around, though. This had to be the most exciting *Cooking with Charlene* Episode in years. I quickly gathered the ingredients and got the oven warming up. "We can probably get away with four hundred degrees if we keep an eye on things and rotate the tray," I said.

"Do it. It'll be faster," Charlene and Gourmet said simultaneously.

The next twenty minutes were complete chaos. Spices flew—toward food, not foes—and the few surfaces that'd been clean after our fight with Foamy Flash quickly became filthy again. Charlene shook her head disapprovingly as the mess piled up, but no one had time for that. Food flew and the sink filled until, finally, the enchiladas made it into the oven.

We looked around the room in horror as Gourmet put twenty minutes on the timer. We'd destroyed *everything*.

Charlene was the first to speak up. "Don't suppose either of you have a cleaning power?"

"No," I mumbled.

"Nope." Gourmet shrugged. "I guess we'd better get her back, huh?"

"Yeah, I suppose you'd better. My set's ruined." Charlene didn't seem afraid to boss around two supervillains.

I nodded slowly. Gourmet shrugged again and stomped to the door. "Hey, cops. Prisoner exchange. Give us Foamy Flash for ten minutes, and we'll let Charlene go!"

Outside was quiet. Then a voice shouted, "Five, and you keep the door open!"

"Seven, and the door stays shut! You don't need to know what's going on in here!"

"Deal!"

Gourmet opened the door and grabbed a very beat-up-looking Magical Girl Foamy Flash. The heroine glared at Gourmet as the door slammed behind her. "What?" she asked sullenly.

"Help clean up," Gourmet said.

"You're serious?" Foamy Flash asked. She gathered herself, expecting a trap.

Charlene cleared her throat. "Yes, we're serious. The place is a disaster zone, and we have a few minutes to cut to a commercial. You use your big cleaning power, tidy up, and *Cooking with Charlene* keeps its reputation as a nondisaster cooking show. Now get cracking!"

"Fine . . ." Foamy Flash said. She started channeling. "It's time for a [**Cleaning Cleanse**]."

As the power channeled, I dug into my pocket, emptying the spice bottles onto the counter. I'd gotten a few texts and calls, and now that we had a bit of downtime, I had to see who needed to talk to me *that* badly.

<Three Missed Calls: Fursona>
<Hey US, I think I saw an owl - Fursona 6:45>
<You know, like the one from the Roadrage Episode - Fursona 6:46>
<Nevermind. False alarm. Just a crow - Fursona 6:49>
<Nevermind the nevermind - Fursona 6:55>

What was she talking about? An owl? The one from the Roadrage Episode? That was Stella-Lunar's bird; if she had been here, the Episode would have ended twenty-five minutes ago. Nothing Gourmet or I could do would be more than a speed bump for a top-three hero in North America. I puzzled through the rambling texts until I got to the most recent one.

<Understudy! Hes here! VV is here! - Fursona 7:13>

"Oh shit," I said.

[A Vigilante is Joining the Fight]
[Name: Vigilant Vow]
[Shifting Alliances: Multiple factions of heroes. Choose your relationship]
[Ally] [Neutral] [Enemy] [[Rival]

Before I could finish, Foamy Flash grinned proudly. "All done!"

A second later, the studio's windows shattered inward, raining shards of glass onto the set. I whirled, trying to activate **[Hometown Villainess]** and go on the offensive.

But it wouldn't work.

Instead, Tails vanished with an almost bubble-like pop.

I gulped and chose **[Enemy]**.

42

Enemy

Familiars flooded through the shattered glass. The camerawoman screamed.

Then, the room went silent. "I swear to clean up crime in this town."

"That's *my* oath!" Foamy Flash shouted, but Vigilant Vow let go of two familiars' legs and stepped through a broken window, ignoring her.

"We won't stop until we've flip-flopped the villains, combed the city for criminals, and brushed off our enemies. I'm quick, clean, and ready to wash the scene." The moment he finished, Bubble-Bill appeared, and my stomach dropped. The rubber-ducky familiar wasn't backing up Foamy Flash anymore.

I'd thought Vigilant Vow's Signature Skill cloned familiars; it explained the army that'd swarmed down The Shoppe-Lifter in the Episode we'd watched in Rocko's studio, and how he'd used so many during the Roadrage Episode. But he wasn't copying familiars—he was *stealing* them. Every time he opened one of his shining crystals, it yoinked the familiar from a Magical Girl, leaving them powerless.

Everything clicked. He'd been using Iyago during the Roadrage Episode, and suddenly, he'd had to leave. Later that evening, Stella-Lunar had backed out of her Episode against 3V1L. He'd stolen her familiar. He'd stolen *her* familiar, leaving her powerless, and Golden Goose had had to fly down from Yorkston to fill in.

He must've been using **[Hard-Candy Hound]** when Magical Girl Candi Crush's powers had stopped working. And now he'd stolen Tails and—

Foamy Flash waved her wand at me, and I ducked. Nothing. She was powerless, but I was still a villain, and in the chaos, she'd forgotten that she'd already lost to me once. I waved my spatula-shaped wand at her. Nothing happened. Right. No powers. Where was Tails?

"Truce?" I asked, holding out a hand to Foamy Flash.

She glared. "I don't make deals with dirty villains! But yeah, this is weird. Truce while we figure this out. Who are you?"

"My name's Magical Girl Understudy," I said. The camerawoman wasn't on me, and that'd be scrubbed for the Ilneat studios, so the confession was okay. "I'm here to help out a friend from superpower studies class. I think . . ."

Gourmet roared and tackled a cat that'd gotten too close to the set. I'd seen it before; Chili Powder's familiar. I had just enough time to think about how ironic *that* was before Gourmet started shouting. "Fight me on your own, you coward! Do it! Come on, do it!"

"No, I don't think I will." More and more familiars filled the room; there had to be a dozen. He'd gone all-out, but at least he didn't have Iyago. Only a single opalescent crystal floated near his head. "I beat you this way before. Why would I change a winning plan?"

He turned toward me. "Magical Girl Understudy. I told you to quit. If you won't listen, you'll have to lose. Bubble-Bill?"

The room filled with gigantic bubbles. I dodged left. Foamy Flash ducked right—straight into Charlene. The bubbles popped a split second later, throwing the hero and Extra toward the door. Foamy Flash picked up the cooking-show star and shoved her out. Then she turned. "You're a thief and a villain, whoever you are, and I'm going to clean up these filthy streets!"

I winced; somehow, I didn't think Vigilant Vow would accept that. But he laughed. "Yes, I am. I've been wrong about a few things. Cartman had me convinced I was borrowing powers, but I'm not. It doesn't matter, though. **[Familiar Faces]** gives me the power of every Magical Girl in the city, and I've got a great system for collecting their contracts. Whether Magical Boy Vigilant Vow or Dark Boy Empty Oath, I *will* have that minor-league spot, and I *will* see you lose, Magical Girl Understudy. Bubble-Bill: Destroy."

My eyes widened. He'd switched archetypes. Instead of being a vigilante, he'd gone full Dark Magical Boy. But Gourmet roared before the rubber ducky could turn his soapy wrath on me. She'd found the wreckage of Lab Assistant Panic's Two-Shot Protein-Shake Shotgun, and pink protein shake covered her face. Muscles rippled underneath her suit again, and she juggernauted toward Vigilant Vow—no, toward Empty Oath.

"I never asked for this! I have one chance to help my mom, and you're ruining it! Die!" Gourmet screamed. She moved like lightning, grabbing Empty Oath's white hoodie and pulling him into a bear hug.

He screamed as she squeezed him, then shouted, "**[Slip-and-Slide Escape]**!" Before Gourmet could keep laying on the pain, he slid between her arms and onto the floor. A wall of familiars formed between him and the supervillain.

But not Bubble-Bill. The rubber ducky stared at Foamy Flash, no recognition in his painted-on black eyes—nothing but emptiness. He inflated as the Magical Girl watched in horror.

SQUEEEEEEEEEEEEEEEAK!

A jet of bubbles burst forth, slamming into the powerless Magical Girl in an endless staccato of pops. I winced as she went flying, but this was my chance. I had to escape—had to get away. While my fellow Magical Girl went unconscious for a second time that night, I dashed for the door.

I didn't make it.

Before I got halfway there, Empty Oath started talking. "I swear to upstage the villains and put justice in the limelight from opening night until curtain call!"

My blood ran cold.

By the time Empty Oath said, "Villains, time to exit stage left," I knew who'd emerge from that last crystal. He hadn't just stolen Bubble-Bill; he had *Tails*. He had *my* powers.

I couldn't be here; I had to leave. But the damn cat—er, my best friend and familiar—appeared between me and the door. "T-Tails, are you sure you want to do this?"

She didn't say anything, either out loud or in my head. Empty Oath did, though. "At first, I discounted your power completely, Understudy. It was just a weaker version of mine, after all. I can steal *any* Magical Girl's powers as long as I've formed a contract with their familiar—why would I need yours? But then I realized something. Tails, TA-1LZ form." Gourmet raged against the familiars swarming her; though she'd knocked a few out of the fight, she couldn't make headway toward Empty Oath, and her muscled form was already growing weaker again.

My plushie cat hopped into the air and spun, glowing white. When she landed, she'd changed into an armored mecha-cat the size of a big dog, with a Gatling taser attached to her head. She turned toward Empty Oath, but I didn't wait for him to give an order.

I jumped over TA-1LZ's head, legs pumping, and crashed through the door into an army of nervous-looking cops. They formed a wall between me and the elevator or stairs; I couldn't fight through them without my powers.

Instead, I ran left.

"Tails has . . . lots of potential," Empty Oath said, almost as if he didn't care that I was on the move. "Go get her."

TA-1LZ crashed through the door a moment later, her Gatling taser rattling. It fired into the police, spraying their line of riot shields, batons, and pistols mercilessly. As the shield-carrying cops fell, those behind them took taser shots, and by the time their return fire started, TA-1LZ had knocked out a dozen officers. The louder bangs of pistols firing echoed behind me, and I glanced back—just in time to see Fursona bounding over the ragged line, taking taser fire herself as she landed.

She lashed out with both feet, kicking TA-1LZ back into the ruined, chaotic studio. Then she looked at me. "What the [**Beep!**] is happening, Understudy? And why didn't you answer my—"

I wrapped her in a hug. "Sorry! I'll explain later. Vigilant Vow's gone villain. He's in there, fighting Gourmet and Foamy Flash. He's the one who's been stealing powers. I can't fight him. I've got to leave!"

Fursona nodded slowly. "I told you this was a bad idea . . . Can you transform?"

I tried, leaping into the air and landing. "No. I need Tails, and she's—"

TA-1LZ bounded through the door, [**Head-Cannon**] spinning.

"—that," I finished.

"Right," Fursona said. She pointed down the hall. "I'll cover you! Go!"

I turned and ran. I didn't think about whether she could handle TA-1LZ or Empty Oath's other familiars. I didn't even think about whether Gourmet would be okay. The whole situation had gotten so far out of control that all I could do was run.

I turned one corner, then another. A pair of cops stood there, and I ducked back; if they saw my villain form with no powers, they'd arrest me, and the whole show would be a disaster. I breathed, waited ten seconds I didn't have, then ducked into another studio room.

The room was empty save for a news desk, four camera cranes, and a weatherman's green screen. I breathed a sigh of relief. A plan. I needed a plan. Some way out of this that didn't make me lose, kept Fursona out of trouble, and let Gourmet walk away with her win. What could I do? What were my options? I could . . . surrender to the cops. That'd remove Empty Oath as a threat to me for a bit, but I didn't *have* a lawyer to bail me out. I could try fighting my way out, but without powers, that'd just leave me in police custody, too.

Or . . .

I had an idea. An incredibly stupid idea. I still had superhero damage; it was the only power Empty Oath hadn't stolen. I could use that.

I crept back to the door, waited until I was sure TA-1LZ and the cops weren't outside, and dashed back toward the *Cooking with Charlene* studio. My heart pounded. For this plan to work, I needed to accomplish three tasks. The first two could be in any order, but the last could *only* happen after I finished the others.

Task One: Find Fursona. I needed my sidekick, or I wouldn't survive Part Three— especially if TA-1LZ got a hold of me, which she would. Plus, I needed to know she was safe. Well, safe-ish—what I needed from her was pretty dangerous. If she got knocked out of the fight here, after I'd left her, I'd never forgive myself.

Task Two: Get Empty Oath's attention. Gourmet was strong, but Empty Oath had said he'd beaten her before. I needed her to win the Episode, so I needed my rival's attention on me, not her. If I could get him fighting Fursona, even better.

Task Three: Exit the building. I was not looking forward to this part but could only see one way out.

Fursona was shockingly easy to find. Unfortunately, I came around the corner at precisely the wrong time, just as she ducked a barrage of tasers from [**TA-1LZ's New Head-Cannon**].

[**HP 2/9**]

As I twitched on the ground, Fursona smashed into my familiar, shoving it into an empty studio and slamming the door. "Holy crap, Understudy, I thought you'd have left by now."

"Can't," I murmured as the shocks faded. I curled into a ball momentarily, then forced myself to stand up. "Too many police, and I'm stuck as a villain. Besides, I need to make sure Gourmet wins."

"You're really putting yourself on the line for a villain, huh?" Fursona asked.

I nodded. "Look, I promised I'd get her this win. Everything's gone to crap, but I can still come through. I just have to make some poor choices and put us both in a *tiny* bit of danger. Please help me."

Fursona sighed through her modulator. "Fine. We'll do it your way."

Task One: accomplished. "Thanks. Let's go before TA-1LZ breaks free!" I said. The familiar in question fired her [**New Head-Cannon**] at the door and clawed at it; with her size, she'd make it through sooner rather than later. We had to move before she got free.

I grabbed Fursona's paw, and she hopped along while I ran. They'd still be in the *Cooking with Charlene* studio. They had to be. The police outside had scattered as TA-1LZ's tasers shredded them; a few stood around, unsure what to do but unwilling to get involved in such a messy superhero fight. I understood. I didn't want to get involved, either.

I kicked in the door.

Cooking with Charlene wouldn't be airing for a while, I decided. The room looked like a bomb had gone off. Half-conscious familiars littered the floor while Gourmet and Empty Oath battled on what was left of the set. The camerawoman had long since fled, but the camera still pointed at them, capturing their battle. Somehow, though, the oven was still cooking. I looked at the timer; just a few minutes on the enchiladas.

It was now or never. "Vigilant Vow, or Empty Oath, or whatever you're calling yourself! Was that your best? I'm still up, so come and get me!"

The vigilante-turned-villain turned to face me and Fursona. He cleared his throat to monologue, two bird familiars and a bat circling over him while Gourmet fought a cat and a ferret or weasel. I held up my hand. "TA-1LZ is out of the fight! Bubble-Bill is . . . Where is Bubble-Bill?"

"I got the ducky. Ate it *right* up." Gourmet burped a few soap bubbles to prove it.

"Ooookay, Gourmet ate Bubble-Bill. The point is, if you want to stop me, you'll have to fight me first!"

"With pleasure," Empty Oath said. He stepped toward me, right into the center of the room. Task Two: accomplished.

Fursona hopped toward him, but as she did, I pushed her. She staggered into the boy, and they tangled up in a ball of flailing fists and feet, inches from the shattered window.

I took a deep breath. Then another one. Fursona was going to *kill* me if we survived this.

Then I dashed forward and crashed into the mass of fists, claws, and teeth, and we all fell from the twenty-fifth floor.

Task Three: accomplished. Yay . . .

43

Yay . . .

I hated math. I'm sure I've mentioned that, but it's important. As I pushed the fight through the shattered window, I had a chance to do some real-world math.

If three supers all fell out a window on the twenty-fifth floor of a building, and the average height of a skyscraper floor was, say, fifteen feet, that gave the supers . . . about 375 feet to fall.

We started falling, and I tried to keep Fursona's fursuit between me and the ground. I'd never hated math more, and it took me a few seconds to estimate how long it'd take us to hit the pavement. Five seconds? No, that couldn't be right. It had to be more than tha—

WHAM!

[HP -5/9]
[HP 0/9]
[**Tough as Nails! +1 Grit Point**]
[**Play Stupid Games! +1 Drama Point**]
[**Critical Condition! +1 Grit Point**]
[**End of Act Two! Act Three in Five Minutes! No Point Changes**]

I blinked, trying to breathe. A few feet away, Fursona groaned and pushed herself to her feet. Her suit was shredded; I'd bounced off her when we hit the ground, so she'd taken the concrete *and* my weight, but her [**Fursonal Furcefield**] seemed to have helped. I tried to roll onto my stomach and push myself up, but the moment I did, my right arm screamed in protest. Had I broken it? Would the Style System *let* me break it? I couldn't use my arm. "Fursona," I said, gritting my teeth in agony.

She looked over at me, plastic eyes betraying no emotion. Then she gently rolled me over and helped me to my feet, talking the whole time. "Tell me the plan next time, Understudy. That shit could have gotten us both . . . Oh fuck! Annie, you need a hospital."

Did I? Funny. I felt fine now that I was standing. It had been weird when the [**HP**] tracker spiked to -5, though. I hadn't thought it could *do* negatives. That was . . .

That was kind of cool. Really cool, actually. Then again, it took away Style Points sometimes, so it *could*. I just didn't think it would for superhero damage. That was pretty strange. I wondered if . . . uh, something.

Fursona looked over her shoulder. Then she turned toward me. "Let's go. Tokyexico General. Switch back to Understudy if you can. It'll be more explainable."

"Haha. Alright. Alright, I'm switching. I swear to upstage the villains and put justice in the limelight from opening night until curtain call!" Nothing happened. Right. I'd, uh, forgotten. "No Tails, no shoes, no service."

"Understudy, focus," Fursona snapped. Before I could ask why she was mad, she kept talking. "Vigilant Vow went out that window with us. I saw him hit the ground, but he's not here. His familiars are, though, and if we stick around, they're gonna swarm us down. I'm completely out of superhero damage, and your arm's broken—if you're lucky, that's all, other than bruises and a concussion. We need to leave."

She was right. I pulled myself together and threw my good arm across her shoulder. "Okay, let's go."

"We'll take a monorail. It'll be faster than walking, and my car's the wrong way," Fursona said as we hobbled through Mid-Town's evening streets. Extras kept looking at us like we were some sort of show, and I smiled at them until Fursona told me to stop. "You look like crap, your arm's broken, and you're covered in smeared spices. Plus, you're a villain. You're scaring them. Save the public relations for another time, okay?

[Gourmet's Glutton Hour: Act Three in Progress]

I nodded slowly. The movement hurt my head, and I felt woozy—not like a little bit, either. We staggered our way to the train station. By the time I got there, I didn't care about my secret identity, or Empty Oath, or anything but sitting down for a minute. I paid with Anika DuPont's travel card and looked for a spot. A few people made some space, and I nodded gratefully. I'd been hurt before, in Episodes, but never like this.

[Critical Condition! +1 Grit Point]

The train started moving, and I breathed a sigh of relief. "Okay, we're safe. You want an explanation, right?"

"You threw me out of a skyscraper, Understudy. You're **[Beep!]** right I want an explanation," Fursona hissed. But she stared out the monorail's back window. "It'll have to wait, though. This isn't over."

Just then, Tails popped onto the ground by my feet. I glared at the plushie cat, but she just licked a paw for a moment. Then she looked at me and cocked her head. *<What's with the confused look, Understudy?>*

"You know *what*, Tails," I said. But what if she didn't? What if she didn't realize what had happened? What she'd done? I'd have to figure that out later.

"Focus. This train's about a minute from being attacked. Do you have your powers back?" Fursona asked. Extras sidestepped away from us as we talked, and one pulled out a cell phone and started texting.

I stood shakily. "I swear to upstage the villains . . . yes!" The spin moves sent waves of pain through my arm, but eventually, I switched from Magical Girl Ramsey Fieri to Understudy. I still didn't have any superhero damage, but at least I had my basic powers, and I could **[I-Frame Transform]** an attack or two if I had to.

The first familiars crashed into the back window a moment later—a ferret and a crow. Both headed straight for me, and while Fursona intercepted the ferret and threw it out the window, the crow opened its mouth and vomited a black beam in my direction. I staggered as the train turned, and the beam went wide, but it fired a second one before I could dodge.

I braced myself for a superhero damage notification, but none popped up. Instead, my hip caught fire for a moment before the spike of pain dwindled to something semimanageable. I screamed—now the Extras were *really* freaking out—and shouted, "**[Stellar Ray]!**"

[Dramatic Damage! +1 Drama Point]

My beam hit the crow's beam, and for a moment, the train car went technicolor. Then, my beam punched through and caught the crow in the face. It popped, vanishing like it'd never been here.

It wasn't much, but for the first time since Empty Oath showed up and ruined *Gourmet's Glutton Hour*, I was a semifunctional superhero. I was ready when the ferret swam back through the window and launched a pinkish, zigzagging bolt my way. I **[Quick-Time Changed]** into Lab Assistant Panic, not caring if Extras thought I was a villain, and used the **[I-Frame Transform]** to dodge the ray. The power only hurt a lot.

[Flashy Fitting-Room! +1 Flamboyance Point]
[Steel Yourself! +1 Grit Point]
[Critical Condition! +1 Grit Point]

TA-1LZ mowed the familiar down with antibirdcraft tasers a moment later. It also vanished, and I collapsed into my seat. One or two at a time, with my powers and sidekick, Empty Oath's familiars weren't so bad. "I hope that's the last of them," I muttered.

[Familiar Flex! +1 Badass Point]

"I don't think it is," Fursona replied.

"Yay."

[Critical Condition! +1 Grit Point]

By the time the monorail screeched to a halt at the University station, the pain had *really* set in, and I regretted jumping out of a building.

I'd regretted it from the moment we went airborne, but I regretted it even more now. As a superhero, I never considered how much adrenaline helped with pain. Superhero damage did such a great job of taking the edge off every attack, every fall, every *scraped knee*, that when it was gone, and all I had was my own pain-coping strategies, it wasn't enough. My arm was the worst. Or the back of my head was the worst. Or maybe my ribs. The place that felt the most on fire kept changing every time I got a handle on my pain.

We hadn't been attacked in over two stops. I'd spent the last two familiar attacks sitting, trying to help with **[Stellar Ray]**, but anything more intense than lifting the wand was too much. Luckily, the Extras had mostly scattered and gotten off at stops that probably weren't theirs.

The train stopped, and Fursona helped me up. I groaned, then winced, then screamed, but eventually, I got to my feet. "Thanks, Fursona," I murmured.

"Let's go. Hospital, now. You need a doctor and a bed."

"Yeah, definitely." I gritted my teeth and took a few steps off the train. It took more out of me than I'd expected, but I had to keep going. I had to—

"I thought you'd get off here, Magical Girl Understudy." Vigilant Vow, Empty Oath, whatever he wanted to call himself, limped out of the next car. I gasped; he looked almost as bad as I felt. He'd *had* healing familiars—he had to, with the sheer number he'd summoned—but even so, his face was bruised and torn, his nose askew, and one arm hung from his side.

But he did have two familiars. The first, a miniature green dragon, flew circles over his head. The other rolled out of the train car just as the doors closed: a hedge-hog. "Can we not do this right now?" I asked.

[Critical Condition! +1 Grit Point]

"Oh, I'm sorry. Is this all getting too inconvenient for you?" Empty Oath asked, wincing. "You could just quit. If not, I'm sure you'll have plenty of time to regret fighting . . . in the hospital!"

[Episode Finished!]
[Episode: Pilot: Gourmet's Glutton Hour - PG]
[Penalties: 3x Rating Warnings - No Penalty]

[Episode Finished! +5 of each Style Point]
[Winner Winner! +2 of each Style Point]
[Role Focus: Cunning + Grit - Goal Partially Met! +10 Grit Points]
[Alias - Understudy] [Archetype - Magical Girl] [Community Rank - 241/523]
[HP 0/9]
[Styles and Skills]
▶Archetype Skill - Transformation Sequence
▶Combo Skills - Power-Weaving
▶Badass (47)
▶Cunning (50) (Skill Roll Available)
▶Drama (32)
▶Stellar Ray 2
▶Bit-Part Barrage 1
▶Flamboyance (26)
▶Signature Skill - Adaptive Armoire 2
▶Stored Costumes: (Rainy Day, Copy Cat)
▶Starwave Sail 1
▶Quick-Time Change 2
▶Grit (53) (Skill Roll Available)
▶I-Frame Transform 2

For a moment, I just stood there, confused, as Empty Oath's face darkened more
and more. Then I started laughing. I'd won—no, *Gourmet* had won. Without Empty
Oath to interfere, and with Foamy Flash depowered and unconscious, she'd finished
the enchiladas and, presumably, served them to *someone* on camera. The pilot Episode
was over. I'd won.

"What do you mean I lost?" Fursona demanded. Even through the modulator,
she sounded pissed. I didn't blame her one bit. "I went and saved my . . . Understudy.
I fought the villain! I got *pushed out of a building*!"

But before she could finish her rant, I started laughing even more. Each giggle
tore at my ribs, but I couldn't stop it. I'd won, and Vigilant Vow had lost, but unless
something changed, all three of us were going to kill each other in the next minute.
And I was the only one who could stop it.

I leveled my wand at Empty Oath and yelled, "[**Stellar Ray**]!" The beam missed,
but that didn't matter. What did matter was that I'd started an Episode. On campus.
In full view of at least three security cameras.

[Casting Call]
[Episode: Magical Mix-Up! - PG]
[Role: Troublemaker! Episode-Starter: Mandatory Acceptance Required]
[Role Focus: Flamboyance + Grit]

Now, I just had to stay up for a minute—which would be way harder than it sounded.

"Understudy, what did you do?" Fursona asked. Before I could respond, she dashed toward the Dark Magical Boy, kicking wildly. The hedgehog intercepted, and a glowing shield formed, knocking my sidekick away. At the same time, the dragon rushed me, breathing emerald flames that didn't set the train station ablaze but *did* feel hot.

I threw myself into the air, using **[Bit-Part Barrage]**. Something let go in my chest as I spun, but I kept just on target enough to hit the familiar once . . . twice . . . three times. And that was enough. It disappeared.

[Dramatic Damage! +3 Drama Points]

Vigilant Vow growled and started reaching for his crystals—maybe to summon Tails, Bubble-Bill, or some other familiar. But we never figured out what, because before he could touch a crystal with his jet-black wand, a trio of heroes teleported into the station. Dr. Mays started an advertisement for Quilliar Tree Pets, whatever those were.

Dr. Jackson cleared her throat. "Magical Girl Understudy, the conditions of your—Oh my god. Ambulance! Get an ambulance!"

I didn't hear anything else. As **[Bit-Part Barrage]** set me down, my leg gave out. I hadn't even realized I'd hurt it, but I collapsed. The pain overwhelmed me, and the world went black.

44

The World Went Black

WEDNESDAY, APRIL 1

I woke up to a commotion outside my room, an IV taped to my arm, and a bunch of emails on my phone. I was in a hospital bed, in a hospital gown, and was therefore, I deduced, in a hospital. Strange beeps from a few machines and the too-clean smell of overused disinfectant confirmed the hospital theory. I smiled—truly, my brilliance knew no bounds.

I couldn't do anything about the IV or the hot liquid it was dripping into my veins *or* whoever was losing their minds in the hallway, so I reached for my phone. I could manage my emails one-handed while I waited for someone to explain what was happening.

Subject: Recent Episode on TU Campus Determination
To Anika DuPont, aka Magical Girl Understudy
Per our emails and agreement, effective Friday, January 9, you were not to start or engage in superheroic activities on Tokyexico University grounds. Due to your attack on a vigilante outside of an Episode, we've placed you under a temporary suspension from all classes while we investigate.
Helen Barber
Vice President of Student Services
Tokyexico University

RE: Recent Episode on TU Campus Determination
To Anika DuPont, aka Magical Girl Understudy
Our investigation uncovered extenuating circumstances originating off campus, and it appeared that up until the moment you started fighting, you were trying to disengage for medical treatment. Your fellow student-hero Fursona also claims that you used the attack to call for help in an emergency rather than as a way to fight an enemy.

Therefore, the Tokyexico University Board of Review has determined that you are not at fault for violating our agreement. However, the agreement still stands. The Board of Review is examining a pair of requests from the Ilneat producer Rocko and the Tokyexico Council of Heroes to lift your ban on superhero activities on campus. The restriction remains in place for the time being.

Helen Barber
Vice President of Student Services
Tokyexico University

Subject: Agreement Status
To Anika DuPont, aka Magical Girl Understudy
The Board of Review and Tokyexico University Campus Administration have agreed to remove some restrictions from your superheroic activities. The new conditions of your continued enrollment are as follows:

1. You may engage in superheroic activities on campus at the PG (little league) level. If caught in a situation of PG-13 (minor league) level or higher, you must disengage and fight only to defend yourself.

2. You must report any superheroic involvement on Tokyexico University grounds within twelve hours, including Episode name, locations, and known participants. Failure to do so will be considered subverting Rule One. This does not include meeting with heroes on your team, TUSSA meetings, or Superpower Studies classes.

3. You must confirm receipt of this email and your intention to follow Rules One and Two.

This is still considered a probationary period for you, and the wisest course of action would be to keep your superheroics off campus grounds. However, the Board of Review has considered your compliance and service to Tokyexico City and believes more freedom has been earned.

We look forward to your cooperation,
Helen Barber
Vice President of Student Services
Tokyexico University

I wanted to cheer and shout in celebration, or *something*. I'd gotten my freedom back; for the first time all semester, I didn't have to worry about being expelled, and I'd done it by *doing* what they'd told me not to. But I just didn't have the energy. Instead, I looked at my arm. Bruises covered it, especially just below my elbow to my wrist. I winced as I tried to move it and the IV needle caught—lesson learned: keep the arm still. Oddly, though, it wasn't in a cast. I wondered why; it'd definitely *been* broken. I idly rolled my skills and tried to ignore my injuries—or lack thereof.

[50 Cunning Credits Used. Rolling Skill!]
[50 Grit Credits Used. Rolling Skill!]

[New Skill! Set Dressing 1: Temporarily blend in with the background, camouflaging yourself against regular vision and sound]

[Rank-Up! Fursonal Furcefield 1: Damage negation happens 10% more often]

The door slammed open. "For the last time, you two can't go in there!" a nurse said.

"The kid's my hero and my investment. I'm already burning Compact leave time to be here, so if you think your hospital rules are gonna stop me, you've got a lot more nerve than I think you do," Rocko said.

"I wouldn't try stopping them," Fursona said through her modulator. They both crowded into my tiny hospital room. "I tried, and it didn't work."

She shut the door in the spluttering nurse's face.

Rocko climbed up into a chair, grasping and squeezing hands clinging to the back as they stood on one armrest. Fursona leaned casually against the other arm so the flimsy-looking thing wouldn't overbalance. My boss stared at me, and I stared back. Then I burst into laughter.

"Hey. *Hey*! Knock it off, DuPont. You all run your thermostats too low." The Ilneat producer wore an orange down coat so thick they looked less like a gorilla/otter hybrid and more like a basketball. They glared at me from inside a balaclava, and mittens covered their squeezing hands. They'd opted for fingerless gloves for their grasping ones.

Eventually, I got myself under control. Once I did, Rocko cleared their throat, coughing dramatically. "They won't even let me have a cigar in here. Barbaric. DuPont, Marino, I'm using my Compact time for the year to be here, so listen carefully. I'm not here to answer questions, and I'm not here to hear your explanations for that Episode. Good job, by the way. You played a difficult situation acceptably well. Visit me when you're out of this dump if you wanna talk about all that. I'm just here to check on my investment and make sure you'll be up and running soon. Otherwise, Cartman's gonna take that minor-league spot, Dark Boy or not."

I opened my mouth. Then I closed it, feeling like a goldfish. A lot of confusing thoughts were rushing through my head, and I couldn't make heads or tails of any of them. Eventually, I focused only on what Rocko had said, not what he *hadn't*. "I broke my arm and screwed up my leg. I'm out for a while, but Empty Oath wasn't in much better shape."

"Two things. First, Empty Oath checked out of Tokyexico Mercy six hours ago, so quit being a baby and get back to work," Rocko said. Fursona stood up and started talking, but Rocko powered over her. "And *second*, I'm not an idiot. I know how bad this kind of injury can be for your career, and I've got a solution. Well, two solutions. You're already getting one in the IV, but we can patch up the old noggin with a simple pill and get you on your feet in a couple of hours."

They produced a . . . pill. I stared at it dubiously. It was the size of a quarter—maybe bigger—and colored bright red. "I don't think I can swallow that," I said.

"Sure you can. Fursona, find some ice cream. Ice cream helps with giant pills like this. Make sure she eats the whole thing, though. Don't cut it up, or it won't work right. Now, DuPont, that Episode needs a lot of editing, and I'll be damned if Cartman gets it out before us. Come by the studio when you're feeling better!" Before I could say anything, the Ilneat disappeared out the door. As they went, I could see them shivering.

After the horse pill finally went down, Fursona pulled the shade down on the window and started fiddling with her helmet. She pulled it off, and I cringed when I saw her face. Her whole right cheek was one big bruise so big her eye was almost squeezed shut. It looked terrible, but that wasn't the worst of it. The eye I could see alternated between worry and frustration.

I gulped. "I'm sorry, Bee."

"Thanks. That means a lot. What are you sorry for?"

I goldfished again for a moment. "Uh, throwing you out of a building, getting into such a crazy situation, and, um, winning the Episode and making you lose."

"Forget winning and losing."

If her face hadn't sobered me up, that alone would have. Bee *always* wanted to win. *Always*. She had to win, whether it was drinking games, Episodes, or an occasional race to the bathroom in the morning. So if she didn't care, I'd *really* messed up.

She kept talking while I sat, unable to meet her eye. "You pushed it too far last night, Annie. Way too far. We got in over our heads, and we both paid for it. You could have died, and as much as losing hurt, losing you would hurt more. So your apology is a good start, but I need to know what happened so we don't get in that kind of trouble again. First, why didn't you answer my calls or texts? You could have slipped off-set."

"I *was* off-set." I cleared my throat and explained the whole fight with Foamy Flash. It took almost five minutes of answering her clarifying questions, piecing together the timeline, and figuring out what she'd been doing during it.

She nodded slowly, scowl still on her face. "We can fix this with a special vibration pattern and a cool ringtone for me. If you do that, you'll know when it's an emergency and when you can blow me off. And the answer to when you can blow me off is *basically never*, Annie. Especially not when I'm trying to warn you about danger."

"Okay, speaking of that danger, Vigilant Vow went villain. He's Empty Oath, and his power doesn't clone familiars. It steals them. That's why TA-1LZ was after me. He stole Tails, Bee."

"I can't . . . Annie, let me be mad. Please," Bee said. She started tearing up, then turned away from me. "I can't do all of this. Not right now. You almost got killed trying to start a fight with Empty Promise or whatever you called him, with no superhero damage and a bunch of *real* injuries. You pushed me out of a building without telling me beforehand. And now you want to just kind of . . . ignore all that and talk about the next problem we need to fix? I can't do that right now. I need to be mad at you, and you're not letting me!"

"I'm . . . sorry?" I spluttered. Then I gulped. "I get it, I really do. I'll make it up to you somehow. But Bee, I don't know what to do. My powers won't work if he hijacks Tails. I—"

"Annie, you're not listening! You know what? I need some time to cool down, and you need to focus on getting better. We've got a date with Mindstorm on Friday, and you're stuck in a hospital," Bee said. She pulled on the Fursona helmet and buckled it. Her voice came through the modulator. "I'm going to hang out with some friends. I'll see you tomorrow, Understudy."

Then she hopped through the door and disappeared.

I glared at the door for a moment, heart pounding in my throat. It wasn't fair. None of this was fair. This had been a brutal Episode for both of us, but she was putting it all on me. It wasn't all my fault—Empty Oath had ruined it.

But that wasn't what Bee felt.

She was pissed. I'd never seen her this angry. And that *was* my fault, I realized— not because I'd pushed her out a window or worked with Gourmet, but because she needed to feel heard, and I needed to figure out how to solve the Tails fails. I'd missed something, though. Her need was *right now*, and mine . . .

As much as I hated to admit it, mine could wait a few days. I couldn't do an Episode right now if Professor Panic took over the hospital, so solving Empty Oath's familiar theft could wait until Friday. So could dealing with Mindstorm; I couldn't see us winning against her, no matter what we planned, so there wasn't any point in talking about it. I sent Bee a quick text.

<I'm sorry. We'll put Tails and Empty Oath on the back burner. <3 - Understudy 4:17>

I needed to focus on Bee's feelings first. With nothing better to do, I sat back in bed and tried to brainstorm.

45

Brainstorm

FRIDAY, APRIL 3

I stretched out on the couch, relaxing as I took my arm out of its sling. My apartment felt comfortable, welcoming, and, most importantly, silent. After two days in Tokyexico General, listening to machines beep at all hours of the day and night, that last part alone was a reason to celebrate.

But I had an even better one. Bee was ready to talk. And so was I. She sat in a chair across the coffee table, arms crossed and looking stern.

"Sorry," I said. "I was panicking, not thinking. We can work through this, though."

"I hope so. Annie, I'm your sidekick, but I'm also your girlfriend. I know sometimes when we're in an Episode, shit's going to be intense, and you won't have time to tell me the plan, but if you're going to throw me out of a window again or anything like that, give me a little heads-up, okay?"

"Okay. Maybe we should look at battle plans we can make to call tactics quickly for stuff like this." I tried not to facepalm at myself. I wanted to be solutions-minded, and it was going to get me killed.

"Yeah, that'd be something to work on later. The other thing is, I don't want you rolling alone with the villains anymore." She held up a hand before I could protest. "That doesn't mean no hanging out with Gourmet or that you can't use the villain Costumes. In fact, I want you to ask if you can keep Ramsey Fieri because . . . reasons."

"Yeah, I want to keep that one, too," I said. My instinct was to fight her on this. Gourmet wasn't that bad, and it wasn't her fault that shit had gone wrong Tuesday night. "Can you explain what you mean, then?"

"If you want to do Episodes with Gourmet, as a villain, that's fine. But *I'm* your hero in those Episodes. I'm *not* waiting at the bottom of some tower, texting you and hoping you'll pick up. I'm *in* the tower, fighting you. That way, I can keep an eye on you and your bullshit."

"It's not bullshit, it's villain shit, but point taken. I can live with that." It'd be awkward fighting against Fursona, but it was a tolerable compromise after throwing her out a window and stuff. And the alternative was putting up walls. I'd done that before, tried to separate my relationship with Peter from the superpower stuff we were both doing, and looking back, some of those barriers had messed up that relationship almost as badly as the distance had. I wouldn't do that again. I *couldn't* do that again.

"Anything else?" I asked her.

"Yeah, actually. How are you feeling about this?"

I blinked. I'd been so concerned with her feelings that I hadn't considered my own. So I hesitated. She closed her eyes and sighed, and I hurried to cut her off. "I'm not trying to hide my feelings, Bee. I've had a lot on my mind, and I've been trying not to fuck up this relationship, and—"

"You're starting to sound like me," Bianca said. She laughed. It wasn't a long laugh, but it broke the tension. "You didn't think about your feelings because you were too worried about mine? That's . . . sweet."

She stood up and held out a hand. I grabbed it with my nonsore arm; whatever they'd fed into my veins had worked wonders, stitching my bones together and leaving me with *just* massive soreness, but using my right arm still *hurt*. Once I was standing, she tucked her head up against my shoulder and held me. I wrapped my arms around her—both of them.

Some things were worth hurting my arm for.

"Tell me what you're feeling," Bee said. "Don't leave anything out."

"Well, I'm, uh, scared. I was scared when I didn't have Tails during the Orientation Episode, and I knew where she was and what she was doing. She was stuck in my duffel bag because my ex put her there. There wasn't room in my backpack." I laughed a little, too. "But this is different. I know you want to focus on other stuff, though, so here goes. I'm happy you're not more pissed at me. I did push you out of a window."

"You sure did, but what's a little defenestration between partners?" Bianca asked, rolling her eyes. "What else?"

"I'm sorry again for not telling you, and I think your plan to be the villain—er, heroine—when I'm playing the villain is a good one, but I also don't want to make a habit of doing villain shit. The "Gourmet's Glutton Hour" Episode was fun until Empty Oath showed up, but then it all went to hell, and I don't want that. If we can do it in a controlled manner, I'm fine with helping her out again, but not like that."

"Yeah, I didn't like that either." Bee nuzzled her cheek against my shoulder. Her hair tickled my chin, and I couldn't get the smell of green apples out of my nose.

I had a sudden, horrible realization. "You planned this whole conversation out, didn't you?"

"Obviously," Bee said. She pulled away. "Look, this isn't the first time you've just made decisions without talking to me. It happened with APPEAL, and it *can't* be a trend. We're not sidekick and superhero, okay? We've got to be partners. You've talked me into some crazy stuff before by saying you're better with me than alone.

I think I am too, but *with* you, not following you blindly. That's not how relationships work."

"Bee, I'll do better. But, um, on the subject of my feelings, I'm glad you're not pissed."

She narrowed her eyes. Her face still had a bruise, though she'd concealed most of it with makeup, and I winced. "I haven't forgiven you yet, Annie. I think we're on the right path, though. The promises go a long way, but you still owe me." She pressed her lips against mine, and we kissed. Then she pulled away, shivering slightly.

"That's a little better. But only a little."

"I can make it more better," I offered.

She grinned, then winced and held a hand to her face. Then she shook her head. "Maybe later, Annie. I've got to get ready for practicum."

"You didn't bring your Costume?" I hadn't noticed the backpack, but it had become background clutter at my apartment. I'd just written it off as dumped by the door or something.

"No." Bianca shook her head. "Not this time. I'll see you at the practice arena for Mindstorm."

And before I could say anything, she headed for the door.

I pushed the training-room doors open. Fursona waved at me, but it felt a beat slower than usual. Mindstorm did *not* wave at me. "Thank you for . . . joining us, Understudy. Today, we will be holding a make-up lesson. Before Spring Break, we explored dealing with unsurvivable situations. I ran fights of four against one, with the solo super's goal being to survive for five minutes. You'll have the same task together, but against me."

She started to explain the rules. I wasn't listening, but I faked it. I was too busy thinking about Bee and me.

The whole thing was a puzzle, that was for sure. She'd kissed me, and she'd definitely enjoyed it. I'd spent enough time with her that I could tell. But she hadn't talked to me at all on Thursday, and she'd made a conscious decision not to bring her Fursona suit to my place today, so she hadn't intended to forgive me no matter what happened. That raised a whole new question that I didn't really want to think about, but once it surfaced, I couldn't get out of my head.

Did I deserve to be forgiven?

My first thought was yes. Of course I did. But a small, nagging voice in my head wasn't so sure. I'd pushed her out of a skyscraper, after all, and relied on her power to make sure we survived. More importantly, though, I hadn't *told her* the plan. In retrospect, that was where things went wrong.

"Nice of her to tell us her powers," Fursona said.

I blinked. Mindstorm was gone. She'd finished talking, and I hadn't been paying attention. I *had* to pull myself together, or this would be the shortest defensive of all time. "Yeah," I said.

We both stood there for a moment. It didn't seem like we were ready for this, but there wasn't a way out, either. As the seconds ticked by, I cleared my throat. "I guess we'd better get down there, then."

"Yep," Fursona said, and we headed for the stairs.

I hadn't even looked at the arena, but as the doors opened, I winced. She'd set it up as the maze—probably the same maze Waterspout had demolished Candi Crush and me in. "Ready?"

"Yep. Let's kick her butt," Fursona said. Her modulator seemed to be tuned up, and I couldn't tell how serious she was about fighting the supervillain.

"Wait, what?"

Before I could stop her, an alarm rang. A huge digital clock ticked from zero seconds to one. The fight for survival was on.

Fursona hopped into the maze and turned right. I ran to follow her. "Where are you going?"

"We'll have more of a chance of one of us making it separately. We can't beat her, so we have to avoid her," Fursona said. "The win condition is that one of us survives, remember?"

I nodded. That made sense, even if I didn't remember Mindstorm saying it. "See you soon."

She hopped right, and I turned left, making sure my **[Quick-Time Transform]** was ready to shift to Rainy Day. Tactically, my best option was to heal from Mindstorm's initial burst, try to heal more as I switched to Copy Cat, and hope for the best. There were a few problems with that, though. The biggest involved her just mind-controlling me and ending the fight there.

She'd done it before, for super student registration, and she was leagues ahead of us—literally. There was no way we'd make it to five minutes, but maybe we could make it to—

I froze. There was Mindstorm, running down the hall away from me. She hadn't seen me, and that gave me an idea. A stupid idea, but an idea nonetheless. What if I knocked *her* below half superhero damage?

I activated **[Power-Weaving]** and **[Bit-Part Barrage]**.

[Dramatic Damage! +3 Drama Points]
[Floating Points: 1 Drama]

The rays shot toward Mindstorm—then passed through her as she disappeared, revealing a mostly empty hall and a very surprised Fursona.

"Oh shit," I said. "Mindstorm was right—"

"You weren't listening to her briefing, were you? She's running illusions and precognition." Fursona patted her fursuit where a **[Stellar Ray]** beam had smashed its fur. Then she shook her head, and I could almost hear Bee's annoyance through the modulator. "Understudy, just focus on staying alive. That's how we kick her butt.

Pretend Golden Goose is coming—no, that's a dumb idea. Pretend Stella-Lunar's coming to save us."

I nodded, blushing. *Focus, Understudy*, I thought. "Got it. Thanks, Fursona."

"No problem. See you in a couple of minutes." She hopped away again, and I cursed myself for being over-the-top aggressive on this one.

[Combo Dropped! Floating Points Lost.]

The hall stretched out in front of us; I encountered at least two more Mindstorms, and this time, I didn't attack them. Instead, I turned and ran the other way. But gradually, I realized something.

Mindstorm was toying with us. Whenever I avoided a Mindstorm copy thinking it was her, it pushed me in the same direction. If the same thing was happening to Fursona, we'd end up in the same place eventually. It'd probably be the room where Candi Crush and I had fought Waterspout.

Actually, how did I even know the Fursona I'd talked to was real? If Mindstorm was using illusions or getting in our heads—literally—I didn't see how I could trust her. I made myself a promise. The next time I saw a Mindstorm, she was getting a **[Stellar Ray]**. If she disappeared, I'd go that way. If not . . . change to Rainy Day to heal, then to Copy Cat to run.

What? It could work.

It took three more turns to see another Mindstorm. This one was moving away from me, just like the others. Now was my chance to break through her illusions and foil her plan.

I took a deep breath, steeled myself, and said, "**[Stellar Ray]**."

[Dramatic Damage! +1 Drama Point]

The beam punched through Mindstorm, who dissipated. I sighed, tension boiling off me. I hadn't realized how stressed I'd been about this attack. It felt kind of like a hand was crushing the back of my neck. Actually, it felt a *lot* like that.

I tried to turn around, but the hand wouldn't let me move. Mindstorm walked around me, sliding between the maze wall and my left side. "Good try, but . . . no."

A wave of pain hit my *mind*. I struggled to get away or activate **[Quick-Time Change]**, but the invisible hand on my neck held me tight while Mindstorm— the real one this time—burned through my superhero damage like a forest fire through lint.

"Three minutes, twenty-five seconds," Mindstorm said as we wobbled into the observation room. The rest of the class was trickling in, and a few had watched our fight. So had Underdelver and Dr. Tennyson. My head throbbed as she continued talking.

"Not bad. Our best solo survivor was Waterspout. He made it . . . almost seven minutes. All modesty aside, you had a harder challenge."

Somehow, I didn't doubt that. I glanced at Fursona and grinned. She nodded back as Mindstorm kept going. "As we talked about . . . Monday, there are two-hundred-level classes on team combos and synergies, so we won't spend much time on them. However . . . it's important to know the basics. Today, you'll be . . . working with a hero or villain of your choice to figure out some tactics that work well together, and testing them with other teams. Ideally, you'd pick someone you already work with."

I looked at Fursona. She didn't say anything for one second. Two seconds. My heart dropped. Then she nodded. "Sure, Understudy. We can be teammates."

I looked away and nodded, trying to wipe the stupidly grateful look off my face. I had no idea how I'd fix our relationship, but I knew one thing. Fursona wasn't being petty. I'd messed up, and she had no obligation to forgive me or keep being my side-kick. That she was willing to work with me, or talk about steps we could take, or kiss me—especially kiss me—meant I still had a chance to fix things.

And I needed to do whatever it took to earn her trust again.

PART SEVEN

46

Tails Fails

It had been two whole weeks, and Bee still didn't trust me.

Honestly, the giant leap backward we'd taken in intimacy hurt, but it also made total sense. I had a lot to work on, and so did she. After all, I'd pushed her out of a skyscraper; in retrospect, I should have known it'd hurt her.

I'd definitely known it'd hurt her, but I hadn't thought about the emotional damage at all.

So, instead of Bee spending more nights in 1301 Walnut Tower than in her own room, we hung out for a few hours after classes—usually in the SUB. She'd been over twice—both times as Fursona, though, and one was just to drop off my key. It'd felt like she was breaking up with me, but then the helmet came off, and the makeout started. She just needed to set some boundaries for me and herself. That made sense. I'd done the same thing with Peter, and Bee and I were determined to make this work. It was just boundaries.

We'd gone so quickly in the beginning that, now that we'd slowed down a bit, I'd started questioning whether it'd been too fast. Instead of coming over, watching an Episode, and getting drunk, we'd done two actual dates—two! And, since we'd gotten most of the horny, sex-brained phase of our relationship out of the way already, I felt like I could really listen to her instead of fantasizing. Or maybe that was just me being determined not to mess this up.

Oh, and Gourmet had gotten her show green-lighted. She even had three costars; The Crumb signed on immediately, but their hero, Magical Girl Foamy Flash, took a lot of convincing. It wasn't until they announced their fourth cast member, Charlene, that the superhero agreed. Their first real Episode was next week.

I hardly cared. Hopefully, her newfound income would help her mom. But even if it didn't, I'd done my part.

I had other things on my mind. Bee-sized things. And mountain-sized things, too—and ones the size of Tails. That last one was why Fursona was coming over for the third time.

The intercom buzzed, and I let Fursona up into the green room. She hopped over to the whiteboard right away; one thing we'd agreed on last week was that when we were suited up, we were hero and sidekick. Keeping a healthy work/life separation was important to her after "Gourmet's Glutton Hour." "I've been thinking about Tails," she said. She wrote 'Tails Fails' on the whiteboard.

"Yeah, me too." I appreciated that she was finally ready to discuss this, but it'd been two weeks. I couldn't do an Episode without worrying she'd cut out mid-fight, and Empty Oath had the lead again. "I don't know how he's doing it."

"I have . . . a theory. It's just a theory, but it's the only one that makes sense," Fursona said. "But before I tell you, I need to know what he said during 'Gourmet's Glutton Hour'—and no, we're not watching it. I'm not ready to watch you push me out a window."

"Fair," I said, but I winced. I knew *why* she was pissed, but it still hurt that she kept holding a grudge. "He said his power was **[Familiar Faces]**. It gives him different Magical Girls' powers as long as he has their familiars, but most work through the familiar, not him."

"More detail." Fursona wrote 'Familiar Faces' on the board, but paused before writing anything else. Instead, she drew three blank circles, wrote 'VV' in one, and left the others blank.

"He said . . ." I paused, thinking. It didn't help that I'd gotten concussed right after. "He said something about having their contracts. That's about it, other than telling Bubble-Bill to destroy Foamy Flash and me."

"Perfect." Fursona scribbled on the board for almost a minute while I watched. When she'd finished, she looked like a maniac, standing in front of the board with a handful of open markers in her left hand and one in her right, eyes blazing. I'd never noticed she was right-handed. The board was covered entirely with half-legible writing. "Okay, here's what I think happened."

She pointed at the 'VV' bubble. "Vigilant Vow or Empty Oath got his powers two years ago, right? Cartman, his producer, recognized how cinematically cool the power was and started pushing for him to collect as many contracts with familiars as possible. He had to have started with only one—his own—but now he's got dozens, and I don't know for sure, but I don't think he's met Stella-Lunar or the Sugar and Chili Powder girls, right?"

"Right. So he's getting contracts from somewhere. Can we cut them off?" I asked.

"Maybe, if we can figure out the source, but that won't solve the problem. The bigger problem is how long this has been going on and how many Magical Girls lost Episodes because of it, and the biggest problem is whether Cartman knows."

"They know. Rocko knew how **[Adaptive Armoire]** worked, but they wouldn't tell me. Cartman has to know how **[Familiar Faces]** works. They have to."

"Then Vigilant Vow is being used," Fursona said.

I sat on the couch in the green room, thinking about that. I was predisposed to dislike Cartman; Rocko hated the other producer, and so did my mom. Mom had a good reason, though. They'd known she wasn't ready for the powers the System had given her, and they'd put her in a bad situation from the very start. No, Cartman couldn't be trusted. They could be manipulating a high school boy into doing worse and worse things in the name of ratings. They *could* have been lying about how Vigilant Vow's [**Signature Skill**] worked until he was in too deep and had no choice but to go vil.

Vigilant Vow's—I decided I wouldn't call him Empty Oath anymore, even if he wanted it—choices made more sense. I imagined him as a soccer star and trivia team champion, with all the pressure that was put on him. Had he always been successful, or had he needed to work for every victory? How had that affected him when I'd beaten him during the Roadrage Episode, or when I'd taken the lead later? How had Cartman used that to pressure him?

And equally important, did it matter?

Yes. But also, no.

"What do you want to do about that?" I asked. "He still has to be stopped. He's gone full Dark Boy. You never go full Dark. I'd love to say that he's redeemable, but as it stands right now, he's stealing Magical Girls' familiars and powers. He stole *Tails*."

"I know he stole Tails, Understudy. He's probably stolen her a dozen times, and you didn't know. I'm not saying he's not a *problem*. I'm saying you can be friends with Gourmet, of all people, after the ass-kicking she gave us last semester. Can we solve this without violence?"

"Probably not," I said. Then I sighed. "Look, Fursona, I'd love to get him to drop out and find a different studio—hell, I'd recommend Rocko pick him up if he chilled out a little—but he's not going to quit. He's got a massive power advantage over me, and I don't know how to counter it. Plus, Rocko's on our butts again. If we don't get the lead back, he's going to be furious. We have, what? Three weeks?"

"Yeah, about that. Okay, we'll table the 'talk to VV' plan." Sure enough, she crossed out a whole section of the whiteboard. Then she sighed. "So, we're fighting him directly, then. How?"

"I don't know. I've got a guest lecture I have to attend tomorrow, though. I'll be out of Costume at Cherry Creek High all evening, so we can't do anything then." Part of our new relationship rules was talking to each other about our plans so we'd know the other was safe and happy—and also so we could give each other space when we needed it.

"Got it. Want me nearby? I don't have any Friday night plans, and Su-Bin hasn't dropped a movie night on us in a while."

"Yes, please," I said. "I don't trust him not to do something."

"Got it. One Fursona support package for tomorrow night."

"Thanks." I paused. "So . . . we *might* be able to win without fighting him."

"Yeah? I was thinking about that, too. If we can find the right Episodes, we could out-earn him on Community Ranking points. It'd be tough, though, especially with finals a month out. I think our best two options are to beat him directly—but I'm not sure how—or." Fursona paused, and I winced. Whatever she was about to say wouldn't be good. "Or we could be little-league heroes."

My first instinct was to freak out. To yell and scream. But I wasn't a child—childishness and half-baked plans had gotten me into this mess with her. So, instead, I took a breath. "Why?"

"Well, we're pushing the limits of our powers, and we're not growing fast enough to keep up. Since the job fair, we've had four Episodes that could have been lethal for people around us. Five, if you count your patrol with Tele-Portal where people went into the ice. I'm not sure we're ready for the minor leagues, Annie."

Ha! She'd broken first and used my name. I was more professional than her! I wasn't going to say anything, though. We were shaky enough as it was. "Fursona, I get what you're saying," I said.

"You do?"

"Yeah. Shocker, right?" I walked to the whiteboard and erased the half she'd scribbled out. Then I started writing. I wrote 'Strategic Decisions' first. Under it, I created a list. "We need to either step up our game in terms of teamwork, powers, and Episode selection, or we need to chill and grow more naturally. I think our lessons recently in Combat Style Forum could be helpful. We can exploit our powers' synergies and win fights we're outclassed in. But . . ."

"But?"

I swallowed nervously and played with my hair. "I'm . . . not sure that pushing harder is the right call either. I've been pretty obsessed with winning this race. You get that, I'm sure. But there's a chance that if I talk to Vigilant Vow and give him the win, he'll stop stealing Tails. If that solves this problem, he can have the minor-league spot."

"Annie, I don't . . ." Fursona started. "I don't want you to throw away your dream. I think we can prep harder or synergize or something. But if we can't solve Vigilant Vow, backing off for now might be the right call, and I don't see a solution."

I held up a hand. I wasn't ready to give up, and I had one last card to play. "I need to talk it over with someone. A couple of people, actually."

Fursona looked at the door in the green room—the one labeled Rocko Studios—and shook her head slowly. "I don't think the Ilneats will help you on this one, Annie."

"Neither do I. That's why I'm not talking to them. Now, I've gotta go." I stood up, staying in Costume. She wanted to know my plans, so I told her. "I'm going to visit Mister Twister and Brick House. They'll know something about redemption for vils. Then, after, I'm going to the Council of Heroes building. I've got super-counseling."

"Super-counseling?"

"Super-counseling."

47

Super-Counseling

At first, The Cloud was happy to see me. Then, when he realized I wasn't at Tottergarten to play, he threw a tantrum.

I looked at The Narrator as the blue-clad super-toddler summoned lightning and wind, totally out of control. "Are you going to do anything?"

"No." The Narrator sipped her coffee and went back to reading her paper. "If you intervene every time a kid doesn't get their way and placate them, they'll never learn to control their emotions, and the other kids aren't nearby. The only people he can hurt are you and me. Jungle Jim or Teacher's Pet can talk him down in a few minutes."

Thunder clapped. The Cloud rolled on the ground, arching his back and screaming. The Narrator rolled her eyes. "Ignore him. He needs to learn that his powers aren't for getting his way. Otherwise, he'll be a real problem later in life. Speaking of problems, you want to talk to Pranky Jones and Jungle Jim?"

"No. I want to talk to Mister Twister and Brick House," I said. There was a difference.

"Alright. I'll get them. Honeycomb, you've got juice time, right?"

"Yep! Yep, I'm good!" Honeycomb said, passing out juice boxes for the other super-toddlers—and a tiny carton of milk for Kaiju Kid—on the far side of the room.

"Great." The Narrator didn't move. Instead, she cleared her throat. "Pranky Jones and Jungle Jim heard they were needed in the playroom!"

It took less than a minute for Pranky Jones to crash through the door, purple wig askew. I gulped; he might not be Mister Twister, but I still wasn't comfortable with him being around. "What's up, Mrs. N? Kaiju Kid going big? Kid Zoomies needs wrangling? It's too early for the Episode, so what's—"

"Relax, Jones. Magical Girl Understudy's here to ask a few questions."

"Oh. Jim's right behind me. He had to suit up." Pranky Jones gave me a look. "You're not talking about the kids, right? Let's head to the office. Otherwise, they'll crawl all over us and be distracting."

I glanced at Honeycomb, who nodded. "Go on, I've got this." She pulled Kid Zoomies off her arm and set her in a chair, then sighed when the toddler ran around her and latched right back on.

I followed Pranky Jones into the hall with the doors, checking for any of his traps. He rolled his eyes and held open the door to a plain white room with cinder-block walls. A few chairs sat on the linoleum tile floor, and The Narrator's desk dominated one side, but a round table filled the rest—adult-sized, luckily. "Welcome to the office."

Jungle Jim joined us a few moments later, sitting gingerly in a chair that, though full-sized, was still too small for him. "What?" he asked.

"I have a rival who recently turned from vigilante to villain, and I was hoping for some advice," I said. I told them all about the situation, from the race for the minor leagues to our fight at the movie studio and what Vigilant Vow had said—including the bit about being Empty Oath now. They both nodded slowly, occasionally asking a question, until I finally finished with, "And my sidekick, Fursona, thinks I should try to redeem him, so I was wondering what your experience with redemption was like."

For almost five seconds, the office was silent as Pranky Jones and Jungle Jim looked at each other. Then, Jones burst into raucous laughter. The purple-haired villain collapsed on the table, wheezing and giggling, unable to speak.

Jungle Jim was grinning, too. "Understudy, you're missing something important here. Twister and me, we're not redeemed."

I shivered, suddenly on high alert. "If you're not redeemed, then . . ."

"We're . . . we're *retired*, kid. Big difference." Pranky Jones managed to gasp between bouts of laughter.

"Yeah, redemption arcs weren't really our thing. Other than Man vs. Nature Episodes, Twisty and me didn't do a single goddamn thing to help anyone our whole careers. It wasn't until we retired that The Narrator approached us about this place, and this doesn't count. I've still got the Brick House Costume parked in the lair, ready to go," Jungle Jim said. "Now, you want to talk redemption arcs? Talk to Teacher's Pet. That little bastard was on his way to the light side before The Narrator talked him into retirement. He's on vacation, though. The Galapagos, or something. Won't be back for weeks."

"Huh. So, you two don't know *anything* about redemption?"

"Nope," Jungle Jim said. I didn't believe him. They seemed pretty much redeemed from where I sat.

Pranky Jones took a deep breath to recover from his laughing fit. His face darkened. "Look, you want my advice? Kill him."

The room went quiet. Then Jungle Jim nodded. I quickly changed my mind. They were *not* pretty much redeemed. Not. At. All. I blinked, holding Tails in my arms in case they started something.

"Jones is right, Understudy," Jungle Jim said. "Villains don't get redeemed unless their arc's planned out in advance. A few studios do that, you know? Plan the whole season out. Every Episode, every conflict, every moral dilemma. Those are the villains who get redemption, but for most of us? We just get filthy rich."

"It's a hard life," Pranky Jones said woefully, "but someone's gotta live it."

"So, you recommend I kill him? That seems . . . like a lot. He's messed up a couple of my Episodes, but death feels over the top."

"If you want to get him to stop, you've gotta stop him once and for all," Pranky Jones said. "That was the problem with my hero. He'd kick my ass, sure, but then he'd stick me in the cushy side of Almhurst, and a week later, I'd be out and about, terrorizing the city. It got worse when we both moved to Yorkston, but even then, he never stopped me."

"Uh-huh." Jungle Jim hesitated. "Look, you're young and idealistic. We've been in the game a long time, and the world would have been better off if a hero had stopped us. But you want to try an organic redemption arc? Watch *Nautilus vs. The Triad*, Episodes one through seven. You'll see how tough it is and how much work it'll take. Then maybe you can make the right decision for yourself."

He pushed himself to his feet, the chair creaking ominously below his massive frame. Then he stuck out a meaty hand, and I shook it. His grip threatened to crush my fingers even through the superhero damage, and I winced. "Kid, you play it safe with this Empty Oath guy, and he'll mop the floor with you. Beat him first. Redeem him after."

"Thanks, you two."

"Don't mention it. Oh, if he does decide on a redemption arc, or his lawyers abandon him, we'll put in a good word with The Narrator. He can come hang out with us. We'll teach him the ropes."

I shivered as I left Tottergarten, taking the back door so I didn't trigger another The Cloud fit. After meeting with the two supervillains, I wasn't sure if they'd teach Vigilant Vow how to be a good guy . . . or a bad one.

The monorail dropped me off three blocks from the Tokyexico Council of Heroes tower in downtown Mid-Town. Its glassy front wall towered over the rest of the nearby buildings, and perched atop that was the black-and-steel circle where, according to the Episodes, the council held its meetings. The elevator ride to the fifty-fourth floor felt a lot like riding up to the *Cooking with Charlene* studio, but by the time I got there, I could see everything: the parks and malls, Tokyexico University, and even the top of the wall.

And I could look down into the shielded, shimmering Hot Zone, where the studios local to Tokyexico conducted business. None of the buildings were more than a few stories, and most looked like offices or warehouses. Here and there, a few people walked the sidewalks, but for the most part, the Hot Zone was surprisingly empty. Or maybe not too surprising; the Ilneats didn't have much need to do business with the average person, and supers had direct paths to their producers' studios. I'd texted Tele-Portal about it, and her advice was the same as Jungle Jim's and Pranky Jones's.

<Fight 2 win. Fix him l8r - Tele-Portal 3:15>

The elevator stopped, and I tore myself away from the view and wandered down the hall toward the super-counseling office. The door was closed, and as I opened it, I saw a couple of heroes and a villain I recognized as Lord Destructo, whose helmet looked different than in the Episodes I'd seen—melted, maybe. His face seemed bruised, at least from what I could see between the bandages, and his arm was in a sling. The heroes sat in plastic chairs, studiously ignoring the villain, who leaned against the wall beside a door leading farther in with his mace in hand. I nodded at him, checked in on the computer, and sat down.

I wasn't sure what to think about the Tottergarten villains' reactions to Vigilant Vow. They didn't seem to think he'd be redeemable, but he was a *kid*. Putting him in the ground wasn't a solution—not really, at least. I'd win the race, but it'd cost me a lot. Not everything, exactly, but more than I wanted to pay. Death couldn't be the solution.

So what was?

Before I could ponder my way to an answer, the door opened, and a woman's voice said, "Magical Girl Understudy, 4:15 appointment."

"That's me," I said. Lord Destructo nodded slowly, glaring daggers at the other two heroes. Then he stepped maybe an inch to the side, clearing just enough space for me to step between him and his massive, bent warhammer.

Inside was a long hallway and an older woman, who reminded me vaguely of The Narrator. Her curly black hair had streaks of gray, and she smiled warmly. "Welcome, Understudy. We're the last door on the right."

"Thanks." Inside were a pair of comfy armchairs, a coffee table with one empty mug and one half-full one, and a coffee maker on a short counter. A few lamps lit the room, while the overhead fluorescents were off.

The woman gestured at me to take a seat. "Coffee with a cream?"

"And sugar, please," I said. Coffee wasn't my go-to drink, but I needed something to do with my hands, and holding a mug counted.

As she filled up the mug, the woman talked. "I'm Dr. Ayers, but you can call me Angie. Unlike you, I don't have superpowers. What I do have is a doctorate in psychology, a master's in de-escalation, and almost fifteen years of working with superheroes. I'm also fully confidential unless you plan on killing someone who's not a super. That's part of my oath and training."

"Oaths. Right," I said.

"Before we begin, I want to mention that I care about both your superhero and real personalities. I'd prefer we use real first names here, but understand if you'd prefer to remain completely anonymous."

"Oh." I thought about it for a moment. Then I nodded. "I'm Annie."

"Annie, Angie. That's funny, so close to being the same."

"Yeah. I'll just call you Dr. Ayers."

"Fair enough." Dr. Ayers sat in the free armchair. "So, what's on your mind?"

"Two things. The first is that a couple months ago, I almost killed a henchman during a car chase, and it got me thinking about what happens when I *do* kill someone. The other one is more pressing, though." I launched into my explanation of Vigilant Vow again. By the time I finished, I was getting pretty good at it. "But yeah, the villains think I should just kill him, and I don't think that's the right call."

"It's not. I take it you'd prefer to focus on this Vigilant Vow first and your near-lethal experience after, correct?" I nodded, and Dr. Ayers continued. "The Tottergarten villains are correct. Redemption is hard, and your villain must be interested in making it happen, atoning for their wrongs, and in the amount of soul-searching and, frankly, therapy it takes. I will say that most villains don't win and then go looking for redemption, though."

"What do you mean by that?" I asked.

Dr. Ayers sighed and pushed my coffee toward me. I grabbed it and took a sip reflexively; even with the sugar, it still tasted bitter and nutty. She cleared her throat. "I mean, Annie, that those villains are only half-wrong. If you want to redeem him, he's got to lose first."

48

He's Got to Lose First

I closed my eyes, reaching into my backpack to touch Tails's head. Everyone kept telling me what I already knew: Vigilant Vow needed to lose. The only difference between the counselor, Fursona, Rocko, and the Tottergarten villains was what needed to happen next.

The silence pressed in. Dr. Ayers just sipped on her coffee. Clearly, she wasn't going to say anything until I did. But what was there to say? That I didn't want to kick his butt? That would be a lie. I needed to beat him, and more importantly, I *wanted* it. He'd frustrated me repeatedly, and I couldn't just let that happen—not if I wanted to move up to the big leagues.

So, after some consideration, I cleared my throat and started talking awkwardly. "Yeah, that's what everyone keeps saying. So, I beat him, then I help with redemption if he wants it."

"Yes." Dr. Ayers smiled sadly. "Many villains don't want it, but there's a chance if he's still a kid. No one grows up wanting to be the bad guy. They just find themselves in the role and do what they're told. But until you can beat him, he won't see the light, which means you have to keep dealing with him. He has a power that interferes with yours, so let's change subjects and return to your nemesis and redemption later. Tell me about the Roadrage Episode. I watched it in preparation for this meeting, but I want to know your thoughts and feelings before I say anything."

"Okay. The Roadrage Episode. Most of it was fine, right up until the end," I started. She nodded encouragingly. "So, the semis are driving at each other, and my sidekick's in the back with Roadrage, but she'll be fine, and there's a guy in the driver's seat oncoming who's in trouble. I grab him a second before the trucks hit. Then, when I catch him, there's a massive explosion overhead. I go back up, set the Extra down—sorry."

"It's fine. You're talking about an Episode, so the terminology doesn't bother me," Dr. Ayers said.

"Thanks. And for a moment, I feel great. But the henchman driving Roadrage's rig is badly hurt, and I feel like it's my fault," I finished. I looked down into my coffee cup, shivering. "I want to help people with my powers, but I've got a friend with

APPEAL—she doesn't like the term *Extra*—and I'm starting to see their arguments that supers are a danger to people. I guess the big thing I need help with is reconciling helping with all the damage I do. Plus, my last Episode messed up my relationship with my sidekick. I sort of pushed her out a window trying to go for the win."

"I see. I see." Dr. Ayers thought for a few moments, and then she smiled. "This whole issue with Vigilant Vow might be an opportunity to focus on the helping people side of superheroing instead of the fighting side, and let your sidekick shine for a bit."

"How?"

"Well, you don't need all your powers to help people. What kinds of things do the police, firefighters, or EMTs do in Episodes?"

"They help keep Extras away from the thickest fighting, evacuate people, talk with the media . . . Oh. You're saying I can do all that without powers. That could work, and it'd clear the way for Fursona to get the spotlight and decide how to beat the Episode."

"Right. You'll be at a disadvantage without your powers, and until you beat Vigilant Vow and figure out how to stop him from stealing your familiar, you can't do anything about that. So—and I give this advice to *so many* supers—you need to focus on what you *can* control. That's you, your unpowered actions, and how you approach teamwork with your sidekick. Heroes fight villains. It's what they do. But it doesn't have to be all they do," Dr. Ayers said.

"Thanks. Um, what about the killing thing?"

"It'll happen eventually, Understudy. As you move into the minor leagues, there's more and more potential for someone to get hurt, whether an Extra, a henchman, or a hero or villain. Especially with things ramping up. The Council of Heroes expects the Third Power War in the next six months, and they're prepping for it. But it means people will get hurt, whether it's on purpose or accidental.

"You won't be alone when it happens. We'll work through it together. If you're lucky, you'll get a month or so off to process it, but some heroes' death counts are so high they don't even take a day. Golden Goose, for example. This is public information, but it's not widely circulated. She's killed more Extras than any two villains nationwide, not counting the Top Five."

"That doesn't surprise me," I said. "And Stella-Lunar probably has a few on accident, too." I thought back to the first Episode from Superpower Ethics.

"Yeah. That doesn't make it easier when it first happens, but know that you won't be alone and that my colleagues and I are very good at working supers through it. We've got grief groups set up and everything."

We talked for a while longer about my relationship with Fursona ("On the rocks, but very recoverable with hard work"), the situation with Gourmet ("You probably did too much for a hero/villain relationship, but way to help your friends"), and classes ("Make sure you focus here. Keeping up in school is super important for super students"). By the time my session ended, I felt exhausted. I thanked Dr. Ayers and made another appointment for a couple of weeks to follow up, since I'd be *trying* some of the things we'd discussed.

Lord Destructo glared at me with one eye as I opened the door. Bandages covered the other. I nodded slowly. "Excuse me."

He moved a full step and nodded slightly, and I left quickly.

<Fursona, I need your help. My place, 20 minutes? - Understudy 5:17>
<Sure. Chinese food on the way - Fursona 5:18>
<Got it. 30 minutes then. The usual? - Understudy 5:18>
<Sure - Fursona 5:18>

I smiled and turned toward our favorite restaurant. I didn't have a complete plan yet, but I was putting one together. Fursona would be impressed.

Fursona was not impressed.

She stared at the whiteboard, where I'd written 'Things I Can Do Unpowered' across one half and 'Things Fursona Can Do Powered' across the other. My side had a small list, like talking to the media and getting people away from the fighting. Her side was much bigger, including doing the actual fighting, being the center of the camera drones' attention, and taking the lead on Episodes. That last part had her the most worried.

Well, the second-most worried.

"Annie," she said from around a mouthful of lo mien, "I feel like your plan is . . . well, it's suicidal. What if you get caught up in the fight without powers? What if Vigilant Vow decides to target you? What if—"

"Fursona," I tried to interrupt. She was rolling, just like she had last semester.

"—I can't deal with the fighting alone, and we lose? I want to be the shot-caller, but what if I mess it up? There are just too many things to—"

"Bee! Take a breath," I said, letting my professionalism slip. "I know there's a lot that could go wrong. That's why I've got it all scribbled on the board—so we can work through it together. But I can't do that if you're panicking about what's up here. Can I please explain?"

"I just . . ." Bee finally took that breath, then slurped another mouthful of noodles, flicking sauce across her face. She wiped her mouth with her sleeve. Sometimes, I thought, Bianca Marino could be a little gross.

"Can I get you a napkin?"

"No, I'm fine now. I just feel like there are too many things we can't control."

"I agree. But we can't stop doing Episodes, so we need to plan as if I'm ineffective, and these are the things I think I can do and how I can contribute to the team. We're a team, right?" I asked, hoping she'd agree, but worried she'd bring up the "Gourmet's Glutton Hour" Episode again. She'd been doing that a lot, and even though I'd been in the wrong and apologized, it was a winning strategy for her. Every time she did, I just sort of . . . gave up on whatever we were arguing about.

That had to stop if we were going to move forward, so I hoped she wouldn't this time.

"Yeah, we're a team," she said instead, and I smiled slightly into my pineapple chicken.

"So, Miss Whiteboard Champion, what do you recommend we change?"

"Well, for starters, threat assessment," she said, taking the whiteboard marker from me. I sat down and dug into my meal, closing her box so it'd stay warm. "I know not every Episode is one you pick out, but we need to discuss the ones we pick better. If you're asking not to be a combatant unless you have your powers, we can't target any more PG-13 minor-league Episodes. I can't realistically solo any of them."

"Agreed," I said, even though I didn't agree at all. Without minor-league Episodes, it'd be much harder to catch up and prove we could hack it. But I pushed that misgiving down. Getting her on board was the most important thing—that and letting her feel in control.

"Second, in-Episode communication. We need a way to talk even if we're not together. That way, I know if you lose your powers. I won't assume you're powerless, and I don't think you should, either. You haven't lost your powers for more than ten minutes at a time, right?"

"Right. So, you want to know if I'm powerless during an Episode and if I regain them?" I asked. I had sweet and sour sauce on my mouth, and there wasn't a napkin nearby. I groaned inside; I'd have to be a hypocrite, but maybe she wouldn't see.

"Right. How about this? A text to Bianca's number during an Episode means you've lost your powers. The phone buzzes, and I don't have to look at it to know," Bianca said. I nodded, and she turned to write that on the board. I took the opportunity to quickly wipe my mouth.

Over the next fifteen minutes, we took turns coming up with ideas for handling a variably powered Understudy. By the end, Bianca almost looked pleased with what was on the board. Almost.

"There's one more thing I need from you, Annie," she said, "and I don't think it's something we can just write on the board. I need your promise, once again, that you'll tell me if shit hits the fan."

I looked at her, trying not to roll my eyes. I'd committed to that half a dozen times in the last couple of weeks. But it wasn't Fursona asking. It was Bee. And honestly, I could see why she wanted me to promise yet again.

So, I untransformed. And I started unbuckling her suit. I got one strap undone before she turned around and did the rest. Underneath, she wore shorts and a tank top, just like usual. She didn't smell like green apples. She smelled like sweat and nervousness, and I checked myself before I said anything flippant.

Instead, I turned her around and wrapped my arms around her. "Bee, I love you, and I'm going to do better at communicating, especially in Episodes. I'd say I need you to stop worrying, but I understand why you do. It's okay for you to be nervous about all this. We've had some big bumps the last month or so, and I really appreciate you giving me a chance to make things better."

"I know." She leaned back into me. For a moment, I could feel her relaxing, her back against my chest and her hair against my chin. Then she stiffened and pulled away. "You have that guest lecture tomorrow, right? Do you think Vigilant Vow will try something then?"

My first instinct was to say no. That he wouldn't dare attack an Ilneat's talk to get at me. But then I thought about it, and I nodded slowly. "Yes. Yes, either he'll be there or someone else will. It'll be dramatic and flashy, and it's such an obvious Episode location. Will you be ready to go and be close by?"

"Yes," Bianca said, and she leaned back into me for a moment before she pulled away and grabbed her chopsticks. "7:30, Cherry Creek High."

49

Cherry Creek High

The Cherry Creek High auditorium was nicer than anything in Riverside, including the community theater. The building itself was both more expensive-looking and not as shiny as Riverside High. It was older and had clearly been state-of-the-art when it was made. They hadn't spared any expenses in keeping it up to date, either, and it was newer than Riverside High where it counted.

The auditorium. That was where it counted.

I sat in a cushy theater chair, similar to the ones in Roth Theater, and waited while a woman in a dark blue pantsuit talked at length about Professor Eustace Bagges's accolades and achievements. The Ilneat had degrees from a dozen universities and schools across Ilneat space, most of which I'd never heard of. The only one I vaguely recognized was an honorary from New Harvard. According to the woman, he'd written a dozen books, shot at least three documentaries, and was in the Hot Zone for a year to research "entertainment worlds and their impacts on Ilneat culture."

On some level, it was really cool stuff. And on another, more visceral level, I wanted to hear from him, not her.

<So far, not much action outside - Fursona 7:34>
<You good? - Fursona 7:34>
<Yep. Boring introduction time. No signs of baddies. Tails here - Understudy 7:35>

"So, without further ado, it's my pleasure to introduce Professor Eustace Bagges, author of *Courage and Cowardice on Mornsal Four*."

I clapped politely and reached for a water bottle. All around me, people from sixteen to their mid-forties were either sipping on their own or glaring at those of us who knew the Hot Zone wasn't a myth. I was dressed for a summer in the desert, and some still wore sweaters and jeans.

Professor Bagges was overdressed in their parka and long scarf. They climbed up the podium and cleared their throat, sounding nothing like Rocko or Pataki. "Hello, members of the Greater Ilneat Prosperity Community. Today, I'm going to talk about how the community has benefited some of our longer-term resource worlds, and I'd like to start with Mornsal Four, the place I wrote about in my book.

"Mornsal Four is the perfect example of how Ilneat Prosperity works. Its culture was warlike, with an interest in infighting between various factions and an, I believe you'd call it, military-industrial complex that was out of control. One of its black research facilities suffered a containment breach in 25832 Ilneat Standard—roughly 1693 CE Earth. Before we could intervene, over half the population was infected. Mornsal Four was doomed, and the bioweapons threatened to spread to nearby planets."

The Ilneat pressed a button, and the screen behind them lit up with a short video of the planet's plant and animal life withering as a sickly green cloud spread across the surface. A few horned aliens with four legs and sickle-shaped bones on their forearms ran from the cloud. Then, they vanished.

"After nearly three hundred Ilneat cycles, Mornsal Four is making a comeback. Parts of the planet have become tourist hot spots, and its large plains offer some of the best farming land in Ilneat space. So, what's the difference between then and now?"

I already knew their answer, so instead of looking at the stage like most of the crowd, I glanced at the few people who weren't. As Professor Eustace Bagges talked about how, with the reduced population, the planet needed Ilneat technology to recover, a few people around my age reached into their backpacks. They pulled out helmets— helmets with spiked horns on their heads. The Student Supervillain Society was here!

I reached slowly for my phone, trying not to tip off any of the others, who I now recognized as henches.

<Fursona, go time soon. SSS henches in audience. Episode - Understudy 7:41>
<Going to go to bathroom and transform - Understudy 7:41>
<Got it. Be careful - Fursona 7:42>
<Stragglers coming into building - Fursona 7:43>

"Ilneat technological gifts and the newly discovered System, which Ilneat scientists were still examining, helped stabilize Mornsal Four, and . . ." the four-armed professor said. I stopped paying attention as I slid past people's knees. My feet "accidentally" kicked a helmet under a row of velvet seats, and the would-be henchman glared at me.

"Sorry," I mumbled. "I'll get it for you."

"It's . . . It's fine," he said. He rolled his eyes. "You've got places to be."

"Yeah. Sorry again." I got to the edge of the row and started toward the door. I just had to make it to the bathroom, then I could transform and be ready for the—

Bang!

[Casting Call]
[Episode: Eustace Holds the Bagge! - PG]

[**Role: On-Site Superhero! Do you accept the role? (Yes/No)**]
[**Role Focus: Cunning + Flamboyance**]

The door burst in, and a familiar pair of faces filled the frame. The first was a hulking figure with metal fists that revved as he held them over his head. "Nobody move! This is a hostage situation now!" Iron Fist grabbed me with an . . . iron fist . . . and shoved me toward the seats. I almost dropped my backpack but kept hold of it as I quietly sat down.

The second one strode down the aisle toward a spluttering Professor Bagges as the henchmen in the audience pulled on their masks. As soon as they did, Monologue began [**Monologuing**], a wave of emptiness washing over my brain—and the audience's. "That's right. It is I, Monologue, the Sultan of Speeches, King of One-Sided Conversations, and tonight, I have a very special presentation for you. Tonight, we'll be taking Eustace here on a journey, but before we do, the Student Supervillain Society has some things to . . . things to say," he finished weakly as Eustace walked up in the middle of his [**Monologue**].

I accepted the role as his power faded, locking myself into the Episode. Unlike the Orientation Episode, I was ready. Or at least, as ready as I'd ever be.

[**Eustace Holds the Bagge!: Act One in Progress**]

"What's the meaning of this? I was promised safe passage wherever I wanted in Tokyexico as long as it related to my research. The studios *all* promised. If your producers find out—"

"How did you ignore my [**Monologue**]?" Monologue asked, looking confused. Then he shook his head. "Doesn't matter. Iron Fist, grab them while I pick a few Extras as bonus hostages. Meet me in the school office."

"Got it, boss," Iron Fist said. The henches began grabbing audience members and dragging them toward the door. I kept my head down, hoping I wouldn't be selected. If the supers left, I could sneak out and transform, then take Monologue and Iron Fist down with Fursona's help. If not . . .

"You. I remember you." Monologue stared right at me, squinting. Then he laughed. "Remember the escape artist Extra from the Orientation Episode? She's here! What a wonderful moment to continue our conversation. It's only been seven months, but I have so many questions for you!"

Before I could protest that he had the wrong girl, or even shake off his [**Monologue's**] power, he grabbed me and shoved me toward a waiting hench. "Take her, too."

Professor Eustace Bagges protested the whole time we walked to the office.

"Your studios will be hearing about this. I'll break you, you hear me? This kind of behavior will not be tolerated from a resource world's citizens. Don't you know who I am?"

At that last question, Monologue leaned in. I was close enough to hear him whispering. "Of course, we know who you are. And who do you think put us up to this? My producer is going to make a fortune off this controversy—and I get a cut of it. It's too bad I don't have to pay for more college since I'm graduating, but it'll be a nice nest egg for my future as one of Tokyexico's greats!"

Without another word, he nodded to Iron Fist, who shoved Bagges into the office. I followed before my assigned hench had to push me; the less I drew attention to myself, the more chance I'd have of sneaking away and getting in on the impending action.

Cherry Creek High's office looked a lot like every school office, just with more glass and steel frames and fewer cinderblocks. It had been upper-class before Launch Day, and it hadn't faded much in the years since. I sat in a student's chair while Monologue walked into the principal's office and Iron Fist dragged Bagges in behind him. The door slammed shut, and I had a moment to plan.

We'd discussed situations like this in the green room, but we assumed I wouldn't have access to Tails because of Vigilant Vow's power. In this case, I *could* start a **[Transformation Sequence]** at any time. I just couldn't do it without giving up my secret identity in front of a bunch of Extras. So, with that in mind, I had to think on my feet, and I had to do it before Monologue dragged me in there or someone went through my bag and found Tails.

"Scuse me," I said to the hench guarding me. "I've gotta use the bathroom."

"No, you don't," she said. "I promise you don't."

"But I do. I 100% promise I do."

She ignored me, even when I fidgeted awkwardly, so I stopped. Okay. I hadn't expected that to work. It'd be too easy, and Monologue didn't want any of us hostages getting away. Counting myself but not Bagges, there were six of us, and that would be enough to keep the heroes off-balance in any rescue attempt. I sighed and reached into my pocket. If I could text Fursona, I could tell her what was happening.

The henchwoman stiffened and lifted a police baton menacingly, and I stopped. "I just want to text my girlfriend and tell her I'm alright."

"No. Give me the phone." She stood over me, slapping the baton into her hand until I complied.

There went the easy options. I sighed. It would have taken an exceptionally dumb henchman to pull either of those off, but they'd been worth a shot. Now, I had to actually think of a plan. It'd have to be clever and cunning, *and* not get Fursona mad at me.

Did such a plan even exist? I'd have to find out!

But before I could think, Iron Fist escorted Professor Bagges out of the office and then turned to me. "Monologue wants you. No idea why you're so important, but he's convinced you're more important than the otter-rilla here."

The Ilneat spluttered, combing their thick fur with their grasping hands. "You'll be hearing from my solicitor. I've never been handled so roughly in my life!"

"Go on," Iron Fist said. "Take your bag. He's convinced you've got something in there that's important. The rest of you, look sharp. We'll have heroes soon, and you'd better fight hard before you surrender, or you won't get bonus pay."

"Bonus pay! Awesome!" a henchman said. Another elbowed him in the side. He glared and rubbed where the elbow had caught him. "What? You like getting paid too."

I scooped up my backpack, gulping. Monologue was looking for a familiar—he had to be. If he found Tails, he'd recognize her from the Series Finale or footage of us fighting against Lady Lockless. I had to hide her, but I couldn't figure out *how*.

Then I stepped into the office. Monologue sat there, feet on the desk, staring at me intently. He raised an eyebrow. "You've shown up twice during SSS Episodes, and I recognize you from the information desks just before Orientation started. Who are you?"

"I'm Anika DuPont, and I'm starting to get really tired of being kidnapped by you supervillains," I said shakily. I wasn't scared of him—not compared to what he'd find if he looked in my backpack. But I *was* trying to ham it up for his benefit.

"I don't think that's who you are, *Miss DuPont*. I want to know your superhero identity."

"My what? You've accused me of this before. If I could turn into a flying laser beam lady, I would have by now," I snapped back.

"Then empty your bag on the desk."

I groaned. But I didn't see any way out. As I unzipped the bag, praying for a miracle, someone answered, and for the first time all semester I thanked Vigilant Vow. When I dumped my bag's contents onto the table, Tails wasn't there.

50

Tails Wasn't There

So there I was, in the principal's office, with every pen, tampon, and school book I owned scattered across the desk's oak top. Monologue glared suspiciously at the pile. Then he stood up. "I don't believe this. All the signs are there, but no Magical Girl would be stupid enough not to have her familiar nearby. Iron Fist! Get rid of her! Put her with the others!"

Monologue wasn't [**Monologuing**] anymore. Instead, he felt like he was about to lose control. In a way, I didn't blame him; this was the second time he'd caught me out, and this time, I'd only dodged being revealed as Magical Girl Understudy by pure luck. That had to sting. I quickly scooped up my possessions, feigning embarrassment at the tampons and a few other items, and fled the room before Iron Fist could grab me and drag me out.

I flopped into my chair next to Professor Bagges, a watchful pair of henches watching over us, and stared up at a row of television screens over the secretaries' desks. Each showed four angles of the school's security cameras. I started watching them, trying to map out a few blind spots so I could change if I managed to escape. Then I stopped.

On the third monitor, a kangaroo stood in one of the frames. I didn't have to fear; the Justice-Roo was here! She stared right into the camera, waving for a few seconds, then raised a finger and waved it in the air. I laughed. That *had* to be costing her rating warnings, but it looked like so much fun, and a secretary would have a heart attack when they reviewed the footage.

One of the henches yelled, "Hey! You got a hero out there!"

"I've got this. Keep the hostages here," Iron Fist said. He stomped through the door and into the hall, and for the second time this semester, I got to watch my sidekick on the screen.

She wasn't doing badly. Her strategy seemed pretty much the same as the Grant Building Episode—dodge the stronger supervillain's attacks, run around, and try to get him lost in Cherry Creek High. I nodded approvingly. She couldn't hold her own against him, but if she could outmaneuver him and hit Monologue fast enough, she might win the Episode right there.

"I say, this is pretty exciting," Professor Bagges murmured from their chair. The henches had spread out to cover more ground with Iron Fist gone and their boss behind a closed door, so we had a few moments to talk. "You know, you're not the only entertainment world. I once got caught up in a battle between two Ildranean frigates for a space opera, and that's the only time I've been more excited than this."

"I thought you hated it and wanted to sue," I said.

"Oh, I do. My presentation was supposed to show the benevolence of the Ilneat Empire, but being interrupted puts a kibosh on that, as your people say," Bagges said. I blinked. None of *my* people said that. But the Ilneat ignored me. "Truth be told, I'm terrified, but there's also something thrilling about all this. It's scripted, right?"

"Uh, right," I lied. The poor Ilneat was in shock, or denial, or *something*. Either way, they weren't thinking properly. I had to get them out of here before they did something stupid or the supervillains did. And I could totally do that without powers.

It wouldn't be more complex than getting out by myself. I just had to . . . figure out how to free myself.

Fursona was still dodging and ducking. She dipped into a classroom, then dashed through an open door into another as Iron Fist hurried to catch her. Then she disappeared. The villain looked confused for a moment, then started looking around as I laughed. Cherry Creek was a massive school, and he was somewhere on the third floor. Getting to the office from there would be a chore, especially if . . .

Yep! Fursona was shutting fire doors, which locked automatically. Between those and the thick brick walls, it'd take Iron Fist a few minutes to get back downstairs.

[End of Act One! Act Two in Five Minutes! No Point Changes]

All around me, henchmen relaxed. I didn't realize they could see the notifications, but they *did* have superhero damage, so it made sense they'd have some small tie-in with the Style System. A few started talking about classes, some even talking to the hostages, who looked both confused and terrified.

I leaned over and whispered in Bagges's ear, "Hey, want to know a secret?"

"Sure, I love secrets," they said. "Secrets and old tales make for great research."

I looked around. No henches nearby; I could speak semifreely. "I'm a superhero, too. I'm undercover, so you can't say anything, but I'll get you out of here. You have my oath on that."

"Excellent," Bagges said. They fidgeted with their grasping hands. "Will it hurt?"

"Uh, probably not."

"So what's the plan?" Bagges asked me. They fiddled with the translator on their coat's neck and a little light flicked orange. I groaned inside; they were recording this.

"First, we're going to play it cool. Why don't you finish telling me about Mornsal Four?"

The Ilneat's face lit up. "Sure, I'd love that. What do you want to know?"

"Whatever you want to tell me." I did not care about Mornsal Four. I was just trying to keep Professor Bagges busy until an opportunity presented itself.

"Very well. Mornsal Four was actually one of the Prosperity Zone's first outside acquisitions. We've only expanded past the four Ilneat systems in the last three hundred cycles, and it's only recently that we made the breakthroughs in understanding the System that allowed us to start transforming Mornsal from a death world into something useful. But the locals are on their way up. In another hundred or two cycles, they might have advanced far enough to self-govern without Ilneat Empire oversight."

As he rambled on and on, I ignored him.

[Eustace Holds the Bagge!: Act Two in Progress]

"The thing most Ilneats don't care about and most resource-worlders don't know is that there's a process for letting a planet self-govern. Yours is further along than most others the Ilneats have saved. We have a noninterference policy unless your planet tries to wipe itself out, in which case we consider you incapable of direct self-government and work to stabilize your leadership for taking over again. In your case, my understanding is that your governments were still pretty much intact, so they—"

"Shhhhh," I whispered. "Someone's coming."

I glanced up at the TV screens. It was hard to tell, but it looked like Fursona was moving closer. A henchman ran into the principal's office, a look of panic on his face. A moment later, Monologue's voice echoed across the school on the intercom, and my stomach plummeted as Fursona stopped in her tracks.

"Hello, Fursona! I, Monologue, was ready for a hero's interference, but I'm thrilled it's you. I've wanted payback for a long time, ever since you and Understudy ruined the SSS's robot takeover plan. Now, I'm going to get that revenge. Henches, let the hostages go—except for the blonde and the Ilneat. Bring me that kangaroo!"

Oh shit. Monologue had created the best fortress ever by simply taking over the intercom. I panicked inside through my brain fog as the henches filed out, leaving two behind to watch Bagges and me. Fursona wouldn't be able to move a muscle as long as he kept talking, and neither would I.

But one person hadn't been affected by Monologue's **[Monologue]**: Professor Bagges. If they just reached out and picked up a phone, maybe they could interrupt the Sultan of Speeches and give Fursona a chance to escape. I'd figure out how to get Bagges and myself out alone. What I didn't need was this getting even worse.

My head felt fuzzy. How long had Monologue been talking? And was his speech more mind-numbing than Professor Bagges's? I tried to shake my head to clear it as Monologue droned on and on.

The Ilneat just sat there, staring at the two henches, grasping and squeezing hands entwined. I had to get their attention. Otherwise, I didn't see a way to save Fursona, and I didn't trust Monologue not to reveal her identity—or worse. He hadn't mentioned the Job Fair, but that humiliation had to sting.

I tried to gesture with my eyes. Were they even looking at me? I couldn't tell. Then, slowly, they reached for the phone and picked it up. "Hello, this is Professor Bagges! I need your help!" The Ilneat's voice echoed through the school, temporarily cutting off the supervillain's constant talking.

I laughed as Monologue's **[Monologue]** faded momentarily before the henchmen wrestled Bagges away from the phone and slammed it down. On the screen, Fursona kicked a henchman, then reached up to fiddle with her kangaroo ears.

Then the **[Monologue]** started again, and I stared slack-jawed at the screen as Fursona . . .

Didn't freeze.

Through the brain fog, I watched Fursona ignore the **[Monologue]**, kicking, punching, and thrashing henchmen with her tail. Within seconds, the dozen horn-helmeted henches lay on the ground or tried to surrender. Then, before Monologue could do more than open the office door, she barreled through the big glass window and smashed into him feet-first.

The **[Monologue]** cut off, and I grabbed Professor Bagges's squeezing hand. Now was our chance to escape! I kicked the office door open. This was all part of the plan Fursona and I had created. I'd do what I could without powers, and she'd do what she could with them.

[Daring Escape! +1 Drama Point]

I laughed, trying not to sound maniacal, as the Style System message came in. I wasn't suited up, but at least I was earning points.

Bagges and I fled for the main door, and honestly? I felt great! Here I was, saving people and trusting my sidekick to have my back. There was nothing in our way to freedom, and as long as Fursona sat on Monologue, he couldn't stop us with his power.

"What happened? Why couldn't you move while he was talking?" Bagges asked.

"His power's pretty ridiculous. As long as he's talking about himself, **[Monologue]** stuns everyone in earshot."

"So why'd the fuzzy critter ignore it?"

I thought about it for a moment. Then I remembered. "The Piano Man! We had to block our hearing. She must have turned that back on!" It also explained why she hadn't said anything before she attacked Monologue. She couldn't have heard our responses any—

CRASH!

As we hit the door, something fell from the sky, blocking our way. I gulped as Iron Fist stood in the middle of the concrete path, where he'd broken a crater with his . . . iron fists. He glared at us. "Where do you think you're going?"

I looked at Bagges, and they looked at me. Then I turned and dashed back into the building, dragging the Ilneat with me. "Run!"

51

Run!

We ran.

We ran as fast as our legs could carry us—then, when Professor Bagges's legs couldn't go any faster, I picked them up and kept running down the hall. The floor squeaked as I skidded around a corner. I looked back, and my heart plummeted.

It didn't matter how fast unpowered Anika DuPont ran; the super-powered Iron Fist was faster.

I only had one play—one option I could take. So, as I reached a T-junction with a sign saying Language Arts and Social Studies and arrows pointing each way, I dropped Professor Bagges facing right, then ran left.

Why? Simple. If Iron Fist followed me, great! That was the best outcome because the Ilneat could escape easily. Sure, I'd be in trouble, but they'd be safe. I'd planned on being imprisoned, beaten up, tied to a chair over a pit filled with alligators while saws menaced me—whatever. The point was, I was ready for it. I was hoping for it, even.

And if Iron Fist decided that Bagges was the right target? I'd get away, stay close, and wait for Tails to return. Then it'd be Fursona and me against the villains; it'd be a fair-ish fight, and I figured we had around a 30% chance to save Bagges if that happened, but it wasn't my ideal scenario.

Then, there was option three, where he tackled me and caught up to Bagges. I didn't have a plan for that one.

So, of course, that's what happened.

As his iron fist closed around my ankle and dragged me to the tile, I panicked. I hadn't planned on this! This wasn't supposed to happen! I started flailing around, thrashing out with my feet. My shoe caught Iron Fist right in the chin. It felt like kicking a brick wall, and I doubted I'd done *actual* damage, but he let go.

[Extra-Badass! +1 Badass Point]

I scrambled away and started running. Looking over my shoulder, I watched Professor Bagges lash out with his squeezing hands before Iron Fist pulled the Ilneat away, holding them like a cartoon kid punching the air toward him. A camera drone recorded the whole thing. Under other circumstances, it'd be funny.

But under normal circumstances, I'd be suited up and ready to fight. I turned the corner and dipped into a classroom. Posters adorned the walls, gerunds, sentence diagramming, and "how to find the symbolism" references. I ducked behind the teacher's desk, then pulled the rolling chair in until I was wedged into a ball. If Iron Fist came, I needed to be invisible.

<Understudy, what are you doing meow?> Tails's voice echoed in my brain. *<You're hiding under a table like a scared kitten. Get out there and—>*

I held a finger to my lips, hoping the cat would stay still and quiet. My plans had just gotten a lot more realistic. But first, I had to survive Iron Fist's search.

The door to the classroom opened with a squeak, and Professor Bagges started whining. "I swear, Steelface, or whatever your name is, I'll see your whole studio underwater! You have no idea of the forces you're messing with!"

"Steelface! Ha! That's a good one," Iron Fist said. He took a step into the room. Then another. I watched from under the desk, frozen more still than if Monologue were talking. I held my breath and started counting in my head.

At twenty-five seconds, he finally stepped back into the hall, and the door slammed shut. Stale breath rushed from my lungs, and I wriggled out from under the table. "I swear to upstage the villains . . ."

As my transformation sequence finished and I dashed into the hall, skirt beating against my legs, I couldn't help but let out a deep breath. The tension melted right off me, and I realized I couldn't play the damsel for much longer. I needed my powers uninterrupted, and if that meant thrashing Vigilant Vow later, then he was on the way to getting thrashed—just as soon as I found Iron Fist, beat him, and saved Professor Bagges.

He'd be heading for the office, so I had to beat him there. I sprinted as fast as I could, rounded the corner into a main hall filled with motivational posters and big glass windows, and saw him. He carried the Ilneat professor in a bear hug, ignoring the gorilla-like alien's attempts to break free.

"Stop in the name of Justice! [**Stellar Ray**]!" I shouted, waving my wand. The pink-white beam slammed into Iron Fist's back, right between the shoulder blades, sizzling against his super-suit.

[**Dramatic Damage! +1 Drama Point**]

"You're sure you want to do that? Okay, then," Iron Fist said. He shifted his grip, wrapping two of Bagges's arms in one metal hand and making the come-at-me-bro gesture.

I nodded and waved my wand again. If he didn't want to engage, that was fine. I'd wear him down. "[Stellar Ray]!"

[Dramatic Damage! +1 Drama Point]

"Have it your way, Understudy." The supervillain ran straight at me, left arm behind his back with Bagges covered by his body, and right ready to punch, grapple, or slap me. His metal fist jackhammered back and forth, and I activated [Power-Weaving].

I couldn't use [Quick-Time Change] before his oscillating fist slammed into me. The impacts—and there were five in less than a second—didn't do much individually, but together, they compounded, and I went flying into the lockers.

[HP 7/9]

"How do you know who I am?" I asked, playing for time.

He didn't give me more than a second. "Grant Building." As he said it, he swung, but I had [Quick-Time Change] ready this time, and [I-Frame Transformed] the hit. Tails's mind connected with mine; I had a theory that maybe I could dodge Vigilant Vow's power if we were one, and since it was only a matter of time before I lost Tails again, I wanted to test it out.

[Flashy Fitting-Room! +1 Flamboyance Point]
[Steel Yourself! +1 Grit Point]
[Floating Points: 1 Flamboyance]

Landing in my Copy Cat Costume, I tried to piece together a combo, but I didn't have a Flamboyance finisher, and Iron Fist's attacks came in too quickly. I regretted not starting the combo with one of my [Stellar Rays] for a second before I crashed into another locker. This time, the fist jackhammered into my chest and stomach over and over, but [Fursonal Furcefield] held—at least partially.

[Combo Dropped! Repeated Styles Used. Floating Points Lost.]
[HP 6/9]
[Tough Girl! +3 Grit Points]

I wouldn't survive much more of this, though, so when Iron Fist drew back to hit me again, I rolled left and used [Leaping Leopards] to create some space. I didn't have a quick change out of Copy Cat, so I was stuck with melee against a Bruiser, but if my theory held, I'd at least keep my powers no matter what.

<Left! Left!> Tails screamed in my head.

I ducked left again, and a second later, the fist slammed through the door where my head had been a moment before. A camera drone hummed overhead, then turned and watched Iron Fist flail Professor Bagges around. I had to drop the supervillain somehow, or at least pull the Ilneat away. If I could get him, I could use Copy Cat's mobility to—

Wham!

[HP 4/9]

I rocketed toward the ceiling from Iron Fist's violent uppercut, cracking a ceiling tile and falling right into the supervillain, who looked almost as surprised as me. He let go of Bagges long enough for the Ilneat to start running, and I activated **[Doom Ball]** just as I landed on his back.

The claws on my hands and feet ripped back and forth across his super-suit, leaving thin scratches and tears in it as I furiously tried to get as much damage out as possible. By the time he grabbed me and pulled me off him, his entire back was a mess of thin, red slices. But then he held me out by the scruff of my Costume.

[**Badass Damage! +5 Badass Points**]

"You're a pain in the [**Beep!**], Understudy," Iron Fist said. He held his free hand back, ready to punch me. I had only seconds to react, and there was only one right move. I waved a clawed hand at his face.

"Literally, in your case!"

BAM!

[HP 2/9]

I slid across the tiles until I came to rest at the base of some stairs. My head rang from the blow, but I shook it off, watching as his retreating form chased after the Ilneat professor. I had to save him, but Copy Cat hadn't cut it. I slowly, painfully transformed to Rainy Day, used **[Virga]**, then switched to Understudy. **[Rejuvenation]** kicked in, healing me even more.

[**Medic! +1 Cunning Point**]
[**Rejuvenation Activated! HP 7/9**]

After a few seconds in Rainy Day, I felt much more ready to take the fight to Iron Fist. The trouble was . . . that there was no Iron Fist to take the fight to. I groaned and started walking toward the office.

A moment later, Fursona dashed around the corner. She turned, poked her kangaroo helmet back around, and sighed in relief. She fiddled with the helmet and started talking. "Hi, Understudy. They don't seem interested in chasing me, but I couldn't two-*v*-one them. Okay, bad news first. Iron Fist got the Ilneat back, and he's pissed."

"Who, Bagges or Iron Fist?"

"Monologue!" Fursona joked. Then she continued. "All three, actually. Bagges yelled something about a lawsuit—"

"Yeah, they've been saying that."

"—And Monologue's pretty beat up and pissy about some kangaroo. I think we've got a pretty good shot at taking them down. These earplugs are really something. Speaking of which, quick plan?"

"Hit the office, distract the villains, get the professor, escape."

"Got it. Hand signals only," Fursona said. She fiddled with her helmet, then turned to look at me. "I'll get you out if he starts up."

I gave her a thumbs-up and a grin, and we started down the hall. I winced as I looked at the broken-in lockers, the squished lunches and destroyed notebooks, and the shattered door from my fight with Iron Fist. I was supposed to be almost ready for the minor leagues, but he'd dueled me to a standstill one-handed.

We crept closer and closer until I could see the office's glass walls. Fursona held up a paw, then took another step and punched through the glass. Then she grabbed a henchman, dragged him across a secretary's desk, and punched him in the face.

"Ah, Magical Girl Understudy! I must admit, as soon as I saw your furry friend here, I wondered how long it'd take you to arrive," Monologue said on the intercom. I felt his power set in, and a moment later, I was helpless. A half-dozen henches poured from the principal's office, followed by Iron Fist. Just before the door closed, I saw Monologue himself sitting, feet up. He looked ruffled, but not too badly beaten-up.

"I'm afraid, though, that I cannot allow you to interfere," he continued his **[Monologue]**. "My employers wish for me to keep the Ilneat, and should you take him, that would reflect poorly on me."

Fursona grabbed my hand, pulled me into her arms, and began hopping. I was still stunned by Monologue's power, but the earplugs we'd gotten to deal with The Piano Man kept her in the fight. She headed for the doors before Iron Fist or the henches could stop her.

She didn't stop hopping to put me down until Monologue's voice faded to nothing, and I could move and think again. As soon as I started struggling in her arms, though, she put me down. "Understudy, you're heavy."

[**End of Act Two: Act Three in Five Minutes**]
[Alias - Understudy] [Archetype - Magical Girl] [**Community Rank - 256/523**]
[**HP 7/9**]
[**Styles and Skills**]

►Archetype Skill - Transformation Sequence
►Combo Skills - Power-Weaving
►Badass (52) (Skill Roll Available)
►Cunning (1)
►Drama (42)
►Stellar Ray 2
►Bit-Part Barrage 1
►Flamboyance (26)
►Signature Skill - Adaptive Armoire 2
►Stored Costumes: (Rainy Day, Copy Cat)
►Starwave Sail 1
►Quick-Time Change 2
►Grit (7)
►I-Frame Transform 2

"Uh-huh. Do you have a plan for this one?" I rolled my Badass skill.

[50 Badass Credits Used. Rolling Skill!]

"No. I was hoping you did. Monologue's power doesn't have much counter-play unless you can't hear it, does it?" Fursona asked.

"No, not at all. I still want to get him back." The System's letters began slowing, and gradually the power appeared.

[Rank-Up! Doom Ball 1: Adds more attacks to the flurry]

I nodded appreciatively. A boost was a boost. Then I turned my attention back to Fursona—and the problem at hand. "Right now, they've got him, and I don't want them to be left holding the Bagge!"

52

Holding the Bagge

[Eustace Holds the Bagge!: Act Three in Progress]

Fursona and I couldn't agree on how to handle Iron Fist and Monologue. We had one pair of earplugs between us, the intercom made Monologue's range too big for an approach, and neither of us could take Iron Fist and the Duke of Discourse in a two-*v*-one fight. So, in the end, after we'd each thrown out a half-dozen choices, we did the one thing we both agreed would help turn the tables.

We called for backup.

I didn't want to make this a dogpile, but there wasn't another way to win without putting one of us in incredible danger, and Fursona vetoed the sacrifice play right away. I agreed with her, deep down, but on a more surface level, I wasn't thrilled about sharing my win with two more powerful heroes.

Still, when the sky-blue motorcycle side-slid to a stop next to us, tires squealing, I felt a ton of relief. A red-tinted Greek wrestler and blue speed-suited heroine got off, and I waved. "Hi, Milo. Hi, Springlock."

"Hi. What's the situation?" Springlock's fingers danced, and Milo interpreted.

"They're inside. Iron Fist, Monologue, and a dozen or so henches. They have five Extras and an Ilneat hostage. Eustace Bagges, author of *Courage and Cowardice* or something. We think their win condition involves getting their studio a ton of money from . . . somewhere," Fursona said.

"Okay, so, save the hostages? Easy enough. How do you feel about a sacrifice play?" Springlock asked.

"No," Fursona said right away. "We talked about it already. It puts people in too much danger. We've got one set of earplugs that work against Monologue, but that's not enough."

"I'm a Monologue hard counter. Milo doesn't like these strats either, but they work well. Here's what we do . . ."

"So, you and the kangaroo, huh?" Milo asked. We strolled down the street toward Cherry Creek High. "She the Nervous Nellie?"

"Yeah, kind of," I said. "She's got a real 'winning isn't everything' attitude, which is weird because she wasn't like that a couple of weeks ago. She's always been winning-oriented, but I threw her out a window to try and lock down an Episode, and she's changed a ton since."

"Yeah, I'm the Nervous Nellie in our relationship. You probably shouldn't have tossed her out a window, though," Milo said. We kept walking, not bothering to hide our presence at all. We *wanted* the villains' eyes on us, and that made me nervous.

The plan was simple. Fursona and Springlock were both counters for Monologue right now, but with the hostages, they couldn't use any *big* powers. Iron Fist needed to be out of the picture, or he and the henches could probably handle the two heroes together. So, Milo and I were bait.

We stepped onto the campus. Milo kept talking. "Springlock is aggressive all the time. Not just about Episodes, either. I mean *all the time*." He winked.

"Yeah, Fursona's not like that."

"No, but *you* might be. We've been following your race for the minor leagues. It's pretty hyped in the TUSSA Cave. Looks like a lot of fun, but damn, you've been pushing hard. So, here's the thing. You can win and make Fursona happy. You've gotta do a few things differently, though. Want to hear about it?"

"Sure," I said. We pushed the gym door open. We'd picked it because it was the farthest door from the school's main office, and it would force any response to wind its way through the whole school, leaving Monologue vulnerable.

"The first thing you've gotta do is—"

"Milo! How wonderful to see you. You've stepped into the new lair of Monologue, the Sultan of Speeches, Lord of Long-Windedness! Unfortunately for you, you won't see much of it from the principal's office!" Monologue said.

I couldn't roll my eyes or do much of anything but stare slack-jawed, but the small part of my brain that still worked felt jubilant. Fursona and Springlock were supposed to launch their assault a minute and a half after Monologue started. Then they'd use Springlock's power to launch across the street, smash into the office, and stop the [**Monologue**] lockdown. We'd fight Iron Fist and whatever henches came with him.

It was simple, but hardly foolproof. However, it was our best chance of winning. It'd also let Milo and me go all-out on Iron Fist. The Bruiser could take some serious punishment.

So, we waited, slack-jawed and still, while Monologue talked and talked. One minute. Two. An alarm went off inside, and a moment later, Monologue's voice stopped echoing across campus—just as a half-dozen henches stepped outside. Iron Fist wasn't here. The plan had failed, but we could still salvage this. Somehow.

Milo moved first, running toward them as they raised batons. One of them screamed, but before the wrestler could hit them, I spun in the air, firing a [**Bit-Part**

Barrage] right into their formation. Henches scattered like bowling pins as first a half-dozen **[Stellar Rays]** and then an enraged Bruiser superhero crashed into them.

[Dramatic Damage! +3 Drama Points]

"Okay, new plan. They're in there, and they'll need backup!" I shouted and headed for the door.

Milo nodded. He stepped over a few whining, groaning henches. "Stay down. Don't move. Cops are coming."

We dashed through the halls toward the sounds of fighting. Monologue got on the intercom a few times, but not enough to stop us permanently. He sounded more and more panicked each time. Then, as we turned the corner, an office desk smashed through the office window, scattering glass everywhere. "That'd be Springlock," Milo said.

A moment later, two hostages burst out the office door and ran toward us. Both had a few injuries, and I sighed and activated **[Quick-Time Change]**. A quick "Itsy Bitsy Spider" later, and I was ready to be a support hero. "You get in there and help. I'll deal with the hostages," I said from my new, unimpressive height.

"Got it. Be careful." Milo waded into the school's office, where a handful of henchmen and Iron Fist fought with Springlock. Fursona had to be in the principal's office.

I stopped the injured Extras. "Classroom across the hall. I'll fix you up. Then you can help the others as we get them out. It'll be safe there."

One of them nodded, and we fled.

Truth be told, Rainy Day wasn't built for a full support role, but she had a couple of uses of **[Virga]** and enough stopping power to keep the hostages safe. As soon as we'd gotten clear, I used the rain power and began patching up the two former prisoners. Wherever the healing rain fell, their bruises and cuts healed rapidly.

[Medic! +3 Cunning Points]
[HP 8/9]

As the points rolled in, I mentally started building a new build for Rain Day. If I cut **[Rejuvenation]** for **[Audition Notes]**, I could maintain Rainy Day's combo potential and still do a better job with support stuff.

As the Extras recovered, I asked them what was happening in the office.

"Monologue wants that Ilneat to admit they're making stuff up in their book. Something about the situation on Mornsal Four, but I don't get the details. It sounds like it's not Monologue's idea, and he's working as a contracted villain, but I'm not sure why anyone cares so much. It's across the galaxy or something," one Extra said.

The other nodded slowly, biting her fingernail. "Yeah. Look, thanks for helping us out. Think I can leave?"

"Not yet. We've gotta make sure it's safe," I said.

"Alright." She sat down in a student's chair, looking dejected. "This is the worst lecture ever."

Fursona hopped into the classroom, where I now had four grumpy Extras to take care of. "Hey, Squirt. I didn't think that'd work, but we've got Monologue and Iron Fist stuck in the office, we've managed to override the loudspeakers by having Milo talk randomly into a phone, and he's down to just one hostage plus the Ilneat. I'm here to help you move the Extras to the cops outside safely."

The Episode looked like it was resolving itself in the most boring way possible. There would be no flashy, last-minute rescue of Professor Bagges. Springlock and Milo had the office under control except for one room, the police had blocked the entrances, and we'd accounted for all but two of the henchmen. They'd probably slipped away when the fighting turned against them, but until we knew for sure, we couldn't let the Extras out of our sight.

"Got it. Alright, ladies and gentlemen, I'm sorry again about the delay, but we're going to move you to the police now. Fursona, you're in front. I'll cover the rear."

"You sure, Squirt?"

"Yes, I'm sure, and don't call me that in public. You're embarrassing me!" I said, then flushed even redder as an Extra laughed.

We started moving slowly down the hall, away from the office. I stepped out, the last person to leave, and checked behind us—just in time to see a henchman's head pull back behind the corner of the hall. "I've got one!" I yelled.

"Deal with them. Everyone, back door! Go, go, go!" Fursona yelled. She gestured the former hostages forward, paw flapping, and I sprinted toward the hall where I'd spotted the horned helmet.

As I got there and rounded the corner, already saying the words to ready a [**Ride the Lightning**], I saw both the missing henches, hands already up. "Hey, hey! Take it easy! We're done!"

"Yeah, we surrender! They made us do it!"

"Seriously?" I asked. I couldn't be sure, but I thought one might've been the bonus pay henchman from the office. Either way, I was glad they were surrendering without a real fight.

"Yeah. They always make us, you know, 'an offer we can't refuse.'"

"Lots of money?" I asked, checking for weapons.

"Yep. You going to take us to the cops?"

"Yeah. Let's get going." I checked the hall to make sure the hostages were clear; the last thing I wanted was for my henchmen prisoners to traumatize them. Then I pointed. "You two first. I've got you covered. We'll walk through the door, you surrender to the police, and we'll all move on with our lives."

"Understood."

The office looked totally under control. Milo was talking to Monologue through the door while Springlock held a computer midair, ready to throw it if the villains gave her a clear shot. I nodded to her, and she nodded back, glaring at my two prisoners. Then, I continued down the hall and out the door.

"Freeze! On the ground! You're covered!" an officer yelled. I stepped around the two henches and waved.

"Don't worry! They've already surrendered. Just take them in," I said. Then, I headed back in and waited.

It took almost an hour, but Monologue had nowhere to go. Eventually, between him, Springlock and Milo, and Professor Bagges, an agreement began to be hammered out. They'd let Bagges go. In return, we'd back off, allowing both the villains to walk out the back door and disappear. I relayed the plan to the police, who seemed upset. I didn't quite get that; wouldn't they get out because of their lawyers anyway?

And then, just like that, the Episode was over. It had been anticlimactic, but I didn't mind one bit because I hadn't seen or heard from Tails since I'd caught the henches. I'd been powerless for almost an hour—a new record.

[Episode Finished!]

[Episode: Eustace Holds the Bagge - PG]

[Penalties: 3x Rating Warnings - No Penalty]

[Episode Finished! +5 of each Style Point]

[Winner Winner! +2 of each Style Point]

[Role Focus: Cunning + Flamboyance - Goal Unmet]

[Alias - Understudy] [Archetype - Magical Girl] [Community Rank - 229/523]

[HP 8/9]

[Styles and Skills]

▶Archetype Skill - Transformation Sequence

▶Combo Skills - Power-Weaving

▶Badass (12)

▶Cunning (8)

▶Drama (52) (Skill Roll Available)

▶Stellar Ray 2

▶Bit-Part Barrage 1

▶Flamboyance (34)

▶Signature Skill - Adaptive Armoire 2

▶Stored Costumes: (Rainy Day, Copy Cat)

▶Starwave Sail 1

▶Quick-Time Change 2
▶Grit (14)
▶I-Frame Transform 2
[50 Drama Credits Used. Rolling Skill!]
[Rank-Up! Bit-Part Barrage 2: The first ray stuns a target for a moment if it hits]

53

A New Record

I had no idea how Fursona did it with only six slots for powers. I had twenty-four, and I didn't have enough space.

[Set Dressing] was going on Copy Cat as soon as I found room. Being an ambush predator sounded awesome with the Costume's powers, and invisibility was overpowered. I wanted to put it on all my builds, but the space costs would be staggering. Was I trying to do too much? Maybe. But close to uniquely among all the heroes out there, I *could* do it all. I just needed a little more space.

I didn't have much time to ponder, though. Rocko wanted to meet, and the Ilneat didn't sound happy.

"Come on, Annie," Bianca said. She stood by the door to Rocko's, tapping her fingers on the handle. "They'll only be more frustrated if we're late."

I didn't blame Rocko for being annoyed and stressed out. In the aftermath of "Eustace Holds the Bagge," Vigilant Vow and I were tied, with less than two weeks to go. It was now or never.

I stepped through the door.

[Welcome to Rocko's Studio. System Disabled. Now arriving Backstage.]

Rocko sat behind their desk, staring at me intently. I couldn't read their face, but the pair of cigars told me everything I needed to know. They were annoyed. "DuPont, Marino, sit."

Once we'd gotten water and sat down, Rocko stood on their chair. "I expected you to close this deal out by now. I've already made the calls for new merchandise, and the expenses are out of this world. What do you have to say for yourselves?"

"We beat Monologue," Fursona said. "And we did it without getting Bagges hurt."

"Sure, sure, if by beat, you mean you called in backup and turned what *should* have been an exciting 'save the hostages' fight into a boring negotiation. If you hadn't dragged in minor-league heroes, you'd be ahead."

"Rocko, we've gotta be turning a profit here," I said, sipping my bottle. "We just need—"

"We don't 'just need' anything. Do you know how many studios are competing for streaming spots? How tight the margins are? What the average profit for a little-league show is versus how much Rocko Studios is spending?" Rocko asked. I shook my head slowly. "Okay, then how about you leave the finances to me? Yes, we're turning a profit. No, it's not enough with the spending. If you don't win this, the studio's done."

Rocko puffed from a cigar, trying not to bare their sharp teeth. They hopped from their desk and started pacing, running a grasping hand through their thick fur. "I don't know, DuPont. I'm starting to have doubts about all this. Maybe we shoulda stuck with the little leagues. Maybe you need another year in the Junior Minor Leaguers. Maybe you're not up to this."

I stiffened in my seat. Of *course* I was up for this! I just needed something, *anything*, and I could beat him. "Rocko, you know you can count on me."

"But?" Rocko asked, puffing on his cigar and staring me in the eyes.

"But . . ." I hesitated. "Nothing. I'll do whatever it takes."

"Great. Then stop messing around. You don't need big-league backup to win Episodes. You're a big girl now, and you can handle things. So prove to me you can handle them, get out there, and end this race so the money we're spending on merchandise and ads pays off. That's what the audience wants to see, so that's what *Heroic 101* will give them, right?"

I'd never seen them like this before, and I had to steel myself for the question I needed to ask, even though it'd result in a blow-up for sure. "Rocko, I can't fight him. He just steals Tails. I need help. Can't you shut him down or get Tails back?"

"'Can't I shut him down?' No, I can't shut down another studio's super. You want me to use the System to do that? It doesn't work like that, kid. You want me to launch a pressure campaign, or tell the world what he's doing? I can do that. But *not* until you win."

"What do you want us to do, then?" I asked. The Ilneat was out of control, clearly upset. I felt like any wrong move would just set them off more, but I didn't know what else to say.

"I don't care what you have to do to make a win happen. You need to ditch classes? Do it. Missing time with your friends? Take a vacation *after* the job is done. Get out there and hunt the little shit down. He's on the ropes. Finish him off." Rocko practically screamed the last words.

"Why can't you shut him down for us?" Fursona asked.

"Because if I do that before you win, it makes you two look damn pathetic. You two are smart, you're capable, and by the end of this, you'll have proven you're ruthless enough for the minor leagues. I know you'll find a way to win, but you have to *do it*. Can you?"

I sighed and took a sip of water. Part of me knew he was doing this on purpose. But most of me didn't care. Whether he was playing Bianca and me or not, he was right. Beating Vigilant Vow face-to-face was the best way forward. I just didn't know *how*. "Yeah, I can."

"Then prove it. Beat him by next Wednesday. Put him out of the race so we can celebrate." Rocko calmed down. "You do that, and I'll leak that Cartman's been having him steal powers. That bastard's been working overtime to keep it on the down-low. Only a few studios know, but we can change that. We'll put him out of business with a one-two-three-four punch."

As they punched the air, I thought about how unstoppable I'd felt over break—and how big the task ahead of me was.

Back in the green room, my mood was foul. Even a shoulder rub wasn't helping, but Bianca kept trying even as I ranted. "And they asked if I knew how much the studio makes!? Unbelievable! They've never told me anything about finances! Do you know how much you make!?"

"$300 per Episode flat, plus .1% royalties, paid quarterly," Bianca rattled off instantly, still rubbing my neck.

I turned around, flabbergasted. "They told you?"

"They really didn't tell you?" she responded.

"No." Why *hadn't* they told me? I'd never cared—that had to be part of it. And I'd been a kid when I'd signed with Rocko. Maybe I'd been told and forgotten. But either way, I needed to find out. "Look, that's not the point. The point is, they *know* I can't beat Vigilant Vow. They *know* it. This is my dream, and it's going to slip away from me."

"Annie, I get it. I need you to trust me for a minute. Can you do that?" Bee asked.

"Yeah. Yeah, but Bee, I don't have any ideas."

"Okay. Just lay down. I've got you. Let's get you out of fight or flight, then we can work on a plan." Bianca pushed on my shoulder blades, shoving harder and harder. Her hands felt warm as she worked them down my spine. She slowly found every knot and tight spot, kneaded them until they loosened up, and reduced me to a pile of Jell-O. It took almost fifteen minutes—fifteen long, agonizingly wonderful minutes I didn't feel like we had.

Finally, her hands stopped, and she kissed my hair. Then she spat it out, complaining. "Eugh. Bad move, Bianca. Bad move."

"Sorry," I said. I felt more relaxed, but my heart still pounded, and I could tell it wouldn't last long. We had to capitalize. "So, we need a plan."

"We sure do. Luckily, I'm a brilliant sidekick, and while I was fighting in the office, I noticed something important."

"What?"

Bianca threw herself on the chaise lounge. "I'll tell you, but I need some incentives. Go on, lavish your praises upon me." She posed in the best "draw me like your French girls" pose she could muster.

"We don't have time for this," I said, the anger welling up. My fists were balled tight.

"Annie. If we don't have time for this, what *do* we have time for?" Bianca looked at me, her playful attitude disappearing and replaced with a deadly serious stare. "I want to make this minor-league thing work, but more importantly, *this* has to be working."

I sighed and sat up. Then I rubbed my eyes and looked at her. She was right. I took a deep breath. "Okay, oh beautiful and smart girlfriend, please share your deepest secrets with this lowly worm."

"Good start. Specifics?"

"Your hair is the color of the night. Your eyes are as blue as a lake. You're smarter than me, and I know it. Tell me your secrets, uh, you cheesecake?" I got up and messed with her hair while she lay there. "Please?"

"Okay, okay, don't ruffle the 'do," Bianca said. She sat up and swatted my hands away. Then she went to the whiteboard. "Your poetry is awful. I'm gonna be glad to see this thing go, but we need it one more time. While I was in the office, I saw a note. Vigilant Vow is still pretending to be an antihero most of the time, you know? And part of that is that he's working with students."

I rolled my eyes. "Let me guess. He's scheduled to be there sometime in the next seven days."

"Yep. Wednesday, as a matter of fact. But don't you think it's suspicious that he's visiting *this* school in particular? He could visit anywhere, but that schedule has five separate visits to Cherry Creek High by the end of the school year."

"That is pretty odd," I said. Then it hit me, and I started laughing. It was so obvious once Bee pointed it out. He was a student there. He had to be.

"You got there, huh? Great. Give me your class schedule for Monday, Tuesday, and Wednesday. We need to cover that high school as often as possible because we're going to catch him out."

"A stakeout, huh? Okay," I said, breathing a sigh of relief. We had a play. I wasn't totally screwed. Then I stiffened. "Why didn't you tell me before?"

"Because we had time before, and I didn't want to attack a school during school hours. Schedule, please." Bee waved her whiteboard marker at me.

"Combat Style Forum with you, Ilneat Politics at ten on Monday and Wednesday, Props at eight on Tuesday, Psych at ten thirty on Tuesday, and Ilneat One at two on Tuesday," I rattled off.

"Great. The only times we can't cover are Monday from two to three and Tuesday from ten thirty to about noon." Bee started scribbling a schedule on the board, filled with all the times we could watch the school. For the next twenty minutes or so, things felt great. We had a plan, and it didn't even require me to be in Costume to pull it off, much less able to fight. That'd come later—after Fursona did her part.

Tails was *not* thrilled about it, though. *<Nya right! This is really your best shot right meow?>* she whined, but we couldn't see another option.

I played with Bee's hair after she sat back down, and we discussed summer plans. But before we could finalize anything, Bee's phone rang. "Hi. Oh shit, study group. My bad, I'll be there in fifteen."

She put the phone back in her pocket, stood up, and kissed my cheek. "Gotta go, sorry. If I don't show up, Brett won't have a partner today, and there's a test coming up. Byeee."

"Byeee," I echoed. And just like that, I was alone, and things weren't fixed. But the pieces were all moving in the right direction. We had a plan, and I wouldn't have to ditch Mindstorm's class to make it happen if I was lucky.

PART EIGHT

54

Cooked Goose

MONDAY, APRIL 20

I turned slow, lazy circles over the Cherry Creek district, one eye on Cherry Creek High School and one on my phone screen. My foot held the steering bar in place—the closest I could get to autopilot for a sailboard, and I had one earbud in.

There were two reasons for my lack of focus. First, Vigilant Vow's odds of appearing at 1:15 on a Monday were so low I could ignore them. And second, Golden Goose had a new Episode out, and all advertisements and conversation pointed toward it being a doozy.

So, while I kept an eye on the school for the next fifteen minutes before I headed back for class, my other eye was on my phone's screen.

Golden Goose landed between McHammer, Lord Destructo, and their target, the Yorkston Metropolitan Council. As the asphalt cracked and boiled from the force of her landing, the camera focused first on her scowl, then on the two villains' faces. Lord Destructo's was obscured by his helmet, but McHammer flinched and looked nervously at his boss, almost like he expected to be able to cut and run.

"I'll give you boys exactly ten seconds to pack up and go back to your backwater town. One, two," Golden Goose said.

As she counted down, the two villains looked at each other, and the camera drones captured all their hesitation and worry. I felt for them, in a way. If they'd succeeded, they'd have taken control of Yorkston, but they'd clearly missed a signal and hadn't expected Golden Goose. McHammer took a step back, ready to take the offer.

"I don't think so," Lord Destructo said. He was bluffing. He couldn't win this fight. "We've got you where we want you, our lieutenants are fighting across your city, and you've got no backup. If we can't take you on two against one, we don't deserve our—"

"So be it. Ten."

The next bit happened in slow motion. Golden Goose's speed overwhelmed McHammer, and he barely got his hammer between her fist and his chest. It didn't matter; her hypersonic punch slammed through the handle and into him, launching him back into a skyscraper. I winced, then winced again as the impact's shockwave blew out windows all the way up the towering building.

Golden Goose turned toward Lord Destructo. With his lieutenant out of the way, she radiated arrogance and boredom. "Ready for yours?"

He didn't look ready for his.

A bell rang below, and I pulled my attention from the tiny screen to watch Cherry Creek High. The shift from sixth period to seventh was happening. We didn't know which student was Vigilant Vow, so we couldn't be sure which class he had an open hour in, if any. I dropped like a rock and landed on the roof. If he was out of class, he might yoink Tails any time, and being a hundred feet in the air if [**Starwave Sail**] turned off sounded awful. I'd finish my shift from the roof—only ten more minutes.

When I refocused on the Golden Goose Episode, I shivered. They'd moved into a residential area: white picket fences and one-story houses. I had no idea how they'd moved so fast or if their studios had cut something and done a time-skip, but Lord Destructo was pressing the attack, or at least trying to.

His hammer strikes weren't making any progress against Golden Goose; she had near-invincibility as a power, and he couldn't beat that. I saw panic in his eyes. Maybe with McHammer, he could get in a few lucky hits. Maybe.

But solo? It'd be like Honeycomb fighting Tele-Portal.

His hammer cracked after a savage blow to Golden Goose's chest that she tanked without flinching. Then her eyes lit up, and I gasped. Was she firing her laser? In a *residential area*?

Lord Destructo reacted without thinking. Even as his hammer slammed into her cheek and knocked her head just *barely* to the side, I saw his eyes widen. The beam swept through a dozen houses, two dozen, then snapped back onto him. He tried to block with his hammer, but it disintegrated. His armor took a few seconds—more than any super should be able to withstand, but her power doubled, then doubled again, throwing him into the air, metal armor melting slightly as he catapulted away.

A camera drone followed her over the shoulder as she smashed through a demolished house's door. Then, as she loomed over the shattered, defeated villain, eyes glowing red again, she stopped.

He fled down the street, but for just a moment, Golden Goose had lost interest. She picked something up off the house's floor, stared at it, and shook her head. The camera angle only showed the back of her head. Then she balled her fist around whatever it was and took off, flattening what was left of the house's walls.

The Episode ended without a speech.

"Holy shit," I whispered to myself. I wasn't bored anymore, that was for sure. That finish . . . "Holy shit."

My phone beeped, letting me know my class was in half an hour. I summoned my **[Starwave Sail]**, angling low across Tokyexico City and toward campus. I could have stuck out the stakeout, but Mindstorm's class was *not* one I wanted to ditch again.

The whole Combat Style Forum class was together in one classroom. That happened occasionally, especially as more and more students grew comfortable with their **[Power-Weaving]**, **[Power-Chaining]**, or **[Systematic Chaos]** combo powers.

"Today, we'll be starting the final . . . unit in Combat Style, 'Signing Bonuses and You,'" Dr. Mindstorm said. Her voice held an almost bored yet stressed tone as she paced in front of the class.

"As supers ascend to the minor leagues, the Style System always gives them a handful of new powers to play with," Dr. Tennyson said.

I looked at Fursona and winked. *That'll be us soon*, I didn't say.

He tapped his finger on the whiteboard, where he'd written four bullet points, then filled in the first one. "You'll get **[Combo-Breaker]**. It does exactly what it says on the box."

"Hold on," Waterspout interrupted. Mindstorm's face flashed in ugly anger for a moment, but the water-powered Tank hero continued anyway. "Why don't we get **[Combo-Breaker]** before our combo power?"

"That . . . is a good question," Mindstorm conceded. She stared at Waterspout for a full five seconds—long enough for me to worry she was reading his mind or something—and then cleared her throat. "The Style System doesn't always do things in the most logical way. Or . . . rather, its logic doesn't seem geared toward supers countering each other early so much as toward . . . enabling . . . flashier fighting."

Waterspout nodded, but his face didn't look any less confused. Mindstorm didn't clarify further.

"**[Combo-Breaker]**, like your combo power, isn't bound to a specific Style. Rather, you use it just like you've been using your combo power. It causes your next offensive power to 'parry' the building combo rather than doing damage. There's a trade-off there, in that it doesn't move you toward winning the fight," Tennyson continued.

"There are three other perks, though," Underdelver said. "And most supers find them much more valuable than **[Combo-Breaker]**. You can disrupt combos by forcing your opponent to drop them without **[Combo-Breaker]**, after all, and the next two enable that."

Tennyson scribbled two more phrases on the board. "Minor-league superheroes get two additional power slots."

My hand rocketed up. If that applied to all my Costumes, getting to the minor leagues was a massive power increase. "What about when a superhero has multiple builds and Costumes with different powersets?"

Tennyson laughed. Mindstorm rolled her eyes at him. "Two more power slots. That's it. You . . . decide where you want them," she said.

I nodded slowly. Two slots were still powerful. I'd most likely put them on Understudy. I could make her a generalist and utility hero, then specialize the others even more. It wouldn't be as good as gaining ten new power slots, but it'd still be a significant increase in utility. I'd been struggling for so long, and being able to fix that would be amazing. I wasn't the only one thinking about it. As I looked around the room, I saw hungry looks from almost everyone. Not a single super wouldn't benefit from more powers.

But Tennyson plowed on. "The cap on power strength moves up, too."

"There's a cap?" Gourmet blurted.

"Yes. Little-league powers cap at Rank Two. It's one of the few . . . safety precautions built into the Style System, and I don't know how the Ilneats were able to do that much, given how rigid the System is. After Rank Two, powers get significantly stronger. Minor-league powers cap out at Rank Four, and at that level, they pose a serious threat against any super not running Grit defensive powers. I . . . strongly recommend one of your two new slots is defensive," Mindstorm said.

Honestly, this wasn't a good thing for me—not at all. I already had a hard time keeping my twenty-four powers leveled, compared to how I imagined the other heroes and villains did with their six. Widening the gap wouldn't help.

Tennyson took over. "And finally, every super receives a 'signing bonus' on reaching the minor leagues. Depending on your class and specific power set, it could be anything from a few rank-ups to powers of your choice to new abilities you get to select. These 'signing bonus' powers, rank-ups, and skill upgrades are there to patch any holes in your build, strengthen your core powers to be competitive, or allow you to experiment with alternative build ideas.

"That's a lot of talking. For the rest of the day, you have a simple assignment. Go through your builds—if you have multiple, start with your standard persona—and figure out where you want to put those 'signing bonus' powers. Then, decide on your two extra slots. You should have a functional minor-league build by the end of class today. Our practicum will be on recognizing [**Combo-Breakers**] and playing around them, so be ready for that on Friday. Go!"

I stayed in my seat while Gourmet approached to join Fursona and me. Fursona bristled; she blamed the foodie supervillain for everything that had happened during "Gourmet's Glutton Hour," but no one fought during CS Forum. No one who didn't want Mindstorm chewing their asses out or assaulting their brain.

Gourmet sat down in an armchair and grinned at me. "Hey, Snack. Got any ideas for your build?"

"No, she doesn't, and she's not sharing them with a supervillain even if she did," Fursona said.

"Easy, Fursona. We're friends here, or at least not enemies," I said. "No, not yet. My build is stupidly complex. How's your mom?"

"Still in the hospital. Thanks for your help, though. Flare's pissed that I stole The Crumb, but that crazy bastard's the perfect sidekick for *Gourmet's Glutton Hour*. Between the three of us, we're pretty sure we'll make minor league next year, and Foamy Flash won't admit it, but she's happy to deal with villains on a schedule instead of all the time."

"That's . . . good." Gourmet had barely mentioned her mom. Was that a good sign or a bad one? I couldn't tell, and the supervillain's eyes screamed "Don't pry" at me. I decided to listen to them. "So, what ideas do you have for your build?"

"My build doesn't need much. I'll probably use the 'signing bonus' to shop around for more powers that fit *Glutton Hour*. What are you thinking? Rough ideas?"

I looked at Fursona, who shook her head slowly. "You do you, Understudy. If you trust her, fine."

"Okay, thanks," I said. "So, I'm thinking about putting the two extra slots on my main build and shuffling as many powers around as possible to make it a generalist, with most of my utility and a few combo pieces. Then, I can take my Costumes and build a tech support, medic/combo piece, and a melee fighter. They're already on their way to being those things, but that'll let me specialize more. I'm assuming I'll get three or four 'signing bonus' powers, and I want to upgrade two offensive combo pieces, a utility power, and something with Grit."

I really wanted to get [**I-Frame Transform**] to Rank Four as quickly as possible, along with [**Quick-Time Change**]. The ability to shuffle between forms quickly opened up so many doors. If I could always have the right counter immediately, I'd be a true monster in the minor leagues pretty quickly.

It wouldn't help me against Vigilant Vow, though, and time was running out.

55

Running Out

TUESDAY, APRIL 21

The final for Child Psychology had just begun, and Su-Bin was already at the end of her rope.

"I hate babies so much!" she shouted from my couch as the weird baby doll we were supposed to be caring for whined and cried in her arms. She had its fake bottle tucked against her shoulder, its swaddling cloth against her stomach and arm, and a scowl on her face that could have darkened all of Tokyexico.

The only thing worse than the baby robot's pitiful cries were Su-Bin's, but I reached out anyway. "Give me Baby Cash and his bottle. I'll get him calmed down."

I pondered the assignment as she handed me the bottle and transferred Cash to me. It had seemed pretty simple; all we had to do was raise Cash from a newborn up to five years old without killing him. We'd trade him out every Tuesday during class for the next size up, all the way until he went to kindergarten. Real adults did this all the time with real babies—how hard could it be?

We'd been going for a little over an hour, and I had the answer already. Pretty fucking hard.

Whoever had designed Baby Cash was either an eight-time mother or a sadist— or both. For one thing, the damn thing was constantly recording volume levels. If either of us got too loud, it'd wake up and start crying. It also got hungry at all hours of the day—except, mercifully, when we were both in class. But only when we were *both* in class. If I wasn't learning, the expectation was that I either had a sitter or that I had Cash with me—or that Su-Bin did.

"I can't do this," Su-Bin muttered as I gently rocked Baby Cash until his animatronic eyes closed and he drifted to "sleep." "This whole class is ridiculous, and I never asked for any of it."

She looked miserable already. I couldn't imagine how haggard she'd be at the end of the week, and I had another problem. I *had* to do stakeouts. The alternative was disastrous for Fursona and me. What plays did I have? What could I possibly . . .

I burst into laughter. "They said a sitter was acceptable, right? I have an idea, but it'll take some maneuvering. I'll work on it tonight if you can take Baby Cash."

Su-Bin narrowed her eyes at me, suspicious. I held the baby bot and cooed like a real mom, rocking him slowly and running my fingers through his hair. Cash wasn't even real, much less my kid, and there wasn't anything I wouldn't do for him, even though I hated how much work he was.

Finally, she relented. "I'll watch him tonight, but your plan better work."

"It will. I know a few people who won't mind, and I can owe them favors."

"You have to take care of him tomorrow night. I've got an APPEAL meeting to be at."

"Okay." I didn't mind. If everything worked out alright, I'd have babysitting arranged with The Narrator. Surely, she'd trade a few spotty hours of handling a robot kid in exchange for me running an Episode with The Cloud and the other kids. I'd let her know that it'd be most of the school day because my assignment partner and I had bad schedules, and it'd be fine.

"If your sitter's willing to cover at night, too, you should come," Su-Bin continued.

I shook my head. "Evenings aren't great for Mrs. N. She's busy around that time. She can cover during the day, though, probably. I could get someone else, but I'm not sure I trust her, and she's busy in the evenings, too." Honeycomb wasn't ideal, but I could trust The Narrator to be discreet.

Su-Bin looked crestfallen. "Okay, well, if you change your mind . . ."

"I can't. I'm sorry. Tell me about your meeting, though. I'm sure you've got big plans, Miss Vice President."

"Okay. We're changing tactics," Su-Bin said. "Instead of focusing on the heroes and villains, we're going after the studios."

"Are you sure that's . . . wise?" I asked. Rocko wouldn't do anything retaliatory, but showing up to protest outside of Cartman's studio was asking for trouble. "The Hot Zone's not built for humans, and I doubt they want to see protesters."

"Of course they don't want to see protesters," Su-Bin said. "No one ever wants to see protesters. Did you know there have been over twenty documented cases of villains specifically attacking protest groups, and at least three heroes have done the same? It's more evidence of how unbalanced this whole mess is."

"I don't know any heroes who would attack an unpowered person," I said. "Not unless they were armed and interfering in an Episode."

"I'll email you the Pherris Report documenting the proof," Su-Bin said.

I didn't want to talk about this anymore. Luckily, Baby Cash chose that moment to wake up, and I distracted myself by cuddling the robot baby, singing the class-approved lullaby, and changing him when I realized he'd "messed" his diaper. Getting him back to sleep took almost twenty nerve-wracking minutes, with Su-Bin getting more and more frustrated. I wished Bianca were here; she'd know how to distract my irritable, child-free-for-life friend.

Once I got Cash calmed down and in his stroller, I nodded to Su-Bin. "I'm sorry, but I've got class. I'll be done at three thirty, but then I've got to work on babysitting and stuff. Cash is yours for the night."

She pushed the stroller out my door, scowling again as I shook my head.

It'd be a miracle if Cash survived to toddlerhood.

I felt a little bad about running out on Baby Cash. Su-Bin would probably keep him alive, but she didn't love the robot baby—not like I did. So, as soon as I finished Prop Design for the day, I suited up and texted The Narrator.

<Hey, I need your help. Can you watch my robot baby? - Understudy 3:13>
<That came out weird. I need to keep him happy for class - Understudy 3:13>
<Conflicts w/ Episode stuff though - Understudy 3:14>

While I waited, I flew toward Cherry Creek High School. I felt like a creep lurking around a school as an adult, but I needed to know where Vigilant Vow was. Class got out in fifteen minutes, which'd be our best bet at hunting him down. Plus, I could give Fursona a ride back to campus if the villainous Magical Boy didn't shut down my powers.

The bell rang just as I circled overhead and landed next to Fursona, who'd taken up a position on the roof. "Anything yet?"

"No. Seems like he lies low during the day. He's not in any sports or activities, right?" she asked.

"I don't think so. He said he was dropping soccer and trivia," I said. Students started filing out onto the sidewalk and heading for their cars. I peered into the crowd, trying to find anyone who might look like him. Hundreds of kids, so many with dark hair, were leaving the building that I couldn't be sure. Then I saw one who might fit the bill.

He was about the right age, with the right haircut and a white hoodie. His backpack seemed fuller than any of the others. And as he left the building, he looked around suspiciously for a moment. I ducked under the roof's edge, pulling Fursona down with me. "That's him. It's gotta be," I hissed.

"You're sure?"

"80%?"

"Good enough. Get the sailboard going," Fursona said.

It wasn't that easy, though. I couldn't just launch; someone would see us, Vigilant Vow would turn around and go inside, and by the time we tracked him down, he'd burst out of a bathroom with a dozen familiars and a building still half-full of Extras. Then we'd have a mess on our hands, I wouldn't have my powers, and he'd have all the advantages of a crowded battle on his home turf against aggressors no one knew. After all, he'd spent time building up a reputation at Cherry Creek High as their friendly neighborhood Magical Boy.

So, instead, I watched the direction he turned, waited a minute, and then took off.

The plain-clothes villain walked into the rows of houses behind Cherry Creek High, whistling to himself and occasionally looking over his shoulder. He didn't look up, though, and that's where Fursona and I were hiding, a couple hundred feet above.

"You're sure?" Fursona asked again. She still wasn't comfortable on the sailboard, and I could feel her nervous energy.

I wasn't sure at all, but this kid was our best lead so far. "Yes," I whispered.

"So what's the plan?"

"We'll wait until he reveals his identity or gets somewhere no one can see him, then we'll swoop down and either execute Operation Old Yeller or search him for his crystals. If we find them, we've got him beat."

"I'm not sure how I feel about Operation Old Yeller," Fursona said.

I nodded. It was super uncomfortable, but it was the only way I could think of to keep Tails out of Vigilant Vow's grasp. "It's our best plan right now. We'll wait him out and hope it doesn't come to that."

We didn't have to wait long.

Our stalkee turned off into the driveway of a white, two-story house. I winced. If he went inside, that'd complicate things. But instead, he opened the gate, greeted a massive gold-furred dog, and walked to the dog house. He fiddled with it, and the whole tiny house lifted up, revealing a flight of stairs leading underground.

My heart stopped. We had him.

"Do we start an Episode?" Fursona asked.

I shook my head. "No. That'll just tip him off. Distract the dog, then we'll get inside and deal with Vigilant Vow."

I steeled myself, and we dove for the grassy backyard.

The dog turned out to be a gigantic teddy bear. Instead of barking or growling, it ran at us at full speed, then rolled onto its back for a belly rub. I gave it what it wanted for a few seconds, then checked the dog house. A button half-hidden beneath a shingle lifted it up, and Fursona and I crept into the villain's secret base.

"I guess this gives new meaning to 'in the doghouse,' huh?" Fursona quipped.

"Does that mean I'm out of it?"

"We'll see," she answered.

The stairs felt mossy, and the whole place was almost as warm as Rocko's Studio. A yellow light glowed from a small room at the bottom of the stairs, where various pots and bags of soil were stacked against the walls.

"Is Vigilant Vow into gardening?" Fursona asked.

"Who the hell are you?" The student we'd followed poked his head out of another door, one filled with even more yellow light. He blinked at us, then paled. "Oh shit, it's the cops, huh?"

"No. I'm Fursona, and this is— Eugh! What the fuck?" Fursona said, coughing into her voice modulator.

"What is it? You're going to make a mess in—"

The overpowering odor hit me a moment later, a pungent, sickly-sweet smell mixed with something skunky, and I knew exactly what we'd walked into.

"You two aren't supposed to be in here. Oh man, Ricky's going to be so pissed when he finds out. Listen, I know you're supers, but you can't tell the cops. Please? I'll give you some of our product, okay? Come on, be reasonable, alright?"

I didn't feel like responding. I *felt like* putting a [**Stellar Ray**] into the kid's chest. We'd missed our Tuesday chance on a false lead, and not only that, but now we had to deal with this. I texted Su-Bin to let her know I definitely wouldn't be home to take over Baby Cash duties for a bit—not until this mess was resolved.

It wasn't a secret lair. It was a grow room, which meant this wasn't Vigilant Vow's operation at all. We were out of time.

56

Out of Time

WEDNESDAY, APRIL 22

"Should I have bought you a 'baby on board' sticker?" Fursona asked.

"Shhhh!" I hissed. We flew a few hundred feet above Tokyexico on our way to Tottergarten; I didn't want to wake the baby with traffic sounds. It was my day with Baby Cash, but I couldn't care for him until later. Much, much later. Ilneat Politics was over, so Fursona and I were heading to our stakeout.

Which meant, much as it pained me to do it, that Baby Cash couldn't stay with me.

We landed in the parking lot and slipped inside. The moment we did, the sound of super-toddlers screaming and yelling woke Cash, who joined them with his fake robot-baby cries. I groaned and looked at Fursona.

"What? He's your kid."

"Just help me find Mrs. N, okay?" I said, just before The Cloud and his friends hit us like a hurricane.

"Is that a baby?"

"No, that's a doll, stupid! I have one at home!"

"No fair! I want a baby!"

I held the bawling robo-baby up high so the kids couldn't reach him, which worked until The Cloud floated up to the ceiling with Kid Zoomies hanging from his leg. "Can . . . can you just go get Mrs. N?" I asked, trying to fend off the super-kids.

"I'm here. And then the Tottergarten kids went and played on the slide while Mrs. N and the visiting superheroes talked," The Narrator said.

Fursona and I sat at the office table while The Narrator stood in a corner and sipped a coffee. "So, tell me about the baby-bot. How long am I hanging on to it, what makes it cry, and how does it work?"

"Ideally, we'd be by around five to pick Cash up," I said, crossing my fingers that she wouldn't protest and rubbing Baby Cash's back to make him quiet down. If she couldn't help us, I'd need to find alternative arrangements since it was my day. "He's got a noise sensor that'll make him freak out, and if it doesn't get dealt with quickly enough too many times, my friend and I will fail the class. It also records what we say around it."

"Got it. You want five hours? That's going to cost you some time here at Tottergarten. I can handle the rest of the baby-bot's needs pretty easily," The Narrator said.

"How?" Fursona asked.

The Narrator took another sip of coffee. "And then Baby Cash didn't need to cry anymore or run his noise sensor until five in the evening on April 22."

Baby Cash went quiet and shut his eyes.

"That . . . seems like cheating," I said.

Mrs. N smiled. "Everything I do is cheating. I'll make it record a normal babysitter for the day. You have until mid-September to pay off your six hours to me. I know it's a busy time of year, and you won't be in town over the summer, will you?"

"No, I won't," I said. I stood up. "Thank you so much."

"Oh, no problem. Children are my passion, after all."

Even without Baby Cash, I saw a lot of ways our plan could fail, and only one where it succeeded, so instead of focusing on all the ways things could go wrong, we sat on top of the Cherry Creek gym as the entire student body oohed and aahed over Vigilant Vow's familiars. We couldn't fly since he'd stolen Tails, but it wasn't time for Operation Old Yeller yet, so I just had to put up with it.

If he left with the crowd, we'd be screwed. If he kept Tails summoned, it'd be totally up to Fursona to track him down. If he chose to stay inside and untransformed, we wouldn't be able to track him.

"Stop it, Understudy!" Fursona snapped at me.

"What?"

"You're worrying. I'm a worrier, and I can tell when someone else is. This will work. It has to."

"How do you know?" The crowd went wild. I couldn't hear any specific words, but Vigilant Vow must've said something inspiring. As it quieted down, I looked at Fursona, waiting for her answer.

"Because . . . because you want it so much. We'll make it happen. You've just gotta trust that the plan will work and that Operation Old Yeller will go off without a hitch. If it does, he won't stand a chance."

I nodded apprehensively. There were too many ways for this all to fall apart.

The assembly continued, but Tails popped back into being next to me after a minute. I pet the plushie cat in greeting, even though she didn't remember being gone. Then I stared down as the cheering suddenly got louder. A single figure emerged from the door, surfing on a tide of bubbles, with Bubble-Bill riding along in his wake.

We had him.

The setup was almost perfect. He was alone, leaving the Extras behind. As I summoned **[Starwave Sail]** to move Fursona and me to the ground, he turned toward the massive rec center near the school. We landed, I checked that Tails was with me, and we started stalking him down the road.

The rec center covered most of a block, its glass walls showing the pool, weight room, and climbing wall for all to see. People played basketball inside or ran around the elevated track over the lap lanes. But Vigilant Vow didn't go for the front entrance. Instead, he walked around the back and unlocked a double door before slipping inside.

Fursona bounced forward and grabbed the door before it could swing shut and lock, and I hurried behind her. The room behind it gurgled and hummed as water rushed through pipes, into a massive boiler, and was pumped back into the pool. It reeked of chlorine and chemicals, and I wasn't sure where the villain had gone. "Ideas?" I asked Fursona.

"He didn't go into the pool deck. He'd have gone through the main doors instead if he wanted to get there. Could his base be in this room?"

"Maybe." I **[Checked the Script]**. A half-dozen possibilities lit up in my vision, from cabinet doors to a grate below the floor with overflow water from the pool lapping against it. I started checking closets and pointed at the grate. "Could he have went through there?"

"Maybe. Let me check." Fursona pulled on the grate, and it shifted without so much as a screech. "It's well-oiled. They'd let it rust if it wasn't important to someone."

"Yeah?"

"Yeah. The rest of the place is trashed."

I looked around again. Sure enough, the metal cabinets were a mix of taupe-brown and red rust, and every pipe joint looked corroded or built up with minerals like the showerhead in my parents' double-wide. "He went there, then," I said and dropped into the water below. The water lapped against my knees, soaking my leggings up to mid-thigh in cold, chlorinated water, and a *Style System* message appeared.

[Casting Call]
[Episode: The Finish Line! - PG-13]
[Role: Vengeful Heroine! Do you accept the role? (Yes/No)]
[Role Focus: Drama + Flamboyance]
[Good Thinking! +1 Cunning Point]

"This is it," I called up to Fursona, and she joined me in the damp, dark tunnel. It stretched much further than it needed to, lit by an occasional skylight or shoddy-looking electric light.

[The Finish Line!: Act One in Progress]

"Why would a hero, even a vigilante, use this as their secret base?" Fursona complained as we sloshed down the tunnel. I let Fursona take point, the better to execute Operation Old Yeller.

I shrugged. "Maybe this wasn't always his base. Maybe he just moved in here recently." I stepped into a glob of soap bubbles, pushing into the tunnel.

"He'll have a dry place for his—Freeze! It's a trap!" Fursona yelled.

A moment later, the soap bubbles popped, tossing me into the tepid water. My head went under just as my superhero damage changed, and a split second later, I saw two lifeless painted eyes attached to a massive rubber ducky.

[HP 8/9]

I surged back to my feet, spluttering and drenched, at the exact moment Bubble-Bill broke through the water like a jumping whale or a surfacing submarine. The narrow tunnel filled with bubbles, the pops echoing off the walls like machine-gun fire as I returned it with cast after cast from my wand. Fursona tried to dodge and close the gap, but there wasn't room to maneuver. I had to suppress Bubble-Bill if we wanted to push into Vigilant Vow's lair.

"[Stellar Ray]!" I screamed, and the blast lit up the tunnel, revealing a long, steep flight of stairs just past the familiar—and another of Vigilant Vow's swarm!

[Dramatic Damage! +1 Drama Point]

The crow I'd last seen at the end of "Gourmet's Glutton Hour" vomited its black beam at Fursona, stopping her in her tracks. "You take Bubble-Bill! I've got this one!" she shouted and leaped toward the flapping crow.

I didn't want to get stalled here; the environment favored Bubble-Bill, and who knew what Vigilant Vow was up to beyond the stairs. If I could force a quick win here, we could make landfall before another wave of familiars hit us. So, as Bubble-Bill inflated to send another cluster of soap suds at us, I spun in the air, sloshing water everywhere. **[Bit-Part Barrage]** fired, and the tunnel filled with **[Stellar Rays]**.

[Dramatic Damage! +4 Drama Points]

There just wasn't anywhere for the giant rubber ducky to dodge. My rays crashed into it, searing its yellow surface until, after the last beam hit, it vanished. I turned toward Fursona, wand raised, but she'd already finished the crow.

"That wasn't so bad," she said, panting into her modulator.

"No. Let's get moving," I agreed.

We stepped onto the stairs, dripping water, and Fursona put her hand on a door handle. I reached out to stop her. "It's probably trapped."

"With what? I could believe your ex would trap his lair, but he was a Genius. Vigilant Vow doesn't have those skills, and he's new enough on the villain scene and low enough in the rankings that he probably can't hire or coerce someone into building traps for him."

"I'm trying to think less aggressively," I said. "Aggression's gotten us in trouble."

"Yeah, I appreciate that, babe, but now's the time to hit hard and hit fast. Let's go." Fursona threw the door open, and we burst through into Vigilant Vow's lair.

[End of Act One: Act Two in One Minute]
[Alias - Understudy] [Archetype - Magical Girl] [Community Rank - 229/523]
[HP 8/9]
[Styles and Skills]
►Archetype Skill - Transformation Sequence
►Combo Skills - Power-Weaving
►Badass (12)
►Cunning (9)
►Drama (7) (2 Skill Rolls Available)
►Stellar Ray 2
►Bit-Part Barrage 2
►Flamboyance (34)
►Signature Skill - Adaptive Armoire 2
►Stored Costumes: (Rainy Day, Copy Cat)
►Starwave Sail 1
►Quick-Time Change 2
►Grit (14) (Skill Roll Available)
►I-Frame Transform 2

And what a lair it was.

I barely noticed Act One had ended. Vigilant Vow must have purchased a house in the hills over Cherry Creek High because his lair was gorgeous. A huge chandelier hung over the round table in the oval-shaped living room's central, pit-style seating, and trophies from Vigilant Vow's high school career covered a massive case on one side of the room. Fursona, always the nosey one, hopped over. "The names are all torn off," she said, outraged.

"Yes, but it's still quite something, isn't it?" Vigilant Vow asked.

I gasped. I hadn't even noticed him at a side door, yet there he stood, a half-dozen familiars around him. I peered at them; the weasel, a flying fish, Sugar and Chili Powder's two cats, and a pair of birds stood between us and the villain, but thankfully, he hadn't taken Tails, and Stella-Lunar's familiar, Iyago, was nowhere to be seen.

I glared at the villain as Fursona leaped toward him feet-first. "Vigilant Vow, it's the end of the line!"

[The Finish Line!: Act Two in Progress]

57

End of the Line

Fursona wanted us to hit hard and fast, so we did.

We'd already failed the number three thing we couldn't let him do: summon an army of familiars. If he summoned Iyago or Tails, the tide of battle would be too much for us, and we'd have to resort to Operation Old Yeller. So, instead of giving him a chance to put together a speech, we attacked.

The pressure was all on me, though. Part of our strategy involved holding Fursona's strongest powers back as late into an Act as possible while using mine early. The other part was trying to force Vigilant Vow himself out of the fight before he could use too many of his familiar's powers.

Fursona hopped fast toward the familiars, and both the light orange cat and the pink one darted forward to intercept. I grinned. Her attack was a bluff. Mine was the one the five familiars needed to think about.

I only had until Vigilant Vow stole Tails, so I lit up the fireworks.

"**[Bit-Part Barrage]**!" I shouted, aiming straight for the Dark Boy. As I did, one of the birds—a falcon—soared across, spreading its wings wide, and my power focused on it. Ray after ray hit home, stopped by the familiar's sacrifice.

[Dramatic Damage! +4 Drama Points]

But even as the falcon took hits, one slipped through and slammed into the supervillain. I grinned triumphantly, then activated **[Power-Weaving]** into **[Quick-Time Change]** as the songbird ripped a sonic blast my way. The pressure on my ears felt overwhelming, but **[I-Frame Transform]** took the worst of it even as I Itsy Bitsy Spidered.

[Flashy Fitting-Room! +1 Flamboyance Point]
[Steel Yourself! +1 Grit Point]
[Floating Points: 1 Flamboyance]

I glanced at the two cats; Fursona was handling them but wasn't trying very hard. Her best moves were in reserve until or unless things got worse. Then, just as I used

[**Thunderhead**], moving toward Vigilant Vow and the songbird, I received a weasel-shaped welcoming gift to the face.

[HP 7/9]
[**Pause for Effect! +1 Drama Point**]
[**Floating Points: 3 Flamboyance, 1 Grit**]

I peeled the clawing, snarling weasel off of me but couldn't make it disappear—not without dropping the combo I'd built up, and I needed that for Vigilant Vow. Forcing him out of the fight was my job. As I dropped the familiar, it snaked between my ankles and tripped me up. The songbird unleashed another sonic blast a moment later, slamming me into Vigilant Vow's trophy shelves.

[HP 5/9]

I hurried to my feet. The storm cloud continued building, filling the vaulted ceiling with angry thunderheads. I rushed toward Vigilant Vow, whose eyes betrayed absolutely no fear. Just as I activated [**Ride the Lightning**], I realized why. Lightning towered below me, and I channeled it at my rival-turned-enemy. Instead of hitting him, it crashed down on the songbird, which vanished.

[**Electric Lightshow! +1 Flamboyance Point**]
[Thunderstruck! +1 Drama Point]
[**Power-Weaving! +6 Flamboyance, +3 Grit, +1 Drama Point**]

It wasn't the result I wanted, but as Fursona kicked a pink cat through the glass doors, I consoled myself with the thought that we'd knocked three familiars out of the fight. Even if Vigilant Vow used Iyago or Tails now, we had it under control.

I [**Quick-Time Changed**] into Copy Cat and [**Rejuvenation**] topped my superhero damage off. I still hadn't tested whether it'd help against Vigilant Vow's Tails takeovers, but it was worth a shot. The weasel took one look at my cat form and switched targets, going after Fursona.

[**Rejuvenation Activated! HP 9/9**]

And leaving me free to take the fight to Vigilant Vow, just as planned.

The Dark Boy's fist glowed red as I used [**Leaping Leopards**] to leap toward him. He swung his fiery fist, and we collided midair. The impact sent both of us flying—me toward the door to the stairs and him toward the doors he'd come in through.

[HP 7/9]
[**Badass Damage! +1 Badass Point**]

I was on my feet a moment later, trusting [**Fursonal Furcefield**] to take whatever he threw at me. Fursona kicked the other cat, which vanished. Vigilant Vow's glowing fist—a Magical Girl Chili Powder move—disappeared with the light orange feline. I rushed toward Vigilant Vow.

"Not so fast!" he shouted. The weasel familiar weaved between my legs again, tripping me up, and Vigilant Vow turned and ran before I could [**Doom Ball**] him.

The double doors he ran through slammed behind him as he fled. A moment later, the weasel familiar threw itself toward Fursona. I leaped through the air with [**Leaping Leopards**], grabbed it with my clawed hands, and dragged it to the ground. A moment later, it vanished, the oval-shaped living room suddenly silent except for our breathing.

[**Badass Takedown! +1 Badass Point**]

"Damage check!" I shouted into the empty, still air. "Seven of nine!"

"Seven of ten!" Fursona yelled.

<Present,> Tails added in my head.

"Debrief! Understudy's out of juice, Rainy Day is down one combo finisher, and Copy Cat is out of [**Leaping Leopard**] charges but nothing else." Debriefing and staying appraised of each other's firepower and damage levels was something new, along with called strategies. We'd picked up the ideas from our Combat Style class, and it felt good to know exactly where my sidekick was at power-wise.

"I used a couple of [**Double Kicks**], but my [**Power-Chaining**] combo is still intact," Fursona said.

I nodded and pointed at the door. "I think we're ahead of him. Let's keep moving before he regroups."

Fursona checked the door. "Locked from the other side. Who installs steel doors in a residential house?"

"A villain," I said. I looked around; there were other doors to pick from. "Let's start with the left side and work our way around. Maybe there's another way through, or we'll find something in here that'll help us."

I started the transformation back to Understudy, but Fursona put a paw on my wand-arm before I could get going. "You should stay in Copy Cat."

"Why?" I didn't have much firepower left in Understudy, but it felt natural. Sharing headspace with Tails was . . . overwhelming in many ways.

"Two reasons. First, you still don't know if he can steal Tails while you're sharing a form. If it offers you some protection from that, you should take advantage of it. Second, if it doesn't, you may still have passive powers like [**Fursonal Furcefield**]. Being able to ride out his attacks while we carry out Operation Old Yeller would be big," Fursona said.

<And third, Fursona likes the Copy Cat form, me-OW!> Tails said in my ear.

I flushed red and tried to turn away so Fursona wouldn't see, but I was too slow. She saw. "Uh, Understudy, you know it's not . . . uh . . . did Tails say something?"

"Yes, hun. We'll talk about it later," I said. I didn't meet her eye; I knew she liked Copy Cat, but having Tails talk about it was . . . a little much.

Still, her other points *were* valid. I didn't trust Understudy or Rainy Day to have the defenses to survive against an Iyago/Vigilant Vow combination, but Copy Cat was tough, and if there was a chance at not losing my powers, I had to take it. Plus, Act Two hadn't ended, and the catgirl Costume still had most of its heaviest-hitting moves.

"Let's check the place out," I said. There was no time to waste. We had to find a way through, or find something that'd let us press our temporary advantage.

The first door opened to a kitchen, but a quick inspection showed that it'd never been used. The fridge wasn't even plugged in, much less running, and the oven clock didn't show a time. We checked a couple drawers, just in case he'd hidden something, but I doubted he'd even set foot inside here since he—or Cartman—had bought the place.

The next room, however, looked like a jackpot.

Vigilant Vow clearly used this room as his study. A dozen textbooks littered the floor, and the overflowing trash can in the corner was filled with papers. Fursona grabbed one, unfolded it, and shook her head. "They're all combinations of familiars. There must be dozens of them. Maybe hundreds."

I didn't bother looking. He still had his winning combination of Iyago and Tails, so none of the others mattered. Instead, my eyes fixed on the desk—and the glowing computer screen. I slid into the gamer chair, stopping its spin with my feet, and grabbed the mouse.

I checked the computer; in his haste, Vigilant Vow hadn't turned it off, and Fursona had the door covered, so I had a minute—but only a minute. Would he be stupid enough to do business through his emails? As I opened them, I saw several marked with stars, and my heart plummeted. "Fursona, we've got to win right here. It's bigger than Vigilant Vow or the minor-league spot. He's got a line to almost every Magical Girl who's ever put on the dress."

As Fursona hurried over to the computer, I flipped through email after email, back and forth between Vigilant Vow and The Agent. "He's been feeding Vigilant Vow every familiar he pulls from every Magical Girl he signs a contract with. What we've been fighting are the best twelve, but they're not the only ones."

"Oh shit," Fursona said. She grabbed the mouse and clicked on a random email from February.

Subject: Would You Like to Sign a Contract? (HIGH PRIORITY)
VV,
Got another one. I'm sending her to the rec center. It's a candy dog that bestows some fairly strong melee powers. It could rival Bubble-Bill in power, and it'll be a hit with the kids. It's a possible top-twelve familiar.
The Agent

RE: Would You Like to Sign a Contract? (HIGH PRIORITY)
Agent,
Seriously? That's not top twelve. No way.
VV

RE: Would You Like to Sign a Contract? (HIGH PRIORITY)
VV,
Have I ever let you down? It's got some real potential, and it diversifies your image. If you're going to make it in business, perception is as important as reality.
The Agent

"That's . . . actually about what I figured," Fursona said. She nodded slowly. "I figured he had to have a sponsor, but I had no idea who. He was getting familiars from somewhere, though, unless he had a power to just take them, and he mentioned contracts, so he'd made deals."

I stood up and walked back into the living room, head whirling. It made sense. His explosive growth up the ranks was because he had access to every familiar out there, but he'd needed help to get them. I wondered what The Agent was getting out of the deal. Had he been building Vigilant Vow up for something? Or maybe his studio got something out of the arrangement. It didn't matter. "Does that mean The Agent's responsible for all this?"

"Yeah, that's right," Vigilant Vow said from the door, a pair of dogs at his feet. "I didn't know what the power *really* did, and The Agent offered me a line on every Magical Girl who signed a deal with him. Every."

He broke a crystal. Iyago, Stella-Lunar's two-headed owl, emerged.
"Single."
Another crystal. I braced myself as a snake slithered through the air.
"One."

Vigilant Vow reached up, Stella-Lunar's Eclipse Form surging around him, and tapped the last crystal with his wand. I knew what was coming, and sure enough, Tails vanished, then reappeared at his feet in TA-1LZ mode. Her [**New Head-Cannon**] folded out of her back and swiveled to aim at me.

The Dark Boy grinned at me. "So now that you know, you can't leave here." Then his brow furled, because I wasn't panicking.

No. Instead, I couldn't stop laughing. I pointed, but not toward Vigilant Vow. Instead, I pointed right at TA-1LZ and said five words through the laughter.

"Fursona, initiate Operation Old Yeller!"

58

Operation Old Yeller

A few weeks ago, we'd discussed preplanned fight strategies in Combat Style class. A lot of teams used them; The Triad had all sorts of set-piece moves involving Tele-Portal's powers. I'd talked about how they best worked with her, and then Fursona and I had sat down and brainstormed options. We'd been practicing several in Tele-Portal's training room and walking through others that we couldn't practice with The Triad's help.

Operation Old Yeller was one of those.

The idea was simple. We'd noticed that Vigilant Vow didn't seem to be able to summon the same familiar repeatedly. Our fight in the subway car had confirmed that; as our desperate retreat progressed, the waves of familiars dwindled. We thought he had a roughly ten-minute delay before he could summon again, and we aimed to take advantage of that.

Fursona had been holding back, using mostly her unlimited-use powers, for all of Act Two. When one of us called Operation Old Yeller, she went all-out, but not against Vigilant Vow. Her goal wasn't to stop the villain.

She had to put down TA-1LZ fast.

I had to distract Vigilant Vow and Iyago.

I wasn't sure whose job was worse. But I didn't have long to think about it.

TA-1LZ's Gatling taser started spinning, the rapid-fire pops filling the air as Fursona dashed toward her. I covered and tried to look weak. It wasn't hard, honestly. I had my claws, but none of my powers. I could only hope that Iyago and Eclipse Form Vigilant Vow took the bait.

They did.

Iyago's [Starflame] filled the room with fire, but most of it was aimed at me. I ducked behind the round table, which burst into flames. We'd been gambling that Vigilant Vow wouldn't be able to steal Tails when we'd combined, but he'd beaten that, so as the flames lapped over me, I worried [Fursonal Furcefield] wouldn't work, either.

[True Grit! +1 Grit Point]

I exhaled in relief as the flames died down. Tails or not, my [**Fursonal Furcefield**] still functioned! I had a chance at this.

A white beam covered the gap between Vigilant Vow and me, and I watched my superhero damage plummet as pure starlight sliced through my fur and seared me to the bone.

[HP 6/9]

I couldn't tank [**Maximum Starlance**], no matter my Costume, if I didn't get [**Fursonal Furcefield**] triggers. I glanced over to Fursona.

The kangaroo had closed the gap with TA-1LZ, and they scratched and kicked at each other even as my familiar's Gatling taser fired point-blank into my sidekick. Her own [**Fursonal Furcefield**] was getting a workout for sure, but it looked like she was on her way to winning.

I dove away from the table, trying not to scream as the room went black. Either Iyago or Vigilant Vow had used [**Total Eclipse**]. It didn't matter which one; Copy Cat melted off of me, and Fursona's suit started drooping around her as its power faded momentarily. TA-1LZ wasn't affected, and neither were my attackers.

I started running toward a door as the room filled with flames behind me. Just before they licked across my back, I slammed the door shut. It shook, then jumped in its hinges. Outside, I heard Vigilant Vow screaming in rage—and something else. Something . . . fearful.

I flicked on the light as the door shook again, thanking the villain for using solid steel.

It had been a bedroom, but the bed had no sheets or pillows, and the mattress looked old. A chair wobbled on three legs every time my assailants slammed into the door, and the naked lightbulb swayed back and forth on a long cord. Nothing in this room fit with the rest of the house.

I'd been forced back into my Understudy Costume by the [**Total Eclipse**], which meant I had no powers, not even to defend myself. But I did have a hunch that something in this room *mattered* to Vigilant Vow. So, as the door shook harder and harder and pictures rained from the walls outside, I started investigating.

I didn't have time for a deep dive, so I glanced around quickly, looking for something—anything—that'd help me. And then I saw them, tucked in a milk crate in the corner, almost fifty pieces of parchment, rolled and sealed in wax with a paw-print, bird's claw mark, or the impression of a nose.

I'd found Vigilant Vow's contracts.

The door blew off its hinges a moment later, sailing past my head and reducing the bed frame to splinters right next to me. My throat tightened, and I held back a scream of frustration. Then I lunged for the contracts, hoping to destroy Iyago's before the two-headed owl familiar or Vigilant Vow destroyed me.

Operation Old Yeller had failed, but I couldn't—

[**Cunning Tactics! +1 Cunning Point**]

<Oooh, contracts! Yeah, you should bust those up right meow!> Tails said from the floor next to the milk crate.

I didn't waste any time. Still on my hands and knees, I extended my wand and pointed at the milk crate.

"[**Stellar Ray**]!" I shouted.

"Wait!" Vigilant Vow screamed. Iyago dove toward my arm as if to tear my red-tipped wand from my hands with his claws.

The [**Stellar Ray**] crashed into the milk crate, shattered plastic, and shredded the contracts. I only half saw it, though. I screamed as Iyago swooped down. His claws broke skin—then he vanished.

[**Dramatic Destruction! +1 Drama Point**]
[**Good Thinking! +1 Cunning Point**]
[**HP 5/9**]

Vigilant Vow crouched next to me on his hands and knees, tears streaming down his face. Torn contract parchment rained down on us like confetti. "You've killed me," he whispered.

"Not yet, we haven't," Fursona said as her kangaroo fursuit filled the door's space. "But whether we do or not is up to you!"

I climbed to my feet shakily. We'd won. There was no way he'd keep fighting without his Signature Skill—absolutely no way.

He rolled and sprung to his feet, flailing his scarf out. "I've still got one trick and a chance!"

The scarf smashed across my face, surprisingly heavy, and dozens of tiny legs clawed at me. I screamed—as much from shock as from pain. He just didn't know when to quit.

[**HP 4/9**]

Then, before I could stop him, he whirled, spinning the scarf around and slamming it into Fursona. It wrapped around her, tearing at her fursuit, and she started trying to tear the scarf off.

Vigilant Vow ducked under the flailing kangaroo legs and hopped over my sidekick's animatronic tail. Then he was in the destroyed, burning living room. I slid past her a second later, my wand extended.

Understudy didn't have much left in the tank, but the Costume had enough for this. "Stop, or I'll—"

"No!" Vigilant Vow shouted and kept running.

"Fine! [**Stellar Ray**]! [**Stellar Ray**]!"

[Dramatic Damage! +2 Drama Points]

The two beams caught the villain straight in the small of his back, and he fell to the ground. Fursona landed on him feet-first a moment later, driving the air from his lungs. He flailed against her suit helplessly, trying desperately to break free. "Surrender, *please*," she asked, holding a leg over his face.

He spat on the floor, then looked up at the paw. "Go to hell, both of you," he said, loathing in his voice.

"Your choice." The foot crashed down on him, and he went limp.

[End of Act Two: Act Three in One Minute]
[Alias - Understudy] [Archetype - Magical Girl] [Community Rank - 229/523]
[HP 4/9]
[Styles and Skills]
▶Archetype Skill - Transformation Sequence
▶Combo Skills - Power-Weaving
▶Badass (14)
▶Cunning (11)
▶Drama (17) (2 Skill Rolls Available)
▶Stellar Ray 2
▶Bit-Part Barrage 2
▶Flamboyance (42) (Skill Roll Available)
▶Signature Skill - Adaptive Armoire 2
▶Stored Costumes: (Rainy Day, Copy Cat)
▶Starwave Sail 1
▶Quick-Time Change 2
▶Grit (19) (Skill Roll Available)
▶I-Frame Transform 2

"So, that's that," Fursona said. She picked herself up and looked at the . . . kid.

"Yeah." The high school kid in an armored hoodie lay on the ground, unconscious. We'd just wrecked him in like three moves. "He didn't build any Grit, did he?"

"Nope. The bare minimum of superhero damage. I doubt he'd really fought anyone one-on-one before. He never had to—The Agent handed him an army, and his producer told him to use it. So what are we gonna do with him?"

I didn't want to answer that question. Instead, I wanted to celebrate my big win. We'd made it! I was a minor-league show's star now, and Fursona was a minor-league sidekick. All the work we'd put in during Combat Style class, and all the hours sitting in front of Fursona's whiteboard coming up with strategies to generate buzz, the radio show, and struggling for a month against Vigilant Vow's bullshit power—it had all paid off.

But the kid lying next to the shattered coffee table had stolen dozens of familiars. Who knew how many Episodes villains had won because of him? I wasn't in the mood to feel charitable. "Give me the scarf," I said.

Fursona pulled the writhing, thrashing scarf off her suit. "It wasn't doing anything anyway," she muttered.

I examined it. Hundreds of legs thrashed in the air, struggling for purchase as I held it off the ground. It flailed back and forth in the air. "Is this thing his familiar?"

"I think so. Drop it. It looks weird waving back and forth like that," she said.

I dropped it. Then I wandered into the odd-feeling bedroom and unrolled a half-destroyed contract. I couldn't make out most of it, but at the top, I saw the name *Anaheim*, and a little lower, *Chili Powder*. I brought it back to Fursona and then stared at the scarf. It had wrapped itself around Vigilant Vow's neck, exactly like it had been before he'd attacked me with it.

"I think he's completely done now," I said, handing the contract to my sidekick.

She read the names, then looked at the rest of the contract. Then she nodded slowly. "You're sure you got them all?"

"Yeah," I said. "So what do we do with him?"

Fursona looked at me as seriously as a fursuit could. "An—Understudy, you have to do the right thing. I don't think he ever had a chance, with the producer he had and the power he was given. We'll bring him in—we have to. Hopefully, he has lawyers to help him out. But after they get him out or he serves time in Almhurst, he needs to learn how to be a real hero. We can be the ones to teach him what that means, or at least give him a chance. Please?"

I stared at the dark-haired boy. His eyes flicked open, and Fursona loomed over him almost immediately. "Stay down," she said.

"No. No, let me go," he mumbled, but truthfully, he wasn't in any shape to go anywhere.

[The Finish Line!: Act Three in Progress]

A massive energy beam, bigger than any I'd seen in person, smashed through the wall. Bricks and trophies flew everywhere, some slamming into the downed Dark Boy. As rubble catapulted into the room and dust filled the air, a woman's voice carried over the sounds of destruction.

"I swear to defend Tokyexico in starlight and under new moon. To stand against evil and corruption. And, above all, to remain true to what's right and just. So witness star, so witness moon."

59

So Witness Moon

[Episode Update! Rating Change! New Rating: R]
[A Powerful Hero is Joining the Fight]
[Name: Stella-Lunar]

Stella-Lunar stepped through the rubble, Iyago the two-headed owl already perched on her shoulder. I'd seen my role model—my heroine—on patrol around campus last semester, but never this close, and this close, I wasn't sure I liked what I saw. An ominous yellow aura shone from a star that hovered behind her head, and the neon glow between her armored dress's plates filled her section of the room with a similar golden aura—her Star Form. I had no idea how long until she rotated to Moon Form, then Eclipse.

Anger—no, wrath—flashed across her face as she stared at Vigilant Vow. "That bastard made a deal with me, and today, he broke that oath. He knows the consequences for violating my trust, and I'm here to collect."

I blinked, my jaw almost to the floor. Was she . . . talking about killing Vigilant Vow? I took a single step toward her, and her wand went up. "Stella-Lunar, this fight isn't yours," I said.

"It wasn't until Iyago vanished," she spat, glaring at me, anger rolling off her in waves. "Now it is."

"Understudy . . ." Fursona said uncertainly. Her kangaroo head turned toward Vigilant Vow, and she started talking again, but I held up a hand.

"Fursona, I know." I gulped and turned toward Stella-Lunar. Toward my idol. Someone who, I knew, could obliterate Fursona and me with the flick of a wand. I'd always looked up to her, and my voice quaked. "It doesn't have to be your fight. He's done. All he's got is his familiar, nothing else. I know, I just destroyed the contracts."

Vigilant Vow groaned on the floor as his scarf-shaped familiar worried over him. I ignored him. Every ounce of my attention was on Stella-Lunar.

"And who's to say he won't rebuild? He's a threat to all of us!" Stella-Lunar shouted, her wrath turning hot.

The negotiations were over. I had to choose: either let Stella-Lunar through and watch her finish off a helpless villain, or grit my teeth, stall her, and try to get her to see reason.

Her form flickered from Star to Moon, and I made my choice. "I can't let you kill him," I whispered. Fursona stepped up next to me and nodded.

"Then I'll go through you," Stella-Lunar said. Her Star Form's yellow light faded, her Moon Form's white glow filled the room, and the fight to beat Vigilant Vow ended.

A moment later, the fight to save his life began.

Stella-Lunar was stronger, faster, and tougher than me, and she had a decade of experience I didn't. I had exactly two advantages over her. I didn't have to beat her—if she left Vigilant Vow alive at the end of this, I'd won.

And I'd watched every Stella-Lunar Episode at least twice. I knew her move-sets, favored attack patterns, and how long she had in each form.

So, even before she started using **[Tidal Pull]** to set Fursona and me up for a **[Moonbeam]** barrage, I'd pushed my sidekick left and dodged right. Surely, my reaction time would be enough to—

Nope.

The force of her grip drove the breath from my lungs as she used **[Tidal Pull]**. I found myself midair, five feet from my idol—too far for Fursona to hit her. Her wand was already rotating for a **[Moonbeam]** before I'd even lifted mine, and I used **[Quick-Time Change]** and **[I-Frame Transform]** to dodge the pulsing, white-ringed beam.

[Flashy Fitting-Room! +1 Flamboyance Point]
[Steel Yourself! +1 Grit Point]

Fursona wasn't so lucky; she went flying even as my Costume shifted to Rainy Day. I used **[Power-Weaving]**, not expecting to get a combo off against the veteran Magical Girl, then started up a **[Thunderhead]**. "Stella, he's not worth all this!" I shouted as the storm brewed.

[Pause for Effect! +1 Drama Point]

My stomach slammed into my ribs momentarily as everything—heroes, villains, rubble, and trophies—fell through the gathering clouds toward the vaulted ceiling. Stella-Lunar landed on her feet, but the rest of us slammed against the beams and plaster, then rolled "up" into the trench as her **[Reverse Gravity]** power finished. She circled her wand again before I could fire **[Ride the Lightning]**, ripping another **[Moonbeam]** across Fursona, Vigilant Vow, and me.

[HP 1/9]

He couldn't take more hits, so as [**Thunderhead**] finished and the white, circle-bound beam sliced toward me, I threw myself over my onetime enemy, smashing him into the ceiling. The beam ripped across my back from my calf to the nape of my neck, scorching my skin and burning at my dress. I screamed in agony, and a moment later, so did Fursona as it hit her.

[HP 0/9]
[**Gritty Sacrifice! +1 Grit Point**]

"Please, Stella! Let him go!" I shouted. Then I waved my wand and started a [**Virga**]. The rain fell across the battlefield, flying "up" from the clouds "below" us— [**Reverse Gravity**] made it all but impossible to keep my directions straight. I felt the slightest bit of relief as it hit Fursona, Vigilant Vow, and me. The villain looked a little healed, while Stella-Lunar had no wounds to patch.

[**Medic! +2 Cunning Points**]
[**HP 1/9**]
[**Doctors Without Borders! -2 Cunning Points**]
[**Floating Points: 1 Drama**]

The System still counted the power as having healed her, though.

A moment later, we plunged back to the floor through the storm clouds and slammed back into the real "floor." I [**Quick-Time Changed**] into Magical Girl Understudy. Copy Cat was the tougher choice, but I needed to land on a combo finisher if I wanted to strike back.

And I wanted to strike back.

[HP 0/9]
[**Flashy Fitting-Room! +1 Flamboyance Point**]
[**Floating Points: 3 Drama, 1 Cunning**]
[**Rejuvenation Activated: HP 4/9**]

The moment I landed, I spun in the air and aimed my [**Bit-Part Barrage**] at the major-league Magical Girl. "Stella! You're better than this! I've watched all your Episodes!"

"Then you know I follow through," she said.

I let the [**Bit-Part Barrage**] go at the same time she used [**Lunar Dance**], warping space around her. A couple [**Stellar Ray**] beams hit, but most soared into the air or fizzled out at her feet.

[**Dramatic Damage! +3 Drama Points**]
[**Power-Weaving! +6 Drama, +3 Cunning, +1 Flamboyance Point**]

Stella stood up from where she'd braced herself for the impact behind crossed wrists. Then she brushed something from the corner of her mouth. For a moment, I thought I'd actually hurt her. Then she kept brushing, and I realized I'd just gotten her dirty. She hadn't even cared that I'd comboed against her!

"Fine, Understudy. If that's how this is, then that's how this is," Stella said calmly. She used [**Tidal Pull**] again, and I flew through the air toward her, already trying to form some sort of basic defense.

This wasn't even one of her offensive forms.

It'd been almost two and a half minutes, and I estimated that Fursona and I could hold on for another minute—maybe two—if nothing changed. The problem was, something was about to. We'd barely scratched Stella-Lunar's glowing white armor, and the heroine's blasts had all but depleted my superhero damage and my best powers. I'd earned a few Style Points, but the beat-down just wouldn't stop.

Then it did.

The fighting paused for a second, and between panted breaths, I looked at Fursona and allowed myself to hope. We'd pushed ourselves to our late little-league or early minor-league limits, so maybe Stella-Lunar was giving us a reprieve. Maybe I could talk her around.

And maybe pigs flew.

Her white glow faded until her body looked like an inky-black silhouette—one with an orange corona around it that glowed brighter and brighter until I couldn't look right at her. Tiny solar flares arced from her shoulders along her arms, and I knew I didn't have another minute.

"Oh shit. It's about to get rough," I said to Fursona as Stella-Lunar finished shifting into Eclipse Form—the only super, hero or villain, no matter the form, that could fight Golden Goose one-on-one and hope to win. We had to make it for one minute, then survive Star Form before we could fight Moon Form again.

One missed [**Maximum Starlance**] from her told me that wasn't going to happen.

The house collapsed around us, and I threw myself over Vigilant Vow's half-conscious body. Bricks and beams bounced off my back, but I had enough superhero damage left to take it. Fursona kicked out, knocking the worst off of me but crushing the supervillain's leg. I didn't have time to deal with his agonized scream; I was too busy with my own pain. I rolled away from him and whirled to my feet to face Eclipse Form Stella-Lunar.

If I couldn't talk her down, we were screwed.

I started shouting, pushing through my injuries. I'd been hurt worse in Episodes—and recently, too. "Stella, you have to give him a chance!"

"I did. He wasted it." Her voice was cold, almost machinelike. Her arm came up, and she used a power I recognized but couldn't do anything about. [**Starflame**] filled the room, more than Vigilant Vow and Iyago could control. Everything that could burn around us did. I rolled on the tile floor, trying to put out the flames before they *really* hurt me.

I didn't even make it to my feet before the room went dark as [**Total Eclipse**] sucked all the power out of Stella's enemies—including me. "But you could give him another chance! He never *had* one! The whole deck was stacked against him!"

"No."

The next [**Maximum Starlance**] punched into Fursona, sending her flying into what was left of the wall. She bounced off the wall, tried to get to her hands and knees, and collapsed. My stomach churned; I'd brought her here, and I'd committed her to fighting against a force she couldn't handle. Bianca was in there, and I'd gotten her ass kicked again.

She was going to hate me.

I tried one more time. Dropping my wand, I held my hands out. "Please, Stella, slow down. At least think about what you're about to do."

She activated [**Dark Side of the Moon**], and the world went cold. I recognized the power but couldn't stop it. Tendrils of darkness tore at my hair, my dress . . . my *skin*. They threw me against the trophy case next to Fursona, and my shinbone crunched as I landed, twisting in agony. A moment later, Vigilant Vow joined us, something cracking in his chest as he slid across the floor.

Stella-Lunar's orange corona faded, and color returned to her body. A yellow, star-shaped halo burst into being behind her head, turning as she gazed at Fursona, who couldn't even try to fight anymore. The kangaroo crawled a few paces away and stopped, plastic eyes staring at me.

Vigilant Vow said something that sounded almost like "Please . . ."

Fursona reached out slowly and grabbed my hand.

I couldn't have moved if I wanted to, but I didn't want to. The Magical Girl was beyond reason, but my choice to throw myself between her and a defeated supervillain had felt right. It still did. And really, Vigilant Vow was just a dumb kid. He didn't know better, and he didn't deserve what was coming for him. I looked Stella-Lunar right in her shining golden eyes, torn mask half covering one of mine, and said, "Please don't do this."

"It's already done," she said, picking me up by one arm.

As Stella-Lunar tossed me aside and loomed over Vigilant Vow, my world started going black. I'd pushed myself to the absolute limit trying to stop her, and I'd failed. Then, without firing her beam, she grabbed Dupe, the scarf-like familiar, and took off into the sky, leaving Fursona, Vigilant Vow, and me lying in the dust.

I'd won, I realized, as the last light faded. I'd beaten Vigilant Vow. The minor-league spot was mine. And, even more impressive, I'd saved him from Stella-Lunar.

Then the world exploded around me, and I knew no more.

60

Blackout

THURSDAY, APRIL 23

The all-too-familiar beeping and humming of a hospital room greeted me, along with the end-of-Episode message I hadn't had the chance to look at.

[Episode Finished!]
[Episode: Pilot: The Finish Line! - R]
[Penalties: N/A]
[Episode Finished! +5 of each Style Point]
[We'll Call It a Draw! +2 of each Style Point]
[Role Focus: Drama + Flamboyance - Goal Met! +10 Focused Style Points]
[Alias - Understudy] [Archetype - Magical Girl] [Community Rank - 220/523]
[HP 10/10]
[Styles and Skills]
►Archetype Skill - Transformation Sequence
►Combo Skills - Power-Weaving
►Badass (21)
►Cunning (22)
►Drama (46)
►Stellar Ray 2
►Bit-Part Barrage 2
►Flamboyance (64) (Skill Roll Available)
►Signature Skill - Adaptive Armoire 2
►Stored Costumes: (Rainy Day, Copy Cat)
►Starwave Sail 1
►Quick-Time Change 2
►Grit (31)
►I-Frame Transform 2
[50 Flamboyance Credits Used. Rolling Skill!]

Sun poured through a window on the far side of my room, and I could see the Hot Zone from it. I was in the Council of Heroes' Building, in Mid-Town. And, to my relief, a domino-masked Bianca lay in the next bed over. I reached up with my left arm to wave at her, and she waved back. Then she pointed to my other side.

"Hey, you're awake," Stella-Lunar said.

[New Skill! Shock and Awe 1: Force of personality, and explosions, powers this shockwave attack]

That was a Mom power. Why was I getting a Mom power? I tried to think about it, but I couldn't. Everything hurt, and Stella-Lunar was right there.

I tried to reach with my right to grab the wand on my nightstand, ready to keep fighting against my idol, but the motion jerked against the brace pinning it to my chest. It wasn't broken—I could tell that by comparing it to my throbbing leg, which definitely was. The veteran Magical Girl sat in a chair, unmoving, and I took a moment to breathe. The fight in Vigilant Vow's lair was over, and if Stella-Lunar had wanted to end us, she easily could have. I took stock of my battle wounds—and Bianca's.

My right shin was broken, somewhere down by my ankle. Every joint in my body hurt, especially my right shoulder, and I could only see out of one eye. I could only breathe shallowly, and twisting hurt my stomach. Bianca hadn't suffered quite as badly; her ankle was braced, she'd been bruised all over, and her beautiful, curly black hair had been singed short on half her head—then a chunk had been shaved off.

All in all, we'd gotten off pretty damn lightly.

But I wasn't worried about us.

"Vigilant Vow?" I croaked.

Bianca laughed, and Stella-Lunar suppressed a giggle of her own. Looking at her out-of-Episode for the first time, I realized she couldn't have been more than five years older than me—maybe six. The giggle broke through, and she snorted through her nose. "Sorry, sorry. Your sidekick had the same first question when she woke up. I didn't kill him."

"Oh," I said, relief flooding me.

"But I'm still thinking about it."

The mood darkened dramatically.

"I feel like I owe you an explanation," Stella-Lunar said. She cleared her throat and stood up. "On February thirteenth, I'd planned to start an Episode against 3V1L and push them out of Thornton and the Poudre districts. I knew where their lair was, had reliable information that the Three *Vs* would be there, and even had an assault plan built that left them no room to escape. I had backup arranged from The Triad in case they called in more firepower, but I didn't expect to need it. And I had an emergency button I'd never used before."

She sighed. "I saw you predicting some of my moves, so you know how powerful I am. I've never had to call for actual backup from someone bigger than me. Not once. But when I tried to use [**Transformation Sequence**] that night, I couldn't. It wouldn't work. That'd never happened to me before. But, as soon as it happened, I went to my producer. They pointed the finger at Cartman and said the Ilneat had a super who might be causing problems. Together, we went to pay Cartman a visit, and we worked out an arrangement. Vigilant Vow could only use Magical Girls' familiars during times when he knew the Magical Girls weren't using them."

"But by then, I couldn't get into the headspace for an Episode. I had to call for help, and Golden Goose responded exactly how I feared she would. She flew down from Yorkston and wiped out the Three *V*s. Never gave them a chance to surrender or anything. I knew who was responsible for those deaths. I could have resolved things without the Three *V*s dying. Golden Goose doesn't operate that way."

Bianca snorted mirthlessly. "That didn't happen."

"No, it did not. But the first time I realized he wasn't living up to his end of the deal was two nights ago when I couldn't transform again. As soon as I got Iyago back, I left to end things once and for all. The Three *V*s would still be alive if Vigilant Vow hadn't been around. Maybe they would've been in Almhurst, maybe they'd have rebuilt 3V1L with the One *L*, but they'd be alive. I had to stop him before he got more supers—or even Magical Girls—killed."

"Did you know about the contracts or The Agent?" I asked.

"What about The Agent?" Stella-Lunar's eyes narrowed.

I was treading on shaky ground, but I had to tell her everything. If I didn't, she couldn't possibly make a good decision. "I found out how Vigilant Vow was stealing familiars. The Agent was feeding them to him. Every time his Temp Heroes got a Magical Girl he hadn't seen, he'd send them to Vigilant Vow, who'd make a contract with her familiar. He had a whole stack of them, and I destroyed them all."

The Magical Girl's face flashed dark. "If that's true, I'll need to tell the Council of Heroes. They're meeting upstairs to figure out how to address this mess, and they'll probably summon The Agent to talk. That slimeball can probably worm his way out of responsibility, though."

I waited for her to finish sending a message on her phone, a little confused as to why Crossbow or the rest of the Council would talk through text with someone just downstairs from them. It barely mattered to me; whatever happened to The Agent was secondary to my single goal for this conversation. "So, we're good?" I asked.

"I understand why you fought with me from a moral point of view. You're still an idiot," Stella Lunar said.

Bianca snorted, then wiped her nose on her sheet. "Understudy's pretty dumb sometimes, but she's *my* idiot."

"*Fairly OddParents*. Before your time," Stella-Lunar said quickly, smiling, "and quoted incorrectly."

"Okay, let me explain Vigilant Vow, then," I bulled on. "He's a smart-ass kid who succeeded at everything he did, then got contracted by the Style System and got the worst possible producer. I don't think there's a slimier Ilneat in the Hot Zone than Cartman."

"Not for long. They're meeting, too. *We* aren't privy to the meetings, but I doubt he'll be able to work on Earth after this," Stella said.

"Good. They ruined my mom's career, and they were doing the same to Vigilant Vow. They pushed him into deals with The Agent, lied to him about his [**Signature Skill**], and pushed him harder and harder until he had to go Dark Boy to keep up. He's not the guilty party here," I said, sitting up in bed.

Stella shook her head, eyes narrowed. "He's not innocent, either. Understudy, he killed people."

"No, Golden Goose killed people. Vigilant Vow is a victim here," I said. "And even if he is guilty, it's not our role to be the judge, jury, and executioner. Maybe he deserves to rot in Almhurst. Maybe he should see Dr. Ayers here at the Council of Heroes. But that's not our call."

"It's *exactly* our role to be judge, jury, and executioner." Stella-Lunar looked ready to attack me right there. Then she stalked to the door. "I need a minute. Stay where you are."

The moment the door shut, Bianca rolled onto her side, groaning, and stared at me, wide-eyed beneath her temporary mask. "Holy shit, Understudy, you've got a death wish."

"I'm just doing what you wanted me to, hun," I said. My throat hurt from all the talking, but I had to get it out.

"Yeah, I know, and if I could move, I'd get up and hug you. I'm not sure he'll choose redemption, though. It sounds like a really hard path to walk, and his scarf familiar doesn't have the kick Iyago or TA-1LZ does. He'll never make the minor leagues, and that'll sting for the rest of his life."

"I just hope he *has* the rest of his life," I muttered. There was every chance Stella-Lunar wouldn't be swayed by a couple of college girls she'd just beaten the shit out of, and I didn't have any other leverage. I had to do something to change the subject. "Heard anything from Su-Bin or school?"

"Well, the good news is that our absences are excused and that Mindstorm's not as pissed this time," Bianca said. "Something about getting destroyed by Stella-Lunar must have triggered a memory or something. Su-Bin's going to kill you if you don't take that damn baby-bot back soon, though."

"Oh shit, Baby Cash," I said. I pulled out my phone to text Su-Bin and let her know I'd be there soon, but Fursona laughed.

"I already told her we got hit by a car at a campus crosswalk. That's the official excuse explaining some of our battle damage—she thinks we're lucky since we just got our college paid for. You need to text her soon, though. And we *will* have make-up assignments, but I've already emailed Mindstorm and confirmed that they don't involve fighting her this time."

The door opened, and Stella-Lunar came in. She didn't say anything. Instead, she walked to the window and stared out over the Hot Zone, fidgeting with her hair. After a minute, she blew air between her lips in a long raspberry. "You're a pain in the ass, but you've got guts."

I stayed quiet. I'd said what I could, and now it was on her to decide. She paced back and forth . . . back and forth . . . back and forth. Bee and I just watched. Then she cleared her throat.

"I'll make you a deal, Understudy," Stella-Lunar said. She stopped pacing by the window and loomed over me, but I matched her gaze. "You can try to redeem him. It might even work. But I'll be watching, and I've already emailed all the other Magical Girls. They know. All of them. The moment a single familiar disappears, we'll be coming, and you won't be able to stop us when he messes up."

"If," I whispered.

"What?" Stella-Lunar said, brow furrowing. I couldn't tell if it was anger or if she just hadn't heard me.

"*If.* You said when. If you want him to turn, you have to give him a chance. Otherwise, you're just waiting for him to fail instead of believing he can succeed. I've been a superhero for almost six years now, and I know that the Episodes and the studios want all the action, but the Extras still remember when heroes helped people in the media. They remember the saves, not the fights, and I'm choosing to start by saving Vigilant Vow."

Stella-Lunar stared at me for a moment. Then she shook her head almost pityingly. "Good luck with that, Understudy. I hope you're right, but I'll be waiting for when—if—you're wrong." She dropped Vigilant Vow's scarf on my bed, turned on her heel, and walked out of the room.

Just before the door closed, she turned around. "Oh, and congratulations on the minor leagues, ladies. I'll be seeing you out there." The door clicked closed, and Stella-Lunar was gone.

I took a deep breath and shivered. Stella-Lunar was the best, and I'd beaten her, not on the battlefield, but with my words. That had to count for something. Then her words sank in, and I raised my good arm in a fist-pump of celebration. It wasn't just a promise from Rocko anymore. We'd made it to the minor leagues. I couldn't wait to see the Ilneat and start working on my new builds, figuring out my "signing bonus" skills, and practicing counters with Fursona.

"Now what?" Fursona asked from her bed. "Are we done with this? Just fall asleep and heal up?"

"You can if you want, but I've got something else I *have* to do. Now . . ." I started, then hesitated. I had to do one more thing before moving on, and I wasn't looking forward to it. "Now I need to visit Vigilant Vow."

61

Vigilant Vow

My former rival turned worst enemy glared at me weakly from his hospital bed. I'd asked the hospital's staff to clear the room, so it was just him and me.

"I got this for you," I said, and held up Dupe, the scarf familiar. "Stella-Lunar and I had a conversation, and she agreed not to kill you. But you've got to stop."

He didn't say anything, and I resisted the urge to scratch my leg. The cast was too thick, and the healing super had told me that even with Ilneat medicine, the burns and breaks from eating a Stella-Lunar Supernova with no superhero damage would take a week or two to heal.

I was sure it was worse for Vigilant Vow. At least I was up and walking. He wouldn't be for a while. Fursona and I had used every trick we could to survive Stella-Lunar, and he hadn't had that option.

He was also cuffed to the bed so he wouldn't flee while the Council of Heroes and the Ilneats had their meetings.

"I pieced it all together, and I've already told Stella-Lunar what I think happened, and she told the Council of Heroes. You got contracted two years ago, your producer picked you up, and you skyrocketed with an amazing power. That's what the public knows about you. But just before I destroyed your contracts, I learned something else. I know you steal your powers, and so do you, but we couldn't figure out how."

I sat down, taking the pressure off my crutches. I might be up and about, but I didn't have my energy back, even transformed. Tails hissed at Vigilant Vow, but I ignored her. "I saw you last semester at the job fair at Tokyexico University. You were with The Agent. The emails on your computer filled in the rest. When I signed my contract with him, he waited until my power came up for his build-a-hero, got that hero over to you, and you formed a contract with Tails, right?"

He stayed silent, and I looked out the window.

"So, why'd you go Dark Boy?"

He still didn't say anything. I got the distinct feeling that if looks could kill, he'd put me in the ground faster than Golden Goose could. As his eyes bored holes into the back of my skull, I struggled not to turn around.

"Vigilant Vow, or Empty Oath, or whoever you want to be, you don't have to say anything. I know exactly what you are."

"What?"

I smiled into the window glass. I had him. Even if he didn't say anything else, he'd cracked just the tiniest bit. "You're a kid who got in over his head, just like my mom. Stella-Lunar wants to kill you, your studio's getting shut down, and every Magical Girl out there knows who's to blame if her familiar disappears. You're done. The minor leagues are out of reach for you now. It's over."

Silence again. I didn't expect a response. Instead, I squeezed his scarf, feeling the hundreds of legs against my palm. "You can still turn yourself around, though. I really think you can."

I set the scarf on his bed, just over his feet. "Here's your familiar back, along with a few phone numbers. The first one's for a counselor, Dr. Ayers. She's worked with heroes and villains before. If there's anyone who can help you make a plan, it's her.

"The second one is for The Narrator. She runs a place called Tottergarten near TU. Go there. You'll meet a bunch of retired villains, see the next generation of super-heroes, and, if you're lucky, Magical Girl Honeycomb. I didn't see her contract in my quick search, so maybe you haven't wronged her yet. She'll show you the ropes of being an underpowered Magical, and how to do it with grace and self-respect. It's the second step I'd take in redemption if I were you."

I cleared my throat and pulled out my phone. I went to my blocked numbers and removed his from the list.

"The last number is mine. I'll be checking in on you to make sure you're doing well, Vigilant Vow. Text me if you need to, but if those messages are *anything* like the last ones you sent me, you're blocked again and on your own."

When I turned around, he'd rolled over slightly and wasn't looking at me any-more. I nodded slowly. "You don't have to make a choice right now. Think it over. Take your time—it's what you've got. Then make those phone calls and become Vigilant Vow again instead of Empty Oath. Or even better, find a new superhero to be and abandon them both.

"I'm sorry you were tricked and manipulated. I think you can turn it around," I finished. Then, without waiting for a response, I opened the door and walked out, crutches clacking. As I left, I heard him reach for his scarf-shaped familiar.

As the door clicked shut behind me, I breathed a sigh of relief and pulled my phone out one-handed.

<Think it went well. Dunno if he'll turn it around tho - Understudy 11:15>
<I did what I could - Understudy 11:15>
<Good job <3 - Fursona 11:15>

<Discharged? - Fursona 11:16>
<Yes. Done with business. Gonna pay for a ride home - Understudy 11:16>
<Great. See you there in an hour? - Fursona 11:17>

A hand tightened on my good shoulder as I tapped out my response. "Magical Girl Understudy. Just the client I wanted to see," The Agent said.

I held back a shiver and nonchalantly finished my text. Meta-powered or not, letting Bee know my schedule was more important.

<Better make in an hour 15. Some annoying stuff just came up - Understudy 11:17>

Once my text sent, I maneuvered the phone back into a pocket—only almost dropping it twice—and turned around. "No hands, please. I just got the Costume cleaned up after saving your sidekick."

"I've already cleared things up with the Council of Heroes, so you'll be glad to know there's no bad blood between us," The Agent said. He took his hand off my shoulder. "There's no reason for us to be enemies, you know. I did nothing technically illegal, had no idea that Magical Boy Vigilant Vow's power worked the way it did, and was simply doing a favor for an old friend's studio. I'm sure we can come to a common understanding about what happened and who's to blame."

I nodded in agreement. "I know who's to blame already, Agent."

"Oh? And does the fact that what you think you know flies in the face of the Council of Heroes' findings on the events of the twenty-second sway your understanding?"

"That depends on what their findings are. I don't doubt that Crossbow and the rest of the Council investigated Vigilant Vow's lair, or what was left of it," I said. I was playing his game, and I knew it. I also knew I'd lose if I didn't change strategies soon; The Agent thrived on persuasion and discussion.

Still, I followed him in when he gestured to an empty hospital room across from Vigilant Vow's.

"The council found no evidence that I was involved in any way," The Agent said, sitting on the bed. "Absolutely none. I've given them access to my computers, and there's no evidence there, either. Your accusations, while plausible, have no proof."

Sure enough, The Agent didn't have his briefcase. I sat in a chair, trying to think of what to say next. But before I could talk, The Agent filled the silence. "Having said that, this accusation alone jeopardizes my power's usefulness. Therefore, I'm offering you fifty Style Points through my [**Power Broker**] power to keep it to yourself."

I blinked, speechless again. Fifty Style Points was . . . enough to power Flamboyance and Drama into the next power, and as a minor-league hero, I could upgrade to Rank Three powers, too. My mouth watered, but I had other priorities, too. "What about Fursona?"

"They'll receive the same deal you do, of course. Fifty Style Points, to any Styles you'd prefer, in whatever numbers you want to each."

"No thanks."

The Agent looked at me, face expressionless. "Excuse me?"

"No thanks. I've sold my soul to you before, and it turned out terribly for me. Getting more involved with you after what you and Cartman did to Vigilant Vow would be stupid—and I may be dumb, but I'm not stupid. Fursona's going to give you the same answer, so I wouldn't bother asking."

"Magical Girl Understudy, I assure you that—"

"That the Council of Heroes found you'd done nothing wrong, legally speaking? Sure." I stood up and headed for the door, skirt whirling as I turned. "But you know the truth, and so do I. If you didn't, you wouldn't be trying to cover things up, would you?"

He seethed—I could feel the heat coming off of him—but didn't say anything. I headed for the door.

<Thanks, Understudy,> Tails said. She'd never remembered anything she'd done as Vigilant Vow's familiar, and I wasn't about to press, but I knew she felt bad from what we'd told her. Rejecting The Agent's offer meant a lot to her. *<Let's never do Operation Old Yeller again, nya?>*

"Nah, we're done with that. You're safe now, with me," I said and hugged my two-tailed cat familiar.

<Purrfect,> Tails purred. Then she stiffened and arched her back just like a normal cat. *<Problem in three, two, meow!>*

The Agent pushed the door open. "Magical Girl Understudy, don't make an enemy out of me. You'd be much better off as my friend, but if you won't be that, think it over before you say anything implicating me. If you do, it'll be a long, rough road through the minor leagues."

"Oh, that's a threat?" I asked.

"No. It's a promise. You could say that it's an *oath* or a *vow*."

I grinned back at him and fished the phone from my pocket. Tapping the screen, I stopped the recording I'd started when I'd fumbled with it after my text to Bee. "Agent, I've got our whole conversation here."

I tapped the screen a few times while he stared, wide-eyed. "Aaand now Fursona has it too. You're a slimy superhero, but I have a deal for you. You leave us alone, or I'll make this public. Actually, no. I think I'll put it out there now."

"You know that won't be enough to show I'm involved in any of this, right?" The Agent asked.

"I don't really care. It'll be enough that if Temp Heroes start attacking me or interfering in my Episodes, people will *know* why. They'll have their eye on you. Maybe some heroes will still trust you after this, but you'll never have a Magical Girl client again."

As The Agent sputtered at me and I stared him down in the Council of Heroes building's medical hallway, I felt a pressure in my ears, and the world started spinning. As it shrunk to a pinpoint, I waved at The Agent, whose voice turned into a low-pitched drone. I wobbled and landed, only to be greeted by a System message.

[**Welcome to Rocko's Studio. System Disabled. Now arriving Backstage.**]

The Ilneat's voice filled my ears before my vision returned. "Well done, DuPont. Welcome to the minor leagues."

62

Minor Leagues

I sighed in relief as Rocko's studio swam into view. They'd gone all-out, with balloons and a glitter-covered sign reading Congratulations! Bianca wobbled next to me in shorts and a spaghetti-strap top. I realized a moment later that I was still in a hospital gown.

Oops.

The Ilneat looked at my arm with concern. "Oooh, yeah, that's bad—worse than last time. Even with the best I can get you, it's gonna take time. Listen to the doctors, take a few weeks off, and let it heal. But first, we've gotta talk shop. I never doubted you for a second, DuPont. You either, Marino. You're the real deal, and I'm with you to the end of the line."

I rolled my eyes. They absolutely *had* doubted us. But we'd made it anyway.

"So, minor-league stuff." Rocko pulled a cigar out, then offered one to Bianca and me. He'd never offered one before, but I declined. So did Bianca. "Suit yourselves. League-up bonuses. You've done a few minor-league Episodes against low-powered minor-league villains. How did they feel?"

"They sucked," Fursona said, "but they weren't more dangerous than the worst little-league Episodes."

"Yeah. The minor-league Episodes I ran felt more intense, but the danger felt like it wasn't focused on me. I had lots of backup for 'Braking and Entering,' though, and Tele-Portal with me for 'Winter is Coming.'"

Rocko rolled their eyes, a surprisingly human gesture. "Yeah, that's not how it really is. You fought a low-powered villain three-on-one during 'Braking and Entering,' and Black Ice wasn't ready to handle Tele-Portal's shenanigans. Her goal was to set up the power plant, not kick your heinie. And Monologue and Iron Fist had strict orders to keep that Episode little league, since they were in a high school. It's rare for heroes or villains to use schools or hospitals. I think the last one was Haze-Matt last summer.

"So, if you wanna handle a vil like Black Ice or Iron Fist by yourselves, you need some firepower!" They flexed their squeezing arms while puffing away. "Marino, you're getting the standard upgrade package. [**Combo-Breaker**], the pair of power slots, the strength upgrade, and four power upgrades. I'm assuming you don't want more powers, right?"

"Could I get a three-to-one split?" Bianca asked. "I want to roll the dice once for something big, but I'm pretty happy with my power set overall."

"You got it. Easy ask for the System." Rocko turned to me. "Now, DuPont, I've got an offer for you. We can go with the standard package, just like Marino. It'll open up your main build, like I'm sure you've thought about. Or . . . we *improvise*."

"Improvise? I'm not sure I like the sound of that, Rocko," I said. I had a bad taste in my mouth about any weirdness from Ilneats after Cartman's bullshit, even from Rocko.

"Relax. The Style System's still a total enigma, but it can be flexible when needed," Rocko said. They pulled up their computer screen. "So, we reject **[Combo Breaker]** for you. You're always working with Marino, and she'll be all up in the villains' business, so you don't need it. In return, the Style System tries to balance stuff out and feeds you a couple of power upgrades."

"Why do I care about those? **[Combo-Breaker]** seems like it's necessary to stay alive," I said.

"That's what I thought, but then I got to pondering. Marino, what level is **[Double Kick]**?"

"Two. Why?"

"I betcha all your other powers are at two, too," Pataki said. They blew on a party streamer, then took a drag from their ever-present cigar.

"I've been playing down this whole time?" I asked. I kind of knew that already, but the confirmation still sucked.

"Yeah, you're splitting your power upgrades four ways. You're also getting more chances at new powers because you have so many different builds. That's not gonna go away, but we can take care of some of that problem right now. You're averaging about level one on your powers. So, you ditch **[Combo-Breaker]** for a couple power upgrades, one of your new power slots for a couple more, and all of a sudden, you've got like eight of the damn things. That'll make up the gap between you and Marino here."

I paused. That *would* help make up the gap, and they were right. I was hopelessly behind if she was close to level two with most of her powers. It made sense; I had too many powers and too few points coming in. But this didn't solve the problem permanently. "This is a band-aid, Rocko. I need more points, not a couple of powers."

"Smart thinking, DuPont. Unfortunately, the Style System's a little iffy about giving bonus points out for nothing. This is the best we can do."

I thought about it. But at the end of the day, my power sets did most of what I wanted them to do; I just needed more power behind the moves. "Got it. So, to confirm, I'm not getting **[Combo-Breaker]** or one of my new power slots. Instead, I'm getting a bunch of extra power upgrades?"

"Yep!"

"Alright. I want it at three-to-one as well, please. I've got a lot of catching up to do, but I'm hoping for some Extra-rescue powers and stuff."

Rocko fiddled with their computer, and I braced myself for a slew of System messages. Instead, I felt nothing, and after a moment, I looked back at them to see their grasping hand hovering over a button.

"Oh, one more thing. No Episodes. None. Take a vacation while we get the minor-league paperwork in order, figure out our new time slot, and hire some more staff. So much to do on my end, but you two can't do anything about it. Go sit on a beach. Kiss and splash around or whatever you humans do for fun. Smoke a cigar or two—I don't care, just do something that's not superheroics. We'll kick off again in August or September."

"That's important. You two beat the hell out of yourselves," Pataki said. "And it's not gonna get easier in the minor leagues. Relax while you can. Oh, Marino, can I talk to you in the back when we've got this all finalized?"

That sounded ominous, but Bee and I nodded.

Rocko pushed the button. "Officially, welcome to the minor leagues. Launch date for *Heroics 101 Season Two* is late summer or fall."

Pataki blew on their noisemaker, and a double handful of confetti fell from the ceiling as the System message appeared.

[League Increased! Little League to Minor League]
[Calculating Rank-Ups]
[New Power Slots: +1 Power Slot]
[New Power Upgrades: +6 Power Upgrades] (Assign to Powers)
[New Powers: +2 New Powers] (Skill Rolls Available)

With Bianca snuggled up against me, I sat on my couch and checked my emails. The Council of Heroes and Rocko had gotten my absences excused, and even though Su-Bin was pissed that I'd ditched her for three days and left her with Baby Cash, she'd held it together. Now, the baby could crawl. That was *not* an upgrade, and I'd placed him in a crib while I worked on the logistics of finals.

Truth be told, I didn't know what a vacation even looked like. We'd only rarely left Riverside when I was a kid, and Rocko's suggestions seemed overwhelming. So, since finals and powers were more familiar, that's where I focused.

Bee wiggled against me, and I put my phone away and rubbed her back while I fiddled with my new powers. I knew she'd done the same thing—trying to maneuver her builds into something powerful enough to hold her own.

She'd finished long before me, though.

I'd already selected my six powers to upgrade.

[Rank-Up! Quick-Time Change 3: Switch between costumes three times per Act]

[Rank-Up! Adaptive Armoire 3: Store up to three Costumes]

[Rank-Up! I-Frame Transform 3: Transforming has a low chance of redirecting an opponent's power back at them]

[Rank-Up! Leaping Leopards 1: Increased engagement range and impact damage]

[Rank-Up! Virga 1: Apply additional healing to either Extras and Henchmen or Supers]

The last upgrade was a little different. I'd expected **[Stellar Ray]** to move to Rank 3, but instead, it upgraded to **[Starlance]**, a weaker version of Stella-Lunar's **[Maximum Starlance]**.

[Skill Upgrade! Stellar Ray 2 > Starlance 1: The power of a star at your fingertips. Starlance hits harder against armored targets and those with high amounts of current superhero damage]

Bee flopped her head over, looking at me upside-down. "I'm *bored*. Hurry up!"

"Bee, this kind of thing shouldn't be rushed, and I have a disgusting number of choices to make," I said. "I promise when I'm done, I'll give it a rest, but I need to pick some new powers, too, and then figure out what my new power slot should be. Gimme a minute."

"Fiiiine." She pouted. She stood up and stretched, popping her back dramatically. "I'm going for a walk. I'll be back in fifteen."

"Okay. Have fun out there, hun," I said. "Love you."

She hesitated. We hadn't been saying that casually—not since "Gourmet's Glutton Hour"—and I hoped she'd return the feeling. If not, though . . . I'd be bummed but not heartbroken. It'd been a month, but that didn't mean she was over it.

"Love you too, you goober," she said, reaching out to mess with my hair before I could stop her. Then, as I stood to retaliate, she headed for the door, leaving me alone in my living room.

I took care of the open slot first. **[Hog the Limelight]** was a power I'd gotten a while back, and I hadn't been able to fit it in, but my Understudy build had room now. I could use it to shield some Extras while evacuating them using **[I-Frame Transform]** and then heal them in the Rainy Day Costume. It was the logical place for an excellent sacrificial power.

With that done, I decided to work on Lab Assistant Panic and Rainy Day with my new power rolls. The first one was a Badass skill for Rainy Day.

[New Skill! Wind Front 0: Crowd Control is king. Stop enemies in their tracks with an ongoing hurricane-force wind (70 miles/hour)]

This was the power The Cloud had used over Christmas, and he'd had the power to stop Jungle Jim in his tracks. Not every power needed a ton of damage on it, and area denial felt like something Rainy Day wanted, both for controlling battlefields before a combo and for protecting Extras. I dropped [**Quick-Time Change**] with some regret.

[**New Skill: TA-1LZ Stealth Protocol: Cats are sneaky. Robot cats are not. TA-1LZ gains basic active camouflage**]

The Drama skill for Lab Assistant Panic felt much more straightforward, and I dropped [**Check the Script**] for it instantly. Having a stealth option on TA-1LZ opened up so many doors for infiltration, setting up ambushes, and using her as battlefield support. It moved Lab Assistant Panic from a Costume I didn't want to wear to one I couldn't wait to try out.

Costumes and powers figured out, I leaned back onto the couch and tucked my hands behind my head. I had no delusions about fighting in the major leagues—I wasn't ready to handle Stella-Lunar, or even the lower majors. I might not ever be on Stella-Lunar's level, and that was okay. I'd been working toward this goal since August, and I'd made it.

I'd be content—happy, even—not worrying about my rank or pushing to the next league. The minor leagues seemed like the kind of place where a couple of heroes focused on saving lives, stopping low-powered villains, and helping people might be able to make a splash. It'd be lower pressure for Bianca and me, and we could focus more on classes and each other and less on superhero work.

The door opened, snapping me out of my daydream. "Hey, you done yet?"

I stood up and walked over, wrapping her in a one-armed hug before she could escape. Then I gave her a kiss. "What's next on the agenda?"

"Classes, finals, and vacation," Bianca said awkwardly, breaking the kiss. "I'm tired, Annie. We both need a break. Why don't you listen to Rocko? Take a real vacation?"

"I've already decided to." I started tickling her side, and she glared at me, trying not to laugh. "Sorry."

"I suppose I'll forgive you. Get a plane ticket to Tortuga West in July. Come sit on the beach and kiss, exactly like Rocko said. It'll be great. We can spend a week there as Anika DuPont and Bianca Marino, without the costumes, villains, and pressure. I think it'll be perfect for us, and my parents' house is big enough that we won't be sleeping right next to them." She winked at me.

I thought about it. I still didn't know how much Rocko was paying me, but it had to be enough for a first-class ticket. I leaned over and kissed her again. This time, I broke it. "I'll be there."

"Great, just promise me two things."

"What?"

"No shop talk, and no beach Episode."

63

Beach Episode

THURSDAY, JULY 9

I sipped my highly illegal daiquiri as I lay on a towel, soaking up the Tortuga West sun. Bianca sat next to me in a black and white polka-dotted one-piece that made her look like an old movie star on vacation, and the oversized sunglasses helped complete the style perfectly. Her hair had mostly grown back from our Finale against Stella-Lunar, and she'd cut it into a cute pixie.

I'd bought a dark yellow bikini with white straps, and she couldn't keep her eyes off me.

Tortuga West sat at the end of an island chain south of Florida, but we'd gone well past its towering walls and the Marino family's spacious apartment for the weekend. Bahia Honda was almost an hour's drive from Tortuga West, but the ringed island and ancient bridges kept the megalodons out, and there wasn't enough food for Kudzu-Zilla thanks to the goats. So even though the island was in Florida, which was considered Florida-Man's domain *only* outside the city, it was pretty safe.

"So, who do you think's going to be in our rogues' gallery?" I asked, then winced. "Oops!"

"Hey! Shop talk! Drink!"

I swore under my breath, then chugged sweet strawberry flavoring and rum for a moment. The waves crashed onto the beach just past a broken railroad bridge, and I sat there, trying not to talk shop. The rogues' gallery question was important, though. The little league and majors were both pretty uncontrolled—you usually had a rival in the little league, but could do whatever you and your producers wanted. The majors had a different problem; with only fifty or so major-league heroes and villains, no one could cover everywhere. The Triad often fought Lord Destructo even though he was Stella-Lunar's villain, and everyone teamed up to fight Fanfic.

"You're doing it again, aren't you?" Bee asked, winking.

"... Maybe ..."

"Shop think is shop talk. Drink."

Being out of the cast was nice, and I *shouldn't* be worrying about superhero stuff. I polished off my drink, happy my shoulder could move again, and glared at Bee mockingly. "Sorry. So, what's the plan, then?"

"For what? Next year? I dunno, fight some vil—wait!" Bee put a hand to her mouth, but it was too late.

"Drink."

Bee did not drink. Instead, both our drinks went flying as she jumped at me, knocking me off the towel and into the sand. She landed on top of me, and we rolled in the sand. Eventually, I got a grip on her and carried her toward the waves.

She screamed and flailed around, and I had to get a better grip twice. A few people pointed and stared, but I ignored them; it was just beach shenanigans. The waves lapped between my toes, and I stepped into them until they covered my calves.

"Please don't, babe. You don't know what you're doing. Please, please, please!" Bee squealed.

"Don't care," I said, launching her into the waves.

Only after her weight dragged me right into a breaker did I realize she'd grabbed my wrist.

The salt water stung my nose and filled my mouth, and I surfaced, soaked and screaming. A moment later, Bee broke through the water's surface. She glared at me. "Come on! My hair will *never* dry in this humidity, and it tangles like you wouldn't believe!"

I opened my mouth to say something, only to catch another mouthful of seawater as Bee splashed me—and just like that, it was on! Our battle raged across Bahia Honda's beaches and the waves coming in from the Gulf. The Extras watched in fear as two minor-league heroes bashed away at each other's defenses, unable to find a gap, and only once my hands were pruney and Bee couldn't breathe from laughing did we call it a draw.

"Lunch?" Bee asked, running her hands through her hair.

"Yeah, lunch."

Lunch was sandwiches and—to my surprise—water, not more booze. We sat at the little shack's counter, unlit tiki torches behind us, and everything was the picture of a perfect beach getaway. I cleared my throat. "The old dollar-bill pizza place was pretty cool last night."

"Yeah, it's an old building from way before Launch Day. I remember my dad talking about it. He said it was a fire hazard even back then, but it still hasn't burned down, and they keep Kudzu-Zilla out. I think they strip the bills off every few years and donate it to some charity or something."

"Uh-huh. I'm surprised no supervillains have tried to rob the place."

"Is that shop talk?" Bee stared at me, an eyebrow raised, then burst into laughter. "I'm just playing with you. It's in the middle of nowhere, with nothing worth taking besides ten thousand in dollar bills, and it's a cultural icon. Sure, a supervillain could take it with no trouble, but their reputation would be in tatters when it got out who'd done it. No henches who knew about the place would work with them again, and Florida-Man would probably do something. *No one* wants Florida-Man doing *anything*."

"Yeah, fair. Speaking of Florida-Man, are we going to Miami on this trip?" I would have kicked myself if I could. Miami had been leveled twice; once by Launch Day and once by Kudzu-Zilla's fight with Florida-Man, the half-hero/half-villain super who was just out-of-control enough to fight Golden Goose and just unpredictable enough to eke out a win one out of five times. But I didn't want to talk shop, Florida-Man, or Miami.

Bee looked at me seriously. "That's not what you want to ask."

Shit.

She knew I was fumbling. "How? What?" I spluttered.

"I'm not dumb, Annie. You're trying to say something, and it's not about Miami or Florida-Man. Just spit it out, babe."

"Okay." I could do this. I could do this. "Where are we going as a couple?"

Bianca sighed and took a bite of her sandwich. She didn't say anything for a while, and I kept fidgeting with what was left of my lunch. After a minute, she cleared her throat. "I gave you my list of changes that had to happen. You did them as best you could. It was stupid of you to put us in danger in that last one, but I agreed with why you did it, and I was right there with you."

"Shop talk," I said, half-jokingly.

Bee snorted, lifted her glass of water, and took a pull. "Real talk. Annie, I love you, and if I didn't think you could fix that screw-up, I wouldn't have given you conditions. I put up with a lot of shit from Jessie. I told myself I wouldn't do it for anyone who wasn't worth it." She shoveled a handful of sour cream and onion potato chips into her mouth and chewed.

I wanted to hug her and kiss her, but the sour cream and onion smell was intense, so I settled for the hug by itself. "Thanks, hun. I love you, too. I've been trying, and I think we should try to take it easy next semester. We've been pushing hard, and—"

"Shop talk," she said, and pointed at the water.

I laughed and drank. The knot in my stomach was gone, and suddenly, I felt ravenous. My sandwich didn't last long after that, and neither did my chips.

As we returned to our little square of beach, Bee dug through her pack, careful not to reveal the Fursona costume inside, and fished out a comb. "Fix it," she said.

I stared at her. She turned around on her towel to let me get at her hair, which was tangled despite her pixie cut. I rolled my eyes as she looked over her shoulder and mouthed, "Please."

I sighed, took the comb, and slowly worked through her curls, thanking Stella-Lunar and the hospital that they weren't longer. It was nice to be nineteen, on the beach, with a couple of nights away from my girlfriend's parents. Even if Bee was being a butt about stuff, everything felt good.

But what was good? I slowly worked out a particularly nasty knot of hair. "How did it get so bad so quickly?" I asked.

"Now you know why I take half-hour showers. Lots of conditioning to keep these lovely locks light and lively."

The comb broke through the last tangle, and I handed it back. Things felt . . . right.

"Heard from VV yet?" Bee asked.

I checked my phone. "No. Honestly, I don't expect to. I'll send him a message every couple weeks, but if he doesn't want to talk to me, I get it. We ruined his career."

"Yeah, we did!" Bee said, offering a high-five and a goofy grin. I nodded slowly and slipped my hand into hers as we lay on the beach and let the sun bake us. After a minute, she cleared her throat. "Still, it's a shame he didn't turn. He could have been one of the good ones."

"We don't know that he won't. He's got a lot of work to do on himself, and hopefully, he'll lean into therapy and the community service I threw his way. If not, he's got a long, lonely road to walk, and a lot of risk all the time."

"He'll do the right thing eventually," Bee said.

"If the other girls let him."

A cloud passed over the sun momentarily, and Bee pushed her hip into my waist. I rolled my eyes and wrapped my arm around her. Thanks to the Ilneat's special medicine, I'd had my leg in a cast for less than two weeks, but being able to move really felt great.

The cloud faded, but I noticed a few tannish-white blobs flying through the sky as I stared up at the sky. "Do you get many windstorms here?"

"No, not really. Sea breezes, yes, but if it's a windstorm, there's a real storm coming, and there's only one cloud in the sky. Want to try snorkeling later? We can rent flippers and stuff," Bee asked.

"Yeah, I'd like that," I said.

"THE SAND WITCH STRIKES AGAIN!" A voice echoed across the beach, and I looked in its direction to see a whirlwind of white beach sand approaching. "GET OUT OF THE WATER AND PUT YOUR WALLETS WHERE I CAN SEE THEM!"

[Casting Call]
[Episode: The Sand Witch Strikes Back - PG]
[Role: Beachside Bombshell! Do you accept the role? (Yes/No)]
[Role Focus: Drama + Flamboyance]

I looked at Bianca, who'd raised her eyebrow at me, then back at the sandstorm. Up high above it, I could see a girl in a pointy hat; it only took a few seconds to decide we could take her if we wanted to. Bianca's backpack was right there. She could be in her Fursona costume in a matter of minutes, and I could transform faster than that. Snorkeling could wait.

But then I looked back at Bee, and I shook my head. "Someone else can have this one. We're on vacation."

"Nah, there's a local hero who needs this more," she agreed.

As we declined the **[Casting Call]**, a pair of superheroes rocketed past us, heading toward the Sand Witch. I wrapped my arm around Bee's waist, and we sat back to watch the show.

Epilogue

Golden Goose smiled as she landed between McHammer, Lord Destructo, and the Yorkston Metropolitan Council's building. She'd made it in time, of course, and now these Tokyexico upstarts would pay for their crimes. She crossed her arms over her green-and-gold jumpsuit, conscious—as always—of how it played for the camera drones circling overhead. Her earpiece fed her a line, and she repeated it, scowling and looming over the impending battlefield.

"I'll give you boys exactly ten seconds to pack up and go back to your backwater town," she said, glaring and charging up her eye-lasers. "One. Two."

The villains looked at each other. For a moment, Golden Goose thought McHammer would bail. If he did, Lord Destructo had no chance against her, and he'd have to leave, too. Part of her hoped he would. Maybe this time, she could resolve it peacefully—

"I don't think so," Lord Destructo said. "We've got you where we want you, our lieutenants are fighting across your city, and you've got no backup. If we can't take you on two against one, we don't deserve our—"

Her line came in, and Golden Goose said it, adding the almost too-light, casual tone she knew drove audiences crazy. "So be it. Ten."

Her punch hit McHammer before he could react, and as the camera drones followed the supervillain and recorded his armor cracking and his bent hammer, she winced. Then she winced again as he slammed into a skyscraper and the shockwave blew out windows fifty stories up.

But by the time the cameras swung back to her, Golden Goose's signature smile, half-angry and half-bored, was plastered on her face. "Ready for yours?"

The battle had shifted. Rather than Wall Street or Manhattan's buildings, which had been built to handle major-league battles, Golden Goose and Lord Destructo found themselves trading blows in a residential area.

In a way, it made sense. Golden Goose's powers weren't subtle or . . . accurate. Lord Destructo, meanwhile, could use most of his powers freely. A small part of Golden Goose wanted to applaud the supervillain—perhaps he'd found a way to beat the unbeatable.

But, as he slammed his hammer into her chest and she watched its handle bend, another voice filled her ears. "Golden Goose. Golden Goose, this is it. You laser him, and you laser him hard. Then you can land, give your speech, and be done. He'll be in traction for a month, even with his studio's backing. Just do it!"

So she did it.

Her eyes lit up, and Lord Destructo lifted his hammer in time. He swung his hammer as pure energy and heat pulsed out from her. She barely felt the blow as it slammed into her cheek.

But it was enough to push the laser a half inch off-course. And that was enough to flatten a neighborhood.

Golden Goose brought the beam back around and fired it into Lord Destructo for one second. Two. Three. No villain had ever lasted more than five, and as she counted past six and up to seven, she could see his armored helmet melting around his head. He'd done this. Not her, him! Her anger, for the first time in years, wasn't faked. It fueled her eye beams, and the surge in power threw Lord Destructo high into the sky. He slammed into the ground and started to crawl away.

Still burning with rage, Golden Goose stalked after him. This wasn't in the script. This wasn't supposed to be how it went. Why wasn't the voice in her ear stopping her?

"Go on, finish him off. You're the best, and he'll be a good lesson for everyone else," the voice in her ear said.

She pushed her way through a half-severed, flaming door, intending to plow through the house to where her opponent lay in the next street over, writhing in pain. But as she went, something caught her eye.

A playpen with a wooden train track inside it.

Her brain stopped for a moment as the camera drones circled. What had she done? Had she . . . ?

"He's getting away," Snowball, her producer, said in her ear. "Finish him off, dammit!"

Instead, for the first time in years, she ignored him. She reached down and picked up a wooden train. It was blue, with tiny tin-centered plastic wheels, and a smiling face that stared back at her. As she looked back into the train engine's eyes, she saw Lord Destructo staggering away.

"What are you doing? You worthless excuse for a superhero! Finish him off!" Snowball screamed, their voice cracking. "Do it! Go on, do it!"

Jasmine Saxton woke up screaming.

She looked around her penthouse room. Everything was exactly as she'd left it. Her super-suit, the Golden Goose's emerald-and-gold regalia, sat on its stand, ready for her to suit up and take her powers for a spin again. The TV kept running, playing the little-league Episodes that helped her sleep on a loop. Anything bigger reminded her too much of the fight. It had been two months, but the playpen and the train engine were still seared into her memory. She wouldn't let them go, no matter how much Snowball insisted they were just in the way.

She reached for the remote to turn her lights on. Her hand wrapped around something, and she held it close to see it in the moonlight. A pair of painted eyes, faded from years of play and two months of Jasmine's compulsive rubbing and holding, stared back at her. They promised something, but she couldn't tell what.

Jasmine sat up in bed, frozen, transfixed by the eyes. Then, after almost five minutes, she put the faded blue train engine back on her nightstand and got up to find something to drink. Sleep wouldn't come for her. Not tonight.

She'd talk to Snowball about that in the morning.

Rocko closed the screen on their computer and looked at Pataki. Shaking their head, they lit a cigar. "I can't believe this! We're in it to win it now! Primo time slot for the first four months, thanks to some other shows disappearing in the fallout. We're going big! Big plans! Big investments! Big profits!"

"That's not what that meeting said," Pataki said, already smoking.

"Yeah, yeah, 'Don't push too hard, the humans are already protesting, and this mess with Cartman's only making it worse.' Pataki, we've got a button that makes our accounts shoot up here, and we're going to press that button until it won't press anymore!" They stood on their seat, then climbed down, squeezing hands gripping tight while their clutching hands held their cigar.

"Wall, transparent, one way," Rocko said. They loved the view from their studio offices, high in the Hot Zone; it felt powerful. Like they had some authority. Granted, other studios had better views, were warmer, or had more space, but Rocko could ignore them, just like they could ignore the Network's meeting.

Those fools. Didn't they know that now was the time to push the superhero narrative? They'd pushed out Cartman—the moron would never work in showbiz again—and Frizzle, who was supposed to be keeping The Agent in line, had been sanctioned and fined half a year's earnings. That was moon-buying money for Rocko, even if they'd just reinvest it into more *Heroics 101* merch and promo deals. Rocko Studios had been broke before, and recently at that. They could afford to keep their reserves low for a while.

No, the studios shouldn't back off now, and the Network was wrong to ask them to. They puffed on their cigar and stared out over the Hot Zone, contemplating the almost-empty streets.

After almost five minutes, Rocko turned toward Pataki. "Tell me about Project Ultima. How's that going?"

"Poorly," the other Ilneat replied, coughing out smoke. "Conceptually, it's fine, but all the modeling requires at least three different Costume fragments to make it work, and nothing DuPont has comes close."

"More Costumes, then. Got it. Can we bribe any other studios?"

"Doubt it'll work. The System already refuses to cooperate on half of it. Even in the modeling, it's highly unstable. The most I've gotten out of it is four powers."

Rocko nodded slowly. "Four's not enough, but it does everything else?"

"Yes. Every other requirement is *possible* within the System," Pataki drawled. "It's trying to do too much, though, with too little."

"Alright. I'll put DuPont and Marino on it. We need something for Fursona, too, though."

Pataki clenched their squeezing hands and bared their teeth in a laugh—the kind you laughed when the task was just too big. "I still don't know what makes the Fursona suit work, though. None of the modeling suggests that anyone else would get powers out of it, but Marino doesn't have any outside it."

"Then it's a Marino thing, in combination with the suit. You've got a job to do, Pataki. Six months, maybe seven, and she's gotta be running more than one option. Faster would be better. I don't care if she can switch between them in-Episode, but the kangaroo schtick is getting old, and it's not gonna cut it in the minors."

"So that's the plan, then? Build a team of shape-changers and pit them against who exactly? Theseus and Gourmet? Our girls should outclass both soon."

"Not Theseus. You heard his studio lost him, right?" Rocko asked. "They have no idea where he went. But we'll build a good rogues' gallery of faces for DuPont and Marino to face off against, don't you worry."

In truth, Pataki wasn't worried at all, and neither was Rocko. They'd spent five long years nursing *Small Town Super* along, making enough profits to pay for their houses back in the home system—not that Rocko spent time there. All their energies and every spare credit had gone into building up *Heroics 101*, priming the pump.

And now, on the eve of Rocko's success, just as the plan began to pay off, the Network wanted them to back off? Rocko chuckled to themselves, rerunning the numbers in their head. With two years of minor-league time, and if Project Ultima paid off, Rocko Studios should be well beyond moon-buying money and closing in on purchasing the Sol system itself.

It wasn't time for a gentle grasping hand on the reins. It was time to squeeze.

Author's Note

Hello, Aest here! Thanks for reading Magical Girl Undergrad: *Oaths and Outfits*. Two more books are coming in the series, but if you can't wait for the Kindle or Audible versions, check out aestbelequa.com/ for more of my work.

Please leave a review; it means a lot to me.

I'm usually on Discord in Walnut Tower, Room 1301 (Discord.gg/xvkfnNMzfe). Come say hello, tell me your favorite superpowers, and meet the fantastic community!

You can find the work of several talented authors at linktr.ee/coteh.

If Discord isn't your favorite, you can keep up with LitRPG through these Facebook groups:

LitRPG Books

LitRPG Forum

GameLit Society

Acknowledgments

Thanks to Astrid and Crown.

About the Author

Aest Belequa is a LitRPG and progression fantasy author, play-by-post RPG game master, and former teacher from Colorado. He grew up loving fantasy and science fiction and tries to bring that same energy to his writing.

Podium

DISCOVER MORE

STORIES
UNBOUND